C0-ALN-931

JAMAICA RUN

Previous work by Clifford Mason

The Case of the Ashanti Gold

JAMAICA RUN

A JOE CINQUEZ MYSTERY

Clifford Mason

ST. MARTIN'S PRESS / NEW YORK

Library of Congress Cataloging-in-Publication Data

Mason, Clifford.
  Jamaica run.

  "A Thomas Dunne Book"
  I. Title.
PS3563.A7878J3 1987   813'.54   87-4403
ISBN 0-312-00611-X

First Edition
10 9 8 7 6 5 4 3 2 1

To my fourth wife

JAMAICA RUN

1

I had just ended the most beautiful love affair of my life. She was a Westchester girl all the way—gorgeous, the touch of silk in everything she was and did. Money, lots of it. Lover of the good life. And she knew how to make my nights something to remember. But that was all behind me now. She'd finally gotten tired of my seedy corduroy jackets, my cheap sneakers, and my endless bottles of scotch that I'd "stopped" drinking. She couldn't understand how anyone, especially a man with my obvious accomplishments, could live on less than seventy thousand a year. Hell, I was living on 10 percent of $70,000, and doing a good job of it too. But, as I said, that was yesterday.

I had moved to Brooklyn to get the kind of rent I could afford. I had two rooms, furnished, off Eastern Parkway, in what was laughingly called a changing neighborhood. Extremely religious Jews on one side of the street and Jamaicans on the other. They never talked to one another. But they tried to outdo each other for cleanliness and respectability. Talk about well-kept brownstones and polished brass handles on oak doors and a tree-lined street, clean as a whistle. Even the dogs were too intimidated by it all to leave their pooh anywhere close to a sidewalk. My corduroy jacket and sneakers were the seediest things on the entire block.

It was a bright, sunny day at the end of the summer. I hadn't had a case in two months, and the fat bonus from my last job was running out and fast. I lived on the ground floor of one of the well-kept brownstones—Jamaican side of the street. My two rooms were huge. I even had a garden in the back. I had lived in Manhattan all my life, but one way or the other, sooner or later, everything—love affairs as well as the cities you live in—gets left behind.

I was sitting outside in my garden, in a lounge chair, sunning myself like an old sheepdog when my landlady, a Jamaican matriarch if ever there was one, called to me from her window on the second floor.

"Joseph, you phone ringing. Why you don't answer it?"

She was a real Island type. Thick accent, resolute manner, willful, even imperious, completely set in her ways. She surrounded herself night and day with people who all sounded as if they'd just gotten off the boat from Kingston. She cooked only Jamaican food. And her friends, her family, and the people she came in contact with on a daily basis were all Jamaican. Iris Hylton. She was mid-sixties, good size, stout, bad feet, broad features and enough hair on her head for four people. And she was the most magnificent cook I'd ever known. "Joseph, you don't hear me talkin' to you. But stop."

I had tried in vain to tell her that my name was Joe, not Joseph. But she said it wasn't possible. That no mother would christen her son just *Joe*. I replied that she didn't know my mother. But she was unrelenting. Joseph I was and Joseph I would forever be. Like it or not.

"Joseph!"

"Mrs. Hylton, let it ring. I'm not in the mood for talking to anybody. And I really don't want to move from this spot."

"You cahn't have the phone ah ring and you don't answer it."

"Why I cahn't?" I was picking up a little bit of the lingo. You grew up black in New York City and you knew that West Indians always said "Hi, mon" when they meant "Yeah" or "What's happening?" That they call cod "salt fish," and they eat things like green bananas and ripe plantain, and curried goat so hot that you need a new mouth when you've had a plate of it. They drink an endless amount of rum, have parties that last all weekend, and usually end up with the type of high-paying jobs that would have made my Westchester Beauty happy forever and kept her from ever crossing her legs against the event.

"Well, if you don't ahnswer it, I goin' ahnswer it."

"Be my guest. But by the time you get there, they'll probably have hung up."

To my utter amazement the phone kept ringing until she had waddled down the stairs and into my front room and picked it up. She kept saying "Eeehee" and "Yes, that's right." I wondered who the hell could she be getting so chummy with on my phone. "Yes, yes, I will attend to it. Right away. Yes, I agree with you. Don't mention." Then she hung up and came outside in that triumphant manner of hers when she was convinced that she had not only logic, morality and the practical world on her side, but prima facie evidence to back up her argument. All of which usually gave her an air of overwhelming superiority. She sat down beside me, turning to give me the full benefit of her immense presence as she looked down at me while I lay there trying to get the sun on my squinting, wrinkled face.

"Well, and what have you to say for yourself?"

"About what?"

"About that nice girl who just called. She's worried about you. She told me all about you and she. How she tried to get you to go to work for her father, but you was too proud. A nice, upstanding girl like that. A real lady. And what do you do? Walk out on her with your wuthless self. Hmph." And she folded her arms and waited for me to try to answer.

"Mrs. Hylton, I only have one question to ask you. How the hell do you know she's such a nice girl? You don't even know what she looks like."

"I can tell by her voice."

"By her voice. Oh, well, that's a different matter altogether. Hell, if you're using a voice test then I've got nothing to say. You've got to be right and no doubt about it."

"Very funny."

"Yeah. Hilarious in fact. Look, Mrs. Hylton, I moved to Brooklyn for the peace and quiet, the friendly faces, the food, the nightlife, the cheap rent, and even the Japanese Garden at the Brooklyn Museum. But I didn't come because I needed a mother. Now be a good soul, fix me some of that red ginger beer, a nice meat pattie and then leave me alone. I'm trying to concentrate."

"Concentrate on what?"

"That's my problem, I don't know yet. But I'm working on it. Once I find out, you'll be the first to know."

"Wuthless, lazy American bway. If you was a Jamaican man you wouldn't lazy so. You'd be out workin'. And it's not ginger beer, is sorrel."

"Whatever it is, it's delicious." And with that I rolled over and pretended to fall fast asleep. She got up and waddled inside.

I must have actually dozed off because the sun had disappeared behind a cloud when next I awoke. There was a dull ringing in my ear. It was the damned telephone again. I turned over on my side and tried to pretend I couldn't hear it, but it was no good. I rolled over the other way and my hand knocked the red ginger beer over. The glass fell and broke on a patch of asphalt, and the liquid spilled out and settled like a little pool of thin blood on the dirt. I looked at it and saw my face reflected in its center. The phone kept ringing, but I didn't hear anyone in the house. Except for the sound of the ringing, everything was still. By now I had a headache. In disgust, I finally capitulated to circumstance and got up and went inside, picked up the phone, and listened. It was dead. Perfect. I had waited just long enough to get there in time to miss that one last ring. I unplugged it, fixed a rum and water and turned on the TV—soap operas, game shows, talk shows, and a dumb movie with a papier-mâché thing coming out of the mists that was supposed to be a monster from the deep who was going to devour the leading scientists, equipment, buildings and all of every major city in North America was all I could find. I turned it off. Nothing had any credibility, not even the rum. I showered and changed, and decided to take a walk. I called up to Mrs. Hylton, but she didn't answer, and I didn't hear her moving around. The wind had come up suddenly and there was an open window somewhere, rattling. She must have either gone out or gone to sleep, I thought. Anyway that rattling window would wake her up if she actually was asleep. I looked at my watch. It was 3:15.

I walked over to Eastern Parkway and strolled in the direction of Grand Army Plaza. When I got as far as the Brooklyn Museum, I remembered the Japanese Gardens and went looking for the entrance. It was closed. I found a bar on Flatbush, had a few beers, talked sports, and came back to Grand Army Plaza. Where the Brooklyn Public Library is. Workmen were putting up a reviewing stand in front of the Botanical Gardens next to the Library for the West Indian Day Parade, which was two days away. A truck was unloading police barricades, and I was getting hungry. Mrs. Hylton had fixed my red ginger beer, but she'd neglected to make me a beef pattie. There was a bakery a block away that served the best beef patties in Brooklyn. You could get them hot or mild. The crust was crisp and flaky and there were real sprigs of thyme in the meat. I got six hot ones and grabbed a cab for Manhattan. I went to one of my favorite watering holes—Marvin Gardens—in my old neighborhood on the Upper West Side. Chewed the fat with some of the regulars, ordered soup, and surreptitiously got out my patties and managed to eat two when the bartender wasn't looking. Switched to vodka, borrowed the bartender's newspaper and settled in to enjoy the early part of the evening. On the front page of the *Times* there was a story about the prime minister of a small chain of islands south of the Bahamas and north of Haiti who had just been arrested in Miami on a drug charge. The case fascinated me and I called up an old buddy of mine who was chief of a wire service.

"Reggie, how you doing?"

"Who is this?" he asked imperiously.

"Joe, Joe Cinquez."

"Joe! How you been?"

"Fine, Reg."

"Working on a case?"

"Nope, no case. But I did want to ask you what you had on that drug bust on page one of the *Times*. Did you boys carry it?"

"Yeah."

"What's the background?"

"Meet me around seven-thirty at The Balcony and I'll tell you all about it."

"Why The Balcony?"

"Because I live across the street, and I'm going to be too drunk from all the scotch you're going to buy me to do much traveling afterwards."

"Okay, Reg, you got a deal."

Marvin Gardens was beginning to fill up. A lot of good-looking women come in there. And the mating game is played strictly by gentleman's rules—no hot pursuit unless it's on the distaff side. If they want to talk, they talk; *they* don't, *they* let you know it. I finished the paper. Didn't see anyone who wanted to talk, so I left to meet Reggie. I was walking up Broadway, a little aimlessly, stopping to look into store windows—book store windows, record store windows, health store windows, sporting goods store windows, even clothing store windows. Thought about trading in my corduroy jacket and sneakers for something with more panache in both cases, but decided that I didn't want to make any rash decisions before I found out what Reggie was wearing. Then I got the funny feeling that I was being followed. But that didn't make sense. I wasn't on a case. And my last one had been a routine surveillance of a security guard who was a monumental thief. He was in jail upstate New York, would be for the next decade. And that was that. Of course my investigation had been the key element in putting him there, but I didn't think he was ordering any hit men to get even with me from the pen. All the same, I was a little uneasy. I stopped for ice cream—the fancy European brand-name variety that they make in upstate New York, probably near a prison—and just stood on the corner of 96th Street and Broadway enjoying the cone and seemingly unconcerned about what was going on around me. That's when I picked her up, walking quickly, almost with a man's stride. She had on boots and slacks, a beret, a scarf, and a light cotton jacket that came no farther down than her waist. She was tall, good-looking, in a strong-featured way. A high yaller like me. She even had freckles. But she kept going, right past me. Head up, looking neither left nor right. I wandered over to West End Avenue, where it isn't as crowded. Stopped to gab with a couple of doormen of the large, well-kempt buildings that still line the area. Had a clear view of what was ahead and what was behind. Gave it about ten minutes, then headed for The Balcony and my date with Reggie.

He was already there and he was already drunk.

"Reg, what's happening?"

"I'm black Irish, that's what's happening."

"Yeah, Reg, but I'm only five minutes late."

"It's the British pub mentality."

"What do you mean?"

"You're cold sober at five twenty-five because the pubs can't open by law before five-thirty. But you begin to taste it long before you get there. They finally open the doors, and five minutes later you've finished your first one. Five minutes after that you've finished number two. Five minutes after that number three, and then four and then five. By six o'clock you're dead drunk. Drunk as a skunk."

"But this is America. The bars open at ten A.M. and stay open till after midnight. And the subways, the *tube* to you, never stop running."

"I know, I know, but culture is everything. What you've grown up with, the way you've been trained, that's what calls the shots, not opportunity or logic or the right and wrong of it. Don't you see?" He had a lovely lilt to his voice, especially when he was a little worse for the wear. But, boy, was he ahead of me.

"Look, Reg, it's no big thing. You don't want to talk about it tonight, we can do it some other time. I just broke up with this gorgeous girl from Westchester with a lot of money, and I'm living in Brooklyn because of the rent and it gets kinda lonely. And I sorta miss Manhattan. So I thought I'd come over and just hang out, that's all . . ." That's when he slipped. He grabbed the railing of the bar, but he couldn't hold on. He let go and landed flat on his ass. He sat there and took a deep breath and said, "Oh, shit."

I picked him up, grabbed his briefcase and got his arm around my neck, held onto his wrist tightly with one hand, while I looped the other one around his waist.

"Where to, Reg?"

"Jeez. Must be that cheap-bar scotch. Look, the assistant bureau chief in Miami knows all about the story. But be careful. The kinda money you're talking about is so huge that you can't count it all. There's too much money, in fact. You get caught in it and you're dead, laddie, and that's a fact. Too many people ready, willing and able to knock you off at the first say-so just to protect it."

"Where do you live, Reg?"

"Right over there in that building." He pointed to a big apartment house on the other side of Broadway. We had to cross a small park where derelicts and guys selling nickel bags of marijuana hang out. I got him to the building. We stopped at the door so he could steady himself. He made me let go of him. And he battled his way to a fully erect position. Reached for his briefcase and tried to find his keys.

"Hey, Reg, no sweat. I'll take you in."

"No, can't let you do that. Bad for the image. Got to go in on my own steam. Chest out, head up and you're over in a flash.

Learned that at school, I did." And he charged the door and it knocked him straight back and smack into me.

We both landed on our respective asses. An old lady passed by, looked down at us and shook her head. "Grown men, falling down drunk and it's not even dark out. Disgusting!"

This wasn't working out. I got up. Got Reg up and told him, "Image or no image, good buddy, the only way you're going to make it to the lobby is with one arm around my neck." We went back to the first position. Got through one set of doors. Used keys to get through a second set. Made the elevator without a fatal mishap. Got out, found the apartment door, and old Reg suddenly got sober. Or soberer. He turned the key in the door, yelled in "Hi, hon, I'm home," smiled at me, waved goodbye, and disappeared inside. I got to the elevator, realized I had his briefcase, went back and rang the bell. But by then they were into the third round. Pots and pans flying and yelling and screaming and exchanging of the kind of compliments that just add to the heartburn. I rang again, but they weren't listening. I couldn't think what to do.

I went down and found a doorman type, no uniform, very casual. But he wasn't allowed to take packages. I told him it was a briefcase. That the owner, who lives in 11E, would probably give him a tip for keeping it for him. He wasn't interested in briefcases, packages, or tips. So I left. Went back to The Balcony. Had a few. Looked out the window and caught a glimpse of someone ducking out of sight in the uptown direction. I didn't move. I felt stinking about it, but I opened Reg's briefcase and sort of leafed through the papers. There was a copy of the same article I had seen, underlined in red. And some notes scribbled in pencil: "Contact man in woolen cap for info on Aquinas." And farther down, "Kathy, stay where you are." Well, none of it made any sense to me. Anyway, I wasn't on a case, so who cared. Still, it was a hell of a lot more fun than the tube or those new release movies with heroes who all looked like soap opera extras and acted like their pants were on too tight. They didn't have any more credibility than my afternoon rum had had.

I turned around again and looked out the window, but no one was there. At least, not looking at me, so far as I could tell. Then the phone rang behind the bar, and the bartender brought it over to me. "Here, Joe, it's for you. Don't stay on too long, huh?"

"Okay, Billy. Thanks." I took it and said, "Hello."

"Are you the private detective who's interested in the story on the front page of today's *Times?*"

"I am, but I'm not."

"What does that mean?" It was a woman's voice, a little husky, but it sounded interesting. No, I was being hesitant. It sounded downright seductive, but that wasn't the message she was sending out. Her call was all business.

"It means that I am a private investigator, but my interest in the story is strictly academic. No one's paying me, so I'm just doing it until I can find a book I want to read."

"I'll pay you."

"You'll pay me. How much and for what?"

"Are you interested?"

"I could be."

"Okay, you stay right where you are. I'll be there in fifteen minutes."

"Wait . . ." But she hung up. I gave the phone back to the bartender with a shrug.

"Bum steer?"

"Who knows, Billy? Maybe yes, maybe no. We'll see. I better switch to ale. Make it dark. Looks like it's going to be a long night."

"We're all out of ale. How about a Guinness?"

"Guinness it is."

Guinness stout. In Ireland the doctors prescribe it for pregnant women, cancer patients and as the only sure cure for Protestantism. Living in Brooklyn for the two seconds that I had, I had found it in every West Indian bakery and grocery store and bar that had a door open. A little tough on the bladder, but very easy on keeping the head clear. Something about stout satisfied you without making you feel you missed a big night because you didn't get that quick buzz. Anyway, advertising was something I was never interested in. What I felt about a product was my private business. Making money selling it, somehow seemed a cheap, vulgar, disgusting way to go through life. Then I thought about all the alleyways I'd been dumped in. All the blows to the head and body I'd taken. All the blood I'd spilled and all the blood from my body that had been spilled in return, and I had a good laugh at myself on myself. I had one bad leg, one bad elbow, a postnasal drip, asthma, and probably conjunctive heart failure, for all I knew. The plaque buildup in my arteries had to be immense. And my hip was so sore from carrying a gun that I left the damn thing at home almost all the time—unless I knew that I absolutely had to have it.

Fifteen, twenty, twenty-five minutes went by. My bladder was bursting. I was afraid to leave the stool. But I couldn't stand it any longer. I told Billy I'd be right back and made it to the privy just in time. When I got back, she was sitting there, playing with my drink! The same one in boots who'd followed me.

"Well, well. Small world," I said.

"What do you mean?"

"Weren't you bird-dogging me up Broadway about an hour ago?"

"You must be mistaken. I only bird-dog on Saturdays and Sundays, and the surroundings have to be more bucolic than the Upper West Side."

"Bucolic, is it? Now, there's nothing I like better than a fancy word to get the conversation off to a good start. Why did you wait until I'd left the bar to make your entrance?"

"Why not?"

"If you have to be that careful it usually means that you're not sure of the territory. Let me see . . . Who's here who wasn't when I went downstairs." I looked around, but I wasn't sure. I really hadn't checked the bar out when I came in either time. It's a friendly enough place that I go to occasionally, and I've never had to worry about my back when I was there. But the bartender, Billy, eyed me in the direction of the guy. He was young, younger than she was. About thirty. Good-looking, model type. Brown-skinned, short hair. Crew sweater. Very strongly built, very intense face. "Aha, over there. Pretty boy who's eyeing us to death. Tell him to join the group. No reason why we can't all three get acquainted at the same time." She thought about it. Looked at me, looked at him, got up, went over and whispered something. He got up and left without looking in my direction. She returned, smiled, crossed her legs provocatively, looked at me, wet her lips, ordered a glass of white wine and lit a cigarette.

"That was good. I'm impressed. So you really are a private detective."

"You mean you were going to pay me without being sure?"

She said nothing.

"Let's see now. I talked to Reggie O'Connor on the phone around five. You couldn't have known where to find me from that. We talked about where we were going to meet, but I never said where I was calling from. On the other hand, if you didn't know about that conversation you couldn't have known about my interest in the drug arrest in Miami."

She smiled again and puffed her cigarette and gulped her wine, ordering another one quickly. "So what does that tell you?"

"Not very much, I'm afraid. Why don't you put me out of my misery? I hate puzzles."

"Not a good habit for someone in your line of work, I wouldn't think."

"And you'd think right." She fell silent, so I prodded her. "Well, I'm waiting."

"I said I'd hire you. The offer still goes."

"I'm listening."

"My family has property in the West Indies."

"What island?"

"Jamaica."

I was interested. "And?"

"And someone's trying to steal it from us."

"Why?"

"Land is very valuable down there. Especially beachfront property."

"I'd imagine so."

"The land's been in my family for generations. For years it just sat there. Nobody thought much about it. It wasn't in the tourist area. But the bauxite, the stuff they make alumina from, has been overproduced on the island, and they've closed down a lot of the plants."

"So tourism is all they've got to keep the pump primed."

"Pretty much."

"And they're looking at land that they wouldn't have thought about before the bauxite glut."

"Right." She seemed intense enough when she said it to make her story credible.

"So what do you want me to do?"

"There's a lawyer in New Jersey who approached us with an offer to buy. When we said no, he told us that there was some question as to whether the land was really ours or not. He said if he went to court there was a fifty-fifty chance that he could get it without paying us anything."

"Means he's got an in with a minister or someone. Proving that it doesn't belong to you doesn't help him unless he can be sure that when he does, he'll be the one they'll sell to. So why doesn't he just go ahead and try and prove it?"

"Says it's too expensive and time-consuming. They'd rather buy."

"From someone who doesn't own it in the first place? I don't believe it."

"The way he explained it, once they take it away from you it goes on the open market. Of course only the people who know about it will be ready to jump in and buy."

"So what can I do for you?"

"Check out the lawyer. See what you can find out about him, his practice. That sort of thing."

"Lady, that's pointless."

"Why?"

"Because it would be very expensive to do, and when it was all over you probably wouldn't have anything that you could use. What you need is a lawyer in Jamaica. See if he really has something, and put up a lot of legal roadblocks to stop him if he does, and right away."

"I tried that."

"And?"

"The lawyer we hired was crooked."

"Yeah, in a small town all the lawyers know each other. It's tough."

"So you won't help me."

"I can't help you. You need someone in Jamaica. I'm in New York. And even if I were in Jamaica, it wouldn't do any good. I don't know the territory. I hate to turn you down, even though I still don't know how you got on to me. But you'd be wasting your money. It's a tough enough business as it is. You start taking money from clients for a job you can't do and it's just one big headache, believe me."

"Here's five hundred. Take it and see what you can find out. I'm desperate."

She pressed five crisp one-hundred-dollar bills into my hand, using the warmth of her hand to seduce me.

"You haven't been listening."

"It's my money. Let me worry about spending it."

"Why me?"

"Because you come highly recommended."

"I do?"

"Yes."

"But you won't tell me by who."

"Can't."

"That doesn't make any sense."

"Please, won't you help?"

"Let me get it straight. You want me to find out what kind of practice this lawyer has. See if he's got serious skeletons in the closet. Stuff that could get him disbarred. That way you could get him off your back while you figured out your next move. Have I got it right?"

"Absolutely."

"But what if he's clean?"

"Then that would be my bad luck."

"And you're willing to take that chance?"

"Yes."

"Maybe you know something you're not telling."

"If I do?"

"Not smart. The more I know the faster I can get results. Making my job harder is just costing you money."

"Will you do it?"

"If that's the way you want it, I guess the least I can do is give it a week."

"That's all I ask. That five hundred runs out before the week's up, just holler."

"You mean there's more where this came from?"

"A lot more." She gulped her second glass of wine, got up, grabbed my face with one hand, gave me a meaningless kiss on the lips and left.

"Where do I get in touch with you?" I yelled.

"Call me tomorrow. The number's in between the last two bills."

I looked and there was a business card. It read REGINA—FASH-ION CONSULTANT—TO THE TRADE ONLY. And it gave a number and an address in Brooklyn Heights.

There was a limousine waiting for her. She disappeared into it. I didn't bother to check it out. I had two more stouts and packed it in. It was getting onto nine and it was a Friday night. Brooklyn would just about be gearing up for the weekend disco and jump up scene. I wasn't very good at either, but I had to have something to do with my nights now that I was unattached. And anyway, I love reggae music. Reggae dancing was another matter. I don't think I really understood it. All they did was stand in one spot and move their arms and feet. I thought about Reg, but decided I'd drop his briefcase off at his office first thing Monday.

I caught a cab back to Brooklyn. When it pulled up there was a huge crowd in front of the house. I got out, paid him and made my way to the front door. A big, heavyset man in his fifties stopped me.

"You can't go in there. No reporters allowed."

"I live here, buddy, and I've got a key to prove it. And the last time I was a reporter John Lindsay was mayor of New York." Then I heard a familiar voice behind him.

"Is aw right, is her boarder."

It was Mrs. Hylton's sister, who lived on the other side of Eastern Parkway. "Come in, Missa Joe." She could never get my last name, but she insisted on being formal.

"What's the matter?"

"You mean you didn't hear?"

"No."

"Oh, lawd, them kill me sistah!" Then she started crying and moaning. Someone carried her into the living room. I followed. It was packed with people. Some of them I had seen before, most of them I hadn't. It was a hot and airless room, filled with

upholstered, uncomfortable furniture, all mahogany, all well polished. It was a room that was not used to having people in it. I
had only been in it myself two or three times. My front room
was right below it. It took me a while to focus on the disparate
group assembled. There were young, middle-aged, and old. Some
dressed in J. C. Penney blacks and grays, some dressed casually,
and some in almost complete disarray. They were solemn and
seemed bewildered by what had happened. Who'd want to kill
Mrs. Hylton? their faces seemed to be asking anxiously. It was a
question I was certainly asking myself.

"Where's the body?" I asked.

"In there," a short man in his sixties said, pointing to the room
behind us. Before I could move, a thin, almost gaunt younger
man in woolen cap with dreadlocks called out rather menacingly,
"And is where you goin', Rasta?"

"I thought I'd take a look at the body. Do you mind?"

"Is not fe I man to mind or not to mind. But who give you
authority fe go inspec' body of I man dead sistah?" I didn't think
he was saying she was his real sister, just his ethnic one, but I
didn't want to ruffle any feathers. The situation called for deli-
cacy, not toughness.

"Mrs. Hylton, do you mind if I look at the body?" I asked.

"No, you can look," she said weepingly. I looked at him and
he looked dead back with a cold resentment that was closer to a
look of death than it was to anything else. I tried to smile and
indicate that hey, I'm really a friend. But he wasn't interested, I
could see, so I gave it up.

She was still in the dress she'd been in when last I saw her.
Her thick hair matted on her right temple with what seemed like
an awful lot of blood. Whoever hit her had enough power to
shatter her skull with one blow. It could have been with anything
from a wooden stick to a metal club. Her slippers were on her
feet. That bothered me.

"Who put her slippers on?" I asked. No one answered. "Mrs. Hylton?" She looked furtively at the man who'd pointed to where the body was.

He spoke up. "I did."

"Who found the body?" No one answered. "Mrs. Hylton? You, sir?"

"The gentleman's name is Black. Missa Black to you." It was my dreadlocks friend.

"And what's your name?"

"But you is police or what?"

"No, just trying to be helpful. I live downstairs." That seemed to shock him. It took the steam out of him anyway. Or so I thought.

"So you live downstairs, so what dat make you. God or what?"

"Now, now, Trevor, no call to be rude to the gentlemahn." It was Mr. Black who was sticking up for me. Well, at least I knew his name.

"Look," I said, "I'm a private investigator. That's how I make a living. I even have a license to prove it. Mrs. Hylton was a friend as well my landlady. And I'd like to help. Anything that was touched, rearranged, or changed in any way may make it harder to find out what happened to her."

"Everybody know what happen!" a woman screamed out. "Is Rasta kill her!" That brought a general stirring and Trevor got angry.

"You know fe sure say is Rasta, eeh, Misses?" he asked.

"Who else could ah cruel so?" she responded.

"Who else? Ethiopia is not the land of oppression. Babylon is the oppressor." He was getting intense.

From my short sojourn in Brooklyn I knew that Babylon was the land of the Pig—as in imperialist, no-good oppressor.

"Have the police been called?" I asked.

"Yes, I call them," said Mr. Black.

"Well, then they should be here any minute, their efficiency notwithstanding. I guess you called family and friends first." He nodded yes. "That's all right. They can't lock you up for that. But they're not interested in who killed her. Oh, they'll go through a lot of the motions. Ask all the right questions. But they're overworked, and let's face it, it's not Park Avenue. It's nobody famous. Nothing that the papers will pick up. Like an ax murder, or three children killed by a deranged mother at feeding time. Know what I mean? So before they get here, I'd like to know a few things that can really make the difference in tracking down what happened."

"Why you keep sayin' 'What happen'? Why you don't say who kill her and done with it?" It was the same lady who was convinced that the Rastas had done it.

"Because, ma'am, rule number one is never to assume anything. She may have fallen, although it's unlikely. But I've seen a lot of unlikely things turn out to be fact in my time." That seemed to cheer Trevor up, although he wasn't giving me any Brownie points for it.

"Exackly. Unnuh can assume all you wahn't, but the truth is the light, and it shineth on Tafari and on I fa'evah." And with that he made a flourish and exited majestically. One hand behind his back, the other propelling him forward. He didn't get any farther than the middle of the street. The cops had just pulled up and they grabbed him as a suspect leaving the scene. I heard the sound and the commotion as he was being apprehended.

"All right, quickly. What happened? Come on, they're on the sidewalk!" The lady who had solved the case spoke up.

"Her sister found her and call me, and I call Missa Black, and we call 'round to everybody between us."

"What time was that?"

"Around seven."

"What about the slippers?"

"Her sister put them on her."

"Why?"

"Because she never like to have anybody see her feet, 'cause them used to swell. But I couldn't get shoes on her, so I put on the slippers." It was the sister talking.

"Where did you find her?"

"In her bedroom on the floor."

"No shoes on, no slippers on?"

"No, none."

"Who brought her down here?"

"Missa Black and Missa Josephs."

"The guy outside who tried to stop me when I came in?"

"Yes."

"Have you called the undertaker?"

"Yes."

"Well, if he doesn't get here in time, get him down to the morgue right away, so he can protect the remains. You understand?"

"Yes." Mr. Black.

The cops were making it through the door finally.

"I'm leaving. If they want to talk to me, I'll be downstairs. Mrs. Hylton, I'll be here to help in any way I can." I covered the body and got down the stairs before they had a clear view of the hallway. It took them a long time to get to me, but eventually two of the finest came downstairs, their uniform jackets unbuttoned at the neck. They seemed harried, bored, and not a little unconcerned, all at the same time. After I told them what time I had gone out, when I came back, what my blood type was, and how America got into the Spanish Civil War, they wanted to know my current occupation.

"Unemployed." They eyed one another.

"On welfare, eh?" the younger one asked with a smirk.

"No, I'm still living off the bonus from my last job."

"Bonus!" he pipes up. Eyes his partner, who's not quite so eager to go along. Then he asks, "What kind a bonus did you get, buddy, an extra jock?" and he starts giggling.

"If I said yes, would you be able to spell it, or would you leave that page of your report blank?"

He changed on a dime, was about to start something that his partner didn't want to have to finish, so the older guy took over.

"Aw right, Mister, what do you do for a living, when you're working?"

I told him. Showed him the license. He copied down the number and pushed sonny boy out of there before he could get into any more trouble. "The lieutenant will want to question you further. Call the precinct in a few days." And they left.

I fixed a rum and waited. Things had quieted down by now. I was hoping someone would take me up on my offer. When no one did, I poured a second drink, suddenly realizing that my rum had finally found its credibility. Nothing like a tragedy to shake you up. I was about to lose all hope when I heard steps at the landing. It was Mr. Black who came down. He waited at my door. I told him to come in, but he hesitated. Something was holding him back. I got up and went over to see if I could ease the way. But it wasn't that he had any problem about coming in, he was just waiting for someone. It turned out to be Mr. Josephs. As soon as he came down the stairs they came in together. I gave them seats, offered each a drink. Black said no, Josephs said yes. I got my third and sat too, and waited.

Black spoke first. "I want to apologize for Trevor's behavior."

"No need. I'm sure he and I will get along fine before it's all over. Did they let him go?"

"Yes, as soon as we explained to them who he was." said Black.

"Who is he?"

"Mrs. Hylton's son."

I was stunned. "Her son!"

"Yes." Black again.

"But she never talked about him."

"No, once he turned Rasta, she disowned him."

"No, he disowned her," Josephs corrected him.

"Is anyone really suggesting that he had anything to do with it?" Neither of them answered. "Well?"

Black cleared his throat. "We're not saying he would have hurt her himself, but he ran with a nasty bunch and they may have tried to rob her."

"Without him knowing about it."

"Maybe." Josephs.

"I think I hear a difference of opinion here, in the voices mainly, but we can let that go for now. How can I help?"

"We discussed it, and we're agreed that we'd like to hire you to find out what really happened."

"No problem. If she was actually attacked physically, I'll find out who did it and what they did."

"How much?" Josephs.

"One dollar."

They looked at each other. They didn't like it.

"No, we want you to really work on it, regular, and we want to make it worth your while."

"Don't worry, I will."

"But how you goin' to live?" Josephs.

"That's my problem. Who's the boss?" They both pointed to the other one and spoke at the same time, saying, "He is." I smiled.

"Okay. Who do I contact when I want to talk?"

"Mr. Black."

"Then this is my offer. I'll take the case for the price I said, but anytime I want a good Jamaican dinner of rice and peas and curried goat, you have to make sure somebody cooks it for me. Agreed?" They both finally relaxed and broke out in broad grins.

"Agreed," they said in unison.

"But it's not going to be easy. And I'll need all the help I can get, especially since I have another case."

"That pays?" Josephs.

"That's the only kind worth talking about."

"How come you take somebody else's money, but you won't take ours?" Josephs, and he was really hurt.

"Because my other client is a stranger. But Mrs. Hylton . . . well, I've already said it. I liked her. I liked her a lot. And she was good to me. She was good to everybody. That's why so many people responded when you called. The same thing that worked with them is working with me. It's the Iris Hylton magic. She was special and no doubt about it."

That seemed to satisfy them. We shook hands and they got ready to go. "But," I added quickly, "don't try to help me by doing anything on your own. If I need something, I'll holler. Otherwise, sit tight and keep your ears and eyes wide open. You hear or see anything, let me know, but for God's sake, don't do anything on your own. You got that?" They both nodded. "Then we've got a deal."

We shook hands and they left.

2

I wanted to do a lot of things all at once. I was definitely out of the doldrums and no doubt about it. My hip even felt better. And all other ailments of mind and body, real or imagined, had suddenly disappeared. I heard them locking up upstairs. The ambulance, with siren whizzing away, had left with Mrs. Hylton's body. Lights had clicked off, and the place was left to darkness and to me. I went up, but got no farther than the landing. Someone had locked the door from the inside. I hadn't counted on that. I came back down, went down to the basement through the door just off the entrance to my rear second room, the one that opens out onto the garden in the back. I turned on the light at the bottom of the stairs and looked around. The level on the waterline of the oil burner was very low. As I remembered, Mrs. Hylton had a man who came in twice a month and looked after it for her. I didn't want to fool with the damned thing and blow up the house. Especially since I was the only one in it. There had been a young woman on the top floor when I moved in, but she left soon after. I never knew why. And it remained unoccupied after that. Mrs. Hylton had the first and second floors to herself.

I found a screwdriver and some nails and went back up and worked the lock and got it open. My lock pick kit was still in storage along with all my files and souvenirs from the cases where life and death had been an issue. I found the light, turned it on and went back into the front room. It had rejected its previous visitors. The pillows and cushions had all fluffed back up, and the carpet looked unstepped on. The long table in the anteroom where she had lain had nothing on it but the drape that had covered her.

I went upstairs to her bedroom. The door was closed, but not locked. I went in, turned on the light, and looked around. The outline of her body on the bed, where she had slept, near the edge closest to the window, was still clearly visible. That always amazed me, how some bodies would do that and others wouldn't. And I don't think it was a matter of mere heft. Something to do with the bones. Anyway, she had been sleeping on her side, her face turned toward the window. But the blood was on the carpet at the foot of the bed, near a dressing table. Some of it had spilled on the dresser itself, what they used to call a vanity bureau in the old days. I don't think the police had even bothered to come up there. She had grabbed the end of the bed, or someone had. There were clear fingerprints of the left hand on the inside of the highly polished mahogany, made while the body was facing the door, back to the window. Which could mean she got up and came around to face her attacker or face the door, one.

There wasn't much else I could find out without help from a lab. My footprints would certainly be added to the evidence. Nothing I could do about that. I turned off the light, closed the door behind me, and heard someone at the front door with a key as I was turning around. I looked and saw a youngish woman, early thirties, with a scarf around her head, a woolen sports jacket and a skirt on, coming through the second set of doors. The first set were huge oak doors. The second set were glass-encased in wood frames. The glass was frosted and with an ornate curlicue design going around its borders and curtains that only came down as far as the glass. She hadn't looked up. I moved out of the light. She went into the front room, turned off the light that I had left on, came back out into the hallway and started up the stairs. I moved to a front room and went in and listened at the door. She stopped at Mrs. Hylton's bedroom. Went in, turned on the light. Turned it off, came back out and went upstairs to the third floor. I heard her walking around for a long time. She seemed quite comfortable up there. I came out into the hallway, and was about to go up, when I heard the front doorbell ring. She came out and I went back in. She went down and opened it. Then she came back up, followed by another set of footsteps. When they had gone past me, I opened the door ever so gently and took a look. I only saw the back of him, but I was convinced it was my old friend Trevor.

They were up there a long time. I looked around the room I was in. It was a very tidy, neatly furnished single room, like an efficiency. With everything except the cooking facilities. There was a sink for washing up, a bed, dresser drawers, a closet. The closet and the drawers were empty as far as I could see. It didn't seem worth it to turn on a light. The bed was made, but hadn't been slept in for a long time. I sat on it and it seemed to be all mattress. I looked under the spread. There were no sheets or pillowcases on the pillows. The dresser had a comb and brush and a hand mirror on it. There were three picture frames on the walls. The first two had cheap, tacky pictures in them, one of birds, the other a scene of the countryside, complete with lowing herd and farmer boy. The third one seemed empty except for the backing. I looked and in between the two pieces of cardboard was an original. It was the face of a young man, very black, in dreadlocks and beard, smoking a pipe. I took it to the window and opened the venetian blinds to get a better look. It was a strong face, direct, with a certain coldness in the eyes, but something else too—a strength that commanded respect. The face, the way the man's hair was combed, or not combed, and the shirt he had on were all reminiscent of Trevor. But it was not Trevor's face. The painter put his initials—R. H.—in the lower right-hand corner. It was dated a year ago. Then I heard loud sounds coming from upstairs. Then yelling. Then Trevor's scream. "Bitch, that money is mine!" Then the woman began to scream. I ran up the stairs and pushed in the door. Trevor had her by the arms. She was on the bed. He was bending over her. From what I could tell, he was shaking her rather violently, but nothing more. He froze when he saw me. The guy just didn't like me. It was as simple as that.

"Hi. I was asleep downstairs and I thought I heard voices up here and, well, what with everything that's happened . . ." He got off the bed and moved away from her. She stood and straightened herself up. It was only then that I recognized her. It was the same woman who had lived there before. No wonder she knew her away around.

"Trevor, I want you to leave," she demanded.

"But I not leavin'. And there's nobody here who can make me leave."

That was a direct challenge to me.

"Don't look at me, buddy. I'm not licensed for that kind of work. I just find out who dunnit. Somebody else does the laying on of hands."

"Mr. Cinquez, I have to talk to you, alone."

"Does it have to be now?"

"Yes."

"Well, we can always go downstairs to my rooms."

"Your rooms. Eh, eh. You is Englishman or what?" He chuckled acidly.

"Well, room sounds kinda tacky, and I do have two of them."

"Is aw right, res' you self, both a you." Then he came to her and pointed a menacing finger in her face. "But you, you sheg roun' wid me and I destroy you. Remember, when in Rome, do as the Romans do. And Brooklyn, love, is my Rome. Ah oh!" And with that he flourished and whirled past me and out the door. Boy, did he have style.

"What does 'sheg roun' mean?" I asked.

"It means don't double-cross me, or fool with me, you know, don't try anything funny."

"Yeah, I get it. Great language. Is it some kind of patois strictly from English, or is it mixed in with African?"

"I don't really know, but probably mixed in with African and some Irish and Scotch."

"Irish and Scotch?"

"Yes, a lot of the early whites who came to the West Indies were Irish and Scotch workers. Some of them were even indentured servants, although they never want to admit to it. So the dialect, the patois of Scotch and Irish indentured servants, went into the pot along with everything else. We even have a group of Germans in one of the parishes in the interior who were brought over to work a plantation a hundred years ago and they just stayed."

"You're kidding."

"No, they're there now, blue eyes, blond hair, and all—and very browned, suntanned skins."

"So then you're from Jamaica too."

"Yes, I'm Mrs. Hylton's daughter-in-law."

"You mean you and Trevor?"

"Yes."

"Well, you two certainly are an unlikely pair, I must say."

"Oh, Trevor only became a Rasta a few years ago. Before that he dressed up in a three-piece suit every day and went to work in an insurance company."

"You're kidding."

"Believe me, I wish I were."

"Was Mrs. Hylton, Mrs. Hylton, or was she Miss Hylton who was Mrs. Hylton for respectability's sake?"

"That's a very roundabout way of asking if Hylton was her maiden name or her name by marriage."

"Yes, I guess it is. But I'm treading on pretty sensitive ground here and I don't want to offend anyone."

"It's all right. You're a friend, you don't have to mind your manners."

"How did I become a friend?"

"Mrs. Hylton gave you her stamp of approval before she died. It's all you need."

"I see. You two stayed in touch?"

"Constantly."

"How does her sister come to have the same last name?"

"Two sisters married two brothers."

"You're kidding." She laughed.

"What's so funny?" I asked.

"That's the third time you've said that."

"Said what?"

"You're kidding."

"I guess it is, but you're coming up with some pretty amazing stuff. Look, it's fairly certain she was killed."

"Everyone seems to think so."

"I want to get the no-good so-and-so who did it. Man or woman, relative or stranger. But I've got nothing to go on. I'm hoping to be able to talk the police into actually doing an investigation—a real one with lab tests and the rest of it. In the meantime what can you tell me that might be of some help?"

"That's why I wanted to talk to you."

"Yes, go on."

She took a letter out of her pocketbook and handed it to me. It was dated two months earlier. It was from a Mr. Williams, addressed to Mrs. Hylton. Sent from a place called Yallas P.O., St. Thomas, Jamaica. He was warning her that somebody was taking away her land. And she should do something about it. Right away. When I finished the letter she spoke. "I want you to go to Jamaica and find out about this for me."

"You want me to."

"Yes, Mrs. Hylton made me her sole heir."

"You're kidding."

But neither of us laughed when I said it.

"Now you see why Trevor's angry."

"Yes, I guess he has a right to be."

"You like him, don't you?"

"I admire him."

"Funny, he has that effect on certain people. Men mostly. They think they see a kind of strength in him. He used to be strong. Now, he's just willful. Look, I'm not doing anything for myself. If it were up to me, I'd chuck it all. I don't want her money. But it's a trust from a dead woman. A woman who was good to me and whom I loved."

"I understand. But how're you going to convince Trevor that you shouldn't turn everything over to him and walk away?"

"Don't worry about Trevor. I can handle him."

"You won't mind my saying so, but you weren't doing too good a job of it when I came in just now."

"I didn't say it would be easy, but I can do it."

"What's your name?"

"Kathleen."

"But Mrs. Hylton used a different name to address you when you lived here,"

"Yes, after Trevor changed religions he disowned me because I wouldn't join him in his new life-style."

"I see."

"So I went back to my maiden name—Campbell."

"Right. Now I remember. Are you going to move back in?"

"Not really, but I will try to spend as much time here as I can until things are straightened out. There's so much to do and no one else to do it."

"What about the sister?"

"Once she finds out that there's no money for her, I don't think I'll be able to count on her much."

"She doesn't know?"

"No. I told Trevor just now. Nobody else knows."

"What about Mr. Black and Mr. Josephs?"

"They'll do whatever Mrs. Hylton would have wanted done."

"Who's the lawyer handling the estate?"

"Smedley Braithwaite."

"Must be West Indian."

"Yep. Jamaican all the way."

"When did she change her will?"

"She changed it twice. Six months after Trevor became a Rasta she disinherited him and left everything to her sister. But about a year ago they got into some sort of row."

"Over what?"

"I don't know."

"Could it have been money?"

"Possibly."

"And what happened?"

"She changed it again."

"That's when she made you the sole beneficiary?"

"Yes."

"Did she ever tell you why?"

"Yes and no."

"What does that mean?"

"It means she hinted that there was a problem having to do with who owned what, but she didn't actually come out and say what it was in so many words."

"I see. Were there any conditions attached to your becoming her sole heir?"

"Yes and no again."

"That's the second time on 'Yes and no'—three strikes and you're out."

"And don't I know it." She'd suddenly made a provocative statement. "She told me that she was going to leave me as sole possessor of all her earthly property and that if anything happened to her I'd be a very rich woman. But that she was only doing it until she could find another way to protect what she had spent a lifetime earning."

I waited. "And that's all she told you?"

"That's all. I didn't really expect her to die. She was a little overweight, but she was in good health basically."

"How much are you worth?"

"Now that she's dead."

"Now that she's dead."

"Three million dollars."

"What!"

"That's what the lawyer says."

"You're kidding."

"I've got you—four to two." She smiled.

"You can say that again." I needed a drink, maybe two or three or four. Talk about your British pub mentality! "You know, of course, that that gives you a hell of a motive for murder."

"But what do I do? I was just trying to help her. Now that she's dead I've got a mess on my hands."

"If I rouse the local guardians of the peace to actually look into the case, you're the first one they'll come after."

"Let them. I'll be glad to get it on the record so that everyone will know where I was and what I was doing. That way the rumors don't even have to start."

"Then you do have an alibi for this afternoon?"

"Yes, I was at work."

"Visibly at work, in a public place with other people around to verify the fact?"

"Yes."

"Okay."

"Do you want me to tell you the who, what, where, when and why of it?"

"No. Save it for the police."

"So what do we do now?"

"I've already taken the case, for one dollar. That's still my price for finding out who killed her. If I have to go to Jamaica to help save her land, I'll need expenses. If you need help and it turns out to be something complicated, we'll discuss that when the time comes. I think I'd better see your lawyer with the fancy name and take a look at that will. Set it up for tomorrow, or for as soon as you can. Has anyone been in touch with this Mr. Williams in Yallas P.O. since the letter arrived?"

"No."

"And you don't know him?"

"No."

"What about Black and Josephs? Think they know him?"

"They might."

"One more thing. How'd she make all that money?"

"I don't know."

"Well, somebody knows."

"Yes, Trevor knows and her sister knows."

"But if they're not forthcoming, we need an alternate source of information. When you call Braithwaite tell him to have the accountant there."

"I don't think there is one."

"There's got to be one, unless her money's in Jamaica. I need to be able to get in touch with you, day or night, so give me both numbers." She did. "Do you think you're in any danger?"

"No, I don't. Why should I be?"

"Well, if you're the sole heir, killing you and leaving all that money around could mean that someone was planning to pass off a phony will. Which isn't that far-fetched. It just happened in Miami with the guy who was the head of a bank in Ohio that failed. All the wire services ran the story. Smedley Braithwaite would have to be in on it since he knows about the real will. It's too much of a long shot otherwise. One thing's for sure, she knew there was trouble, that's why she gave it all to you, even if it was in name only. But then whoever killed her didn't know that. She thought she'd protected herself by doing what she did. She didn't count on the killer not knowing she'd done it."

"Or not caring if he or she did know."

"If that's why she was killed."

"You mean there could be another reason?"

"Of course. Several, in fact."

She thought about that, then said, "Any way you look at it, it's all pretty gruesome."

"Murder usually is."

"What's going to happen to all that money, even if we do manage to save it?"

"That's up to you."

"But I told you, I don't want it."

"You may not want it, but you're stuck with it."

"You mean it's really mine to dispose of?"

"Yep. Unless the will's contested."

"Trevor will contest it. Of that I'm certain."

"Well, you aren't planning to spend any of it right away anyway, so I wouldn't worry about it."

"But what about your going to Jamaica? You said you'd need expenses for that. And I'm afraid that if we wait and do nothing that someone will steal poor Mrs. Hylton's land."

"Look, don't take on more than you can handle all at once. Mrs. Hylton left you with a lot of problems. But they're really *her* problems. You do the best you can and that's all you can do. I think your biggest worry is going to be deciding how to dispose of the money once it's really yours. There'll be a great temptation to spend some of it, even a little bit, on things that Mrs. Hylton didn't plan on having her money spent on, good intentions notwithstanding. You're only human, after all."

"Yes, but it was a trust from a dead woman. That's the kind you have to keep."

"If you can. But no one's perfect. We can't even make our own life work out the way we want it to, so how can we ask ourselves to do for someone else what we can't even do for ourselves? It's not fair."

"You're just trying to make me feel that I'm keeping her trust even when I'm not."

"No, my dear, I'm just trying to get you to face a reality that you're going to have to face sooner or later."

"Well, can't we at least take it one step at a time?"

"That's usually my line."

"Meaning?"

"Meaning, by all means, yes."

"So what do we do first?"

"The will gets probated. And you either do or you don't get the money, depending on what you have to contend with, from Trevor or anyone else. You should anticipate getting it, since once you do, you'll need to set up all kinds of accounts and put people in charge of whatever portfolios people who are good at that sort of thing get put in charge of. If you never get the money, you've lost nothing and you're off the hook." A look came into her eyes that seemed to say she hoped she would never get it. I knew enough about human nature to know that no matter how much she thought she felt that way now, once she actually had the money, she'd begin to feel differently. How differently would depend on how much integrity she really had. Three million dollars was an awful lot of corruption to be let loose in anybody's moral system all at once.

We left it at that. She wanted to be alone in the room. I gave her my number downstairs and left. I needed to get out of there, but thought I should change my shirt before I went nightclubbing in the environs of Eastern Parkway on a Friday night. West Indians can get awfully fancy when they get dressed up for the weekend dance. And I didn't want anyone to think I was slumming. The fact is that I really didn't want to change my shirt. But I didn't want to look too much the outsider either. The phone rang before I could make a decision.

It was Mr. Black. "Yes, sir, how're you?" I asked.

"Fine, thank you. I understand that Miss Campbell is in the house."

"News travels fast in your circles."

"Sometimes."

"Yes, she's in the house. In her old room."

"She talk to you?"

"A lot. If I'd known about the three million dollars, I'd never have agreed to one, I can tell you."

"But we wanted to offer you more, but you wouldn't take it."

"Just kidding."

"So she say the estate worth three million."

"That's what she says."

"Who tell her so?"

"The lawyer, Braithwaite."

"That man is a crook. Watch him. Watch him good." I think that meant watch him closely.

"I intend to. How did she get all that money?"

"But Kathleen never tell you?"

"No, she never." I think that meant she hadn't.

"Well, some of it she work and save, and some of it she get through a will."

"What will?"

"I don't know. People she used to work for. Rich white people."

"As a domestic?"

"Housekeeper," he corrected me.

"You know the name of the family?"

"No, but her sister know."

"What's her telephone number?"

"She won't give nobody the number."

"Really. An address." He gave it to me. "Why'd you call?" I asked.

"We havin' a meeting and we'd like you to join us fe a little while."

He gave me the address. I took a cab over. It was a locked door on Empire Boulevard. I didn't know the neighborhood. A guy looked through a peephole and said, "Yes?" I asked for Black.

"Name, please?" I knew it wasn't going to work but I gave it to him. "Repeat, please." I did, slowly. "Yes, that's right. Come in." And he opened the door. There was a huge sign on the wall that said PRIVATE CLUB. MEMBERS AND GUESTS ONLY. I guess I was a guest. It was lit not too tastefully. A lot of blues and greens. There was a bar at the end of a long room. They obviously used the room for dancing. There was a jukebox and a pay phone on the wall. These guys were serious about turning a dollar. Around a corner to the left there was another, more private room with tables, some booths, and a door leading to a kitchen. They were middle-aged men and fattish women mostly, at the bar and in the first room. In the second room there were men at the tables and some men and women in the booths. My group was all male and at a table in a corner away from the kitchen.

Black got up as I came over. We shook hands and I sat down. Everyone was drinking rum or stout. I had rum, Jamaican, of course. I think it was the only kind they sold. Black introduced me to the other two men. One was Chinese, in his forties. His name was Winston Chin. The other man was in his early thirties. His name was de Souza. He turned out to be a cop. "Where's Josephs?" I asked.

"At work," Black said.

"So what can I do for you gentlemen?" I asked as the waitress came back with the drinks.

"We feel that we have a community problem here. One that affects dozens of Jamaicans in New York who own property back home." Black.

"What kind of problem?" I asked.

"Several of these people have been attacked recently." Chin.

"Why?"

"We're not sure. In some cases they've been forced to sell their land." Chin.

"But not in all cases?"

"Right." Black.

"In the cases where they didn't have to sell, why were they attacked?"

"That's what we'd like to find out." Black.

"Is that why you and Josephs wanted me to investigate Mrs. Hylton's death?"

"Yes, partly." Black.

"People don't get beaten up for no reason," I offered.

"That's exactly the point." Chin.

"In the cases where they did sell, who did they sell to?"

"Different individuals. But we think they're all part of one group." Chin again.

"And do you gentlemen all own property in Jamaica?" They nodded yes. Until then de Souza hadn't spoken. I turned to him and asked him why he carried a gun. He seemed surprised that I had noticed, then he smiled and said, "Of course, you're a private investigator."

That's when Black said, "Mr. de Souza is a police officer."

"What precinct?" I asked.

"The Forty-fourth."

"That's the one that those two yo-yo's who came with the ambulance are from."

"You got that right." At least he wasn't going to bore me with a "we're all brothers in blue" routine. Maybe I'd get to like him, even if he was a cop. Not that I disliked cops out of hand. But I had developed a decided distrust for most of the ones I ran into when I was on a case, until they gave me good reason to feel otherwise. They usually gave you a hard time because they didn't really think you had a right to do what you did if you weren't one of them—unless you belonged to a big outfit or had a blue-chip client. But this one could be quite useful if I could get him to cooperate. Help me with some of the research.

"Draw me a map of the island," I said. They seemed surprised at that. I waited. Finally someone realized that in order to do it they needed pencil and paper. They sent the waitress for it and Chin drew the map.

"Where's Yallas P.O.?" I asked. That seemed to surprise them. De Souza pointed to a spot near the capital, Kingston, on the south coast. Black made him move it over a little more to the east. It looked like an hour's ride from the capital, depending on the condition of the roads. "Now, show me where each one of you has property, put crosses, and also for anyone else that you know of. Include Mrs. Hylton's property too." There was some discussion at this point over several locations. Chin had to make a list of names so they could keep track. When they finished, there were eleven markers on the map. Half of them were clustered near Yallas P.O. on the southeastern shore of the island. Four were near the center of the island and three were way west, on the northern tip.

"What's this place called?" I asked, pointing to the center section.

"Bamboo," said Black.

"And this one?" pointing to the northwestern tip.

"Negril," all three said.

"What do the three areas have in common?" I asked.

"Nothing," said de Souza.

"Are you sure?" I asked.

"Nothing that would be worth beating anybody up to get."

"Aw right, let's try a different approach. What do they have that would make them valuable by themselves?"

"The south coast has some beachfront property and all the property in Negril is near or on the water." Chin.

"And Bamboo is rich in bauxite." Black.

"Other than that, you're talking about agriculture. Winter vegetables, coffee, produce, spices." Chin.

"But the best places for those things are in other parishes. The winter vegetables are all being grown by Israelis in St. Ann." Black.

I didn't know it then, but knowing about the parishes was the clue I needed to crack the puzzle.

"Well, we need time to get a better picture," I said.

"But we don't have any time." Black.

"Why not?" I asked.

"Because Josephs has been given three days to sell or else." Chin.

"Is he afraid?"

"Yes, very. Wouldn't you be?"

"I don't know. I'm afraid all the time, so it's hard to tell."

"You don't look to me like a man who's afraid any of the time." Chin again.

"It's only a cover, believe me, because it's usually a mistake."

"What is?" Chin.

"Not being afraid." I don't think they got it. "When does Josephs get off from work?" I asked.

"At two A.M." Black.

"How do I get word to him to contact me right away?"

"You don't have to. He's coming here as soon as he finishes." Black.

"Well, that gives us about four hours to wait."

"You could wait here," said de Souza. "We're having a dance tonight."

"You mean I can stay and join the fun while I wait for Josephs?"

"If you wish." Black.

"Well, well, just when I thought I'd have to go looking for ole Muhammad, he falls right into my lap." They didn't get that either.

We ordered another seventy rounds of drinks, give or take a hundred. I asked a lot of useless questions about Jamaica. They filled me in on some of the ethnic mix. Turns out that the Chinese used to own all the grocery stores and import and export companies. But they were afraid of nationalization under the last government and left in droves. Chin was bitter about all the money and land he had given up or sold. He was determined to hold onto his piece in Bamboo, no matter what.

Then the place began to fill up and a fairly good-looking crop of women began to show. Black and de Souza tried in vain to fix me up, but none of the women were interested. There were a lot of good-looking guys too. They came later. No one was doing anything but sitting around in safe little groups and talking. I was thinking of going home and taking a nap, for chrissakes. If I sat there and drank all night, I'd be too stewed to do anything by the time Josephs arrived. The music was going great guns, but nobody moved. Hell, I wanted to dance so badly that I was thinking of getting up with a pair of plates and doing it all by myself—Greek style. But I knew that wouldn't go down too well. So I just sat and waited like a good little boy. Then, they played one of the calypsos that they'd played a dozen times before and as if by a prearranged signal, everyone jumped up and started dancing. I looked around and I was the only one sitting down! This was not working out, and it was already midnight. I was desperate and no question about it.

Two or three calypsos and reggaes later—they were beginning to both sound alike by then—I started to head for the exit, just to get some air, when de Souza stopped me.

"Josephs just called. He says he's leaving work early."

"Why?"

"He sounded like there was something on his mind, but he didn't come right out and say it."

"How far away is it?"

"About fifteen minutes. It's downtown, near Boro Hall. The big gas company. He's a security guard."

"Does he wear a gun?"

"No."

"Get him back and tell him we'll pick him up, unless he's afraid of getting hit in the building."

He disappeared to make the call and that's when I got lucky.

She was an East Indian mixed with black and, boy, was she gorgeous. I went over and asked her to dance. She got up, said nothing, and we were close and I was enjoying every minute of it. Then they changed the beat and we had to break it up. She began to show me some moves I didn't know were in the book. She turned and danced on me from the back, if you know what I mean. Talk about fantasy time. That's when de Souza reappeared and grabbed me.

"We gotta go. He's waiting for us."

I never even got a chance to ask her her name. "Your timing stinks," I said.

"We'll be back, don't worry," he said.

"But suppose she doesn't wait," I protested.

"I can always track her down for you. It's a pretty close community. Everybody knows everybody, one way or the other."

Well, that made me feel a little better. We jumped in his car and shot down Eastern Parkway, made the big turn on Grand Army Plaza, headed west on Flatbush Avenue, and got over to Montague Street in no time. The Brooklyn Union Gas Company was a huge building on the corner. Everything was dark. We rang the night bell. Nothing. De Souza went to the corner and phoned up. He came back looking grim.

"No answer," he said.

"Then let's break in," I said.

"This isn't television. I can't go in there without a reason. My lieutenant is a racist. He'd have me nailed to the wall. Believe it."

"Yeah, well, that's your problem. I'm going in."

"Wait," he said. "I have an idea." He went back to the phone booth and made another call, maybe two. He was gone a long time and I was getting very restless. The silence was almost eerie. He came back unhappy. "I called the precinct. There's been no report of anything wrong here. And I called Josephs's home. No one's heard from him."

"Come on, we've wasted enough time." He wasn't happy about it, but he was game. I broke the glass on the front door (it wasn't easy) and had a hell of a time unbolting and unlatching. I was at it nearly two minutes when alarms finally went off. But between the two of us we managed to get the damned door open.

"Want to stay down here?" I asked.

"No, to hell with it. Let's go."

In we went. We got to the second floor when an old gent with a thick Italian accent, in uniform, threw up his hands and said, "Don'ta shoot! Don'ta shoot!"

De Souza identified himself and asked for Josephs. Our friend said he should be on the sixth floor. We sent him down to meet the press or whoever showed up and went to the sixth floor.

We found Josephs lying face down, halfway between the hallway door and the staircase. His head and shoulders were inside and the rest of his body and his legs were in the stairwell. He was lying in a pool of blood, shot once through the head.

"Well, call it in, officer," I told de Souza. Boy, those guys hated to take the initiative on anything that wasn't assigned to them. He found an open door and turned on the light and called. Josephs's watchman's clock was beside him. The key was in his hand. He had just recorded his last check of the floor, apparently. It said 12:55 exactly. Why hadn't the old man on the second floor heard the shot? Would it be possible to find out how the murderer got in and out? Maybe whoever did it was still in the building? I looked at my watch. It was 1:49. I touched the blood. Rubbed some of it between my index finger and my thumb. Smelled it. It was less than an hour out of the body. Then I smelled something else. It was a sweetish, sickly smell, one that I had come across before. I couldn't tell if it was some sort of incense or a lotion or what.

De Souza came back. "Eucalyptus," he said.

"Eucalyptus oil," I said.

"Right."

"You go up, and I'll go down,"

"No," he corrected me, "you go up. I don't want you shot by any of my brothers in blue. They stop me, I can at least prove to them who I am."

"But I don't even have a gun." said I.

"I still think I should go down."

"Okay," I said, and I went up.

The police found nothing, not even an abandoned gun or a footprint. I went up as far as the roof, but all I found were empty spaces and a lot of darkness. If there was anyone lurking in the shadows who knew his way around, giving me the slip would have been the easiest thing he or she ever did. There were just too many places to hide. Getting out of the building was the only real problem they had. From the roof it wasn't possible.

I descended in time to see a real investigation going on. I mean the whole team showed up—robbery, homicide, the private agency that answered the alarm first—the works. Before it was over it was a zoo. Josephs's body wasn't taken away until they had measured and diagrammed and searched and taken dozens of photographs. A far cry from the blue plate special they gave Mrs. Hylton.

De Souza went back to the dance, but I went home. I'd lost my taste for calypsos and reggaes, for the rest of the night anyway. I was tired again. There was something about the case that was dragging me down. I just couldn't get up a good head of steam and sustain it. It was all fits and starts. I was allowing myself to get involved in something I didn't really want to get involved in. I was doing it because it was there to be done—that came under the heading of the nobility of the work ethic. And I was doing it because I thought I owed it to Mrs. Hylton. I was convinced that if I didn't track down her murderer no one would. And she deserved that much at least. That came under the heading of noble because it was noble.

When I got back to the house, the light was still on on the

third floor. But I didn't go up. I turned on the TV. All I got were porno flicks and horror movies and reruns of shows that I hadn't liked when they were new. I turned out the lights, turned off the television and lay in the darkness of the quiet night, staring out the back window. It was a clear night, the moon shone brightly, lighting up the garden. I thought I saw movement out there, but I figured it had to be my imagination. Then it happened again. A slim figure, moving among the shadows, from tree to tree. I got up, took my gun out of the refrigerator, checked it, sat up in bed and watched and waited.

Yep. It was a man, and he had a machete! My God. He came close to the building, then he disappeared. He couldn't get in unless he came through my door; that is, if he didn't plan on climbing up the side of the house. But I heard nothing. I went to the door, opened it, and stepped outside into the night. He had disappeared. I came back in and locked the door. I went up to the second floor without turning on a light and listened at Mrs. Hylton's bedroom door. He was in there all right. How he'd gotten in, I didn't know. I waited for him to show, but all I could get was noise—soft noise, but noise nevertheless. At first I thought he was opening and closing drawers, then I wasn't sure. Hell, I thought, I might as well face the son of a bitch and check his jock. I knew where the light switch was. I threw open the door, flicked it on and went into a semicrouch all at once. He was on the other side of the bed, down on his hands and knees, looking under it apparently. He looked up, saw me and crashed through the window. I could have fired, but I didn't.

I rushed over and watched him. He landed on his feet and disappeared into the night. With that kind of agility he was an awesome enemy. But he was a dreadlocks all right and no doubt about it. A friend of Trevor's? Maybe. I'd never seen him before in my life. He had Trevor's build, the slimness and the suppleness of body. If anything, he was an even more elongated version. But the face was burnt-out—pockmarked and sinister. Nothing handsome there. Wolf's eyes. Not the deep, rich eyes of Trevor. Anyway, he was gone.

I went upstairs and knocked on Kathleen's door. Nothing. I called to her. Nothing. I tried the knob. Nothing. Getting desperate, I began shoving and banging. But it was locked. I shot the lock and kicked it open. She was lying in a pool of blood. On the bed, face up. She'd been hacked at a diagonal from the right eye to the left rib. It was a mighty blow, probably inflicted by a weapon similar to the one my crocodile-eyed friend was carrying. And she was dead.

Things were beginning to happen at a frightening pace, I had gotten into a nice leisurely rhythm with Mrs. Hylton around to feed and nag me. When I got bored I went to Manhattan. When I wanted to be alone, I just stayed in my "rooms"—Trevor's sneer notwithstanding. But now it was all beginning to unravel.

The deaths were piling up and I didn't know what the hell was going on, much less what I was doing. I was tempted to call my erstwhile client Regina and give her back her $500, but I had decided she was part of the puzzle, and anyway at least somebody was going to pay me for all the work I was going to do. What would happen to Mrs. Hylton's three million dollars now that Kathleen Campbell was dead was a question I wanted answered and fast. Trevor was suspect number one and no doubt about it. Of course, the sister might be a beneficiary in strong standing, especially since she had been named in the previous will and could get a good lawyer to fight to reinstate her claim under some legal guise or the other.

I looked around. There didn't seem to be anything in the way of clues. She had changed into a nightgown. It was a short, delicate affair that showed most of her legs and arms and part of her stomach. She was quite a beautiful woman, even in death and with that horrible, immense gash across her body. I covered her up and went back downstairs, leaving the door to the first floor open.

The phone rang as I was about to pick it up.

"Hi," came a seductive voice.

"Hello," I answered guardedly.

"What happen? Why you never come back?"

"Come back where?" I asked.

"To the dance, of course. Where else?"

That's when I realized it was my East Indian beauty. We had hardly said two words to each other, so I didn't really have a clue as to what her voice sounded like.

"Having fun?" I asked.

"Yes, but not as much as I'd like to."

"Look, is de Souza there? It's very important that I talk to him."

"Just a minute." And I heard her call him.

"Thought you might be lonely, so I had her give you a call."

"And I appreciate it, but we've got problems."

"Yeah, I know. Everybody here is scared, let me tell you. We're having a meeting right now."

"Well, don't adjourn it too quickly because I've got another item for the agenda. Kathleen Campbell is dead. I found her in her room just now. Killed with a machete."

"A machete," he repeated almost in disbelief. "You mean what we call a cutlass in Jamaica, a long knife?"

"Right. Call it in and get somebody over here with brains, a lieutenant or somebody. I need fingerprints, the works, you know, like what they did for Josephs."

"I'll get on it right away. You'll be there?"

"I'll be here." I hung up and went back upstairs and checked the entire house. I came back down and searched the basement just to make sure. But there was no one in the house but a dead woman and me. As I came back up I heard something at the front door. I went outside from my floor and looked up. Trevor was at the door, trying to force it.

"Down here, Trevor," I called to him. He stopped, hesitated, looked down at me and reluctantly accepted my hospitality.

"Did she go out?" he asked as he came toward me.

"No, she's up there." I went in first when I saw him hesitate. "Close the door behind you."

"Why? You afraid of muggers?" He almost laughed as he said it.

"You won't think it's so funny when you see what I've got to show you."

I suppose I shouldn't have done it, but I wanted to see his reaction. Of course if he was guilty, then he was prepared to give a performance anyway. But he was shaken, like hell, and no mistake about it, when he saw her. He actually began to cry. I wanted to leave him alone, but I didn't dare.

"The police will be here any minute. You'd better hang around, they'll want to talk to you."

"You called them?"

"No, de Souza did. Know him?"

"Yeah, I know him. When did it happen?"

"I don't know, I was out all evening until about fifteen minutes ago."

"You were at the club on Empire Boulevard?"

"You know about the club."

"Everybody knows about the club." He almost sneered.

"Just before I found her I saw a man in your mother's room, the one she was killed in."

"What kind a man?"

"A Rasta, or at least he was dressed like one."

"And what do you mean by that?"

"Trevor, why don't you give it up? I'm neither for you nor against you, unless you're a killer. The guy had dreadlocks, he was carrying a machete, what you call a cutlass. He was in pants and shirt. His face was pockmarked and he had an evil look about him. A little taller and thinner than you. Know him?"

"Where you say him was?"

"In your mother's room, looking under the bed."

"Looking under the bed!"

"That's right. When I came in and turned on the light, he saw me and jumped out the window and ran."

"Snakey! Ah goin' bun' him rass." And with that he bolted past me, down the steps four at a time, and out the front door. I looked through the window and saw him tearing down the street in one direction as a police car turned the corner coming in the opposite direction.

As I watched Trevor disappear, I thought to myself that he was actually traveling faster, going in his direction, than the police car was, coming in its. It was going so slowly that it seemed to be moving in the opposite direction. But it was getting closer so I knew that had to be an optical illusion.

When they finally pulled up and got out, I was already bored with the prospect of having to endure another "interview" with New York's finest. But it had to be done, so I went downstairs, opened the two front doors and stood there as they got out and climbed the stairs. The man in the lead was in a dark suit, white shirt and tie, no hat. He had a stoop to his shoulders, a chewed-up cigar sticking out of his mouth, and a bored, I wish to hell I was somewhere else look to him. He was about five feet ten and 190 pounds. Swinging nightsticks, the two jerks in uniform from my previous encounter brought up the rear.

They had parked the car in the middle of the damned street and left the flashing light on. I guess they wanted someone to spot them in case they got mugged. He was Lieutenant Quinn, Timothy Quinn, but they must have called him Red when he was a kid. He had freckles covering his face and all his body hair: eyebrows, eyelashes, everything. He was red all over. He stopped halfway up the stairs, looked up at me, and said, exasperatedly, "You must be the black Philip Marlowe."

"Right, just call me Sam Spade and grin when you say it."

"The day I grin at you, Chubby Checker, will be the day they bury Ireland."

"You mean it's still there—in the North Sea? I thought the Brits had sunk it long ago."

"You wish. Now get out of my way before I turn you into a welfare case."

"Yeah, it must kill you to come out to the rice and peas district—just because somebody got killed—to listen to a smart ass like me tell you what happened."

"You said it, bud" was his next sally as he came up to the landing I was on and stood there looking me in the eye. Thank goodness his cigar wasn't lit.

"Do we need the rear guard or can we handle it alone, until the rest of the team gets here?"

"The rest of what team?"

"The guys who take the pictures and dust for fingerprints, like on television."

He turned to them and rolled his eyes. They grinned broadly. "This is it, bud."

"Oh, I get it," I said, "those two are the chief medical examiner's female assistants, but they're in disguise."

"I'm going to tell you something, bud"—and he pushed his finger into my chest as he said it—"I could stick you in a cell and forget about you for a week, if I wanted to."

"Well, twenty-four hours certainly."

"For sure, but I never waste my resources. Which doesn't mean that I'm going to let you smart mouth my officers. You watch yourself, or you won't know the ceiling from the floor when I get through with you."

"You're kidding. Do you mean to say that you would unleash those two stalwarts in blue on me? Or would you do it yourself? What're you going to use? The stub from your cigar?" That's when de Souza showed up. He at least had parked near the curb. Quinn wasn't happy to see him.

"Is this the guy you told me about, Hank?"

"Yes, Lieutenant, that's him."

"Boy, you sure can pick 'em, that's all I gotta say." And with that he brushed past me and into the house. He headed straight back, got lost, turned around and said, "Aw right, where is she?" But he didn't look at me, so I didn't answer him.

"Well?" He was getting testy.

"The old broad—" Young Baby Blue started.

"Watch your mouth!" I shouted.

"Now you've been warned," said Quinn.

"And I say, let's do it and get it over with, but I'm not going to listen to his bucket mouth."

Quinn thought about that and sent Handsome Johnny out to the patrol car. The older one told him where the back room was, but de Souza spoke up. "That's not where she is, is it?" he asked me.

"No, that's not."

"So where is she?" Quinn.

"Right this way, Lieutenant." And I led them upstairs. He changed as soon as he pulled back the cover and saw her.

"Damn. Pete, see if you can get a photographer over here." Pete went downstairs, leaving de Souza, Quinn, and me in the room with Kathleen Campbell's remains. "Okay, hotshot," he began. "Tell me what you know." He eyed me, then de Souza, and he took a seat and looked at his cigar as if it had deserted him. He put the stub in his coat pocket, ashes and all, and reached into an inside pocket and came out with a fresh one. He went through the ritual, unwrapping it, licking it, biting off one end —I never could figure how they knew which end to bite off, but they invariably looked at both ends before making their move— and finally the huffing and puffing until he got a good light. When he'd finished all of that, he looked at us as if we were retards and said, "Well?"

"Well what?" I shot back.

"Well, what happened?"

"Are you asking me a friendly question, or are you insisting on my cooperation regardless?"

"What is it with you, bud? You think your New York crap cuts any ice over here? This is Brooklyn. We take you New York fags and chew you up, then we spit you out in Brooklyn."

"Oh, gee, and I thought this was New York. But you're right, it's Brooklyn, as in boondocks, bush league, back alley, and bullshit."

He got up, came over, blew on his cigar so the light would glow, and stuck it in my cheek. I hit him in the stomach. He swung a left. I hit him on his chin with a quick right that snapped his head back. De Souza drew his gun. Quinn stumbled, caught himself, then said, "Cuff him." De Souza hesitated. "Cuff him, you son of a bitch," he yelled. De Souza got out the cuffs, then we heard a scuffling downstairs. Quinn went to the door and yelled down, "What the hell's going on?"

Pete called up, "There're these two guys down here who want to talk to de Souza."

"Who are they?"

Pete asked who they were and called up, "One guy's Chinese, the other one's black."

"I didn't ask you their pedigree, for chrissakes."

De Souza butted in, "They're friends of mine."

"You shut up," he told de Souza. De Souza looked like the lost dog of the world when he realized that he was in trouble with his Lieutenant. "Send them up," he yelled down, "but you two stay down there. And watch the street. I've got enough trouble up here, I don't want to turn the place into a zoo." Then he looked at de Souza, who still had the cuffs out.

"You still want me to cuff him, Lieutenant?"

"You still want me to cuff him, Lieutenant?" he mimicked. "What a drip." Black and Chin came in. "Who're you two and what do you want?"

Black answered, "May we view the remains, please?"

Quinn went over and drew back the bedspread, looked at the body, looked at them, said, "Satisfied?" They nodded yes and he covered her up again, picked up his cigar, cleaned it off, and relit it. "Well?" he said to them.

"Well, we have an interest in the case," said Black.

"What kind of interest," he asked.

"We believe that there's a connection between this murder, Mrs. Hylton's and Mr. Josephs's."

"Who the hell is Mr. Josephs?" he asked. That surprised Black so much that he didn't know what to say. "Well?" Quinn persisted. "I'm waiting. Who is he?"

"The gentleman who was killed at the gas company just a while ago."

"Hank, you know about this?"

"Yes, Lieutenant, I'm the one who called it in."

"So why the hell didn't you tell me?" Hank didn't answer that. "I suppose your boyfriend was with you?"

"I may be his boyfriend, but before this is over, you'll be my lay for the week," I told him.

"That's it, cuff him."

De Souza came over, almost apologetically, with the cuffs.

"Not a smart move," I said.

"Who asked you?"

"These two gentlemen happen to be my clients. I've got a friend who's the copy chief of a wire service. He doesn't usually run this type of story, but I think I can get him to make an exception in my case."

De Souza was slowly putting on the cuffs by this. When he'd finished, Quinn said, "All through talking, wise guy?"

"Oh, yeah, I've got you where I want you."

"That's what you think. I'm going to teach you a couple of moves that they don't even know about in Harlem."

"There isn't anything you can teach me that they don't know about in Harlem."

"You two guys finish what you got to say and go. I've got to question your friend here."

"We can wait until after you question him." Black again.

"Not for the type of questioning I have in mind you can't."

Chin came over, looked at me closely, turned me around, opened my shirt, and looked at my chest. Turned to Quinn and said, "Well, there're no marks on him."

"Not yet anyway," Quinn replied. He wasn't about to be intimidated.

Then Black spoke up again. "I don't like the look of that cut. It's vicious. You think say Trevor could a do it?"

"I don't think we want to discuss the problem in front of Brass Knuckles here," I said.

"This is an open case, bud. You withold any evidence and I'll bust you good."

"Oh, now you've got a better charge. I wonder which one will go on the sheet first, insolence or interference in a case?"

"You two finished?" he asked them with finality. Black looked at Chin, Chin at Black, then Chin spoke.

"We'll call you tomorrow. What's happened here tonight proves that you have to get on a plane right away."

Quinn said nothing. They left. He locked the door, came over to me and set himself. Then he hit me in the stomach. It was a good hit. I saw stars, but I stayed on my feet. He didn't like that. He tried the other hand, getting more body into it. I staggered. The next one would have had me on the ground and no question about it, but he just smiled, straightened up, and relit his cigar. He'd made his point.

"Uncuff him," he said. De Souza did, a lot faster than I had expected him to. "You've been warned. The next time, I'll have you crapping in your pants for a week. Now get outta here and don't let me see you again, ever. This case is off limits to you, period. And don't you forget it."

"In the first place, gonzo, I live here, and in the second, this case is a lot bigger than what you're looking at. And you couldn't keep me out of it if you changed your name to Willie, so don't even try."

"When you say live here, do you mean in this room or somewhere else, like the basement maybe?"

"Oh, the basement definitely, but it beats Hell's Kitchen by a wide margin. Come down and see me sometime. I may even give you a tip or two on what's going on." And I left.

Of course I'd been foolish, baiting him like that, but the only thing you get for good behavior is condescension. If they start out thinking you're a cheap peephole creep, you stay that way unless you change their minds fast. If de Souza had had the clout, I could have avoided the Irish menace altogether. But as it was, he was the man I needed to talk to. Well, now I never would, and that was that.

As I lay there watching the dawn about to come up like thunder, I thought about the living and the dead, avoiding the biblical cliché of the quick, since if they'd been that in the one sense, they'd have been it in the other. Mrs. Hylton, with her elaborate legal maneuvering that didn't save her life. Kathleen Campbell, so articulate, so becoming, winsome almost, in a pseudo-British way, neat, informative, well contained, brave, so sure of her own strength and now so very dead. Josephs, assertive, full of pride, willing to pay his way. And Trevor, at least he was still alive but arrogant, full of hate for my light-skinned, bourgeois facade, and yet so stunned to find out that friend Snakey had been crawling around under his mother's bed while he was trying to protect his religion's reputation from my imagined sneers.

Three murders in one night in Brooklyn. Several things could have been happening—all of which held the promise of a very romantic adventure under a tropical sky. Someone could be buying up all the fallow land in an island in the sun, because there was offshore oil, or maybe to make it a base for Russian missiles, or for a chance to make a killing with beachfront hotels—although I doubted that one—or because a mad scientist had found a way to make plutonium out of sand! Or maybe gold out of coconut oil. It couldn't just be winter vegetables and bauxite, or could it?

And there were so many other intriguing threads woven into this burgeoning fabric of suspense or was it pulp fiction. My friend Reg O'Connor knew something about it. A leggy beauty with style and a sense of danger about her knew something about it. There was a lawyer who Black said was crooked. Then there was Black himself, Chin, and God only knew who else. Maybe time was the key. A satellite was going to orbit the earth twice by Thursday and blow up the world unless someone gave them all the sunken treasure in the Spanish galleons lying in half a mile of water off Port Royal, and paid for the cost of recovery, in three days or less.

I was getting tired of playing guessing games. I pulled the shades, stripped to my underwear, put the gun under my pillow, and fell back onto the bed. Sufficient unto the day . . .

3

I woke up with another dull headache and Mrs. Hylton's voice ringing in my ear. A lot had happened in less than twenty-four hours. I was on a case with two dead women for clients. A lot of people wanted me to do a lot of things for them. And I felt responsible, for what I wasn't sure. I hated playing the Lone Ranger. But that's what it seemed to be coming down to. I showered, shaved, and made coffee while I tried to sift the priorities. I had to check out two different lawyers, go to the island of Jamaica. In addition to that I had to get Brooklyn's finest to do tests in the house, then I had to get the results, once I'd gotten them to do the tests. That would probably be the hardest part. If I did go to Jamaica, I'd have to learn a lot more about the island, as well as the case, before I got on a plane, unless I was just interested in getting a suntan no matter what. I was confused. I got dressed and left the house without incident.

I walked over to the other side of Eastern Parkway and checked out the other Mrs. Hylton's building. It was a huge apartment house. And I was conspicuous by my presence. A lot of guys were standing around in front and they eyed me as if they thought I was fuzz or a bailiff or the city marshal or something. But I didn't let that stop me. I went in, found the bell and rang up. She buzzed back without asking who it was. I got to the floor and knocked on the door. She seemed surprised when she opened it and found me standing there. I think she was expecting somebody else, but she recovered quickly.

"Come in, please, Missa Joe," she almost purred. I did. It was a close apartment. Small rooms, overly furnished, a lot of plastic covering everything. She was one up on her sister. No one ever went into that living room.

"Come into the drawing room, please."

I followed her, took a seat on a sofa that had so much spring to it that I thought I was sliding off, even with both feet planted on the rug and me pushing backwards.

"Can I get you something?" she asked.

"No, I've already had coffee, thanks."

She sat, rather primly, and waited. "Mrs. Hylton, frankly I'm a little confused. So much has happened so quickly that I'm having trouble keeping up."

Before she could answer, the phone rang. "Excuse, please." She got up and went to a corner, turned her back to me, picked up the phone and mumbled into it. She kept saying "Eeeee-heeee." It sounded like the Jamaican version of "Uh huh" or "Okay." Then she hung up and and came back to where she had been sitting. She was acting differently and no question about it.

We hadn't had much to do with each other. I'd seen her maybe four, five times. Once her sister had a cookout in the back and we talked for about five minutes. But it was just small talk. I didn't really know a damned thing about her. But I did know that she was nervous about something. Was it guilt of some kind? How much did she want her dead sister's money, if indeed she really did want it? I decided to check her pulse.

"You were saying, Mr. Joe."

"I was saying a lot is happening and happening rather quickly. When's the funeral?"

"Ten nights after the death."

"Why ten?"

"Because we have to have nine night."

"You do?"

"Yes. That's how we do it in the West Indies. And we call it nine night."

"You call what nine night?"

"The period of mourning."

"Is that like sitting shiva?"

"I don't know what that is."

"Your sister knew."

"In many ways Iris was more educated than me."

"How come?"

"She came here before I did, and was well taken care of for several years before that."

"I see. Where's her husband?"

She hesitated, then said, "Why, I think he's in Jamaica."

"But you don't know for sure."

"No, he's definitely in Jamaica."

"And your husband?"

"My husband."

"Yes, your husband."

"What about him, please?"

"Where is he?"

"I don't know."

"When did you last see him?"

"I . . . I . . . I don't remember."

"Well, give me a ballpark figure. One week, one month, one year."

She thought about that for a long time, then said, "I think he's dead."

"You think he's dead."

"Yes."

"I see. And exactly where is he buried, if he's dead, may I ask?"

"I don't know."

"But your sister's husband would know."

"I suppose so."

"Only suppose. Aren't they brothers?"

"Yes."

"Then doesn't it stand to reason that if one brother was dead, the other brother would know about it?"

"Yes, I suppose."

"And wouldn't it also stand to reason that his widow would know about it?" She didn't answer that. "Why was your sister killed?" I asked her.

"Somebody must have wanted to rob her. Them have plenty dangerous types walkin' 'round in Brooklyn these days. Plenty." She seemed to be reassuring herself that there were types who were indeed dangerous, and that there were indeed plenty of them walking around in Brooklyn.

"When you say 'rob,' you mean fifty-dollar rob, a hundred-dollar rob or what?"

"Whatever they could get, I suppose."

"How about three million?"

"But it wasn't sitting down in the house waiting to be picked up."

"Then what was?" She didn't answer. "I'm going to Jamaica next week. Anything I can do for you while I'm down there?"

"No, nothing." She was getting more and more tense.

"You do know she's dead?" I asked.

She nodded "yes."

"Now that Kathleen Campbell is dead, who's going to get all that money?"

"I don't know."

"Don't you?"

"No."

"Well, you are her sister."

"Yes."

"So what does that tell you?"

"Nothing."

"Has her lawyer contacted you?"

"No, not yet." Not yet, I thought to myself. Sounded like she expected him to.

"When he does, will you tell me?"

"Why?"

"I'd like to know what's going on."

"What's your interest in the case?"

"I'm glad you used the word 'interest.' I believe your sister was murdered for her money, and I intend to prove it because I liked her and because she was good to me, at a time when I needed someone to be good to me. Do you have any objections to that?"

"No, none whatsoever."

"Good, then will you help me?"

"How can I?"

"I just told you. When the lawyer contacts you, let me know."

"Well, if you think it will help."

"I think it will."

She fell silent and I sat there looking at her, while she tried to appear calm. She had one thumbnail close to drawing blood from the fleshy part between the index finger and thumb of the other hand. When she realized I was watching her do it, she suddenly stopped.

"Mrs. Hylton, are you in any sort of trouble?"

"No."

"Are you sure?"

"Yes, I am." She was choosing her words carefully. There was no need to play games with her.

"Well, suppose we assume that your sister was killed for her money. Let's also assume that the money was legally protected so that even if someone had possession of documents like bankbooks, securities, whatever, that that still wouldn't be enough to get them the money unless and until that person was established as the legal heir." I paused, then said, "That person would have the best motive for murder possible."

"Meaning me, I suppose."

"Meaning you." I looked at her closely. She gave away nothing, so I continued. "It would be difficult to imagine you as the actual killer in either case. I suppose you could have knocked your sister's skull in, although you don't really seem that strong.

She was twice your size. Still . . . Then there's the Kathleen Campbell killing. If she was killed while she was sleeping, then you could have done it. Otherwise, it would seem rather difficult, unless you're good at wielding a machete. There was just one blow. Which takes us to the next point. An accomplice."

"Of course, someone could be doing it unbeknownst to me."

"If he or she were, then they'd have to have a pretty good idea that they'd be able to get you to cooperate with them once they'd removed all the heirs between you and the three million."

"I suppose."

"When did you last see Trevor?"

"Not since yesterday."

"In the house?"

"Yes."

"Do you know someone named Snakey?"

"No." I didn't believe her.

"Why did your sister change her will, leaving everything to Kathleen Campbell and nothing to you?"

"Who told you that?"

"Kathleen Campbell."

"Well, it's not true."

"Oh."

"Not completely true, anyway."

"Explain that."

"I think you'd better take it up with the lawyer."

"Is he working for you?"

"No, I wouldn't say that exactly."

"What would you say, exactly?"

"We're working together."

"Oh, how come?"

"I don't understand you."

"What do you two have in common that would make it worthwhile teaming up for?"

"We both want to see justice done."

"And that means seeing that you get all of your sister's money."

"No, not all."

"You mean you want to share it with Trevor?"

"Him don't deserve a penny. All him do is cause the poor woman trouble."

"That's not a good enough reason for disinheriting him. After all, he is her son. From where I sit, he's got the best claim, unless she said otherwise."

"Then he would have the best reason for killing her and his wife."

"Do you honestly think he would kill his own mother?"

"Do you honestly think I would kill my own sister?"

"It's been known to happen."

"With sons too."

"I guess so." The phone rang again. She didn't move. "Aren't you going to answer it?" I asked.

"Not necessary." Then it stopped.

"Look, Mrs. Hylton, I hope we're on the same side. If the money belongs to you legally, and you didn't do anything illegal to get it, then I'm glad for you. All I want to do is solve a murder."

"Just one?"

"No, three, in fact."

"Three!"

"Yes, didn't you hear about Mr. Josephs?" Her eyes went wild. She began to shake all over.

"Him dead?"

"Yep. I found him. A policeman from Jamaica named de Souza was with me. He was killed on the job."

"Oh, my God." And with that she got up and ran into the back room and slammed the door. I waited for a while. Then I went to the door and knocked. But she didn't answer. I called to her. Then I tried to open the door. It was locked. "Mrs. Hylton, will you be all right? Do you want me to stay or to help you in any way?"

"No, no, please leave. Just leave," she pleaded.

"All right." And I left.

4

Well, I'd taken the beauty in boots's five-hundred dollars, so I had to at least find out what the guy who was on her back was all about. I went over to the Brooklyn Museum and called.

"Hi," she purred.

"Hi. I'm about to earn my advance. Who's the guy and where's his office?"

"His name's Richard Aubuchon. His office is in Bowling Green."

"I thought you said he was from New Jersey?"

"Well, he lives in New Jersey, but he works in New York."

"So, give me the Jersey address too."

"I'd rather you just stick to the New York address."

"Didn't I tell you not to make it difficult for me."

"Yes, you did, but I'm a naughty girl. I just never listen."

"Okay, I'll call you tonight, if I find out anything."

"Call me anyway, around nine, and we can get together for a drink. There're a lot of nice places in Brooklyn Heights."

"Sure." She gave me Aubuchon's address and I hung up. It was one of those big complexes put up by the first or second largest bank in the world, I wasn't sure which. His office was in the tallest building. He shared space with a lot of other lawyers from what I could tell. They called themselves Legal Associates. It wasn't until I got to the double doors with all the names listed on it that I stopped in my tracks. The second name on the list was none other than Smedley Braithwaite. Aubuchon's was first. But it was Saturday and not much happening. A couple of cleaning people, a few weekend executives. Girl friends and wives sitting impatiently in cars out front—that sort of thing. Legal Associates was closed, but I saw a light on in a room somewhere off to the left. The door was locked, but not bolted. I slipped it and went in. I made the left and came face to face with a Dapper Dan in summer linen, Paul Stewart shirt and tie, Brooks Brothers slacks and jacket. Everything, down to the handkerchief, was *Town & Country* centerfold.

"Yes, can I help you?"

I thought about it and decided I didn't want anyone to know I had an interest in Richard Aubuchon just yet. "I'm looking for an attorney."

"Just any attorney?"

"No, I have a name."

"What is it?"

"Braithwaite, Smedley Braithwaite."

"I'm Smedley Braithwaite."

"Hello, I'm Joe Cinquez."

"I'm not familiar with the name. Were you recommended by someone?"

"Well, I'm not exactly a client."

"I see. Excuse me, I have to get this in the chute before the mail pickup." And with that he went through the doors and across the hall to the mail chute and dropped a large brown envelope down it. Then he came back in.

"Wasn't that door locked when you came in?"

"No."

"Funny, I thought I'd locked it. Saturday you know, not too many people around. We have to be careful."

"Yes."

"Sit down." He indicated one of the plush chairs in the waiting area in full view of the hallway. He wasn't taking any chances. I sat across from him. We eyed one another. He took out a cigarette, lit it with a fancy gold lighter.

"Have one?"

"Don't smoke."

"Good for you. So how can I help you, Mr.—"

"Singkwey, spelled CINQUEZ. Here's my card." I got up, went over; he got tense. I was standing over him suddenly. Had caught him off guard after he'd gone to so much trouble to put some distance between us. I showed him my license. He looked at it for a long time before he handed it back to me. Then he got pensive. I mean he was in deep thought. I went back to my chair.

"This is about Iris Hylton, isn't it?"

"Yes. It happened last night around seven or eight o'clock from what I can tell."

"I talked to her sister afterwards."

"She called you at home?"

That bothered him. "Yes, why do you ask?"

"Well, it seems odd. I thought you were Iris Hylton's lawyer, not her sister's."

"I've handled the legal affairs of both sisters for some time now."

"I see. Any conflict of interest?"

"No, why should there be?"

"Well, Iris did disinherit her sister . . . What's her name, by the way?"

"Who, the sister's?"

"Yes."

"Enid."

"And then went to great pains to see to it that Enid had no chance of reclaiming the money by leaving it all to her ex—daughter-in-law, Kathleen Campbell."

"Not ex. Trevor never divorced her."

He was a curious type. I thought. Telling me things he didn't have to, on the one hand, and yet being so unhappy about my involvement, on the other. "You know, of course, that Kathleen Campbell is dead."

"You're mad!" he blurted out.

"No, it happened in the early hours, around two or three A.M."

"But how could it . . . she . . . it . . . she . . ." He began to stammer and twitch at the neck. Then he caught hold of himself. Got up, paced. "Did you actually see the body?"

"Yes."

"And you know Kathleen Campbell?"

"Yes."

"I see." Then he was quiet for a long time. He finished one cigarette and started another. "Does Enid know?"

"Yes, I just left her."

"What did she say when you told her?"

It was Josephs's death that had upset Enid, not Kathleen Campbell's, but I decided to switch the reactions. "She ran into her room and locked the door and asked me to leave." I lied.

"And what did you do?"

"I left."

"I see. I suppose you're wondering why her death is having such a startling effect on everyone."

"Yes, I was."

"When I made the will leaving the bulk of the estate to Kathleen Campbell, I warned Iris that she was putting both herself and Kathleen in extremely dangerous positions. But she was adamant. Nothing that I said or did could dissuade her."

"Why did she have to do it in the first place?"

"Trevor had threatened to kill her."

"And she believed him?"

"She believed him enough to do what she did."

"Well, with everyone knowing about it, I still don't see how he could have expected to get away with it."

"He wanted her to finance some absurd scheme of his. She refused and that started the bitterness."

"What kind of scheme?"

"He wanted to build beach condos in St. Thomas."

"You mean the Virgin Islands?"

"No, that's the name of a parish in Jamaica."

"What is?"

"St. Thomas."

"How many parishes are there?"

"Fourteen. It's the way the island's divided politically, like the states in America."

"Where's Yallas P.O.?"

"Well, I don't know where the post office itself actually is, but Yallas is in St. Thomas."

Just then another Dapper Dan showed up at the double doors. He was dressed for leisure time in Banana Republic khaki. Curly haired, tanned, built like a tennis pro or a gymnast. Braithwaite tried to signal him off, but it was too late. He had his key out and we were staring at each other before he caught on. He fumbled around and then made a pretense at a casual entrance.

"I'll be right with you, Dick. My office is open," Braithwaite advised quickly. *Dick* tried to slip by, but his attaché case had R. A. in gold metallic lettering. I got up.

"I'm sorry, I'm Joe Cinquez."

"Uh, pleased to meet you," and he tried to get by. I held out my hand. He took it, barely shaking mine as he let go before I could get a good grip.

"I didn't get yours." But he kept going. "He's in an awful hurry," I protested.

"Yes, he is."

"Taking a trip, is he?"

"Yes."

"Kingston or Montego Bay?"

"You're very clever, Mr. Cinquez."

"You called him 'Dick.' There's a Richard Aubuchon listed as one of your colleagues. His name is right over yours, as a matter of fact. And I noticed the initials on his attaché case."

"Yes, that's Richard Aubuchon. You don't know him, I take it."

"No, never laid eyes on him before in my life."

"I see. Will you excuse me a minute."

"Sure." And he went inside and I heard them talking behind a closed door. What they were saying it was impossible to tell. I contented myself with waiting it out. Braithwaite came back out, relaxed, took a seat, lit yet another cigarette and waited for me to start it up again.

I decided to go back to where we were when Aubuchon showed up.

"How did Mrs. Hylton get her money?"

"It was bequeathed to her."

"All of it?"

"The bulk of it. The part that's in question."

"I'm afraid I don't understand."

"The money Iris earned on her own, most of which she used to buy her house—that money doesn't amount to more than a hundred, hundred and fifty thousand, tops. The three million is an entirely different affair." He was telling me things that I could have found out anyway, sooner or later. And he was doing it for a reason.

"Isn't Mr. Aubuchon going to join us?" I asked.

"Oh, I'm sure he will as soon as he's finished with the few odds and ends he came in to take care of." I didn't believe him.

"You were saying?"

"Yes, the three million was given to her by an eccentric English doctor."

"Really!"

"Really."

"You have my complete attention."

"She'd worked for him in Jamaica. He taught at the university down there. Iris was a religionist."

"A what?"

"A devotee of our remaining vestige of African religious culture. It's called Pocomania—which in Spanish means 'a little madness.' "

"How is this culture practiced?"

"They dress up in white and chant and sing and dance until they've become hynotized by the spirit of the thing and descend into a semiconscious state. Then they twitch and moan and roll around on the ground, which is always an extremely reddish clay so as to reinforce the visual effect of the trance."

"Did the doctor become a devotee?"

"I'm not sure if he practiced it in public, but there was some involvement. How much I'm not sure."

"So how do we get from that to his giving her three million dollars?"

"Well, when he decided to do it he was afraid that it would be contested by his family in England, so he got the money out some-how, and she had already converted it to dollars before she died."

"Three million. No bank would handle that kind of money for an individual without some sort of government sanction."

"You're right. I don't honestly know how they managed it, but they did. I didn't become involved until long after. I never knew Iris in Jamaica, you see. She came to me through a mutual friend about a year after she got here."

"Who's the friend, if you don't mind my asking?"

"But I'm afraid I do. Privileged information."

"Aw right. So all you know is that she had the money in negotiable documents when you met her."

"Right. Certificates of deposit—which she was converting into other assets."

"Who helped her with the conversion?"

"I'm sorry, Mr. Cinquez, that's all I can tell you."

"I understand, and you've been quite generous. So what happens to all that money now?"

"That's another story, and one that I'm afraid I haven't time for today. If you want to, we can finish this next week. I'll be glad to tell you everything I can." Then he paused. "So it's pretty certain she was murdered."

"Pretty certain."

"I see." Something about people being killed really bothered him. Almost as if it meant he too might be in danger.

"So, do I get to say goodbye to Mr. Aubuchon?" I asked with a stupid grin on my face.

"I'll see if he's got a moment to spare." And he went in and came back out. "Yes, if you wait a minute, he'll be glad to say goodbye to you. Uh, I have a phone call to make, please excuse me."

I didn't really want to let Aubuchon know I was checking up on him. But I wanted to look in his eyes, feel his body heat, find out what type he was. I sat, flipped a magazine for the cartoons, got up, crossed the lobby twice, and then got restless. I went back in to where they had been and looked, but there was no one around. I called out, checked all the rooms on both sides, then found a side door which led to a back staircase. They were both gone.

I had been careless and not a little haphazard about it all, mainly, I suppose, because I hadn't really taken the case, although I had said I had, and had wanted to. It started out as a way to get Westchester off my mind, then slowly it took on a life of its own, but I was still dragging one foot. Where were Iris Hylton's papers, bankbooks, things like that? I never even thought to look for them in her bedroom, as often as I'd been in it. That was stupid—pure and simple, on the face of it. I consoled myself with the fact that it was all I could do to keep up with the bodies, much less find time for on the scene research. But finding out where she had the money, and how she had really gotten it, was at the top of my list as of the moment that those two pretty boys skipped out.

I called Black. He was glad to hear from me. I told him I was all right. He knew Iris Hylton's bank. But he didn't think the three million was there.

"Why?" I asked.

"Because there's something funny about that money. It was

handled differently. She kept things to herself, so I can't be sure. But that money seemed to be more of a trust. In fact, I think she was keeping it for someone else."

"Then why was she killed?"

"I don't know. When are you going to Jamaica?"

"Any day now. Tell de Souza to call me tonight," and I hung up. I took a cab back to the house, went up to her room, searched through the drawers, in hatboxes, under the bed—maybe that's what Snakey was looking for—but I could find no bankbook or any documents that indicated where she kept her money. Or what form it was in—gold, English pounds sterling, dollars, coal, oil, or coconuts.

I went downstairs, got Reg O'Connor's briefcase, called him, he was in, I told him I had the briefcase. He told me to bring it over.

On the ride back into Manhattan to his office, I tried to make a determined effort to be systematic. To start thinking ahead. To get involved. I hoped it would work.

Reg was as cheery as an Easter Bunny. He was getting a little fat in the middle and a little red in the nose, but he couldn't have been more fulsome.

"Joe, you old drifter. You went back to the pub and got my briefcase. Now that's what I call a friend."

"Well, not exactly, Reg. I had it when I, uh, left you at your door, but didn't realize it until I'd gotten to the elevator. When I went back and rang the buzzer, you didn't answer, so I left."

"Yes, those damned buzzers never work when you want them to. I must speak to the landlord about that."

Well, that was certainly a wondrously smooth, "official" version of why he never heard me leaning on the damned buzzer.

"I hope it's all there."

"Sit down and take the load off your feet." He winked at me, opened a side drawer, took out a pint bottle and poured two doubles into paper cups, downed his in one swallow as he handed

| 73 |

me mine, put the bottle back, and immediately assumed the demeanor of a priest. I needed at least two tries and then some to finish mine. But I wasn't going to let ole Reg down. Not me!

"I see you've solved the problem of the British system of getting drunk."

"The whole point of it is not to get drunk, old boy. A shot here and a shot there and you never feel a thing."

"What about last night?"

"Well, Friday is Friday, after all."

"Of course. How silly of me to even ask."

"So what can I do for you, Joe, me lad?"

"Tell me about Regina."

"Don't know the lady."

"You have to. She wasn't very smart about it. She told me too much for it to have been any other way. Trying to get work for me, Reg? And if so, why so shy about it? I'm grateful if anything. Five hundred dollars is five hundred dollars after all."

"Joe," he started out, taking the bottle out of the drawer again and taking another shot here and another shot there as he spoke. I turned my cup down, which only drew disdain from him. "You want to live long, you know when to play and when not to. A lot of items come across my desk. I read each one carefully, very carefully. The ones I run must be safe first and last. And I don't really care what else they are as long as they're safe."

"Safe?"

"Safe. No lawsuits from the rich and famous, no midnight phone calls from the mob, no bricks thrown through the window by extremists."

"Must make life a little dull."

"Not at all. You were asking me about a story that we ran."

"Yes, I was."

"Now you take a story like that. You'd think it was risky, what with the drug angle bit, but it isn't."

"No?"

"Not at all."

"How come?"

"It's quite simple. The story is filled with the idea of danger, but apart from the poor slob of a black prime minister, who gets hurt? No one. So it's almost perfect, isn't it? Dangerous without being dangerous." And he smiled and took another slug. Reg was trying to tell me something but the bourbon was one leg up on him. I tried to be patient and hoped he'd find the courage to say what he wanted to before he was no longer able to. But his grin just got bigger and his stare more vacant.

"It's absolutely the perfect story for us. The perfect. Of course there's an element of danger in everything. You get up one morning, shower and shave, and defecate. Go to work and get run over by a truck when you step out the door for lunch. It's all in the roll of the dice, isn't it?"

"I suppose so, Reg, I suppose so. Anyway, I've met the lady, taken her money, and in fact have a date to see her this evening. And by all that's holy in the name of St. Bourbon and St. Scotch, I shall do my best by the dear, sweet thing. You have your property and, I assume, I have your good wishes, so I'll leave you to the sweet ministrations of the nectar."

I got up and left. Reg was just sitting there, the glass in his hand, smiling and staring into space. And that's how they found him. I know because the picture on the front page with the caption "Wire service copy chief found shot dead" showed him that way, except for the hole in his forehead where a single bullet had entered.

5

It was Sunday morning and I was tired. I had a hangover and I felt stale, the way also-rans feel the morning after. Regina hadn't answered the phone when I called at nine o'clock, so I went home. But then de Souza called around ten and tried to cheer me up by talking me into coming to the club. I did, but my East Indian West Indian beauty was out of town and I ended up with an Ashanti princess by way of Rockaway Boulevard who announced at two A.M. that her husband would soon be over to pick her up. That's when I went home for the second time that night and went to bed.

I got up bright and early, and found a newsstand on the eastern side of Grand Army Plaza, bought the *Times*, and headed back with it tucked safely under my arm. It was 10 A.M. and half of Brooklyn was already getting ready for the annual West Indian Day Parade. In about two hours Eastern Parkway would look like the evacuation of Europe after the Second World War. I hastened indoors to escape the melee or maybe it would be the mayhem. It could even go to holocaust from what I'd seen of past West Indian Day Parades.

Beyond the picture, there wasn't much on Reg's killing. They found him about two hours after I'd left. Well, the deaths were piling up and fast, but I wasn't going to get anyone of West Indian descent to cooperate with me on anything until the next day. Of that much I was certain. That's when the phone rang. It was Regina.

"Have you seen the morning papers?" came her question hotly.

"Well, I usually only read the sports and the TV sections—but if you mean Reggie O'Connor, not only did I see it, but I saw him."

"When?"

"Yesterday. And he was sitting just the way he's sitting in the picture—except, of course, that he wasn't dead."

"Oh, Joe, I'm frightened."

"Where were you last night?"

"Never mind about that now. When can you go to Jamaica?"

"Today, tomorrow, next week. Why?"

"Why? I told you why."

"Oh, yes, property in the family. And what do I do when I get there, wrestle Dick Aubuchon to the ground and make him admit he's a rat?"

"Rick, he likes to be called Rick."

"Does he? Well, not by everybody."

"And how would you know?"

"Because I was in his company yesterday, briefly, when an associate called him Dick."

"Are you sure?"

"Sure about what, that I was in his company or that he was called Dick?"

"Both actually."

"Describe him."

"No, you describe him," she hissed.

It was time to stop being so likable and find out what the hell was going on, and the only way I was going to do that was by getting a little hard-nosed. And there was no time like the present to begin.

"Why is it so important for you to know whether or not I saw Richard Aubuchon yesterday?"

"Will you stop playing games at a time like this? Can't you see that I'm in a desperate situation?"

"No, I'm sorry to say I can't see that at all. But I'm perfectly willing to be persuaded that you are." I think she was thinking about hanging up, but decided against it.

"Meet me at Grand Army Plaza in an hour."

"My dear, nothing short of the promise of an extended longevity, replete with wine, women and song, could lure me out into the chaos of Grand Army Plaza today. Besides, I just came from Grand Army Plaza."

"On the steps of the library. It won't be crowded there." And she hung up.

And here I had been planning an afternoon of baseball and booze, while I tried to figure out who killed Reggie and why, and if it had anything to do with Iris Hylton and her three million dollars.

I made coffee, read about the Mets losing after they'd had a three-run lead going into the eighth, got disgusted, and decided to meet Regina after all. The phone rang. I had a feeling it might be Westchester and didn't answer it.

Outside all was madness. There were vendors lined up for miles on end on both sides of Eastern Parkway, selling everything from fritters made from conch (the Italians call it scungilli) to codfish to ripe bananas (and God knows what else) to books and emblems and notions and oils and incense. I was eating a fritter and drinking a ginger beer when I thought about the oils. I quickly finished my fritter and asked the young man, dressed dramatically in white turban, flowing black robe, with a silver decorative piece in his nose and gold in one earlobe, if he had any eucalyptus oil. He gave me some to sample. It wasn't quite right, I told him. I tried another brand—number 41—that was on the money. I bought a vial, thanked him, and tried to get to Grand Army Plaza, but the festivities had already begun. The first floats were rather stiff and commonplace. But then I heard drums of passion and looked down the long line of entries and saw what had to be the most amazing sight ever beheld in New York City in broad daylight by man or beast.

There were about fifty dancers, seminude. Some had mud plastered on their bodies. Others had half of their faces painted and half unpainted. There was a lot of decorative brass and copper. Some was in the form of skirts, some in the form of cowbells, some were emblems, some were swords, and some were shields. And talk about dancing. Wow!

I threw my ginger beer in the air, almost swallowed my eucalyptus oil whole, and rushed to join the party. The poor cops didn't have half a chance of keeping things under control. Looking into their frightened, uptight faces, I almost felt sorry for them. I think they all wanted to be someplace else.

But before I could completely go native, I saw a familiar face on the other side of the parkway. Snakey himself, in the flesh. He didn't see me. He was moving toward the plaza, looking left and right, seemingly not in too much of a hurry to get where he was going. I put the eucalyptus oil in my pocket, assumed an indifferent demeanor, crossed over to where he was, and began to track him. The more I thought of him rummaging around under Mrs. Hylton's bed the angrier I got. He veered right at the plaza itself. Which was a bit of a problem for me, since the crowd thinned out over there. But he had a purpose and seemed unconcerned about his back. Right where the plaza rotunda begins, he stopped and chatted with a guy who was leaning against a car. The guy opened the car door and took something out. Then they both lit up splifs that were the size of chimney stacks. I mean everything was everything! Can you dig it! If not, follow the asterisk for a translation. I used my fancy mnemonic system from the course I had taken five years ago—when I had just gotten my license—to remember the plate number on the car. It was Jersey. It was ANR 7109. My mnemonic was Annie Knew Ralph—1709, switch the 17. How the system works is too boring to go into.

Snakey settled in to finish his splif. I moved directly behind him, in front of a building that was quite substantial and well kempt. The tenants were all out, arms folded, black and white alike, as if they were protecting their manse from the horde. I sort of sat on the edge of their tension and tried a weak smile.

Snakey never turned around, but his buddy did. He was shorter, a little beefy in the face and broad featured. He looked like a cab driver type. But the car didn't appear to be a gypsy cab, not that that meant anything in Brooklyn.

Snakey finally finished his smoke. He and the guy exchanged something. It seemed like money, but I couldn't be sure. Whatever it was it definitely required some give and take on both sides. He was doing more than paying the guy for the grass, that was obvious.

Just then a blonde in shorts and sandals—thirtyish, well endowed, on the big side about five feet six, 139 pounds, big bones, broad featured—came out of the building, crossed over, and went directly to where Snakey and his friend were standing. Snakey looked up as she got close. If he had been standing at an angle slightly more to his right, he could have seen me with no trouble. But she had his complete attention. She knew the other guy too. She took a drag or two, then she and Snakey headed west away from the parade and the activity. I was sitting there, trying to figure out how to get a line on her when the old hens fed it to me like a computer printout.

"Well, Gretchen's hanging out in fast company these days. Whatever happened to Bob?" says the white-haired old lady with the Jewish accent.

"Don't know, but she better watch that one, he's a rough customer," says speckle-haired older lady with Barbadian accent.

"Does Mrs. O'Gilvie know what she's doing?" asked another.

"Mrs. O'Gilvie can't control her," reported yet a fourth.

Her name was Gretchen and she lived with a Mrs. O'Gilvie, who could be her mother, aunt, grandmother, or just her landlady. But I didn't think she'd be hard to find. I didn't want to be conspicuous by asking any questions just then. I crossed over to the library steps just as Regina was standing up and brushing herself off.

She assailed me with, "Well, I'd just about given you up."

"Oh, and why should I take your appointments any more seriously than you do?" was my clever rejoinder.

"And what does that mean?"

"It means last night."

"Oh, last night. Sorry about that. Something came up."

"Yeah, well, tell me about Reg O'Connor."

"Let's go where it's a little more private."

We crossed over to Prospect Park and found a secluded bench without too much trouble. Everybody was at the parade.

"Okay, kid, let's have it."

"First, I want to know if I can trust you, and if you'll really help me."

"I told Reg I would just before they shot him."

"Can you prove it?"

"Not unless you can talk to Reg."

"I'm not sure I like you."

"Now we're getting somewhere. All the pussy-cat sultriness, the 'Let's have a drink and talk' come on, none of it's really necessary. You paid me to do a job and with some luck I should be able to do it. But we can conduct our affairs on a businesslike basis. You don't have to keep trying to seduce me with your manner. And why do you go around so provocatively dressed all the time? Don't you ever take a day off?" I was wound up and ready to bust a gut and no doubt about it. I usually get like that when things aren't going right. I apologized.

"I'm sorry, Regina. Reg was a nice guy. I liked him. He was the kind of guy who would always do a favor for you, know what I mean?"

"I was in love with him."

"And what did his wife have to say about that?"

"The bitch. She was his biggest problem."

"Oh, bigger than the bullet that killed him?"

"Well, at least he's out of his misery."

"That doesn't sound like love to me."

| 81 |

"I said I loved him, I didn't say I was blind. I knew he was a hopeless alcoholic who didn't have the guts to get out of the jam he was in."

"And what kind of jam was he in?"

She thought about it, took out a cigarette, lit it, took a long drag, crossed her legs and got melancholy. She just couldn't help being provocative. It's the way she went through life. She was gorgeous, and no question about it. But she wasn't my type. Astrologically speaking, I was convinced we didn't even belong in the same room at the same time.

"Reg, God bless him, was sitting on a story that was too big for him. And he didn't know what to do with it. He'd spent his whole life trying to play it safe. But never could. He talked playing safe, but he was always taking chances. When you called him Friday, he was actually looking for your number because he wanted you to protect him."

"Me?"

"Yep. But then he changed his mind and got brave. So I decided to get you involved with a cock and bull story about land in Jamaica."

"Why?"

"Because land in Jamaica is actually the problem."

"And Aubuchon?"

"Reg was convinced that Aubuchon was the key to the whole thing."

She was still holding back on me, but I was beginning to get the pieces to fit anyway. "And it has to do with drugs?"

"Exactly."

"Was Reg trying to get a piece of the action?"

"Yes!" she hissed.

"For?"

"For running the story."

"Oh!"

"Yeah. They wanted the prime minister busted because he wouldn't play ball."

"I see. It's getting big all right."

"Too big for you, hotshot."

"No, I've handled bigger."

"I doubt it. The kind a money we're talking about would bust a calculator."

"True, but the actual cash flow is somewhat smaller."

"Not in the drug business. It's strictly cash all the way."

"Maybe. In any event, now that the man in your life is no longer with us, what is your continued interest in the story and the cash?"

"I want to get even."

"You want to get even."

"Yeah, for Reg's sake if nothing else."

"And what do you call getting even?"

"Either get the bastard who pulled the trigger or make him pay for it."

"I see. What's your plan?"

"That's where it gets tricky. If you're a thief or a fink, I'll have to deal with you the way they dealt with Reg."

"And how do you propose to do that, my pretty?"

"Take a look at your back."

I turned and the pretty boy with the muscles and the intense face was standing near a tree. He could have been carrying a weapon but he was too far away for me to actually tell.

"And that's your protection?" I asked.

"That's it and it's plenty."

"Lady, you're in trouble."

"No, you're in trouble." And she beckoned to him. He rushed the tree and tore off a limb with a grunt and a kick.

"Very impressive," I said, "If you're into destroying nature's ecological balance."

"That could have been your head."

"I doubt it. I usually keep my head close to my body." She was desperate. If I didn't shiver and shake I had the feeling she was going to clam up. "Okay, okay," I relented. "He's awfully good. If that was my head I would definitely have lost it. That make you happy?"

Then she started to cry and the karate threat came charging over. I surrendered before he got within two yards. "I didn't touch her. She started crying all by herself," I protested.

"It's all right, Jay, he's not going to do it."

"Do what?" I asked.

"Kill the prime minister."

"What prime minister?"

"The one they busted."

"You're kidding."

"No, that's why they killed Reg, because he promised to do it." Jay had finally opened his mouth.

"Then why didn't *they* do it themselves?"

"Because federal narcotics agents have been sticking to him like a leech for over a year."

"There's no such thing as a hit that's too big," I offered, trying to sound my most authoritatively hard-boiled New York, Private I genre.

"It has nothing to do with its being too big. It has to do with its being too risky."

"Same difference."

"Look at it this way. If you can get something done that you need to have done without putting yourself on the line, wouldn't you do it?" he asked.

"Maybe. But killing a member of the press isn't exactly smart business either."

"A deal is a deal."

"I have a feeling there was more to it than that." That shut them up. "Was Aubuchon the payoff man?" Nothing. "What was Reg supposed to get for doing the job?" Nothing. "Okay, you want me to *hit* the P.M." I was trying not to laugh. "When do I have to do it?"

"You mean you will?" Jay with enthusiasm.

"Try me." But Regina smelled a rat.

"How much?" she asked dryly.

"Oh, I don't know, make me an offer."

They went into private session while I waited. Then they came back.

"Five thousand," Regina said.

"Not enough," I said with a straight face.

"Well, that's all we've got."

"Why doesn't Jay do it, since he's so good? That way you'd save the five thousand and still get what you want. Although how killing the prime minister helps you, I'm not quite sure I understand."

"Reg had to kill him to get his cut. That's the way they wanted it." Regina.

"Go on."

"They were going to set it up for him, but he had to pull the trigger."

"First you say he ran the story to get the P.M. busted, then you say he had to kill him."

"They came to Reg with the offer, then they set the P.M. up so that he would get busted."

"You mean they approached Reg about running the story before it happened and then made sure it did by tipping off the Feds?"

"You've got it." Jay with enthusiasm.

"I see. Then why bother killing him?"

"Because he still wouldn't play ball."

"Tough customer?"

"Tough customer." Jay again with even more enthusiasm.

"They tried to get his voluntary cooperation. When that didn't work they voted for the final solution, is that it?"

"Right." Jay again.

Just then I looked up and saw three suspicious-looking characters approaching us. Two were black and one was white. "Don't look now, Jay, but I think we're going to put your fierceness to the test."

Jay wasn't happy at all about that idea. The guys looked like pros. I didn't have a gun and I was hoping they were not inconsiderate enough not to return the compliment. At least they weren't showing anything. But they meant business all the way. They spread out. I thought about making a run for it, but Regina had on high heels. It was too late to tell her to take them off and still manage to get away. In bare feet she probably wouldn't have gotten very far anyway.

"Don't tense up on me now, Jay. Regina, get behind us and use those heels of yours like a hammer."

They rushed us.

"Hey, wait a minute," I protested. "Can't we talk this over?" The next thing I knew, I was on the ground. This big brother, who looked stronger than he actually was (thank God for that) was trying to pin me for a ten-count. But he couldn't quite manage it. We ended up back on our feet, only he had me in a half nelson. He was trying to get the other arm in position, but I ran him into a tree before he could and broke his grip. He started swinging away. He wasn't fast either. I blocked him off without even a scratch on my elbow. That's when I saw Jay being chased by the second brother while Regina was trying to destroy the other ethnicity with her metal-tipped heel. But she couldn't quite manage it. He had her by the wrists and was dragging her away. I backed off from my guy and picked up a brick. He took out a blackjack. I hit him once and he lost it all. I took his blackjack and turned, but the other guy had a gun out. He held it to Regina's head, said nothing—just looked at me and backed to the street and into a waiting car. They sped off. I never saw Jay or his pursuer again. My man was just recovering. I gave him his own blackjack behind the left ear. He sank into the grass with complete abandon. I went through his pockets. Nothing by the way of an ID. Just money. I dragged him behind a bush and went to the corner, found a phone and called the precinct and asked for de Souza. He wasn't there. I got brave. I asked for Quinn. He was there.

"Hello, Lieutenant. This is the private investigator you assaulted night before last."

"What do you want, Daisy Chain?"

"Lieutenant, will you stop being so redolent of manner. It doesn't become you."

"I'm busy, make it fast."

"I need a favor."

"I don't think you're playing with a full deck."

"I'm not. But I still need a favor."

"I'm waiting."

"I'd like you to send the lab boys over to the house on Hancock Street."

"I've already done that, hotshot."

"Yes, but Mrs. Hylton's bedroom is as important as the room Kathleen Campbell died in. It might even be more important."

"Which room is hers?"

"The back room on the second floor."

"Anything else?"

"Yes, I just witnessed a kidnapping." I waited for him to ask me if it was my own, or something equally clever, but he just waited, so I pushed on. "A woman, black, in her early thirties." I gave him her name and address and a general description. "She was the girlfriend of Reg O'Connor and has some theory about why he was killed. You know about his death, of course. It made the front page of the Manhattan newspapers, but I figure some of the news from the Big Apple filters across to Brooklyn once in a while."

"Exactly where and when did this happen?"

I told him.

"Anything else?"

"Yes, there were three of them. I've got one behind a bush waiting for you."

"I'll be right there."

I hung up and went back to check on my friend, but he was gone. He seemed out when I left him. I thought for sure he'd be good for another ten to fifteen minutes. Maybe my moving him helped wake him up. I stood on the sidewalk and waited for Quinn. The parade was in high gear and the acts were still coming up to the judging rotunda in an endless stream. All was gaiety and festiveness. I hadn't been in the mood for the damn singing and dancing to begin with, first thing on a Sunday morning. And now that it was getting louder and more hectic, it just added to my feeling of impotence. I hoped Regina wouldn't be added to the list of corpses.

Quinn got there sooner than I had expected. "Where is he?" he asked unceremoniously.

"Gone."

"What do you mean gone? If you got me out here on a wild goose chase, so help me . . ."

"He had no ID on him when I searched him. I hid him over there behind a bush. I went to call you and when I came back he was gone. But if he's in a mug book anywhere, I can find him. And the license plate of the car that the kidnap victim was taken in is Billy Billy 4094. Connecticut. But it probably won't get you anywhere."

"Show me the spot."

I did. He looked around skeptically. "Something like that could have happened here. But I'm not saying it did."

"There's no reason why you should. You weren't here. I was."

Then I saw the third member of the trio jump over the park wall and into the street. "There's number three," I yelled and ran after him. Quinn jumped back in the car and U-turned and drove past him and up onto the sidewalk to cut him off. He jumped back over the wall and headed into the park. I followed with Quinn behind me.

The guy was fast, a lot faster than I was. But I didn't lose him. He cut across an open glade, turned to see where I was, and tripped on a rock. He got up and I was close enough to nail him with a gun, but not close enough to grab him. Quinn yelled at me and I moved to my right without breaking stride so he could get a clear shot. He fired once and missed. By this time the guy had made it to a clump of trees. Before Quinn could get off a second shot, there was a yell. A woman came running out of the trees past our guy, screaming, "Don't shoot, don't shoot. I have my baby in there." By the time we got to the woman and the trees he was nowhere in sight and I was out of breath.

"You missed him."

"You were in the way."

The woman had calmed down. Quinn apologized. Her baby was fine. The bullet had hit a tree trunk and stayed there.

We went back to the station house, and I looked through a lot of mug books. I found the guy I'd knocked out and left under the bushes after the fourth book. Calvin Davis. Originally from Cleveland. Last known address: the Bronx, White Plains Road and 220th Street. I thought about that and remembered something Mrs. Hylton had once said about a West Indian community in the Bronx—White Plains Road in the 200s—but I said nothing to Quinn.

"Well, there's the one I had in the park waiting for you, Lieutenant."

"What about the others?"

"What about them?"

"Aren't you going to look for them too?"

"I was looking for them."

"And?"

"Didn't see 'em."

"Keep looking." And he left.

I yelled, "Aw right, Lieutenant, I'll go through two more books and then I'll quit." I did, but didn't find either of the other two guys: The one who'd dragged Regina off or the one we'd just chased in the Park. He came back with coffee as I was finishing up. He was suddenly quite friendly. He wanted something.

"Now tell me all about Reg O'Connor's girlfriend."

I told him most of what I knew. There was really no point in not telling him.

"You have her card?"

I gave it to him. He copied the information and gave the card back to me and then got up to dismiss me.

"What about the lab report?" I asked.

"What about it?" he snapped back.

"When do I get it?"

"Who said you were going to get it?"

"Nobody said. But I asked and you didn't say no."

"All right. Call me tomorrow. It should be ready then."

"Thanks, Lieutenant." And I left. Outside, I saw Frick and Frack, the two uniformed geniuses. The younger one wasn't so cocky. The older one seemed preoccupied. I wanted to find de Souza, but I didn't want them or Quinn to know about it. I waited in front for a while. A brother in uniform came out. I asked him about de Souza. He told me he hadn't seen him for several hours. I caught a cab and headed for home.

When we got within a half mile of the reviewing stand the cab driver quit on me. I got out and walked the rest of the way. They had finished the judging and the politicians were getting in their two seconds in the sun—handing out buttons, crowding around one another, waving and smiling at, and to, all and sundry. But nobody was going anywhere. The crowd was as thick as ever and seemed a sure bet to stay that way for another two–three hours.

I was looking to get lucky, and I did, but not the way I had expected. The third member of the trio, the one I had chased into the park less than two hours before, was coming my way, hell bent for leather. I turned and bought a small press news-paper—the kind that accuses everyone in an official position in America of being a facist—buried my head in it and watched him pass me and head in the general direction of the park. I followed. He went right back to the spot where we'd all had our little tussle. I watched him from the sidewalk. He was looking for something. He bent down a few times and picked up what might have been it, but wasn't. Finally, he gave it up and that's when he saw me.

I hopped the wall and we were at it again. He ran deeper into the park, but when he realized that he couldn't shake me, he decided to turn and try a different tack. He picked a good spot. Secluded, but with enough room to move in. He stopped, turned, and took out a gun and faced me. As I came up to him weaponless and out of breath for the second time, I felt like a consummate ass, but I kept coming, at a slower, more ambling gait, of course. I didn't want him to think I was going to charge his onrushing bullet. I had been convinced all along that he didn't have a gun. But I mistook discretion with the draw for no draw at all; unless, of course, he had acquired it after our first encounter. I pulled up and pretended to be more winded than I really was, talking to him while I bent forward, hands on knees, but he didn't get too close. He came within eight, ten feet, studied me. I tried to relax him, make him feel more confident. That had to be priority one, as the aggressive, ad agency boys are wont to say. I straight-ened up, hand on hips, still breathing heavily, and made my move on priority two.

"You did that real good. Your boss is gonna be proud of you.

I have a deal for him that's gonna knock his eyes out. I was with the newspaper guy hours before he got it right in the forehead. And he gave me something that will make that prime minister in the West Indies play ball for the rest of his life."

"What kind of something?"

That's when I got closer, about four feet.

"That's close enough," he said.

"Sure. I'm clean. Look, see." And I held up my hands. "Hey, look, take me to him and I'll make it worth your while. He'll be happy to see me, I promise you." That's when a park ranger, in uniform, on a horse, no gun, cowboy hat and walkie talkie, came riding up. My friend heard the horse's hoofbeats behind him.

"Watch out, he's got a gun," I yelled. I wanted to rush him, but he didn't turn around. I think he wanted to kill me as his priority one, and then deal with whatever was behind him. I was an instant away from ducking for cover—not that I would have made it—when the hoofbeats got too close for his comfort. He turned to look and I sprang on the instant. He was on his way back when I hit him. He fired a shot that came so close to my temple that I was deaf in that ear for the rest of the week.

But we were down by this and tussling. The gun fell from his hand as soon as he hit the ground. We rolled around once or twice, then got to our feet. All the while the damned ranger stayed on his horse enjoying the show for chrissakes.

My man was built like a ten-ton truck. Muscles bulging from everywhere. He started at me and I retreated into a defensive position. He was throwing lefts and rights with the ferociousness of a mace and chain. Each one raised a whelp on my arms the size of a coconut. But he couldn't get inside. That frustrated him. He set himself for a karate kick, but I beat him to it. One swift one in the balls and he was down, his stomach in his mouth. I hadn't laid a hand on him. I got his gun, told him to stay on his knees, and requested that the defender of the grass use his walkie talkie.

He suddenly got very efficient, pulled out handcuffs, cuffed my friend, got on his walkie talkie, and talked gobbledygook into it, then took out a pad and started writing like hell, checking his watch, checking the date. Then the horse got restless and he gave me the reins. We were mobbed in no time. More rangers, spectators, a patrol car. Then they got into a hassle over jurisdiction. I told them to call Quinn.

"Wrong precinct," one guy piped up.

"Maybe," I said, "but he's working on a case and this guy can give him some answers."

"And who're you?"

"Me? Nobody. I just happened to stumble along."

"Oh, no," spoke up grass ranger. "He's the one who subdued the perpetrator and assisted in his being apprehended." I was suddenly a hero. They took us to Quinn's precinct.

"Well, well, quite the hero, are we?" said Quinn when we all walked in.

"If at first you don't succeed, Lieutenant."

I waited around while they booked him. He refused to make any phone calls. After the rangers were all sent back to the grass and Quinn went off somewhere, I wandered into the hall to get coffee, or what was probably two-year-old chicory passing for coffee, when I saw de Souza. He was in another room. He beckoned to me. I went over casually, not sure of why I was trying to be surreptitious, when he suddenly waved me off and disappeared. I did an about-face and went back to the room I had been in. When Quinn returned he seemed worried.

"I just got a call from the FBI."

"How come?"

"That's the first question I asked myself. Do they have spies in the precinct, for chrissakes?"

"But you realized that they probably picked it up when you ran a check on Davis."

"Right you are."

"And?"

"They want to know what I know."

"About what?"

"Everything."

"So what'd you tell them?"

"I didn't. Those hotshots give me a pain in the you know what."

"What're you, Irish or something? You can't say 'ass'?"

"Look, don't you start."

"Relax, Lieutenant, we're in this together."

"Where'd you get this together stuff?"

"Figure it out for yourself. It's a big case. Your end is probably incidental. But they need you because they can't put the puzzle together unless they have all the pieces. And I know a lot more about it all than you do."

"You son of a bitch. You been holding out on me."

"Well, I'm not sure that that's what I'd call it. In the first place, you never asked me. In the second place, you told me to bug off. And in the third, you've just been using me as much as you can and throwing me a bone or two to keep me on the string."

He said nothing to any of that. He knew I was right. And he was probably surprised that I hadn't gotten pissed over it. He certainly would have.

"You have the lab report on Mrs. Hylton's bedroom?" I continued.

"Yeah," he said reluctantly.

"Good. Let's run over there and go over it. We'll know a lot more when we're finished than we do now. And we'll be in a much better position to deal with the ole Federal Bureau of you know what." I hadn't expected him to go for it, but he did. He called de Souza, told him to get a squad car, and the three of us left tout suite. We had trouble getting through Eastern Parkway. The West Indians were still out by the truck and van load.

But de Souza knew all the shortcuts. He whipped around here, and turned corners there, and before you knew it we had pulled up in front of the house, probably a lot faster than if there had been no parade and Quinn or I were driving.

Inside, all was quiet. There were somber shadows in the hallway as the light through the front window played in long lines against the walls. The double mahogany doors were open. That never happened, even when Mrs. Hylton was lying in state and the clan had gathered. They had all gone down the narrow hallway and entered by the door at the end of it, in front of the stairs leading down to my "rooms." Whoever it was, was either in a hurry, careless, or innocent.

I went in. Quinn tried to stop me.

"I thought the room we wanted was upstairs," he said.

"It is," I said, "but someone's downstairs who shouldn't be."

"What do you mean?"

"Just trust me, Lieutenant," I replied, and I went in. And there she was, standing there, Kathleen Campbell, only she was dressed differently. I was stunned.

"You're, you're . . ." I stammered.

"Yes, I'm her twin sister, Marlene. You are?" And she came forward, hand extended. She had on scarves and delicate cotton, all bright colors, an earring in her nose, and a shawl glamorously covering her hair. The skirt flared to thick boots that only added to the allure and the general effect of good taste.

"My name is Joe. I found your sister."

"Oh. Yes, so I'd heard."

"This is Lieutenant Quinn and Officer de Souza. They're investigating your sister's death."

"I see."

"When did you find out about it?" I asked.

"I didn't until just now."

"How's that?'

Before she could answer me, Quinn butted in.

"Hold it, hotshot. Any questioning of relatives will be done by me. Okay? But first we got to go over the room the murder was committed in." He turned to de Souza and said, "Take her name and number and have her come in tomorrow morning."

"It seems as if we have a case of bureaucratic entrapment," I said. "But that shouldn't stop us from getting to know one another." I wanted to ask her what she was doing there, rummaging around in that part of the house, but decided that with Quinn playing major authority it would be a waste of time. We smiled at each other, exchanged numbers, and she left.

As we went up the stairs, I felt myself thinking of something and not knowing what it was. Suddenly I realized that when we shook hands, I had smelled it, but was too taken by the fact of her being Kathleen's twin for it to register. But it was unmistakable and now I had it on my hands—eucalyptus #41.

In Mrs. Hylton's room, Quinn took out the report and began reading aloud. "She probably died where you said she did, right here where the blood was found on the carpet. Traces of her hair on the rug indicate that the blow was struck while she was standing or sitting nearby and then she fell to the floor. Of course we can't be sure."

"Any other hair found anywhere around?"

"No."

"What about footprints?"

He hesitated. I could tell he was holding out, but I pretended not to notice.

"There were some shoe prints, but they were too blurred for the boys at the lab to make any sense out of them."

"What about fingerprints?"

"Hers on the dresser and the inside of the bed."

"Pointing in which direction?"

"Towards the window."

"Are you sure?"

"Yes."

"But . . ." I started, then stopped.

"But what?"

"I thought they were in the opposite direction."

"Well, let's see," he said and went to the bed to compare the prints on the report with the ones I'd seen when I was there. "They aren't here."

"I know," I said.

He turned to de Souza. "You know anything about this, Hank?"

"No, Lieutenant," de Souza said.

"Well, somebody's been in here."

"It seems that way," I observed. "What else you got?"

"Just a minute. If someone's been in here destroying evidence, then we better get the lab boys back. Hank, call the precinct."

Well, the FBI certainly had him hopping. De Souza went downstairs to make the call. I got impatient. "Well, Lieutenant?"

"No one else's fingerprints in this room," he said.

"But?"

"There was another set on the doorknob."

"Inside or out?"

"Out. Hers were in."

"So she could have opened the door for someone."

"If she opened the door for someone, then why would someone else's fingerprints be on the outside knob?"

"The prints are unrelated, or it happened at different times, or the other person held the knob anyway, either before or after or during the time she opened the door for that person."

"Maybe," he said.

"Have you identified them?"

"Not yet."

"But it's a good set."

"Yep."

"Man's or woman's?"

"Can't tell without a matched print."

"Well if you do find out, will you give it to me when you get it?"

"Sure." But he didn't look at me when he said it.

"Anything else?" I asked.

"No, that's it," he said, although he said it guardedly. He was trying to appear casual, but boy, was he holding back. And he wanted to ask me a lot more questions but couldn't without giving away what he had.

"Well, I guess that wraps it up," he said suddenly.

"Aren't you going to wait for the lab boys?"

"We probably won't get them back here before tomorrow. I'll leave Hank to keep guard until we can check it again."

"A little like closing the barn door after the cow's gone, wouldn't you say, Lieutenant?"

"Maybe. Let's look at the other room."

We went up to Kathleen Campbell's room. He took out another report. It was only then that it dawned on me that the reports had been done rather quickly, but I suddenly found myself being as uncommunicative with him as he was being with me.

"It's the same set, look."

It was the same set. "The left hand in both cases," I said.

"Exactly," said he.

We went in. "They found traces of hair from a wig in the bathroom. Two other sets of fingerprints, neither of which are on file. But the set from the door were not found in the room."

"And Kathleen Campbell's prints?"

"Found in the room, but not in the bathroom."

"And nowhere else?"

"Right."

"Strange. Why wouldn't her prints be on the doorknob? She certainly had to open it to come in. And we know that her prints can be identified since you have a copy of them taken, I suppose, from the corpse."

"What do you mean can be identified?" he asked.

"Well, there have been cases of people suffering from burns so severe that they removed the prints from the fingertips."

"Yeah, well, her fingertips had prints on them all right. Who else came in here?"

"I did. And my prints are on file in Manhattan. And Trevor did."

"Who's he?"

"Her husband, the son of the woman who was killed downstairs."

"What! Why doesn't somebody tell me what the hell's going on!" And he went to the door and yelled down, "Hank."

De Souza was two flights down on his way up.

"Yes, Lieutenant?"

"Do you know this Trevor character?" he yelled down to him.

"Yes, Lieutenant."

"Well, get an APB out on him, quick!"

"Yes, Lieutenant."

"I don't think he's the guy you're looking for," I offered.

"Why not?"

"Because Kathleen let him in."

"How do you know?"

"I was in Mrs. Hylton's room when she went downstairs and opened the front door for him, and the two of them came up together."

"What time was this?"

"Around ten-thirty."

"Friday night."

"Right."

"So why didn't you tell me about this before . . . I know, I asked you to bug out. Well, I'm sorry. Forget I said it, O.K.?"

"Sure, Lieutenant. Sure." If he believed that, I had a bridge I wanted to sell him.

"Did you find my prints on the doorknob or anywhere in Mrs. Hylton's room?"

"No."

"Strange."

"Why do you say that?"

"Well, when were the lab boys here?"

He got shifty-eyed suddenly and said, "I'm not sure."

Sure, you're not, I thought. What I said was, "Can you check it?"

"Yeah, I can check it." Then he paused, cleared his throat, and asked rather tentatively, for an Irish cop working Brooklyn, "Uh, what time were you in there?"

"The same night, Lieutenant, around three in the morning. That means the lab boys came afterwards—sometime Saturday in the day. That also means that someone wiped my prints off the knob because I definitely left them there. I had no reason not to. I was not trying to cover my tracks."

He thought about that, then said, "You wait here, I'm going to make a call," and went downstairs to find de Souza, and the phone presumably. I kept thinking about Snakey. I went back down to Mrs. Hylton's room and looked under a large dresser—an armoire that stood near her bed. I'd heard Mrs. Hylton refer to it as a clothes press. She kept her winter coats and things like that in it. I felt around in the bottom. It was clean. Everything in the room was cluttered and packed in as tightly as possible, one on top of the other. Hat boxes, shoe boxes. Sometimes there were shoes, sometimes hats. As often as not there were clothes, rags, newspapers from the islands, and just a lot of junk stuffed in them. I had seen all of that the first time I looked around. Now that clean surface at the bottom of the armoire was staring me in the face. Some of the coats and dresses came all the way down and touched it, but there still was a lot of room to "stuff" things in down there. I looked in front and there was a solid panel of wood that seemed glued onto the base of the armoire.

I was just about to find out once and for all what was inside that base when I heard Quinn on the stairs. I went back to the door and waited for him.

"Find anything?" he asked with a clever smile.

"No, what about you?"

"They were here Saturday, around noon."

"Well, I wasn't, so you can't prove it by me."

"Why should I want to?"

"You shouldn't. I'm just saying."

"I don't get you."

"Forget it, Lieutenant. So the lab boys came Saturday around midday. But either they missed a lot or someone cleaned up before they got here, right?"

"What do you mean they missed a lot?"

"I mean they overlooked little things like the doorknob or just didn't bother with them."

"What're you talking about?" And he reddened considerably.

"Lieutenant, don't get sore with me. I didn't tell them what to do, you did."

"Tell them what to do about what?"

"Not about what, just what to do, period, when they got here. I know how it works. They want to know how thorough you want them to be and depending on what you tell them, that's how good a job they do." He began to open his collar and get nervous. He was one step away from violent. "But now with the FBI interested, you're kinda in a bind. You have to get 'em back in here to do a real job this time. Only your captain is gonna want to know how come you needed two shots when one good one should have been enough."

"Look, fella, you don't understand. Those guys work hard. They're all over the lot."

"Yeah, Lieutenant, I know. You have to conserve your resources." That didn't go down too well. He couldn't decide what to do, come out swinging or try to get my sympathy. I continued.

"You should have seen the job they did on the gas company employee's murder. 'Course it was downtown, not your precinct. But it was Brooklyn. I mean those guys know what they're about. The measuring, the photographs, the fingerprint teams working in tandem. One guy powdering and scraping, another guy taking photographs and putting samples in plastic bags. The whole bit."

"Aw right, aw right. You've made your point. We didn't take it too seriously."

I looked at him, but nothing passed my lips. Only because by then I realized that I was up against it, but good. It was getting closer and closer to the time to get on a plane for Jamaica.

"Two murders in one house in less than twenty-four hours and you didn't take it too seriously. What're you going to tell the FBI?"

"Nothin'."

"Nothing!"

"Nothin'."

"Okay, it's your funeral."

"What's the matter, hotshot, you scared of the little old FBI?"

"No, Lieutenant, but they know more than you do. At least try to trade with them."

"With those guys? Are you kidding?"

"No, Lieutenant, I'm not kidding."

"They'll pick you clean, believe me. I've seen 'em do it. They did it to a buddy of mine. With them it's strictly a one-way street, believe me, I know."

"Okay, have it your way, but if you try to hard-nose it you'll just end up having to give it all to them anyway and getting nothing in return if they force it out of you."

"Let's talk," he said suddenly, and pulled out a bottle of bourbon.

"Oh, Lieutenant, you embarrass me. Come downstairs, I've got clean glasses, ice and fancy stirrers. I can even give you a mixer."

We went down and he called to de Souza, "Hank, wait by the phone. Okay, buddy, your place it is." I thought about telling him I had a phone, but realized that he really wanted us to be alone, so I said nothing.

We went down, I opened the door, turned on the light—and the place was a shambles. Everything was ripped apart.

"That girl," Quinn said. He called de Souza. "That girl who was just here. Pick her up, now!"

"Suppose she's not home?" de Souza asked.

"Then look for her. I want her and fast." Then he turned to me. "All right, hotshot, what do they want that you've got?"

"Jeez, Lieutenant, if I knew that I'd be glad to tell you."

"Don't play dumb with me, fella."

I didn't like the sound of that. I thought we'd gotten to a level of mutual understanding, racial harmony, peace, love, and, above all, cooperation. Obviously, I was wrong.

"Relax, Lieutenant, let's have that drink and discuss it." I picked up a glass, about to pour rum into it, when he came over and knocked it out of my hand. I moved away, picked up a chair, placed it on its legs and moved to the cookie jar where my gun was. "Lieutenant, if you try any crap with me, I'll whip your ass for you. You don't have any buddies to help you now."

"I don't need any to take you," he said and went for his gun. I beat him to it and he froze.

"Think you're smart, don't you?"

"No, but I do think you're stupid. Just because someone turned the place upside down, you think that's the cue for bringing out the rubber hoses, and if you do, I'll tell you everything you want to know. Well, I've got news for you, cutie puss, you're much too desperate to ever get to the bottom of this one. Talk about in over your head. You're so far in that a helicopter couldn't pull you out with a mile-long line."

He thought some, picked up a chair himself, sat and said, "I'm sorry. This thing's got me going in circles and swinging at shadows. I thought you were playing me for a sucker, that's why I got sore. Okay?"

"Sure, Lieutenant, sure."

"Can we have that drink now?"

"Sure." I put the gun in my pocket, made sure he saw me do it, went to the refrigerator, got ice, came over to where the broken glass was, when he said, "I'm sorry about the glass."

"As big as this mess is, that's the least of it, Lieutenant."

I got two more glasses, put in ice, gave him one glass, poured my rum, watched him pour his bourbon, and we sat across from one another, sipping slowly, eyeing each other and thinking about it all.

"You know, you're right," he said.

"I am?" I answered, a little astonished.

"Yes, we've got to stick together on this thing."

"Well, I wouldn't go that far."

"No, I mean it. Look, there's something in it for both of us."

"There is?"

"Sure. I get the bust and you solve the case for your client. What could be fairer than that?"

"Both of my clients are dead."

"Both?"

"Yes. Kathleen Campbell and Mrs. Hylton."

"What about the woman who was kidnapped?"

"She's a client too. But I'm not sure I'll keep the contract."

"You mean you'll take her money but you may not do the job? Kinda hitting below the panty hose, isn't it?"

"I've been hitting below that for a long time now, Lieutenant."

"I'm sure you have." I saw him thinking, but he said nothing. I continued, "But if I take your money, I do the job, or I give the money back."

"All of it?"

"All of it—minus what it cost me to find out that it was a mistake to begin with."

"And you took her money?"

"Privileged information."

Then the phone rang. "Excuse me," I said and went to it. It was the Kathleen twin. "Hi. When can we meet, it's awfully important?"

"Pick your spot," I said.

"There's a place in the Village where writers and actors go. It's on Hudson Street. The Black Stallion."

"Sounds good to me. When?"

"Eight o'clock."

"Right," and I hung up.

"Who was that?" he asked.

"A girl I met at a dance last night," I lied. I don't think he believed me, but what could he do. "Well, Lieutenant, here's to success," and I raised my glass. He raised his, and we drank. "And to crime. Without it we'd be out of work."

"That doesn't mean we should drink to it," he said.

"Of course it doesn't, Lieutenant. And I respect your position." As I said it, I finished my drink and poured another. He waited as long as he could before joining me.

"I hope you won't hold out on me with the dame?" he offered.

"What dame?"

"The one we found upstairs, the one I told de Souza to pick up."

"Oh, that one."

"Right, that one."

"Of course not."

He knew I was lying. "So what do you think they were looking for?" he asked.

"Beats the hell out of me. I didn't know I had anything down here worth going to that much trouble for."

"Well, what about petty theft?"

"No." And I showed him the TV and the stereo and tape deck.

That convinced him that whatever it was it was something he wanted to know about. That made two of us.

We had a few more drinks and bored each other with small talk and more promises to work together for each other's good and to foil the bad old FBI. After he left I tried to straighten up. When I thought I was quite alone, I went back upstairs, let myself into Mrs. Hylton's room, and pried open the base of her armoire with a large screwdriver. The front panel came off after some work. It had never been sealed but it fitted in too tightly. There had to be another way that she got to it. But there were all the papers I'd been looking for neatly stacked in metal boxes: bankbooks, a will, letters of credit, another will, letters of transfer, a couple of deeds. It was unbelievable. I was looking at millions of dollars in property and cash sitting in the bottom of a wooden cabinet. The metal boxes could hardly be counted on to protect them in case of a severe fire.

I was too intent on what I was doing to hear him. And I was just raising my head up when I was hit from behind. The blow stunned me and I struggled instead of going limp, my second mistake. He hit me again and this time I saw his shoes, but I lost consciousness before it registered. When I awoke it was late and there was a knocking sound inside my head. I roused myself, tried to hold my head together—it felt like two parts of a mushed pumpkin—and finally realized that the knocking sound was coming from the front door. I got up, stumbled through the door and down the steps and moved the curtain back. Kathleen Campbell's twin was standing there. It was still eerie seeing her, except that the dress and the whole style were so dissimilar from her dead sister's. I opened the door, still holding my head, and wondered why she hadn't let herself in the way she had earlier, but I decided not to question her.

"Hi," she said. "You don't look too good."

"I've felt better," I said and led the way down to my rooms. She followed, locking the door behind her.

"A drink," I offered as I was about to pour one for myself.

"No, thanks, and you don't need one either. What you need is a good pot of coffee." And she took the glass from me.

"What're you having?"

"Tea."

"How can a tea drinker make a good pot of coffee?"

"You'd be surprised. Here, sit, relax, let Mama take care of you."

She put me in my easy chair, got my feet up on my ottoman, fluffed a pillow behind my head, dimmed the lights, and put on the kettle and the coffee. Then she began to rub my head and dab the damned eucalyptus number 41 on my forehead from a tiny vial she had in her hand.

"I think you should know that I've been looking for someone who wears eucalyptus number 41."

"Why?"

"Because the smell of it was all over the hallway where a Jamaican watchman was found murdered Friday night."

"I see, and you think the scent was left by the killer?"

"Could be. It's a good bet. The place was sealed off. I found no one on the roof and there was a police officer in the lobby waiting for reinforcements."

She got up, turned the flame down on the coffee as she talked. "Anyone smart enough to get in in the first place, and commit the murder in the second, would certainly be able to make good his escape."

"Or her."

"Of course. I was speaking generically. So do you want to have me arrested?"

"No, not yet anyway. Why don't you tell me what you're doing here."

"We had a date, remember."

"But that was in Manhattan an hour ago."

"Well, you didn't expect me to just sit there all night, did you?"

"No. But what made you come back to Brooklyn? The chances of finding me here couldn't have been that good."

"But I live here."

"You live where?"

"Here, in this house."

"Since when?"

"Since as of now."

"You've lost me."

"It's quite simple."

"My dear, it's anything but that."

She went to get the coffee and the tea. When she came back with them, my headache was gone and I was on my feet.

"How do you take it?" she asked.

"I'll take it as is."

I took a few sips, waited for everything to come into focus, and then looked at her. She was my type of gal, but right then and there I had more important things on my mind. "You have the floor," I told her.

"When my sister was killed the other night, I was on a plane from London. I called her Saturday."

"But there's no phone in that room."

"She has an apartment on the East Side."

"Go on."

"There was no answer, so I went to the apartment and found a note telling me to come here and wait for her."

"What time did your plane get in?"

"Around eleven."

"Where did you spend Friday night?"

"At a hotel."

"Which one?"

"The Summit. It's on Lexington, right behind the Waldorf."

"I know it. Why the Summit?"

"I'm a stewardess. It's a hotel that many airline people stay at."

"How did you get into her apartment on Saturday?"

"I have a key."

"Where are your things now?"

"In the apartment."

"You checked out of the hotel?"

"Yes."

"I see. So what do you mean you're living here?"

"That's what her note said. If anything happened to her I was to live here for ten days."

"I don't think I understand."

"Neither do I, but that's what the note said. Here, I'll show it to you." And she took out a folded piece of personal stationery —linen, with the initials KC in large blue letters in the upper left-hand corner. It was dated the tenth. It said, "Meet me at the apartment on the Saturday morning after you get in. If anything happens to me, you're to stay in the house on Hancock Street for a week at least, but no more than ten days. You'll get a letter by then telling you what to do with my property. Love, Kat."

"What property is she talking about?"

"I don't know."

"The tenth was over a week ago."

"I know."

"And you haven't seen her in all that time?"

"No, I just got off my tour. She knew when I would have a layover with leave. We'd planned to spend the time together if we could."

"How did you get into the house earlier?"

"I used a key."

"And why didn't you use it just now?"

"Because it didn't work."

"Where is it?"

She took it out and handed it to me. I went up, she followed, and I tried the key. It didn't work. I tried my key. It didn't work either. Then I tried my key to the downstairs entrance to the ground floor. That worked, but it was a different key. Then I realized that when I led her down the first time the door had been bolted. That bolt had been taken off months ago. Now someone had put it back on. I opened it without realizing it because I was still groggy. Whoever knocked me out must have been very busy. At least I was still alive. We went in through the ground-floor entrance. I went back up. She followed. I took off the bolt and latch, then we went up to Mrs. Hylton's room and I looked in the base of the armoire. There was nothing there. I turned to her.

"What were you doing downstairs in the back room earlier when we came in?"

"Trying to get my bearings."

"Wasn't the door locked?"

"No, just closed."

"Had you ever been in this house before?"

"Yes, when Trevor and Kathleen got married the reception was held here."

"And you haven't been back since?"

"No."

"But you didn't come ready to move in?"

"No. I didn't really expect to have to, not right away at any rate. I expected to find her here. If I didn't I was prepared to wait a few hours, leave a note, and then come back and spend the night, if that was actually necessary."

"So that when the note said spend ten days here, it wasn't something you expected to have to do."

"No."

"Had she ever done that sort of thing before?"

"No."

"Have you ever been in this room before?"

"No."

We went back down to my part of the house. I made two cups of tea. Gave her one, put a toddy in mine, and thought for a while. "How many keys did she give you?" I asked.

"Two. A front door key and a key to her room."

"And you've never been in her room either?"

"No."

"Didn't she use that room when she and Trevor were married?"

"No, they didn't live here. She only moved in after their breakup."

"Now tell me how and when you found out she was dead."

"To tell you the truth I didn't think she was. When I left you I went to the morgue and it wasn't until I actually saw her that I accepted the fact that she was."

"But you didn't seem to be that disturbed."

"Only because I kept expecting to hear from her. I didn't know you, and I certainly wasn't going to say anything in front of the police."

"But I told you that I was the one who found her."

"You could have been lying."

"But why? Did she get involved with people who lied about things like that?"

"Let's just say that a lot of strange things have been happening lately."

"But you said you'd just found out that she was dead."

"I got a call."

"Who from?"

"I don't know."

"Where'd you get it?"

"At the apartment."

"When?"

"Just before I left. I was sitting there trying to make sense out of the note and wondering why Kat didn't call me or something, when the phone rang. It was a man's voice. He asked who I was. I told him, he paused, then he said, 'Something's happened to your sister, you'd better get over there right away. As a matter of fact, I think she's dead.' That's when I rushed over."

Something about it wasn't right, but I'd learned from long experience that some things you just don't find out by asking questions.

"Let's go up to the room." I took her up. Blood was still on the bedsheets. The few things that Kathleen Campbell had brought with her were all at the morgue along with her body. Marlene looked around. She seemed very uncomfortable. She suddenly had a chill and it made her shiver.

"Where did you find her?" she asked.

"Lying across the bed in a nightgown. She'd been hacked across the body from her right shoulder to her left thigh."

"What does that tell you?"

"Nothing much, except that it took a good deal of strength to inflict that kind of wound. And that the person who did it probably knew how to use a machete, what you Jamaicans call a cutlass. And that the person is right-handed."

"Well, that's a lot."

"True, but it still leaves too many suspects around for it to be enough to tell us who the culprit is."

"Can we go back down, I don't like it in here."

"Of course." And we left. "How close were you and your sister?" I asked.

"Not very, and then again we were."

"Yeah."

"Because we were twins we were kept apart, sent to different schools and things like that, so we wouldn't end up as each other's clone. But we were always together during holidays and some- times on weekends. If anything, it helped keep us closer over the years because we cherished our time together, came to value it rather than take it for granted."

"So you knew things about each other."

"Yes, many things."

"Did you know Iris Hylton?"

"Not well. She seemed like a nice woman, open, expansive, generous. From what I can tell she was well liked."

"Is it possible that she and Kathleen were close enough for her to entrust a large sum of money to Kathleen?"

"How large a sum?"

"Three million dollars."

"That is a large sum. Why would she give that kind of money to Kathleen? Why would anybody give it to anyone else for any reason?"

"Not give, entrust."

"You mean to keep for her until she asked for it back?"

"Precisely."

"Seems to me a bank's the best place for that sort of thing."

"Usually, but in this case we have an added problem."

"Which is?"

"Iris Hylton wanted to remove motive for murder from someone's mind. Who, I don't know yet."

"You mean make Kat her heir?"

"That's what I mean."

"Well, in a situation like that Kat was totally reliable."

"Why do you say that?"

"Because the same sort of thing happened once before."

"It did."

"Yes. I'm not sure of the details, but a Mr. Black would know. It had to do with a relative of his, I think."

"How much money was involved?"

"Nothing like three million. Fifty, one hundred thousand at the most."

"And you don't know the details?"

"No, all I know is that Kat kept the money for about six months. Put it in bonds or something—made a modest profit, about five thousand dollars. Kept that and returned the original amount intact when they asked for it."

"Very interesting."

"Of course, I'm not trying to imply that she made a living out of doing things like that."

"What did she make a living out of?"

"You mean you didn't know?"

"No."

"She worked for a lawyer."

"As a legal secretary?"

"More than that, more like a legal clerk."

"Was she studying law?"

"Oh, yes. I think she planned to take the bar exam next year."

"Who'd she work for?"

"I don't know. She'd just changed jobs recently."

"Who was her former employer?"

"I have the address in my book back at the apartment."

I went to the phone and called Quinn. He wasn't in, but I did get de Souza.

"What do you know about the FBI interest in Calvin Davis?"

"I can't get near that file. Quinn has it under lock and key."

"I need anything you turn up on Kathleen Campbell."

"Did you talk to Black? He had some dealings with her."

"Over what?"

"Something to do with money that he didn't want to put in a bank."

"Why?" I asked.

"I guess he was hiding it."

"You mean it was illegal?"

"That's what I mean."

"I've heard of a lot of ways to launder money, but that has to be the strangest. How did he know he could trust her?"

"I guess that was a chance he thought was worth taking."

"I guess so." I looked at Marlene, she looked at me, and I knew that she knew a lot more than she had told me. "O.K., Hank. What was it you wanted to tell me earlier?"

"That they were setting you up as a fall guy. How, I don't know. But I heard Quinn say, 'We'll make the black P.I. the fall guy.' "

"Thanks, Hank. You find out any more, you know where to reach me."

"Right." And he hung up.

I turned to her. "Well?"

"Well?"

"Was Kathleen involved in laundering stolen money?"

"I don't know if the money was stolen or not, but it was questionable."

"What was? The money or where it came from?"

"The money wasn't counterfeit, if that's what you mean."

"Can you be sure of that?"

"Reasonably sure."

"So she had done that sort of thing before."

"No, but the lawyer she worked for had. I think that's how she got the idea."

"Tell me about it."

"A lot of Jamaicans with money left the island when the last prime minister began to turn to socialism. I admired the man myself. He brought a lot of welcome changes to the island: minimum wage, land reform, the removal of illegitimacy as a legal stigma. And he got rid of the Masters and Servants law."

"The what?"

"The Masters and Servants law."

"You're kidding, of course."

"No, I'm not. You know how the old colonial mentality is, it dies hard. We actually had a law on the books more than a decade after independence that defined the relationship between masters and servants."

So much for third-world egalitarianism, I thought. "So he passed a lot of good laws."

"Yes, but he wrecked the economy in the process. It wasn't

all his fault, but he wasn't that smart when it came to minding the store either."

"Did he have a poor background in economics?"

"No, he had graduated from the London School of Economics."

"What was the problem then?"

"The rich, the privileged, had been that way for three hundred years."

"Are we talking about black rich and privileged or white rich and privileged?"

"By the time independence came the rich and privileged were more than fifty percent black. By the time they started leaving in droves, eight years later, they were practically ninety percent black."

"But their blackness didn't extend to helping their poorer brothers so that both groups could find the millennium together?"

"Not in the least. Jamaica is the most hidebound, caste-oriented country in the world. Even worse than India."

"Black Englishmen."

"Well, they usually call Barbados Little England, but Barbados has nothing on Jamaica."

"So where does that leave us?"

"A lot of the rich had a lot of Jamaican dollars that they wanted to turn into U.S. currency."

"Didn't they try to do it before they left?"

"Yes, but the U.S. dollar drain became so great that the government had to put a limit on the amount a private citizen could convert."

"What was the limit?"

"Fifty dollars."

"You're kidding."

"Nope."

"So what did a guy with hundreds of thousands of dollars do?"

"What they couldn't convert on the black market they smuggled out of the country and tried to convert after they got here."

"Let me see if I understand you. Legally, a citizen could take out fifty dollars. If he wanted to take out more in U.S. dollars he had to smuggle it out?"

"Correct."

"And if he was stuck with a large bundle of Jamaican dollars that he couldn't convert, he smuggled that out too and then tried to convert it afterwards."

"Right. Things got very hectic by the end of his second term."

"The prime minister's."

"Yes. People were abandoning land and businesses. Money was being smuggled out in plaster casts and under nuns' robes. Money would be deposited in one country for one person and the person that the money was deposited for would deposit money in Jamaica in the name of the person who'd made the foreign deposit."

"Or in whatever name was agreed on."

"Correct."

"So the only real problem was finding something to do with the Jamaican dollars in another country—or having all that money in Jamaica that was only good in Jamaica?"

"Right again."

"How much Jamaican dollars would you say was running around?"

"Hundreds of millions of dollars' worth."

"That much?"

"That much. I myself saw an airline executive in a hotel in New York with a million dollars in Jamaican money that he'd brought out in one trip alone."

"What could they get for it?"

"Very little unless the buyer had an interest in Jamaica."

"If he did, all he had to do was buy it up at five to one, ten to one, I suppose."

"More like twenty to one or fifty to one."

"It went that cheaply?" I asked.

"Sometimes it didn't go at all."

"But once he bought it, he smuggled it back into Jamaica and then he could buy up the place?"

"At one period doing that was no problem. There was very little check on how much money you brought in and where you got it from."

"But now?"

"Now they want you to deal only in U.S. dollars."

"So the Jamaican dollar abroad has ceased to have any real value unless you can prove how you came by it?"

"If the business is legitimate. If it isn't you can still cut a deal."

"Of course. Somehow this is all tied into drugs, but I don't know how just yet."

"Why do you say that?"

"A woman was kidnapped from a Brooklyn street earlier today who wanted me to go to Jamaica to protect land that she said belonged to her. But her boyfriend, who was a wire service chief, was killed because he was involved with a prime minister of a small island in the Caribbean who was arrested by the U.S. government for smuggling marijuana into America."

"Well, a lot of ganja is grown in Jamaica."

"Ganja, sounds like an Indian word."

"It is. It's the Hindi word for weed. It means marijuana in Jamaica, grass, reefer, whatever you want to call it."

"That might explain the killings."

"What might?"

"The fact that a lot of . . . what do you call it?"

"Ganja."

"Great name. Sounds like you can get high just from the smell."

"You can, believe me."

"That good, huh?"

"That good. It's highly valued. The best brand is a seedless variety, sin semillas, which means seedless in Spanish."

"Oh, that's what those guys on the corner of 87th Street and Broadway are talking about when they say, 'Buy a bag of sensy.' "

"That's it."

"Do you indulge?"

"Occasionally."

Just when I was developing a warm feeling too. Shucks. One thing I can't stand is a woman who smokes. And one who smokes grass, forget it. "Where do they grow the stuff mainly?"

"You name it, they grow it there."

"You mean north, east, south and west, it doesn't matter?"

"That's right."

"But some spots are better than others?"

"Of course."

"Name one."

"Guy's Hill."

"Where's that?"

"In Clarendon."

"Clarendon is a parish?"

"Right."

"Name another."

"Balaclava."

"Where's that?"

"In St. James."

"Another parish."

"Yes."

"Any more?"

"Well, a lot's grown in St. Thomas."

"Right you are."

"Oh!"

"When can I get a plane to Jamaica?"

"Any time you want."

"Will you arrange it for me?"

"Sure. I'll even put you in first class and go with you."

"Can you come and go as you like?"

"I have some leave coming. I can take it now."

6

Of course I couldn't leave until I'd found Regina. Marlene went back to the Manhattan apartment. We both agreed that that would be safer than her staying in the room Kathleen had been killed in, Kathleen's note notwithstanding. I had dinner alone at a Thai restaurant on Flatbush Avenue. The food was excellent. And except for a small pinball machine near the bar, so was the ambiance.

It was around eleven when I wandered back to Grand Army Plaza. The sanitation department was still cleaning up. It had been quite a parade. Then I thought about Snakey and Gretchen and crossed Eastern Parkway and stood in front of the building. I decided I might as well put the evening to some profit. I rang a few apartments, but no one buzzed back. I kept at it until I finally got a response. I guess if they're not expecting anyone they don't even bother to talk. But the intercom was a little faulty and after two or three attempts at communicating, we gave it up, and he buzzed me in anyway. Maybe he liked the sound of my voice. Inside, there was a neat directory. Mrs. O'Gilvie was listed in 4G. I took the stairs, knocked on the door, and Gretchen answered. I hadn't expected that and it caught me off guard.

"Yes, may I help you?" She was a little provocative; dressed in shorts and a skimpy top and sandals with a small heel. She was quite attractive up close, although the face wasn't actually a pretty one.

"Is Mrs. O'Gilvie in?"

"No, she's not."

"Will she be in later?"

"No, she's gone away . . . on business, family business."

Something was making her nervous. I decided to play an old

credit agency trick. "I'm a private investigator. I've been hired by an insurance company to find a Mrs. E. O'Gilvie. There might be some money coming to her."

I gave her my card. She took it, looked at me, looked at the card, then said, "Won't you come in."

It was a neat little apartment. A small living room, a dining room–kitchen combination right behind it, and a little hallway that led off to the right where the bedrooms probably were.

She offered me a seat and then asked, "Was the front door open?"

"No, someone was going out as I was coming in."

"And they let you in?"

"Yes."

"They're not supposed to do that."

"Probably a visitor who didn't know the rules."

"What is the name of the insurance company and how much money is supposed to be coming to her?"

"I'm afraid I can't disclose any of that until I actually talk to Mrs. O'Gilvie. It's why I'm working at such an odd hour. We get stuck with a lot of false claims once people know there's money involved. We prefer to insist that people prove their identity before we disclose anything like amounts or where the money is coming from or any of that sort of thing."

"I see. Well, how can I help you?"

"You can't, I suppose, since it's the lady whose name is on the bell that I want to talk to. It means making a second trip, I guess. But I got the impression from your answer that it will be some time before she does come back. May I ask where she is?"

"Abroad."

"Oh, dear, that will complicate it."

"May I ask is the sum considerable or just something that you want to get rid of to avoid an IRS audit or just to balance the books or something like that?"

"It's a sum that would make anyone's life relatively secure for quite a while."

"How relatively secure?"

"Well, that all depends, doesn't it?"

"Yes. Can I offer you a drink?"

"If it wouldn't put you out."

"Not at all."

"Rum, vodka, or scotch?"

"Rum is fine."

She got up, went behind the half wall. I watched her as she took out a bottle, poured two drinks, put in ice and came back.

"How's this?"

"Fine, just fine." I shook the ice around and waited.

"Well," she began, "if I could be sure that Mrs. O'Gilvie was the person you were looking for, then I'd have something to offer. If she isn't, then it's all pointless as far as my interest is concerned, isn't it?"

"I suppose. Of course time is money, and anything that you did by way of making my investigation easier would be of value to me."

"I see."

"Yes, I work on a comfortable expense account. And I'm very generous with it. You see, the mere fact that it's the same name can mean something."

"How's that?"

"Well, I could find out something that would help me the next time. No, I've learned not to turn up my nose at any information when I'm investigating a claim of this sort."

"I noticed you didn't mention her first name."

I had been afraid of that, but I couldn't duck it now.

"That was done on purpose. The initial is the same as the one in the directory. But I'm waiting for someone to fill that in." I waited.

Of course she could have given me a phony name, but I didn't think she wanted her Mrs. O'Gilvie to be the wrong one.

"In other words, if I give you the wrong name, that will be that."

"For the most part. Of course, I'll finish my drink. I'll even buy you one if you wish, anytime."

She thought about that. She was interested and no doubt about it. Greed was probably the motive, although she obviously enjoyed playing the coquette as well.

"So where do we go from here?"

I had to think about that. One thing was sure, I wanted to get out of there before Snakey showed up and I'd have to start ducking cutlasses.

"Well, my problem is that you don't seem to be able to put me in contact with Mrs. O'Gilvie. Once I see her, the rest will be easy."

"Why?"

"Because we know what our Mrs. O'Gilvie looks like. Names, documents, all of that can be changed. But a face is a different matter."

"A face can be changed too."

"Of course, to disguise an identity, not to make a new one that you don't even know exists."

"What you're saying is that your Mrs. O'Gilvie doesn't know she's come into this money."

"That's exactly what I'm saying," I'd suddenly decided.

"Suppose I showed you a picture."

"Pictures are hard. A recent picture? Full face, up close? What?"

"About ten years old. Posed, face and shoulders. Touched up, but only to get the wrinkles out and lighten the skin, that sort of thing."

"It might. But I'd still want to see her."

She either couldn't or didn't want to produce Mrs. O'Gilvie. "Suppose she were out of the country?"

"Where out of the country?"

"In the Caribbean."

"Show me her picture. Tell me where she is and I'll give you five hundred dollars." I was blowing Regina's advance on the wild chance that Snakey under the bed and Mrs. O'Gilvie in the Caribbean was a combination that would somehow pay off.

"Make it five hundred to see the picture and five thousand to see Mrs. O'Gilvie and you've got a deal."

"And whether or not she's the real Mrs. O'Gilvie is my affair?" I asked.

"Yes," she replied quickly.

"But you're selling yourself short," I offered.

"How am I doing that?"

She was so sure that her Mrs. O'Gilvie didn't have a large amount of money coming to her that she was more than willing to take the five hundred and run, no questions asked.

"Suppose she is the real Mrs. O'Gilvie?"

"You mean there'd be a bonus."

"There should be."

"Of course."

She recovered quickly and in the one way a woman always can and not lose whatever allure she has to begin with. She came over, took my glass and freshened it, brought it back. She was close, standing. I was in the chair. She looked down at me, oozing sultriness. "You'll think of something to make it up to me, I'm sure."

"That's usually the man's line," I offered, not too gallantly. Before she could recover a second time the bell rang. She got nervous.

"Uh, that's a friend. Look, I want to keep this between us. Okay?"

"Sure."

"In your line of work, I'm sure you've done things like hide in closets."

"At least closets," I assured her.

"Well, do we have a deal or don't we?"

Before I could answer, the bell rang again, and she went to the intercom. They debated it. She said she'd be right down, but he wanted to come up. She buzzed him in, then turned to me.

"I'm going to put you in the next room. I may even have to go downstairs for a while. Just sit tight. But can I see something, just to show good faith?"

Luckily for me, I had Regina's advance with me. I let her see all of it as I took out two fifties and handed them to her.

"I think I can trust you," I said.

"I'm trusting you," she said and pushed me into one of the bedrooms off to the right, as she was clearing up. I think we both made it just in time. He was pounding on the front door before I could get my bearings. He headed right for the bathroom. I think he just made it too.

The room was not too unlike Mrs. Hylton's. Bigger, more modern furniture. No armoire, but the same sense of mustiness, of everything of importance being in that one room. The bed was to my right and the window in front of me. There was a closet left, off the window, a sewing machine between the bed and the window, one of those old Singers with a foot pedal. There seemed to be a lot of tables with papers, covered with throw cloths. A brass bed. I moved toward the window and stumbled. I grabbed for the bed and the dresser, instinctively, and at the same time—one hand on the bed and one on the dresser. I froze. Then I heard his voice. "What was that?" It was Snakey all right.

"I don't know, probably the kid upstairs playing basketball in his room again," she lied.

While I stood there, daring not to move, even with my back to the door, I suddenly realized that fingerprints on the doorknob weren't the key. Why had Mrs. Hylton grabbed the bed so tightly with her left hand? Were there prints of her right hand on the top of the dresser across from the bed in the same position that this dresser was across from this bed? That could mean she grabbed for the bed because she was struck. She was already up. Had already answered the door. Had already let the person in, in fact. There could have been someone hiding in the room already, but that seemed unlikely. Why kill her after she'd gotten up, if killing her was the object? Kill her in her sleep, unless the killer hadn't wanted to kill in the first place.

I slowly unfroze, as I heard them talking on. I moved over near the window and looked out and waited. Gretchen kept trying to change the subject every time Snakey brought up Jamaica and Mrs. O'Gilvie. I don't think she wanted me to know more than I had to. I heard them leaving, waited for about a minute, then turned on the light. There were several pictures of a woman in her fifties. Some of children with an older woman—grandmother, aunt maybe. A few of men. Then in a corner a very interesting shot, a group of people, all blue-eyed and blond, but really brown-skinned. They looked like aberrants—freaks of nature—like left-overs from Mengele's experiments in South America. *Germans in one of the parishes who had been brought over as indentured servants by the English a hundred years ago*, Kathleen had said.

I took the picture that Gretchen had described and went into the front room and listened at the door. There was no one out there making sounds that I could hear. I came back, poured a drink and sat and waited for the inevitable. I suddenly had a premonition and started up, fully expecting another blow on the head from some dark figure lurking ominously, or however they lurk just before they knock your brains out. But there was no one in the room but me. Before I could sit back down, there was a key turning in the lock. I stood there, weaponless as usual, and waited, hoping that she knew what she was doing. I certainly didn't know what I was doing. That was obvious.

In she came, finger on the lips. She closed and locked the door behind her and went to a window left and looked out. Then she came back.

"Sit down, please. It's possible that you could be seen from the street if you went near the window."

"This high up?"

"Yes, if someone were in the park."

"Okay." And I sat back down.

"I see you found the picture."

"Yes."

"Well?"

"It's possible. There's certainly enough here to make a trip to Jamaica worth taking." She flinched when I said Jamaica.

"You heard us."

"No. Let's just say that it was a logical conclusion."

"I don't follow you."

"You don't really have to. Just tell me one thing. Is Mrs. O'Gilvie really somewhere in Jamaica, and if she is, is she coherent and functioning and capable of receiving a large sum of money, or is she in an insane asylum, demented or paralyzed or worse?"

"You are a very suspicious man."

"Yes, I would say so."

"She's in excellent health."

"Good. Give me back the two fifties and I'll give you a five-hundred-dollar bill. I don't have enough in smaller ones."

She hesitated. "I don't have the two fifties."

"Your friend's expensive, isn't he?"

"Yes, very. It's the only way I can get rid of him when I really want to."

She was a nickel and dime hustler, desperate for a couple of hundred dollars to keep her man happy. Getting her cooperation wasn't going to be that difficult.

"I suppose you want me to pay for your ticket as well."

"And his. He won't let me go alone."

"So how are we going to do business when we get there?"

"You check into a hotel and sit tight, and I'll bring her to you. How's that?"

"Which hotel, where?"

"Kingston, the Pegasus. It's the best hotel on that part of the island."

"Where is she?"

"Near Kingston."

"But not in Kingston."

"No."

"What's your name?"

She laughed. "Yes, I know your name, but you don't know mine. It's Gretchen Schultz."

"Schultz. Are you Jewish?"

"No, German."

"Yes, I know, but most Germans in New York are Jewish."

"Maybe Schultz is Jewish in New York, but it's not necessarily Jewish in Germany."

"Have you ever been to Germany?"

"No."

"Oh. So your Schultz is German German, but you're not from Germany."

"No."

"New York?"

"Well, I've lived here for several years."

"Yes."

"But I was born somewhere else."

"Where?"

"Jamaica, if you must know."

"Really. That seems odd. I thought that former British colonies were populated mostly by Anglo-Saxon types."

"They are, mostly."

She didn't take it any further, but I didn't really need her to.

I had stumbled onto more than I had had a right to expect to stumble onto. I was content to leave it at that.

"Okay, let's go over the game plan. I go to Jamaica and check into this hotel in Kingston . . . the Pegasus."

"Right."

"I sit around the pool drinking rum colas and soaking up the sunshine while I wait for you to show up."

"Right."

"You bring Mrs. O'Gilvie to me, leave us alone for an hour, and that's that."

She didn't answer right away. I waited. "Well?"

"I didn't mean I'd bring her to you, actually."

"Go on."

"You won't be able to see her at the hotel."

"Can you tell me why?"

"No."

"Okay. So where and when do I see her?"

"That I don't know just yet. But it will be on the south coast and within three days after you get there."

"When do I have to get there?"

"Next Thursday."

"That will give you enough time to set it up."

"Yes," she said, almost admitting that there was something that was going to be done that required a fast shuffle.

"Suppose I want her to come back to New York with me."

"If you can get her to agree to come back to New York, that's between the two of you. Our deal is strictly for the meeting and nothing more."

"And for the meeting you want how much?"

"Five thousand dollars."

"That's a lot of money."

"That's what I want."

"You want it in Jamaica or in New York?"

"In New York."

"Before or after?"

"Would you give it to me before?"

"No."

"Well, then?"

"Let me understand you. You're going to let me see her and then come back to New York, and then you'll come back and get your money?"

"Right."

"I don't understand. You're not naive. And you certainly can't trust me that much, so what's the deal?"

"You'll pay."

"I will."

"Yes."

"Why?"

"Because." And she just smiled. It was the first time since she came back that she was relaxed.

"How do I get the tickets to you?" I asked.

"I'll call you day after tomorrow and tell you how I want you to do it."

"Do you want me to book mine and reserve a room now, or should I wait for you?"

"Give me twenty-four hours."

"Okay." And I got up. "Is it okay if I leave?"

"Yes, but you're forgetting something."

"No, I'm not forgetting anything." And I took out Regina's advance again and gave her the other four hundred.

"I thought you said you didn't have it all."

"I just wanted to find out if you'd given away the two fifties."

"And you found out."

"Yes."

"Satisfied?"

"Partly. Look, whether or not I pay you five thousand will have to depend on a lot of things happening right. It may end up only being worth two or three thousand. Or maybe only one."

"You'll pay the five."

"I will, huh?"

"Yes."

She was awfully sure of herself, but I was damned if I knew why.

"So that's it?"

"That's it." She came close. "Another one for the road? I have no plans for the rest of the night."

"Maybe some other time." And I gallantly kissed her hand and left.

When I was younger maybe. Who knows. But it was the sort of thing that was no longer that compelling. The age of flights of romantic fancy had definitely passed us all by, what with the ravages of so many virulent diseases and the need for everyone to suddenly have to talk first, to get to know one another and then get involved later. In any event, I certainly wasn't interested in ensconcing myself in her apartment, with Snakey on the loose. I went home, followed by I didn't know who.

Marlene's voice was coming through the line before I knew what side of the bed I was on. I had tried to ignore the incessant ringing, but that wasn't possible since I'd forgotten to put the phone near enough to the bed to be able to kick it off the receiver without getting out from under the covers. And she wouldn't hang up.

"Are you awake?"

"Yes, I'm awake."

"You don't sound like it."

"I may not sound like it—but I am."

"What time did you get in last night? I called you twice before I went to sleep."

"Oh, checking up on me."

"No, but he called again."

"Who called again?"

"The same man who called to tell me Kat was dead."

"You recognized the voice?"

"I recognized that it was the same voice, but that's all."

"What did he want?"

"He wants to meet. He says we have something in common."

"What?"

"Three million dollars."

"I don't get it."

"Neither do I."

"When does he want to meet?"

"Tonight. Ten o'clock. A restaurant on Twelfth Avenue called the Boondocks."

"You're kidding."

"Nope."

"You know it?"

"No, you?"

I'd never heard of it and I told her so. "Look, it sounds like a pretty sleazy place to me. I mean Twelfth Avenue, and with a name like that."

"He wants me to wear a hat and sit near the piano."

"The piano. Well, maybe it isn't such a greasy spoon after all. Okay, what else?"

"That's all."

"He didn't ask you to bring anything with you?"

"No."

"Did he say anything about coming alone or not?"

"No."

"That's strange. It's almost as if he doesn't care."

"Or wants to see who I'll bring with me."

"That's possible. And he didn't tell you anything else?"

"No."

"His name?"

"No."

"Did you ask him what it was?"

"No."

"That was a very strange conversation. When did he call?"

"As soon as I got in. That's why I called you."

"What time is it?"

"Eight-thirty."

"Okay. Give me an hour to get dressed and have my coffee, then call me back and I'll meet you. If we're lucky they're open for lunch. We can check it out then."

"I've got a better idea. Have coffee here."

"My dear, nobody makes my coffee for me. But nobody."

"That's not true."

"What do you mean?"

"I made coffee for you last night."

"I'm talking about morning coffee."

"I have Jamaican."

"You're kidding."

"No. Pure Blue Mountain."

"Damn." I was tempted, but I told her, "It's still a long ride. I'd never make it. Call me in an hour, but save some of the Blue Mountain."

"You want it all your way, don't you?"

"Not all. Just as much as I can get."

All the while, while I was making the coffee and getting dressed, I kept thinking that the three million dollars was out there somewhere and there was someone who knew about it, had plans for it, but couldn't get it without help. And they were desperate enough to think that Kathleen Campbell's sister could give them the help they needed. Maybe she could and just didn't know it. There certainly was no reason for her to take me into her confidence if she wasn't playing it straight. I didn't have anything she wanted. If I did, I didn't know about it. Then I stopped, realized that someone else thought that I had something, and they had ransacked my place to find it.

Well, well, maybe Ms. Marlene was playing me for a chump

after all. That thought got me to Manhattan even faster than the promise of her Blue Mountain coffee.

She met me in the lobby and we grabbed a cab and went over to Twelfth Avenue. It was 11 A.M. We got out and stood there, feeling rather foolish. It was a quite substantial establishment. "Shall we go in?" she asked.

"No, there aren't more than five, six people at the bar. We'd stand out too much. Let's go over to the river."

We walked along the boondocks, in effect. There's always something special about being near water. The air changes, the sounds are mysterious, the scene, more often than not, arresting. She put her arm through mine casually and snuggled up.

"There's a wind, do you mind?"

"No, not at all, but I think you ought to know," I said, "that I suspect you of having dishonorable, even criminal intentions."

"Such as?"

"I haven't figured out that much yet."

"Rather clumsy of you, wouldn't you say?"

"Most definitely, but then no detective worth his salt would worry about a position taken just because he didn't have any facts to support it."

"Why not?"

"Because that's what hunches are for."

"Hunches."

"Yes, hunches."

"You mean you would actually act on a hunch?"

"Not only would I act on a hunch, but I'd even put my life on the line because of one if it were a strong enough hunch."

"Well, it's all very well and good to talk about what you would do. But the proof of it lies more in what you have done."

"Meaning?"

"Meaning have you ever laid your life on the line because of a hunch?"

"Oh, yes, many times."

"With what result?"

"Well, that all depends on how you evaluate results."

"Meaning the hunches were wrong."

"No, I wouldn't say that, not all of them."

"Most of them?"

"Fifty-fifty."

"So you say." Then she added, "So then your suspicion of me is based on a hunch?"

"Part hunch."

"And part fact?"

"Not an Agatha Christie fact. But circumstantial certainly."

"Go on, I'm listening."

"You've been very trusting of me, open, letting me into your confidence almost unhesitatingly."

"And?"

"Well, it makes you think, doesn't it?"

"In other words you're holding it against me."

"Holding what against you?"

"My openness, the fact that I've taken you into my confidence."

"Well, I wouldn't go that far."

"Well, I would, and I think that's awful. You're no gentleman, I can tell you that."

"Yes, but look at the facts."

"Agatha Christie facts or wobbly ones?"

"Dashiell Hammett."

"Go on."

"There's three million hanging around somewhere that someone—who shouldn't—knows about. That person thinks you can help them get to it."

"The voice on the phone."

"Or someone he's fronting for."

"And?"

"And there's the fact that someone ransacked my"—I hesitated before I said it, thinking of Trevor's sneer—"rooms, at about the same time or just before you were found on the first floor wandering about."

"And you're accusing me of having something to do with that?"

"I'm not accusing you of anything. I'm just saying that those facts exist."

"Well, you can call them facts if you want, but they're about as persuasive as *facts* as my use of eucalyptus oil is."

"Brand number 41."

"Maybe where you buy it, it's number 41. But where I buy it it's Whispering Waters." And she showed me the little vial. I opened it and took a whiff. It was the same stuff all right. So much for the deductive method. "Pretty common, eh?" I offered rather lamely."

"I wouldn't know, I never took a survey."

"Sorry."

"Look, you met my sister, talked to her. You may have been the last person to see her alive, except for whoever killed her. I don't know. But if you'll remember, when you said you were the one who found her, I said, 'Oh! Yes, so I'd heard.' "

"As a matter of fact, you did."

"You never asked me about that."

"Only because I didn't want to seem too . . . inquisitive." I knew it the minute I said it, but it didn't help. She started laughing almost uncontrollably. "What I mean is I didn't want to seem aggressively so."

"You mean you thought being sneaky was the better option?"

"You needn't be nasty."

"Oh, needn't I."

"I guess I had that coming."

"You most certainly did, but we'll let that go. Before I left for Brooklyn, I called Mr. Black. I had met him once or twice. His number was written on a pad in Kat's bedroom. He was the one who told me that you had talked to her and that you were trusted by the group."

"The group?"

"Yes, from the club. Don't you know anything?"

I guess I didn't. "You mean the members of the club are called the group?"

"Not all of them, only certain ones. Anyway, he said you were going to Jamaica to find out who was stealing their land and to see if you could do something about it for them. That they'd hired you. That's the only reason I trusted you."

"The only reason?"

"Well, after I saw you, I kinda liked you too, but now, forget it."

We had walked almost up to where an aircraft carrier was docked. We decided to take a closer look. They were letting people on board. We still had some time to kill, so we took the tour. You never really get over being impressed by how huge those damned things are, especially when you go inside and take the open elevator all the way down and stand on the ground floor and look up. The amount of space captured within those metal walls is so huge that you always end up being in awe of it. And yet, undefined, in the open air, it's just so much space. I was thinking about that when I suddenly realized that Regina had to be held for a reason that had less to do with why Reg was killed and more to do with money and the personal safety of whoever was getting the money or planned on getting it. I had given Quinn enough time to get something out of Calvin Davis. That was all I had, unless Jay called.

I decided I would return Marlene's favor. I studied her for a minute, then said, "Look, after we check out the Boondocks, I have to break into an apartment in Brooklyn Heights. Want to come along?"

"Should I want to come along?"

"I don't know. But since you've been so open with me, I'm going to return the compliment."

"You're sure it's the wise thing to do?"

"Only time will tell."

"By then it might be too late."

"That's just the chance I'll have to take."

"Well, all I can say is I hope it's not because you have a hunch."

I was beginning to like her.

We went back to the restaurant. By the time we got there the place was mobbed. They did a big lunchtime business and no mistake about it. Mostly construction workers. Some businessmen. The guy behind the bar was friendly, black, middle-aged, hair slicked down. We squeezed into a corner.

"Hi," he offered.

"Hi," I said by way of a return.

"What can I get you folks?"

"Just some soup."

"Anything to drink?"

"Glass of wine for the lady, beer for me. You're really busy."

"Lunchtime. It quiets down after two and doesn't pick up again until around five."

"Do you have music?"

"Yeah, piano." He pointed to it.

"That's nice. Maybe we'll come back for dinner."

"Good. Want to see a menu?"

"Sure."

He got one for us. It was mostly soul food—smothered pork chops, macaroni and cheese, collards, candied yams, fried chicken, porgies, that sort of stuff, with peach cobbler and hot apple pie for dessert. It got my interest.

When he came back with the soup and the drinks, and before he rushed off again, I asked quickly, "What kind of music do they play?"

"Well, the owner used to be a jazz pianist, that's his picture up there, back in the days when he had a trio." He pointed to a large old black and white on the wall above the bar of a young man in black tie and tux, hair slicked down, sitting at a piano, looking out and smiling at the camera. "And he won't let anybody in who can't play jazz."

"Maybe I know him. What's his name?"

"Billy Angus."

"No, doesn't ring a bell. He's not from New York."

"No, Kansas City. Excuse me." And he was off.

Marlene turned to me very slightly and said quietly, "Pretty clever, getting all that information without even half trying."

"He's the talkative type. Black establishment, they like to attract as many substantial black folks as they can."

"Well, I'd hardly call you substantial," she offered.

"My dear, I was thinking of you, obviously."

"I bet you were."

We finished our soup. I left a nice tip. The guy told us not to forget to come back. Ask for him, Ray. We said we would and caught a cab to Brooklyn.

Regina lived in a modern building. There were TV monitors in the lobby, everything glass enclosed, an intercom, double locked doors. But there was no one around watching the lobby.

"Well, how are you going to do it, genius?"

"The front door is the hard part." We went over and I looked at the lock. It had a metal lip to prevent anyone from getting between the lock and the door and forcing it. But the lock itself was simple. Strong, but simple. I needed a tool. There was a gas station across the street. "I have to get past that first door," I told her.

"Why not just wait for someone to come along?"

"Once we get inside we can try the old press the buttons trick until someone lets us in. But we can't expect anyone to let us in to both doors."

"Why not? How else would a visitor get in?"

"There's probably a guard in the lobby. When he's there, the door to the street is open. If you start pressing a lot of buttons, he'll stop you from coming in even if you get someone to buzz back."

"So you have to get in before he returns."

"Right."

"I still don't understand how visitors get in when he's not there."

"They have to use an outside phone after they get here, and the person they're visiting has to come down and let them in."

"Talk about security."

"Yep. And the tenants want it."

"It's certainly different from growing up in Jamaica."

"I guess so."

I made her wait on the corner, went over to the guy at the gas station, and paid him five dollars for an old oil can opener. Went back and worked the street door lock. We got in just as an elderly gray-haired lady was coming out of one of the elevators.

I pretended to look for a name when she came to the door. She eyed me keenly. Marlene stepped back. She came out. I tried a smile and made a motion for the door. "And what do you think you're doing, sonny?" she asked imperiously, and with that she gave me a swift kick in the shins. I let go of the door and let out a yell at the same time. It closed, and before I knew what had happened, she was gone.

Marlene thought it was all very funny. "Well, well, so much for Plan A."

I had to think fast. "Look," I said, "I'm going to play a—you should excuse the expression—hunch. When I ring the bell, if a voice comes on, you answer. Ask for Regina. If they want to know who you are, say you're looking for Jay. Tell whoever it is that you're a 'friend.' And make 'friend' sound significant."

"So why didn't you do that in the first place?"

"Because I didn't want anyone to know I was coming. Not that I expect to find anyone in."

She rang, a man's voice came on. It wasn't Jay. I didn't like it, but I had to go forward. I nodded to her.

"Hello, is Jay there?"

"Just a minute." He clicked off, then he clicked on again. "Who is it?"

"A friend of Jay's."

He went off again, came back on, and asked, "What's your name?"

I shook my head.

"Look, who is this? Is Jay there? Can I talk to him, please?"

There was another click off and then the buzzer. We went in just as the lobby attendant showed up from a stairwell. We smiled as we passed him. He went to the door and took the lock off the outside one, then came back in and sat down at his station behind a long table, taking out his little radio and his newspaper and settling in. We took the elevator to the floor above Regina's, got out and looked around. Regina's apartment was in the middle, next to a service door.

"I want you to stay up here for ten minutes. Someone comes out of an apartment, hide in the stairwell. If you get caught, pretend you're lost." She suddenly got nervous.

"This could be dangerous, couldn't it?" she asked.

"It already is. If I don't show in ten minutes, call the number on this card from the street. Ask to speak to me. If I don't call you by name, get ahold of Lieutenant Quinn or Officer de Souza at this precinct." I gave her both numbers. "Got it?"

"Yes, be careful."

"I will, and thanks." She looked at me as if she wanted to kiss me on the cheek, but decided not to.

I took the stairs down to Regina's floor and stood there, listening at the door. There was no sound or movement. I looked at the elevator indicator. The elevator was on the way down, but I couldn't tell from what floor it had come. I decided to go in. I tried the door. It was open. I pushed it in with my foot and stood there. I heard mumbling sounds and went in, closed the door behind me and bolted it. When I got into the front room proper and looked around, I saw no one.

It was an open apartment with a terrace. Lots of plants, nicely done. Kitchen to the left and enclosed. I came back and stood at the bedroom door, which was to the right of the front door. It was closed. I tried it, but it was locked. I had to get a spatula from the kitchen to slip the lock. The door swung open and there was Jay, trussed up and on the bed. Tape around his mouth, ankles, and wrists, hands behind his back. He was squirming and making a lot of sounds. I yanked the tape from his mouth. It hurt, but he didn't yell. He had grit, that kid did. He began to breathe heavily.

"My God, I thought they were going to kill me," he said breathlessly. He tried to undo the tape from his wrists by bringing his arms forward under his feet. But he didn't quite manage it and got caught halfway, with the tape from his wrists getting caught on the tape from his ankles.

"Take it easy, Jay, I'll get it off for you."

First I had to get his hands behind his back again. That really hurt. His shoulders were obviously quite sore by then. Poor Jay. He had been through it and he didn't have the temperament to endure the pain and maintain his, well, equanimity at the same time. I cut the tape with scissors that were on the dresser. He moaned from relief. Then I cut his feet loose. I helped him up and rubbed his wrists for him. He was shaking a little bit.

"Come on, Jay, take it easy." I looked at him and he was ready to go into shock. I slapped him but he didn't focus. I slapped him again and he shook his head. That seemed to help. I took him to the terrace and made him take deep breaths. I found the

liquor cabinet and got him a shot of the first thing I found—
which happened to be rum. He coughed and spat it out. I patted
his back.

"You all right?"

"Yeah. I can't stand the taste of liquor."

I gave him some water.

"Okay, Jay, what happened?"

"I was here going through Regina's things, trying to find something that would tell me something, anything." I wasn't sure
what he meant by that, but decided to let him finish before saying
anything. "When they came in and caught me by surprise."

"They had a key?"

"They must have."

"Regina's?"

"Yeah."

"So they still have her."

"I guess so."

"What did they want?"

"I don't know. Whatever it was, they didn't ask me for it. They
taped me up and went through the drawers and things."

"They didn't seem to leave much of a mess."

"No, they'd open a drawer, look through it and then close it.
When the intercom beeped, they decided to split. They locked
me in here and left."

I wasn't buying, but I said nothing. He sat, took a deep breath
and finally seemed to be composed. I asked him if he wanted
anything else.

"No, I'm fine now. Thanks."

That's when the phone rang. It was Marlene.

"You all right?"

"I'm fine. What time is it?"

She hesitated. Then I realized I had said I'd use her name.
"Sorry, but forget the signal, everything is okay. I just want to
keep names out of it at this point."

"Are you sure?" she asked.

"Quite. I told you to call me in ten minutes."

"Well, it's ten plus. And there are two characters staring at me. They were across the street when I came out. They're eying me and the building both."

"Describe them." She did. They sounded like the two-thirds of the trio that was left over.

"They could be dangerous. You'd better come back in. Wait till I get to the terrace before you do. Head straight for the door. I'll have my hand on the buzzer."

"Okay." She hung up and I went right to the terrace as she crossed the street. Once she got to the side the building was on I went to the intercom and leaned on the button. Then I waited. Did it again. Then I went to the front door and watched the elevator. It was on the way up. It stopped at the floor I was on and Marlene stepped out.

"Any trouble?" I asked.

"I think we caught them by surprise."

"Yeah?"

"Yeah. When I crossed back to the building and came in, they were crossing the street, but they stopped when I went over to the guard and told him he was cute."

"You're learning fast."

"I'm a big girl and I've been surviving in a man's world for a long time now."

"I guess so. There's a guy in there who you'll meet, but we won't use any names. Okay? It's for your own protection."

"Okay. Anything you say. You're the boss."

"Let's not get carried away."

We went in. I closed and locked the door. "Jay, this is a friend."

"Hi," Jay said. He wasn't interested in talking.

"Those two guys are still out there, Jay."

"Huh?"

"The guys."

"Oh, yes, the guys."

"There were two of them, weren't there?"

"Yes, two."

"Well, they're across the street watching the building. They're the same two from the park, aren't they?"

"Huh?"

"I said, aren't they the same two from the park?"

"Yes, yes, I think so. It all happened so fast. I . . . I don't even remember what they looked like."

"Either time."

"Right, either time."

"But one was black and one was white?"

"Right. That much I remember."

"Good. The question now is what were they looking for."

"Do you think they've done away with Regina?" And he began to cry.

"My, my, what a lurid little imagination we have. Of course not. They may have roughed her up, but I don't think they've killed her."

"Then why couldn't they find what they were looking for? If she told them where it was, why didn't they just go right to it instead of searching all over as if they didn't know where to find it? Oh, my God. I know she's dead. I just know it." And he started to cry again.

Marlene was touched and went over and sat beside him and put her arm around his shoulder and tried to console him. I wanted to tell her not to bother, but I figured, what the hell. I went to the door and peeped out. There was no one that I could see in the hallway. I went to the terrace and my two friends were gone. At least they were no longer in the spot they had been in across the street. I came back in.

"Now try to think, Jay, what could it be?"

"You mean that they were looking for?"

"Yes."

"I don't know. Honestly."

"Well, let's think of something. And let's look while we think."

"But we don't know what we're looking for."

"And that's the challenge, isn't it? Now you take the living room. I'll take the bedroom, and you"—and I looked at Marlene—"take the kitchen and the closets in all the rooms. Okay?" They both nodded. "Then let's go. And if you see something that you think might be it, yell out. Don't be bashful. It's going to take three heads to be better than one if we're going to come up with the answer to this puzzle."

We started off in our separate directions. Jay was having as much trouble getting it together as he had had trying to untape himself.

"Stay away from the window and the terraces, Jay," I said from the door.

"Huh? Oh, yeah, sure." He got up and took a step and bumped his knee, said, "Ouch," and fell back into a chair.

"You all right?" Marlene asked.

"Yeah, yeah, I'm fine." She looked at me and motioned me to the kitchen. I followed her. "He's really out of it," she whispered. "He's not going to be much help to you."

"I know. Just let him do what he can. If we don't find anything, I'll go over the living room myself."

"Yeah, but he may need medical attention."

"Maybe. I'll keep an eye on him."

Just then Jay yelled out, "I got it. I got it." We both rushed into the living room and he was sitting in the middle of the floor on the rug, with a large framed picture in his lap that he was staring at. He began to cry and to breathe heavily, and he said, "Oh, my God. Oh, my God."

"Take it easy, Jay," I said as I got behind him and looked down at the painting and tried to figure out what it had that made it so important. Marlene was on one side and I was on the other. She looked at me. I looked at her, but neither of us could glean any special significance from it. It was a picture of a large field with trees that had thick trunks and delicate leaves. There was very little sky. There were four animals: a cow, a jackass, a wild boar and a horse. And there was a carrion bird on one of the trees looking down at the entire scene. The colors were bright reds, greens, some blues and strong blacks. There was something about the style that reminded me of something else I'd seen. Then I realized it was derivative of Henri Rousseau, the animals particularly, with their expressionistic gleam of the eye and the way they seemed not to be a part of the landscape while at the same time being in it.

"Henri Rousseau," I said.

"George Rhoden," she said.

"George who?"

"George Rhoden. We have a Jamaican painter named George Rhoden who paints in that style."

"I don't see a signature," I said.

"Neither do I."

"Why do you think this is it, Jay?"

"Because it's all there."

"What is?"

"The whole thing. Can't you see it?"

"No, Jay, I can't see it."

"Look. See the lines." And he traced the lines with his fingers. "They separate the counties."

"Right," said Marlene. "Cornwall, Middlesex, and Surrey."

"Sounds like a map of the Lake District of England," I offered.

"Those are the names the English gave us," she replied by way of a defense.

"Then why don't you change them?"

"You'd be surprised how people like to hold onto things like that, even if the implications of it, culturally speaking, aren't very flattering."

"So what do the counties mean, Jay?"

He began to shake and convulse. Then he coughed and a thin line of blood came to his mouth.

"My God," Marlene said.

Jay grabbed his stomach and rolled around on the floor. He was in extreme pain.

"We'd better call an ambulance," Marlene said.

"I have a better idea. Go downstairs and get your friend to do it. They'll come a lot quicker if the building calls it in."

She did. I helped Jay to a couch.

"What happened to you?" He was sweating profusely. I opened his shirt and there were marks on his stomach and his ribs. Contusions, by the look of them.

"I've been hurt bad."

"Those guys?"

"Yes."

"Why didn't you tell me?"

"I felt ashamed after the way I ran out on you yesterday."

"Nonsense. You need help and fast." I felt around. He seemed to have a couple of ribs broken. But what was making him bleed I didn't know. Marlene came back with the guy from the lobby. They took Jay downstairs and I stayed in the apartment. I searched the place from top to bottom, but I couldn't find anything. Finally, I came back to the painting. I looked at it, but saw nothing. Then I remembered. It wasn't Rousseau at all. It was the face of the Rasta man that I'd seen hanging in the room under Kathleen Campbell's. There was something about the way he used color and about the strength of his images and the sense of flatness that it all had, almost like Gauguin, but yet more like Rousseau. He was an unusual painter, whoever he was. I looked at the back of the canvas and there were clear lines like rivers or trails going everywhere, but they were not the same ones as the county divisions that Jay had pointed to. And there were at least a dozen of them instead of the two that divided the island into three counties. I decided to wait for Marlene to come back. I fixed myself a rum from the same bottle that I'd poured Jay the drink he didn't liked. Then the phone rang. It was Regina.

"Jay?"

"No, we've just sent him to the hospital. This is Joe."

"Joe! Joe! How the hell did you get in? What happened to Jay? What are you doing in my apartment? Huh? What?"

"Easy, one question at a time."

"One question at a time, my Aunt Fanny. What are you doing in my apartment and what happened to Jay?"

"I just told you. He's sick so we sent him to the hospital."

"Who's this *we* you keep talking about?"

"My assistant and I."

"Since when did you start having an assistant?"

"Since you got kidnapped."

"A woman no doubt."

"No question about it."

"Well, I need to talk to Jay."

"As soon as I find out what hospital they sent him to I'll call you and tell you. Uh, what was that number?"

"Very funny."

"You mean you're keeping things from me, and you hired me to recover the old homestead in Jamaica."

"Very funny," and she hung up.

I waited. She called back. "Look, I'm sorry."

"No need to be. I'm just glad you're alive. We were worried about you."

"Thanks. How did Jay get hurt?"

"Two of the guys from the park. The third one's in jail. I put him there."

"Are you okay?"

"Sure."

She was silent.

"Look, Regina, how did those guys get in?"

"They took my key."

"What were they looking for?"

"You don't know?"

"No, I don't."

"Where the ganja is grown."

"Why do they want to know that? They aren't going to go into farming it, are they?"

"I think so. That's what all the fuss has been about."

"Where are you?"

"I can't answer that."

"Why do you need to talk to Jay?"

"I can't answer that either."

"Have you made a deal with them?"

"Not the kind of deal you're talking about."

"Well, whatever kind of deal it is, why did you make it?"

"To save my life, why do you think?"

"That's reasonable. So are you still in need of my services or would you like me to send you a bill and get lost?"

She thought about that. Then she said, in a whisper, "I'll be in Jamaica next Wednesday, if all goes well. Meet me at the Pegasus Hotel in Kingston. I'll be registered under the name of St. Clair."

"And what are we going to do when we get there that we can't do here?"

"Everything. The deal is going to go down and you've got to be in the game to win anything."

"Regina, I don't know what you're talking about, but I hope for your sake that you're not getting greedy."

"Look, I'm talking about one million in cash, more if I really wanted to make a killing."

"And how can I help?"

"You're my protection."

"You mean bodyguard."

"That's right."

"And what about Jay?"

"I need him for other things. But the three of us are going to have the biggest payday of our lives and soon." And she hung up.

Well, Gretchen certainly had the right time if Regina knew what she was talking about. I needed a meeting with Black and the group right away. If ganja was the key to it all, then somehow what happened to the prime minister from the small island was having an effect on the price of marijuana in Jamaica. If I could put that neatly into a puzzle that was forming in my mind, then everything should come into focus. Maybe even the unanswered questions about Mrs. Hylton's three million dollars.

Marlene called me from the hospital. Jay had internal hemorrhaging caused by the beating he had taken. He was in intensive care, but he was young and he was strong, so the prognosis for his pulling through was good. I asked her if she was all right. She said she was. I told her I'd pick her up at her place in time for our appointment at the Boondocks.

I found Jay's keys, wrapped the picture in a sheet and some newspaper, then called de Souza at the precinct. Luckily for me he was in. "Hank, I need a big one."

"What is it?"

"Can you get a patrol car over to Brooklyn Heights and park it in front of a certain building for me for about an hour or so?"

"Not me. But I can get my buddy Jimmy Little to do it, I think. His girlfriend lives around there, and he's always trying to check her out. Seems he thinks she tricks on the side. Know what I mean?"

"That's the kind of thing that can keep a fellow up at night." I offered, by way of showing that I understood the problem. I gave him the address and waited for him to call me back.

"No sweat. He's right around the corner. How long you want him to sit?"

"It shouldn't take more than an hour. I'll call you and tell you when."

"Okay, but if he gets a call he'll have to split."

"Understood. And thanks, Hank, especially for not asking what it's all about."

"Hey, man, I'm not stupid. I know what you're up against. I just hope you pull it off, baby."

I thanked him and hung up, then waited by the window until I saw the patrol car pull up and park conspicuously across the street next to the gas station. I went down to the basement with the picture tucked safely under my arm, found the service entrance, and went out that way. I caught a cab a block away and took it back to Manhattan. Found a good stationery store, wrapped the picture some more. Went to the post office on 34th Street, put the package in one of their jiffy bags and mailed it to myself in Brooklyn, insured, certified, return receipt requested. I valued it at $50,000 for want of more specific information as to its true worth. Then I went home, got the gun out of the cookie jar, and went back to the apartment. The patrol car was gone. How long it had stayed I had no way of knowing. But I had to go up, even if it meant that I was walking into my own trap.

I turned the key in the door, pushed it open and stood there. I felt nothing by way of another presence alive and/or hostile, or just benign. I put my hand in and turned on the light. It seemed safe enough. I went in. I had the place to myself. Once I was absolutely certain about that, I turned off the light, left the lock on, and the chain off, and went to the far corner of the living room and sat in the big hammock chair under Regina's plants, and took out a magazine and tried to see in the half light.

The phone rang several times intermittently. I knew what that was all about. I didn't answer it.

I had almost dozed off when I heard them at the door. I quietly put the magazine down, got up, and stood in the corner behind the chair, arms folded in front of my chest, gun out and in hand. They came in quietly, closed the door behind them, and began looking at the pictures on the walls of the living room. They were intent of purpose and didn't see me. They looked at one, then another. Said nothing to each other. But after examining each one they would look at one another and shake their heads no. It was the same two, the white guy and Calvin Davis. The white guy finally told Davis to turn on the light. He went to the door and flicked the switch. As he turned, he saw me. The white guy looked at him, then he turned and looked at me and he froze.

"Well, well, gentlemen, you took your own sweet time about it. What's the matter, Jay didn't tell you what you wanted to know, but Regina did. Imagine that. Well, I'm afraid you're a little late. The picture in question isn't here. The police have it. You are two naughty boys. And the FBI wants to talk to both of you. They don't know it yet. But I'm going to give you to them, gift wrapped. No charge. What do you think of that?"

The white guy spoke up. "Can we make a deal?"

"No, I'm afraid not. I'm fresh out of deals. Jay's in the hospital in intensive care. He could bleed to death. Now, I'm going to make a phone call."

I went to the phone, picked it up with my left hand, pressed the buttons and waited. Calvin made a dash to his right to get behind the wall that faced the front door. I fired once. I heard him fall against the closet door. He yelled out, "Oh shit." My man just stood there, hands clear. Quinn came on. "I've got two pigeons for you. One's been shot, the other one's looking me dead in the eye." I gave him the address and put the receiver down.

My main man started to deal again. "One hundred thousand."

"For what?"

"You let us walk."

"Well, I need at least one live one."

"Okay, you let me walk."

"You hear that, Calvin? You've been sold out."

Calvin just howled from pain.

"You no good son of a bitch. You'll get yours if it takes me the rest of my life. You'll get yours. And I mean get it," said main man.

"Sure you do, good buddy, and you mean it whether I let you walk or not, so shut up, unless you've got a move you want to make? I think I asked you a question?"

He spat on the floor.

"Oh, tough guy. Well, you're good with the girls. Let's see how you make out with fellas." And I went over to him. "Up with the hands." He didn't move. I gave him the gun in the stomach, muzzle end. He retched, but grit his teeth and held his ground.

"Oh, you can take it, huh. You want to try for two?"

His hands went up. I patted him down. Came up with the gun. Made him turn around, spread his legs and put his hands against the wall. He was safe. I took the bullets out of the gun and tossed it around the wall. Calvin opened fire.

"Tut, tut, Calvin, when the police get here, I'm going to tell them what a bad boy you are."

"Hey, man, I'm sorry," ole Calvin sang out. "Can we make a deal?"

I went back to white brother and whispered in his ear. "Well, what's good for the goose, as they say." Then I went to the edge of the wall and said, "How do I know I can trust you, Calvin?"

"Hey, man, I'll throw out my gun."

"Do that."

He did.

I looked around the corner of the wall and he clicked away with the empty gun. He was lying in the corner, bleeding from the leg where I'd hit him.

"Tut, tut again, Calvin. Are you a mess. When the police get here I'm going to tell them that a mad dog killer is near the door and they should spray it with machine gun fire before they come in." Just then the phone rang. I went to it. It was Quinn.

"We're downstairs. What's the situation?"

"I'm up here with the two left over from the park. One's cooperating, but there's this black dude at the door with two guns. He's a mad dog killer and he's ready to throw down on anybody, police or anyone else. You better come in shooting."

"Where will you be?"

"I'll be in the room, near the terrace. Once you open the door you'll be able to see me. I'll tell you what the situation is before you cross the threshold."

"Okay." And he hung up.

"They'll be up in two minutes, Calvin. I hope you have a bulletproof vest on." I heard Calvin scuffling. Then the elevator opened. As soon as he'd stopped moving there was a knock at the door. Then Quinn's voice.

"Joe?"

"Fire away, Lieutenant."

Then Calvin tried to get farther into the closet as they opened fire. Then Quinn again.

"Joe?"

"I think you can open the door." All the while, white brother kept his position. They opened the door and I saw Quinn with a machine gun, de Souza behind him, and another policeman I didn't know. Quinn looked at me, I looked at him.

"Your boy's to your right," I told him. "Ask him to throw his gun out and you should be okay." Before Quinn could ask the question, Calvin started yelling, "Don't shoot, don't shoot, I ain't got no gun."

Quinn looked at me, half suspiciously, then he came in and fronted the closet, motioning de Souza and the other guy into my part of the room. They cuffed the white brother, then Quinn said, "All right, come out."

I went to witness the surrender. Calvin just wouldn't open the door. Finally, when he did, he was curled up behind Regina's shoes, afraid to look up. It was a funny sight. I had been a little rough on ole Calvin, but I didn't like what they had done to Jay and the way they had kidnapped Regina right from under my nose. I guess I was getting even. Maybe I overdid it, a little, but it happens like that sometimes.

Back at the precinct, Quinn was licking his lips. I had to hang around while they were booked. The white guy said nothing. He wouldn't even give them his name. He just wanted to make his one call and that was all they could get out of him. Of course the only thing they really had on him was breaking and entering and a weapons charge, since he didn't have a license to carry the gun. But that didn't surprise anyone. Calvin had tried to be the Lone Ranger, so there was also assault for starters with him. Then they took him to a hospital. I found de Souza, but we just nodded. It wasn't the right time for talking. I slipped him a note telling him to contact Black and tell him to call me first thing in the morning. Then I went back to Quinn's office and sat and waited to see what he was going to give me.

When he finally came back in he was the proverbial pig in mud, his happiness overflowing.

"Well, we got 'em where we want 'em."

"You got who where you want 'em?"

"The FBI."

"Oh."

"Yep." And he started rubbing his hands together. "Those bastards have to come to me now."

"They do?"

"They do."

"Why?"

"Because that's the way I set it up."

"Good for you." And I waited, but he just kept looking at me and smiling. Finally, I said, "You want to tell me about it?"

"I'll do better than that, buddy boy. I'll take you to the scene of the crime."

We got into a squad car: he, the other guy who was with him

at Regina's, and a second uniform driving. We said nothing. But Quinn was beaming. We headed across the Brooklyn Bridge, went up the FDR Drive, turned off at 96th Street, and crossed over to the West Side.

"Out of your territory, aren't you, Lieutenant?"

"Don't worry, this is a cooperative effort."

We pulled up in front of Reg O'Connor's apartment house. I smelled a huge rat the size of a skunk, but I said nothing. We got out. There were two other squad cars—both from Manhattan. We went up. There was a uniformed captain with a lot of confetti on his chest. One guy in plainclothes and three other uniforms. The rest were downstairs. The apartment was open but nobody was home.

"She's gone, Tim," said the uniformed captain.

"Have you found anything?" Quinn asked.

"No. Who's this guy?" he asked, looking at me testily.

"He's the guy who caught them."

"Oh. Let's go in."

We went into the apartment. I'd never been in it before. It was a mess.

"Remind you of anything?" Quinn asked me.

"If you mean my place, they did a better job here." The place had been torn apart. Things were ripped to shreds, mattresses cut open, furniture broken and smashed.

"What were they looking for?" I asked. Quinn and the captain eyed one another, but they said nothing.

"There're pictures of her, but we don't have a real description," the captain said.

"If you're talking about Reg O'Connor's wife, I know the lady. I can give you a very detailed description."

"You can," said the captain. "Good. Shoot. Get this, Jerry," he told the plainclothes who was with him. Jerry took out his pad and pencil and looked at me expectantly.

"What are you doing, Captain, taking lessons from the FBI?"

"What's he talking about?" the captain asked Quinn.

"Hey, Captain, you can ask me what I'm talking about. I speak good. I can talk up for myself. Lieutenant Quinn didn't bring me over here on a leash."

The captain didn't like to have things get away from him, even in small ways.

"Look, fella, if you want to help, help. If you don't, take a walk."

"There's nothing here that I'm really interested in. You've got an empty apartment. The man's dead and you don't even know what the wife looks like." I turned to Quinn. "I think the guy I handed you from the park gave you a bum steer and if you let the lawyer spring him, you're left with egg all over your face, no matter what guarantees the lawyer gave you. So if you have no further need of me, gentlemen, I bid you good day." I got as far as the elevator when Quinn caught up with me.

"Take it easy, fella. The captain's a little rigid, but he's fair. Let's talk." I followed him back in and he and the captain and I went into the bedroom and closed the door. The captain opened his collar, but kept his hat on the center of his head. He sat on a chair, elbows on his knees, hands clasped, leaning forward. He never looked at me when he talked.

"This thing's getting messy. The FBI has a bullshit bust that they can't really do anything with, so they're trying to get us to do their work for them. I've got one murder in Manhattan and you've got two, maybe more in Brooklyn. But we keep coming up with empty leads. I say get that bastard back and sweat him." I looked at him as if he were a fool.

"Rubber hoses and hot lights. He's been there before. By now they've probably offered him the moon to keep his mouth shut. What the hell can you give him? Immunity from a gun rap." I didn't like him, but he surprised me. He didn't take umbrage. He just kept talking.

"It's not a hard case to figure out. They've got tons of the stuff, and there's nothing we can do to stop it from coming in. But that's not my problem. My problem is this goddamned formula."

"What formula?" I asked. Quinn looked at him. The captain nodded and took out a cigarette and said, "Sure, what the hell. Everybody else knows about it. And you owe him." That surprised Quinn. I don't think he ever thought of owing anyone who wasn't in the force. But since it was obviously the captain's show and he did outrank Quinn, and Quinn obviously respected him, he said, "There's this new strain of marijuana that they grow in Jamaica that's supposed to be so powerful that one good drag is like smoking an entire joint of the regular stuff. They call it super sensy because it's an offshoot of the seedless variety that's been the prime weed up till now. This stuff is supposed to be so powerful that it makes you grow hairs on the outside of your nose."

"Let's not get carried away, Tim," the captain cautioned.

"Anyway," Quinn continued, "someone's trying to grow it in New York on a small, experimental scale at first. The idea is to imitate the soil and climate conditions of the islands in order to get the same result."

"How did you come by this information, Lieutenant? And who's trying to grow it?" I asked.

"Well, before we answer that," said the captain, "how about a description?"

"Sure. Her name's Caitlin O'Connor."

"We know that," he said. "She's about five feet six, brunette, thin, wiry in fact. Pale complexioned, solemn face with sad eyes."

"Weight?" he asked.

"About a hundred and eighteen pounds."

"Any distinguishing features?"

"No, not really. I think she has a mole on her left hand near her thumb, but I'm not sure."

"Smoker or nonsmoker?"

"Smoker, definitely."

He got up. "Okay. Finish filling him in, Tim. I'll be right back." And he left the room.

Quinn looked at me, hesitated, then gave me the rest, hard as it was for him. "We don't know who's growing it. But we were told that this is where the experiments were taking place."

"You said something about a formula. You mean one that's written down?"

"Yep."

"And that's what you expected to find here?"

"That and evidence of some effort to test it."

"So you were going to give the FBI the guys, keep the formula and trade with them after they realized they had nothing with which to solve the case, get your convictions and leave them with empty arrests?"

"Something like."

"You and the captain."

"You got it."

"Very interesting. Let me ask you, Lieutenant, what good is the formula without proof of murder?" He said nothing. "Oh, I see. You were going to let the FBI solve it for you. Then you were going to swap with them." He said nothing to that. "Do you think the murders in Brooklyn are connected to this formula business?"

"I don't know. That's what we're gonna get the FBI to find out for us."

"Assuming they're dumb enough to play it the way you orchestrate it."

"Look, guy . . ." But before he could get it out, the captain was back in.

"You two all through?" Quinn didn't answer.

"I have a question for you, Captain," I said, putting a few two and twos together. "Tons of marijuana, as you say, come into New York every day, and there's nothing you can do about it. It isn't even your job. But the stuff that was coming in from the

| 161 |

small island where the prime minister was busted was coming into Florida, not New York. The FBI wants to find out who's trying to kill him for stuff that doesn't come from Jamaica, so how do you expect them to solve your case for you. Even if the gang is dealing in both islands, the FBI will have all the information if they solve their case, and whatever they give you will be half a loaf and after the fact. Which will still leave you with a lot of work to do."

"It never works out that neatly," he offered.

"No," I admitted. "But there's a lot there anyway."

He thought about it. Sat back down, unbuttoned his collar again. This time he took off his hat, set it neatly on a table, rubbed his hands across his temples, almost nervously, went back to leaning forward on his elbows, moved his feet up and down as if he were working out a stitch, and finally asked, looking ahead, "And what do you suggest?"

"I suggest laying your cards on the table. All of this 'who's going to outsmart who' is childish. I'm not saying you don't have to watch your step, but you still have to face the facts. You don't have enough to use them the way you want to. You'd be a lot better off going in now and making a deal. Hold something back if you have to, just in case they double-cross you and grab all the glory, but set it up so that you get what you need for your end before it's too late to make a difference."

"You know, the guy's right, Tim." That really surprised Quinn. "I said all along, I didn't believe in this 'we'll con them into giving us what we want' bullshit."

Quinn said nothing.

"So if I'm right, what's stopping you from taking the advice?"

"Tell him, Tim," he said.

Quinn cleared his throat. He was violating every rule known to man that he had held sacred all his life, and all in one afternoon. Finally, he got it out. "It's not up to us," he said and swallowed and looked down at his feet.

"Then who is it up to?" I asked rather simplistically.

"The commissioner wants to run for mayor," the captain said.

"You're kidding," I said.

"Nope. We haven't had an Irish mayor for a while. He thinks it's time, what with an Irishman in the White House and an Irish senator, and he wants to be the guy."

Well, well, well, I thought, and all of Quinn's posturing had absolutely nothing to do with how he felt about the FBI, but rather how the police commissioner of New York City felt about getting a chance to run for mayor. "So it's out of your hands," I finally said.

"Completely."

"Well, maybe I can help."

That got their interest. "You do, fella," the captain said, "and I'll see to it that the commissioner makes it worth your while. And I mean really worth it. He's got a lot of friends in high places. You could land a contract with one of those high-tech companies that would set you up for life."

"Gee, thanks, Captain, but I'm not interested in helping the commissioner get elected mayor. And I certainly don't want any of his high-tech contacts. I'll tell you what I do want, and I want it in a hurry when I ask for it, and no bull." I waited. They said nothing. "I'm going down to Jamaica this week. I may need some firepower before it's all over. Let the embassy down there know about it. I may even have to smuggle out some of the stuff myself."

"And what are you going to do for us in return?"

"You mean for the commissioner."

"Same difference."

"Well, for openers, I can tell you that there are a lot of Jamaican dollars going back and forth. And checking the banks to find out how the currency is manipulated will open some leads for you."

"What else?" he pursued.

"I'm working on it. I'll have something for you before I leave.

But don't follow me. I flushed out all three of the goons for you. Now I'm working on the thinking side of the operation."

"You got it," he said.

Quinn was about to open his mouth, but didn't. I knew that the captain couldn't really help me unless and until he actually talked to his boss. And even then they probably would only give me a crumb or two, if that. But it could end up probably being better than nothing.

I left them chewing it over and went back to Brooklyn to change. The phone rang as I was about to leave. It was Black.

"I got your message," he said.

"I wish I could subscribe to your network system, it's faster than any I know."

"Sometimes."

"Three things. I need to talk to you about Kathleen Campbell and Jamaican dollars. I need to know how much the group knows and exactly what you guys are really all about. And I'm going down in a day or two. I'll be at the Pegasus in Kingston."

"Good hotel, a little expensive. Why'd you pick it?"

"That's a long story. What about the meeting?"

"Tonight, late."

"Make it midnight at the club."

"No, not the club."

"Where?"

He gave me an address in Manhattan, uptown. "Chin's apartment," he said. I took the telephone number, then I called a cabdriver who I use for occasional jobs of the type I had in mind and told him where to meet me and what to do. Then I left to pick up Marlene.

We got to the Boondocks half an hour early. I went in first, sat at the end of the bar nearest the door and renewed my conversation with the bartender.

"You alone tonight?" he asked.

"No, but she has a meeting, so I'm just sitting over here so I don't get in the way."

"Oh," he said. I don't think he liked the sound of that, but he said nothing. I looked around, saw no one I knew, sat back and enjoyed my drink. About ten minutes later Marlene came in as we had arranged, sat right behind the piano player and ordered a drink from the waitress. When she didn't acknowledge me, the bartender went to the back and came out with a short pudgy man who was an older version of the one in the picture.

"What you got going, buddy?"

"I don't follow you."

"Ray here says you came in this afternoon with the young lady over there, asked a lot of questions then left. Now you're back and she's sitting in one place and you're sitting in another, and you two are acting like you don't know one another."

"Oh, that, that's nothing. As I told Ray, she has a business meeting and she doesn't want me interfering. You know how women are nowadays. They want to act independent and prove that they're just as good as a man, and all the rest of that nonsense."

"You're telling me. My wife drives me crazy with that stuff. Ray said you seemed like nice folks this afternoon, but you can't be too careful. It's hard for a black business to get a liquor license. When we do, we have to be mighty careful. Least little thing and the ABC has us up on charges."

Just then Aubuchon and Braithwaite came in. They didn't see me, but I didn't expect that to last too long. I nodded. She got up and pretended to straighten her dress and sat back down again. They went over and introduced themselves and sat with their backs to me. Aubuchon faced her, but Braithwaite sat at the end of the table and kept looking from left to right. He hadn't gotten around to checking out the corners just yet. But I knew it was only a matter of time.

"I said you want a drink on the house?" Billy Angus almost yelled in my ear.

"Yes, sure," I said hastily.

"But just remember, no trouble."

"No trouble," I promised, and he went back to the rear.

"I think I'll move to a table and give them some room," I told Ray. He didn't like that, since it was obvious that if I left the bar and sat in a corner near the front window, they wouldn't be able to see me. But he said nothing. I moved with my new drink just as the piano player started his set with "Laura." He was smooth and lyrical, with a good melodic line that he extended almost gracefully. He was halfway through his fourth number when I thought I heard a commotion. Ray called to me, "She's fainted or they drugged her one."

"Let them play it out," I said.

Aubuchon came over to the bar, but he was at the other end and too intent on getting her out of there to think about looking around.

"The lady's fainted. All she needs is some air. How much is the bill?"

Ray told him, took the money, but didn't have time to give him change. They had her up and were trying to get her to walk. At least that's what they pretended they were trying to do, as they took her out the side entrance.

I was about to pay for my drink when Ray waved me off. I didn't argue the point. I went out the front way. They had a private limo waiting. I crossed the street, got the license number, and waited. When they turned on the lights, I signaled my cab. He pulled up and I got in. The limo turned up 12th Avenue and we followed. They took the Henry Hudson Parkway all the way up to the Cross County, then went up the Thruway heading north and got off at Rye and turned in at the Hilton. I told him to go in and park far away. I got out and watched them. The limo pulled up, but only Braithwaite got out. He went in while they waited. Then he came back, gave the bellhop the luggage, and went back in. The car circled around to the side and pulled up near a side door. I didn't have to move to see it all. They saw Braithwaite through the window enter the room, tip the bellhop, close the door, come to the window and signal, then go out again and come to the emergency side door, open it, and they took her in that way. She was still on her feet, but barely.

I waited. The limo driver came back out and drove away. That's when I sent the cab back to Manhattan. I went in, registered. Told them that my bags would be there in the morning. Went up to my room and called de Souza. Told him I couldn't make the meeting. He asked me where I was, I hesitated from habit, though I didn't know why. Told him I couldn't talk about it, but that I'd call him first thing in the morning. He told me when he'd be in. I hung up. I had to get inside that room. But how? I went down a flight to the floor they were on, listened at the door. Heard nothing. Went to the front lobby, found the bar, and sat and had a drink.

Then I saw Braithwaite come out and head for the front exit. I followed him. He gave the bellhop a bill and the bellhop took a key from a rack and disappeared. I went back inside and stood next to a window with tall plants. The bellhop came back with a car. Braithwaite got in and drove off. I went out and watched. He parked near the fire exit, right in front of the door they were in. I wandered over, looking back as I did so. The bellhop had gone off to get another car, presumably, and there was no one around. Braithwaite was just getting out of the car when he turned and saw me. He tried to pretend innocence. Maybe he thought I just happened to be there. Whatever. I said, "Hi," held out my hand to shake his, and he took it. I spun him around and got a good grip on his Adam's apple and squeezed until he was close to passing out. Then I turned him around, hit him in the belly twice and he sank to the ground. I put him back in the car, in the back. Opened the trunk. There was plenty of room.

I was just putting him in when the fresh air revived him and he started to struggle. I tapped him once with the tire iron. That quieted him. Then I locked the trunk and drove the car out onto the highway and about a quarter of a mile down and onto a dirt road. Left it there and came back. Went to my room and dialed Aubuchon. He picked up the phone with a "Where the hell have you been? She's coming around. We'll have to give her another . . ." Then he stopped and said, "Smedley?"

"Uh, no. Is this room 113?"

"Yes, it is. Who is this?"

"This is hotel security. We found a gentleman with your room key on him who looks like he was mugged in the parking lot. Could you come down to the main lobby right away."

"Describe him."

"Uh, sir, I'm afraid if you don't come down we'll have no choice but to come and get you."

"No, I'll be right there." And he hung up. I made it down the stairs just as he was locking the door. He headed for the front and I went out the side door and broke the window and went in. She was in the closet. I got her out, she was still half dazed, and out the door, closing it, and up to my room before he had figured it out. I rubbed her wrists and tapped her face gently. Wet a towel and dabbed her face with that. She finally came out of it.

"You okay?" I asked.

"Yes, I guess so. But I was scared for a while."

"I know. Sorry. I didn't expect them to play that rough."

"That's okay. You got me out of it. What did they give me anyway?"

"I don't know, but whatever it was it couldn't have been too strong. It was wearing off. One of them told me, thinking I was his partner, that he'd have to give you another dose. But he didn't have time, thank goodness, which is why he locked you in the closet."

The phone rang, I picked it up. It was the front desk.

"Yes."

"Excuse me, sir, but could you come down to the lobby for a moment, please?"

"Of course, what seems to be the problem?"

"One of our guests has the problem and we're trying to get to the bottom of it."

"Yes. I need to come down anyway. My assistant just arrived and she's staying the night. I'll need a second room."

Old Aubuchon was trying to flush us out. That was silly. He could do nothing in an open confrontation.

We went down and while Marlene conspicuously registered, he and I eyed each other. The manager came over. "This is Mr. Aubuchon. He says he got a call from security. But security didn't make the call."

"Oh, really. You look familiar," I said. "Have we ever met?"

Aubuchon suddenly changed his mind about the whole thing and said, "No, I don't think so." Then he turned to the manager. "I'm sure my friend will show up." And he left. The manager and the clerk shook their heads and apologized to me. "The house detective saw you standing around and you didn't have any luggage when you checked in. So we thought you might have made the phony call. I'm sorry we bothered you."

"No problem," I said and turned to look at the detective. He was in tennis shorts and shirt, no less. Young. I never would have guessed.

Marlene and I went up to the new room and ordered from room service. Then we relaxed and waited. The phone rang again. It was the front desk. "The gentleman would like to talk to you. We didn't give him the room number."

"Don't. Tell him I'll call him in his room in fifteen minutes."

I did. "Where's Smedley?" he asked.

"What did you want her for?"

Just then there was a knock on the door. Marlene got up to get it, but I stopped her. I put Aubuchon on hold, went to the door and looked out. There was a guy in uniform with a tray, but I didn't like the look of him. I kept the chain on and signed for it through the door. Told him to leave the tray and closed the door. I went back to the phone and asked Aubuchon if he was still there. He'd hung up. That convinced me.

"I think he's got something working," I told her. "He's either got help that he just acquired or he called it in or had it set up from the start."

"What do we do?"

"We're fine for the time being. Tell me about the conversation."

"You mean before I got drugged?"

"Yes."

"They introduced themselves as lawyers who represented Kathleen. They gave me their cards."

"Do you still have them?"

"Yes." And she took them out of her purse and handed them to me. They were the right names all right, but they had Kingston addresses on them. "Do you know this area?" I asked her.

"Yes, Constant Spring. It's a well-located mall with only the best of tenants."

"I see. Did they indicate that they had offices or a practice in New York?"

"No, and I didn't get into it. You told me not to be too inquisitive. Just enough not to arouse their suspicions."

"Right, I did. What else?"

"They wanted me to go to Jamaica with them. According to them, Kat has considerable property down there and I'm her heir. They wanted to leave tomorrow." She paused, then said, "They were very clever. I'd relaxed, thinking that that was all there was to it. Hell, I'm in my backyard in Jamaica."

"What about Smedley?"

"He wasn't brought up there."

"Are you sure?"

"Quite. When I asked him what school he went to, he gave me an elementary school."

"What's wrong with that?"

"It's never done. You always give your high school. Then if someone wants it, you give them your elementary school. Or if you do, you say that was the elementary school, and then tell them what the high school was. It's automatic."

"So you think he went to high school somewhere else?"

"Yes. Either here or in London."

"But he could have relatives in Kingston just the same."

"He probably does."

"Anything else?"

"No. It was after that that the lights began to spin round." Then she held her head and reached for something to hold on to. I grabbed her and lay her down on the bed and went back to the wet towels. Then I remembered the tray with the food. I went to the door, looked out. Saw no one and got the food. Locked the door and chained it again and came back in. I went over to put the tray down when I noticed that her purse had a rather hefty bulge to it. I put the tray right next to the purse, pretended to pour the tea and take the covers off the food plates as I looked in the purse. She had a small silver-handled gun. A .28. They don't make too many of those. I came over to her with the tea.

She got up. "Do you think we ought to? After all, you did say you were suspicious of the waiter."

"You're right. Let's get out of here." I figured it was as good a time as any to test her. "We'll turn left when we get in the hallway, go to the front of the building, take the stairs down to the main lobby, find some magazines and pretend to read. Give it a while, then make our next move."

"Which will be what?"

"Either back to my room or out the door."

"Okay." And she got up.

"You ready?"

"Yes."

"Sure?"

"Absolutely ."

"Then let's do it. If you feel faint, just grab my arm." She picked up her purse and we went out. There was no one in the hallway. Down in the lobby we were eyed by everyone at the front desk. We sat and read, not saying anything to each other for about fifteen minutes. Then I spied the detective coming in from the front, a little muddy, his legs scratched, dirt splattered on his whites. He wasn't too happy. When he saw me, he tried nonchalance. He must have been looking for something, I told myself. Maybe a car with a corpus in the trunk. He disappeared into the interior of the hotel. I went to the house phones, which were in full view of everything and called Aubuchon's room. There was no answer. I waited, called again. He picked up the phone and said, "Well, did you find him?"

"You're in the habit of assuming you know who you're talking to on the phone, Mr. Aubuchon," I told him.

He seemed to want to hang up, but probably felt silly doing it. "Yes, it does seem that way, doesn't it?" he said.

"You were asking me a question when we were rudely interrupted the last time."

"And you countered by asking me a question."

"So I did."

"How do you propose we exchange information?"

"Good question. We could all meet in the coffee shop, or in the jacuzzi or the lounge, the steam and sauna, or even among the Nautilus equipment."

He was silent. I think he was actually thinking about it.

"I didn't bring a swimsuit so I guess we'll have to make it the lounge."

"No, the fixed drink act may be too much of a temptation for you. Let's say the coffee shop. Things tend to fizz or bubble up in hot liquid, and their taste is more easily exposed."

"Not all things," he said.

"No, not all," I agreed.

We sat across from each other. Marlene was to my left in the corner seat. He was trying to appear calm. He was anything but.

"I only have one question before we begin," he said. "Is Smedley alive?"

"If he weren't, would I tell you?"

"What does that mean?" he demanded rather vehemently.

"He's alive." Smedley must have meant a lot more to him than met the eye.

"But where is he?"

"Aren't we getting ahead of ourselves? You're supposed to tell me why you drugged Marlene, and I am then supposed to tell you where Smedley is."

"I'm not playing games," Aubuchon threatened.

"And what does that mean?" I asked.

"It means I'll have Billy blow you away if you try anything cute."

I turned and Billy was none other than the big guy posing as the waiter earlier. Either he had been in the limo and came back or Aubuchon had him in the hotel when he got there. Billy was seated in another booth, he got up, came over and sat beside me, he was out of uniform. He pushed me in close to Marlene. I felt the muzzle of something cold, big and hard against my ribs. A .44 maybe.

"Frisk him, Billy," Aubuchon said. Billy did. "Nothing," he said.

"Nothing," Aubuchon said. "Are you sure?"

"I'm sure," Billy said.

"Why didn't you ask me?" I offered. "I rarely carry them."

"Well, this is one time you'd wished you had," Aubuchon said.

"Why? You going to beat it out of me?"

"No, out of her." And he hissed when he said it.

"Oh, you have something against beautiful women?" I asked. I think he wanted to slap me.

"Look," I continued, "this is all very silly. What are you going to do? Shoot me and then drag her kicking and screaming out the front door? How far would you get?"

"You'd be dead, so you'd no longer have to worry about it," he said.

"Besides, she doesn't know where Smedley is, I do," I said. Just then Marlene slipped the .28 into my boot.

They were waiting for something to happen before they made their move. That much was obvious.

"Look," I said again, "why don't we leave the lady out of it."

"But it's the lady we want, you keep forgetting. You're the dispensable one, she isn't."

He was beginning to get on my nerves.

"I still think making you shoot me down here is my best bet."

His eyes blared and he nodded to Billy, who banged me in the ribs with whatever weapon he was carrying. I wanted to blow him away right then and there, but I didn't know what Aubuchon had and Marlene could easily end up getting shot too, but I decided playing possum was not the right move.

"So he's going to wear out my ribs, is he? What else is new?"

Billy was about to try again, but I moved away and he missed. That really made him mad, but he didn't overplay his hand. He was willing to wait.

I stood up. Billy made the mistake of trying to get the gun out. I put one foot on his hand and wore him out with my right fist while he tried to hit me with his right. My left was free to ward those blows off. But either he had an iron jaw or I needed to go to the gym more often. I kept him down, but all he did was blink and try to get up. People started yelling and screaming.

Aubuchon tried to drag Marlene away, but she bashed him

over the head with the sugar jar and he decided to leave alone. As soon as he was gone the gun went off. That brought their whole army, about ten guys. Some in sneakers and sweatshirts, some in suits with badges. Everybody was into the disguised cop routine ever since "Baretta" had given way to "Hill Street Blues." They all had walkie-talkies. The guy with the gun hadn't shown up yet, so they stood around trying to decide their next move.

The bullet had gone between my legs and halfway up Marlene's skirt before it lodged in the padding of her chair. When the guy with the gun showed up, he held it correctly and seemed to know what he was doing. He said, "Freeze."

"He's got the gun in his left-hand pocket, be careful," I told him. He pointed his gun right at Billy. I moved away, held my hands up so as not to make anyone nervous, and turned to Marlene and winked and nodded down. She took the gun back without anyone noticing. Billy stood up slowly, hands on his head. He knew the routine. One of them took Billy's gun and they marched us all into a back office. A new, more impressive manager came out. He had the police and his Manhattan office calling him back simultaneously and right away, as well as soon.

I was in the clear without any difficulty. I let them look through my pockets, but I didn't want them to search Marlene's bag. "She's my assistant," I said.

"But she has no ID to that effect," said the new, impressive manager.

"It was an undercover job." I said. He still wanted to see the contents of her purse rather than what she showed him.

"Sorry," I said, "privileged. We're still friends, let's try to keep it that way."

"Meaning what?" he asked.

"Oh, a lot of things. How did he"—I pointed to Billy—"get into a waiter's uniform and bring us our food from room service? The tray is still in the room. It's poisoned for all I know." Just then Billy bolted. He knocked down the guy at the door and was through it in a shot. All ten of them tried to get through it at the same time. By the time one of them did, Billy had disappeared into the night. That settled it. We were moved to a luxurious suite and afforded every courtesy.

"Well," I said, as I opened the complimentary bottle of champagne and poured, "this is turning out to be quite an evening. Jamaica should be dull by comparison."

"I doubt it," she said.

"Why are you carrying a gun?"

"Whatever the reason, don't pretend that you were surprised because you weren't. I saw you peek in my purse when you brought the food in."

"Did you? How observant."

"Yes, and it helped you even if you were clever enough not to have to use it."

"How so?"

"Because it gave you courage. You knew that you could match him, gun for gun, if it came to that."

"Very good. To you, my dear." We drank and she came over and kissed me.

"Thanks."

"Think nothing of it. That's just my way of complimenting you for being a good soldier. You always seem to think of something, no matter how sticky things get. What is it, instinct?"

"No, luck."

"Come on, you're being too modest."

"You just stay loose and pick your spot. The biggest mistake you can make is not to know it when you see it."

"Sounds easy, but when I saw the look in his eyes, I thought we were dead."

"We were, almost. But in my business 'almost' can be an eternity."

"I guess so. What about Aubuchon?"

"He's probably hiding out."

"But they didn't seem too concerned about him. I found that odd."

"I don't think they wanted to add to their embarrassment by asking questions they had no answers for."

"But you didn't bring him up either."

"Because he's no good to me locked up somewhere trying not to answer a lot of dumb questions that the police would ask him. No, I want to get my hands on him alone and in private."

"How are you going to manage that?"

"We'll just have to wait."

"Wait?"

"Yep."

"You don't really think he's still around?"

"Yes. And he's going to stay around until he finds Smedley. And since Billy got away, he's not in any real trouble. Think of it. What do they have against him?"

"A lot, I would think."

"Not really. They can kick him out of the hotel, that's about all. Remember, their priority is not solving crime, but keeping the reputation of the establishment unsullied."

She seemed a little perplexed by it all, but decided not to pursue the matter. "So what do we do?"

"That's what I'm working on. I'm convinced the house detective is in it with him."

"Or maybe he's just pretending he is so he can trap him."

"No, that would be too much work for a relatively small problem. Whatever Aubuchon's doing, the hotel wants him to do it far away from here. That's their bottom line."

"I have an idea," she said.

"You have my complete attention," I told her.

"Why don't I pose as a chambermaid and go looking through the rooms until I find him."

"And what do you do with him when you find him?"

"I don't know. Kick him in the shins and yell."

"No, kick him in the shins and run."

"Either way."

"There're only three things wrong with that plan. One, I like you better in the dress you're wearing; two, I don't want you in another room alone with any man, unless I'm the man."

"And three?"

"It would take too long to go through all those rooms."

"Just when I was getting interested in the reasons."

"The business at hand must take precedence, I'm afraid."

"I'll have to teach you better habits when I get you in Jamaica."

"Yes, you must."

We finished the champagne. Thought about each other's bodies, realized we hadn't eaten and went back down to the coffee shop and had a light supper.

The management got nervous as soon as they saw us. I opened my coat and grinned, saying, "No weapons." That actually got a laugh and relaxed the front desk. We were just finishing up when I thought of something. "The house detective's room."

"It's logical," she said. "But how do we get in, once we find it?"

"Let's find it first," I said.

Back at the front desk, I asked if he was around. He wasn't. Would they ring him for me? They did. He wasn't in.

"What side of the building is he on?" I asked, matter of factly, and as though I had a right to know.

"He has a private bungalow behind the arboretum, just after you pass the outdoor swimming pool," said the energetic young man with the thick glasses.

"Thanks," I said and we left.

"You'd think they'd want to keep that sort of thing secret," she said.

"As a rule, they probably do. But I suppose we've made our mark as friends of the firm, or at least as guests who should be given access to privileged information. Sometimes it's amazing how quickly one can get credibility."

"Or lose it," she said.

"Come on, let's go find our friend last seen in a tennis outfit." We did. The bungalow was quite secluded. A small pentagon-shaped affair on top of a little rocky knoll, with steps up to the door and a small porch that went halfway around either side. The curtains were drawn, but lights were on. We went around the left side, which seemed to have the sitting room. One of the floorboards on the porch squeaked, so we couldn't get too close. They kept talking. We went farther to the back and looked in between the blinds. Aubuchon was sitting. He seemed sullen. He had a drink in his lap and he was looking in the direction of the front door. We had a good view of his right side.

The house detective had changed. He was in a terry cloth bathrobe. He was drinking something hot out of a mug.

"What're you going to do now?" he asked Aubuchon.

"Where are they?"

"In the honeymoon suite."

"I've got to find Smedley."

"You can't touch them until after they leave the hotel, I'm telling you."

"O.K., O.K. We'll wait. As soon as they check out."

"Sure. We'll grab 'em on White Plains Road at the intersection of Route 287."

"You got it set up?"

"I will."

"You'll know when they check out?"

"I'll know."

I'd heard enough. We went back to the main building and made ourselves conspicuous at the bar. Had a few drinks. Then Marlene said, "Suppose they find out that we asked where the bungalow was?"

"Well, unless they can be sure that we were up there listening, it may not mean much. Their key man is probably in the cashier's office. He knows when anyone checks out. That's the move we have to watch."

"Do you know the intersection they're talking about?" she asked.

"Yes."

Just then the disco started in the lounge and we decided to give it a try. Some of the security boys who had let Billy slip through their hands were around with walkie talkies, but that was all. Then there was a commotion and people started yelling and screaming. Two guys were locked tight in armholds and rolling around on the well-polished floor. Nobody was throwing any punches, but they were serious. Everyone moved over to see how it would end up.

I suddenly had an idea. I went to the house phones and called the operator. "What's the extension for the house detective? I seem to have misplaced it."

"Why do you want him, sir?"

"Well, there's a fight in the lounge and he was asking about one of the men involved in it earlier."

"Just a minute, sir."

He came on. I used the old handkerchief over the phone trick. "Hello."

"That guy that had a fight earlier, well, he's at it again with another black guy. They're in the lounge. I saw you talking to him and thought you ought to know. Those are the wrong kind of people to be in a nice hotel like this if you ask me."

"Seems as if our friend has gotten himself into some difficulty," I heard him saying. Then to me, "Is security there?"

"Yes," I told him.

"Thanks," he replied. "Keep an eye on him, I'll be right there." And he hung up.

I signaled Marlene and we made it back to the arboretum just as our friend was coming out of his bungalow. Guess he had to change into something more respectable. We waited behind some shrubs that were in full bloom until he'd passed us, and then went up to the door and knocked. Aubuchon called from within, "Who is it?"

"Smedley," I said in a husky, choked voice. He quickly opened the door and I pushed him in and down onto a chair. He tried to get up, but I wouldn't let him.

"Show him the gun, kid," I menaced. Marlene was so astonished that she almost didn't play her part. But she recovered and took it out. "Now," I said, "we're going for a little walk and don't get cute. One shot's all it takes. And remember, even if they do catch us you'll be dead, so it won't matter to you."

Marlene gave me the gun, even though I hadn't asked for it. We went out the back way, found the long end of the parking lot and headed for the exit. We walked down the road, turned in where I'd parked the car—it was still there—and got in. I sat in the back with Aubuchon. Marlene drove. As soon as we started off, we heard Smedley kicking up a ruckus in the trunk. Aubuchon's eyes widened, but he said nothing. We drove to Brooklyn, parked the car, and took Aubuchon in and made him comfortable. I called de Souza at home. He wasn't there. I tried the club and spoke to him while Marlene made coffee.

"Not spiked," she said, smiling, as she gave Aubuchon a cup.

"What about Smedley?" he asked under his teeth.

"Oh, does he drink coffee?" I asked.

De Souza arrived in about twenty minutes.

"We have our second case of kidnapping," I said. "This gentleman, an officer of the court and a member of the bar, kidnapped our precious Jamaican flower here from a West Side restaurant earlier tonight. There are witnesses. She was drugged and abducted, quite simply. Taken out of the city limits and sequestered in a hotel in White Plains. A reputable hotel, I will admit, but still. White Plains. That's almost like crossing the state line."

De Souza wasn't sure what I wanted him to do. While he thought about it, I went to get Smedley. He had to be helped inside. He was a wreck and in pain. Coffee didn't help, neither did rum. I let him lie down on the bed in the other room. Left the door open. He was in full view. Aubuchon got angry as soon as he saw how much pain his friend was in.

"You know, of course, officer, that this is an illegal detention. I intend to prosecute you to the fullest extent of the law, unless you release us immediately."

"Shot in the act of escaping," I said as I shook my head.

"What did you say?" Aubuchon asked.

"I said, you were shot in the act of escaping. In the back, right between the shoulder blades. Just as we were taking you to the precinct for questioning."

"And Smedley?"

Old Smed had managed to sit up by this time and was showing signs of life.

"Oh, a witness to it, of course. He might even testify to what really happened. But you'll be dead, so you'll never know how it turned out, will you?" I smiled and waited. Then the phone rang. It was Quinn.

"Is de Souza there? I've been calling all over town for him."

"You bet he is," I replied. "Want to talk to him?"

"I do."

I gave it to de Souza. "For you," I said.

He whispered into the phone, then gave it back to me. "For you," he said.

I took it, said "Yes?" and waited.

"Having a party?" Quinn asked with a salacious ring in his voice.

"Sho nuff, Cap'n. You know how us cullud folks is afta midnight."

"Good. Enjoy yourself. The captain would like to see you tomorrow in his office in Manhattan, Twelfth Precinct."

"Will you be there?" I asked.

"Yes," he said.

"Then I wouldn't miss it for anything. What time?"

"Ten."

Then I got an idea. I turned so Aubuchon could hear and said rather loudly, "Uh, by the way, Lieutenant, will the police commissioner be there?"

There was silence, then he said, "I don't think so, why do you ask?"

"Well, the captain did make me a big promise, remember."

"And you turned him down."

"If he wants to set up a meet with the commissioner to get to the bottom of this FBI thing," I said, almost yelling it, "then that's okay with me. And we can talk about the high-tech deal after we've taken care of the FBI." Big on the FBI again.

After I hung up, I turned to de Souza and said volubly, "The FBI wants to hog it all, but we've got to save the police commissioner. He's a good Democrat and an Irishman. They're Catholic, you know, the Irish. Anyway, the guy's a square shooter and he wants this one for New York City's finest. And why not, I say. They deserve it. Hell, J. Edgar Hoover's dead, for chrissakes. He's had his glory and then some. It's time somebody else had a chance. Right?"

Neither Marlene nor de Souza was quite sure of what to say. So to keep it going, I hastily answered my own rhetorical gambit with "Right!"

Aubuchon was deep in thought. Smedley asked for coffee. Marlene obliged, then the phone rang again. This time it was Gretchen, of all people.

"Plans have changed. I have to have the tickets right away."

"Sure. When?"

"In the morning."

"How early?"

"By ten."

"Not possible."

"Look, by ten or forget it."

"Then I guess we'll have to forget it."

Silence, then, "Okay, eleven, no later."

"Gretchen,"—that was a mistake. Aubuchon all but jumped out of his seat—"we'll have to talk first, okay."

"When?"

"Later."

"Where?"

"Name it."

She thought, then said, "Do you know the Williamsburgh Bank on Hanson Place?"

"I'll find it."

"It's right next to the Brooklyn Academy of Music."

"Yes."

"In the lobby."

"When?"

"Noon."

"Okay." And I hung up. "Cuff these two to the bed frame," I told de Souza. "We'll need them on ice for at least forty-eight hours." And I got seemingly busy.

De Souza thought about it, then he did it! I was shocked beyond belief, convinced as I had been that he would protest, pleading their constitutional rights. But he didn't.

Aubuchon tried to protest, but de Souza got rough, grabbed him and threw him down. Smedley went quietly. They had to sit on the floor chained to the cross bar. Escape was a distinct possibility. It meant disassembling the bed, but it could be done. Of course they'd still be chained to each other. We left them like that and locked all the doors.

"How long do you think it'll take them to get out of it?" I asked de Souza when we got outside.

"About half an hour."

"That's all?"

"If they're smart."

We found an all-night restaurant, got Jamaican patties and ginger beer, came back, moved Smedley's rented car a couple of blocks away, and waited in de Souza's unmarked car.

In about forty minutes or so they came out of the downstairs entrance, walking closely together.

"They couldn't get rid of the handcuffs," I said.

"No, that's not easy to do," de Souza replied.

They went to the corner and waited until they got a gypsy— about the only kind of cab you can find in that part of Brooklyn. They go anywhere, they're not yellow. We followed. I didn't think they saw us at first, but they kept looking back out of the rear window. They seemed to want the driver to take circuitous routes, but he wasn't interested in playing. The combination of an all male couple, racially mixed, and obviously joined together by more than physical attraction was more than he was willing to deal with. He put 'em out. But they got another one right away and headed across the Manhattan Bridge, and straight to their office in Bowling Green.

It was only then that I realized that they were just being cautious but actually hadn't seen us. They went up. We gave them five minutes, then followed. They were in the back rushing about, cleaning out everything. They still hadn't gotten the cuffs off. They hadn't had time.

We stayed in the hallway. Then de Souza said, "The night watchman could come along any minute. We have to be careful."

"Just as long as he doesn't arouse our friends," I said.

They were finished, finally. They came out and closed the door and locked it. We were in the stairwell. They were carrying a huge manila envelope bulging with papers. They headed down. De Souza said he'd follow them. Marlene and I went into the office.

It took a while, but I finally found it. Mrs. Hylton's cash box. The only thing in it was an old newspaper article.

"That's the *Daily Gleaner,*" Marlene said.

"What's so special about that?" I asked.

"It's the oldest English-language daily in the Western Hemisphere. It was founded in 1834."

"Not really. Alexander Hamilton founded the *Post* in 1801," I said, "and he was black."

"I know. Born in Nevis."

"Right. So this newspaper is well known in Jamaica, I take it."

"It's *the* newspaper on the island."

The article mentioned a Dr. Gillesslee of London who had been declared incompetent by the court to handle his own affairs. He had come to Jamaica to teach at the University of the West Indies and had just transferred all the family fortune down to the island and withdrawn a million pounds sterling out of it. The family got a court order that prevented him from taking any more money out of England. Apparently there was another million left. There was a picture of him taken with a group of Jamaicans. Iris Hylton was in the picture. But she wasn't the only one. So was Black. The caption read: "English doctor in Pocomania scandal." There was no date.

"I think they have Mrs. Hylton's estate in those manila envelopes," I said.

"What can you do about it?"

"Nothing, until I hear from de Souza."

We looked around some more. There didn't seem to be much else. I found the secretary's desk and flipped through her appointment book. She had a note for Wednesday the 15th: "Pegasus. Check in—12 noon." Then, it read, "For 3 days."

"Someone's going to be at the Pegasus for three days, starting on the 15th," I told her.

"What time's the flight?" she asked.

"They check into the hotel at noon."

"That means the early bird. On Wednesday, it's either Air Jamaica or American."

"Good work. If it turns out that our friends have a reservation on that flight, we'll know where to find them."

"If it's already made, I can check it in a matter of minutes."

"Can you do it now?" I asked.

"Sure," she said and called a travel agent she knew. When she hung up, she said, "Air Jamaica. The flight lands at eleven-thirty."

"Are they both on it?"

"No, only Braithwaite."

"I wonder what that means?"

"You want me to have her double check?"

"No. Ask her if the flight is all booked and when the reservation was made."

She did. "The reservation was made a month ago and paid for by credit card. At the time there were plenty of seats. Now it's all booked up."

"So Aubuchon has other plans, or at least he did a month ago. Have her check every day next week for a reservation in his name."

She got her friend back, but she had gotten busy and couldn't do it right then. She told Marlene to call her later.

We left. I took her home. Said good night. She offered me coffee. I said I'd take a raincheck.

"What're you afraid of?" she asked.

"Well, I'm still getting over something. I don't have my sea legs yet."

"Oh, is that what you call them? Well come in, relax, tell me all about it."

I went in, but refused to talk about what she wanted me to talk about.

"Are you just going to sit there?" she asked.

"No, but forget the coffee. I'll take a rum."

"No rum, just cognac."

"Show-off."

"I usually have rum, I just ran out, that's all."

"Oh, doing that much entertaining?" I asked testily.

"For sure. All the fellas call this apartment Grand Central Station when they don't call it their home away from home. It all depends on the mood they're in."

I apologized. She got quiet. I sniffed the cognac and tried to think, but my mind was a blank. We waited awhile, then I got up and began to pace.

"Why don't I put on some music?" she said. And she did. Good old Bob Marley. That helped clear things up. I sat again.

"Feeling better?"

"Much," I said and took a drink.

"Well, you certainly don't make it easy on a girl."

"Woman," I corrected. She laughed and I added, "No chauvinistic remarks, I'm a charter member of NOW."

"I'm sure you are."

"So why don't you want to talk about what you don't want to talk about?"

"Why do you want to talk about it?" I shot back.

"I just thought that with us about to spend so much time together in Jamaica we ought to know where we stand."

"I see. And exactly where is that?"

"Well, I get the feeling that you're in love with someone, or you were and it's on the way out or close to it. Is that right?"

"Something like that."

"But you're having problems getting rid of the feeling, apparently."

"Sort of."

"Yes, well, I just wanted you to know that you're not the only one."

"Oh."

"No. As a matter of fact, I just put him out two weeks ago."

"I see. Where? In Jamaica?"

"Yes."

"What does he do?"

"He's the prime minister's cousin."

"You're kidding!"

"Not at all."

"I think I'll go down alone."

"Don't be silly. It's nothing like that."

"She says the second before they abduct me."

She laughed as she tried to get a word out but couldn't.

"Well, you've certainly managed to change the mood," I said.

"Yes, with poor old Charlie." And she started laughing again. "It's probably the only time he's been good for anything in months."

"At the risk of spoiling the levity, have you gotten over him yet, may I ask?"

"Well, not completely."

"I see. So we both have something we're trying to forget."

"And can you forget?"

"I'm trying. What about you?"

"I'm trying too, but with me it's just a matter of time."

"You're sure?"

"Quite sure. And what about you?"

"I hope that it will just be a matter of time with me too,"

"But you're not sure."

"No, I'm not."

"Must make it difficult for you."

"Somewhat."

"Poor boy." And she came over and gave me a real kiss, then pushed me away. "You'd better go now."

"Of course, but before I do there are one or two points I'd like to bring up. I need another day in New York at least. I don't know when Aubuchon's getting on a plane, or even if he is. And of course, Smedley may be leaving the morning of the fifteenth, or he may not. If he does change flights, we may not know about it until after the fact. Then there's the problem of you."

"Of me?" she asked.

"Yes. They wanted you for something, remember. They know the address because they called you here. Right?"

"Right."

"So, that means that either they've found a way around you or they still have plans."

She said nothing.

"I think I have to spend the night."

"Now, just a minute."

"It's the only way. But not to worry. This is strictly in the line of duty."

"How can it be after . . . I've just kissed you so passionately."

"Oh, that. It didn't start any fires that can't be put out."

"Well, thanks a lot."

"You misunderstand me. What I mean to say is, it didn't only because it's not the right time."

"I'm not sure I consider that a compliment either."

"I'm spending the night strictly as guard dog. All right? I'll bed down on the couch."

"Well, if your intentions are honorable, the couch pulls out."

"No, leave it up. Better not to get too comfortable. Put the chain on and we'll back some furniture up to the door. That should get us through the night."

"You're serious."

"Why wouldn't I be? They tried to lure you out the first time. But once they've exposed themselves, they've got nothing to lose. Anything's possible, including dragging you off."

"Okay, if you think they might really try something."

We barricaded ourselves in and went to sleep. The next morning I couldn't move. I had gotten my head twisted in the corner of the couch and the pain in my neck felt like a permanent injury.

But she was up and the coffee was ready. I hated to admit it, but it was almost as good as mine. It was even better than mine after the second cup.

I left her and went to my meeting with Quinn at the Twelfth Precinct.

When I walked in I felt like the perpetrator of a major crime. They were all sitting or standing solemnly and waiting. The captain was seated behind a huge desk. No jacket, no hat, but as natty as ever. Quinn was standing in a corner, looking his disheveled best. And there were a stenographer and two other men. One in uniform, one out. The captain began it.

"Quinn tells me you want to cooperate with us more fully."

"Is that what the meeting's all about?" I asked.

"Well, no, we did have another item on the agenda, but we thought—"

"You thought that since I did a turnabout you'd grab at that first. Let's hear what you had on your mind before I said what I did to Quinn."

There was a restless moment. The captain coughed. "Well, actually, the situation's changed. But if you're willing to join the team . . ."

"Something's happened since last night. I don't know what." Then I got up. "But if all you want is to get me to join the team, forget it."

"But—" Quinn began.

"Forget what I said to Quinn," I told the captain.

"Was it true or wasn't it?" he asked.

"Oh, it was true when I said it. But that was last night, this is this morning."

"And?" he asked.

"And either you've got something to tell me that I don't already know or you don't. Well? No. O.K. Bye." And I left. As I got to the door, I saw a body move from out of the corner of my eye, but the captain signaled him off. I was on my way back to Brooklyn to get into a clean shirt when I saw Regina on the corner waving to me.

"Are you okay?" she purred.

"Regina, down, girl. We both know that neither of us is interested in the other sexually."

"Aw right!" Boy, she could change on a dime. "Where's Jay?"

I gave her the name of the hospital. "He's in intensive care. Better go and see him."

"Can't. No time. We'll have to call him from the airport."

"What are you talking about?"

"I'm talking about the John F. Kennedy Airport where you and I have to catch a plane in forty-five minutes."

"Plane to where?"

"Kingston."

"To begin with, I spent your five hundred dollars yesterday and I have about two tokens left to my name. I slept in my underwear and I don't have a change with me. I have a twelve noon date in Brooklyn and at least forty-nine other reasons why I can't catch a plane in forty-five minutes."

"Yeah, sure, we'll talk about it on the way." And she dragged me into a rented car and zoomed east to the Midtown Tunnel. "To begin with, there's a contract out on you for what you did to those guys."

"The time not to leave town is when there's a contract out on you. You lose your sense of who's after you. You relax, and two months later someone walks up to you and and you never know what hit you."

"Sounds good, but these guys are serious."

"You mean Dicky and Smedley?"

"Small fry."

"Really?"

"Really. Look, I never thanked you for taking care of Jay for me."

"What's between you two?"

"We're going to get married."

"Really?"

"Really."

"You love him too, then?"

"Heart and soul."

"And Reg?"

"Oh, I loved Reg too, but not the way I love Jay."

"I guess not, it was so long ago."

"Let's forget about my loves and get down to the business at hand, O.K.?"

"By all means."

We were going through the tunnel when I said, "Switch lanes."

"Do you know how much the fine is for doing that?" she asked.

"I want to know if we're being followed. Switch lanes."

She did. The guard in the tunnel didn't see her. When we got to the toll booth, we went right and I got a good look at the cars.

"Get in the exact change lane," I told her.

She did. I got out and told the operator at the booth that we had no change. He gave us change, made us get out of line and back in behind several cars that were in front of us. She took her time and we were on the Van Wyck with a clear view ahead and behind. If someone was tailing us, either they were very good or I was blind.

"Okay, Regina, give it to me."

"I have two reservations for us on the Air Jamaica flight to Kingston that leaves in"—she looked at her watch—"thirty-five minutes."

"Why is it so important for us to be on that flight?"

"We have to be in Jamaica tonight."

"Go on."

"You've heard about the formula?"

"I have."

"Good. Now all that talk about growing the stuff in New York is nonsense. They can't duplicate the climate, let alone the soil or anything else. But the crop is in trouble."

"How so?"

"Don't ask me. Some insect or the other got into Sligoville and . . ."

"Sligoville?"

"Yep. That's where the new superweed is grown. Anyway, they have to harvest it and ship it out fast. Apparently it's much harder to grow than the regular variety and now that the hype on it is in high gear they want to get it onto the streets fast, so they can have them all panting until the next crop comes in. Good for business. Get it?"

"So how do you fit in?"

"There's a war going on down there. The guys who wanted the prime minister of the small island bumped off are trying to move in on Jamaica. And they want me to help them do it."

"But if the map is in Brooklyn, how can you help them, unless you've memorized it?"

She brought the car to a screeching halt and onto a shoulder.

"You bastard. Did you find it?"

"Let's say I did. The question is, why are you getting on a plane without it?"

"Just tell me. Did you find it or didn't you?"

"I found it."

"And what did you do with it?"

"Left it in the baggage room at the Port Authority bus terminal."

"Are you sure we're not being followed?" she asked.

I looked back and there was a car across the highway on another shoulder.

"Not anymore I'm not."

She turned and saw them. "Damn, no-good double-crossing bastards. They promised me."

"What's your next move?" I asked her.

"Jay was supposed to bring it down with him, while they followed me. That was the plan."

"And it was a good one, except for one thing. You didn't trust Jay enough to let him in on it. If you had, he would never have told me about it. But what with the beating he took and he not knowing if you were dead or alive, once he found it, he just blurted it out."

"If he'd known when they got there and worked him over, don't you think he would have told them?"

"Maybe yes, maybe no. But when they came back they knew what they were after. How come?"

"Jay was supposed to have gotten it and gone by then. They were getting angry. I had to tell them something. And it had to be convincing. They were running out of patience."

"So what was the final deal?"

"When Roger—"

"Who's Roger?"

"The guy from the park. The one you caught in the apartment a couple of hours ago."

"Oh, that's his name."

"Yep. Anyway, when Roger called from the precinct, they knew that they'd lost it. So they let me go so I could try to get it back."

"Are you telling me what I think you're telling me? That these guys are ready to come get me as soon as you tell them that it's okay because you've got it back?"

"Don't worry. I'm not going to sell you out."

"So why the 'we have to get on a plane' routine?"

"Because I'm on the level. Jay brings the map down and we're in the driver's seat."

"You're crazy if you think I'm going to fight a whole army so you and Jay can pull a stupid double-cross."

"You won't have to fight anybody. Just relax, O.K.?"

"Yeah. Tell that to that armored car across the highway."

"We'll have to miss the flight, that's the only way it can work. I don't want those guys bird-dogging us all the way onto the plane."

"I'm all ears."

"We can catch an Air Florida flight out of Miami at four P.M."

"Well, getting a flight to Miami shouldn't be too difficult."

"Exactly." And she started up again. As soon as she did, they did.

"Do they know what flight you're booked on?" I asked her.

"Of course."

"Okay. Then just do what I tell you. First, we'll park the car in long-term parking. Do you have any baggage?"

"Yes. One in the trunk and this carry-on."

"Good. Now we're not ready to lose them just yet. So take it easy."

We pulled into long-term parking. Got the bag out of the trunk. Waited for the airport bus. Got on and got off at the Air Jamaica terminal. As we got out I saw them pulling up cautiously. Inside they told us that we'd missed our flight. The next one was at 2:30, but it was all booked up. But we could get on the midnight flight. We had them put us on an Eastern Airlines flight that would get us to Miami in time for the four o'clock Air Florida flight to Kingston. Regina called the hospital. Jay was under sedation, but out of intensive care.

I called Marlene. "I'm at the airport. I've mailed a picture to myself. It'll probably come to the Brooklyn address tomorrow. It's important that you meet the mailman, smile at him and sign for the package. I'd planned on having it sit in the post office until I showed up. But now it looks as if I have to change my plans."

"Why are you going down in such a hurry?"

"When things are going on that you don't understand, the only way to get to the bottom of it all is to follow the bouncing ball."

"What do you want me to do with the picture when I get it?"

"Get a Polaroid and make a copy of the front and the back, in color. Shoot it as close up as you can. Mail the picture to yourself, return receipt, and bring the photo with you."

"Should I get it blown up?"

"Definitely. Do you know a place?"

"Yes, I do."

"Good. When will you come down?"

"When do you want me to?"

"As soon as you can."

"Day after tomorrow."

"I'll be at the Pegasus, I think."

"Let me give you my number in Kingston." She did. "And I have a friend at the Air Jamaica office in Montego Bay. Her name is Joyce Shoucair. Call her if you don't get an answer at my Kingston number."

"Good. See you on Thursday."

"See you." And she hung up.

I turned to Regina. "Where are they?" I asked.

"Two of them are inside, and I guess one is in the car."

"Do you know them?"

"Yep."

"Are they pretending that they don't know you?"

"Yes, they are."

"You mean they think you haven't spotted them?"

"But it's the way I've played it."

"I don't like it. They may be ready to start shooting if we make the wrong move."

"Why would they when they don't have the formula?"

"I don't know, but something's not right. Let's lose them and see what happens."

I went back to the Air Jamaica counter with Regina in tow. I got the manager to come out. Told him I needed to check Regina's bag on the 2:30 flight to Kingston even though we wouldn't be on it. He was reluctant. But we paid full fare for it and he agreed. We had to sign a form releasing the airline from any obligation.

I made sure that our friends saw us.

One guy went to a phone booth while the other stood guard.

Regina and I sat nearby and pretended to be absorbed in watching television and reading magazines.

"What now?" she asked.

"He's making his call. If they have half a brain, they'll check Air Jamaica and find that we have a nine-hour wait, which should tell the other half of their brain that that's not the flight we're waiting for. So we have to effect our disapearance, as it were, before the return call."

He'd gotten off the phone by this and stood by the booth menacingly. A youngish woman came up to him and wanted to use it. He tried, diplomatically, to ask her to use another one, but she was insistent. Finally their disagreement became noisome and a guard went over.

"Casually go to the ladies' room. The one guy can't follow us both. You have the tickets. Keep yours and give me mine. I'll distract him. As soon as he starts watching me, keep going. Take a side entrance out of the terminal to avoid the car waiting in front. Walk to the next terminal and grab a cab to Eastern. Check in. Go through security and wait in the ladies' room until they announce the flight. Wait until the second call and then board. If I don't make it, I'll either meet you in Miami or Kingston. Now go!"

She gave me the ticket, got up casually, and went toward the ladies' room as if she were going in. I got up and moved toward the commotion, pretending to look out the window. I hoped Regina would take her chance as soon as she got it. The guy was certainly distracted. He started staring me down. By then the airport security had calmed the young woman and the other one down. But she was insistent. She got inside the phone booth and, of course, once she did, she took her own sweet time about it. The one who had made the call conferred with his buddy, who pointed to the ladies' room. Number One quickly dispatched Number Two to stand guard at the ladies' room. That's when I casually wandered back across the lobby and took the escalator up to the second level. Number One was frantic. He started pounding on the door of the telephone booth. The guard came back over. They yelled and shoved each other around. But I guess the lady suddenly realized that she could get her teeth knocked out and hung up and left. Number One went in, looked at Number Two, who looked at me. Number One signaled him to stay put. I disappeared down a hallway. Found an exit and walked over to the next terminal. I didn't see her. But that meant nothing. I suddenly realized I didn't have a sou to my name. And no credit card either. The banks had taken all of them away for nonpayment of debts years ago. All I had was the ticket. I caught an airline bus and went the whole route. The driver said, "Last stop, buddy." I pretended to have missed the Eastern stop. He said I'd have to get out and wait for the next bus, which would be along in ten minutes. I didn't really want to stand outside where I might be seen, so I asked him if I could sit and wait. He gave me half the time. His checker came and then he was ready to shove off.

I got out and crossed over to a cargo building. That got me thinking about how the ganja was brought in. Miami is easier than New York. And, of course, with all the drugs that find their way into the streets of Manhattan, Staten Island, Brooklyn, and the Bronx, they'd solved their distribution problems long ago. Just the same, knowing the specifics of it, as far as Jamaica was concerned, would help.

My bus showed up and I got on it without incident. When I got to the Eastern terminal there were no familiarly ominous figures about. I made it to the gate and sat in the lounge and waited, only because I wanted to be on hand if Regina needed me. They started boarding, but she was nowhere in sight. The last call came. Still nothing. The clerk turned to me and said, "If you don't board now, sir, you'll miss the flight." Before I could decide what to do, the phone at her desk rang. It was Regina.

"Hi, I'm all right. I switched the Eastern ticket to a straight through flight on American. I'll be in Kingston an hour after you."

"How do I know you're all right?"

"Ask me anything." Just then I saw the two guys trying to get past the passenger check-in. Their problem, of course, was that they had guns. I quickly told her, "I believe you. You can tell me all about it when you get to Kingston." I hung up and made it just as they were closing the door to the boarding ramp. My two friends never got past security.

We lifted off and I relaxed with a complimentary juice—I had no money with which to buy a drink—then settled back to nod my way to Florida. I had closed my eyes when I heard a sweet voice say, "Have a drink, compliments of Eastern, Mr. Cinquez." I looked up and there was a stewardess, pretty, petite, and smiling, with a liquor tray in her hand.

"How did you know my name?"

"Marlene Campbell sends her regards."

"That was fast."

"She caught me just as I was about to board."

"I see. Anything she wanted you to tell me?"

"Yes. She said she got a call. She was offered one million dollars, Jamaican. In Jamaica."

"Did she say anything else?"

"No, that's all."

"Thanks, I'll have a Bloody Mary."

"When you get to the Air Florida terminal, ask for Amanda. She'll take care of you for the second leg of your flight."

I looked at her leg and thought to myself that the first one hadn't been too bad at all. She gave me a second drink and sashayed down the aisle.

When I got to Miami, I looked around for a post office. Sent de Souza a letter at the precinct, telling him where I was, headed for Air Florida, and caught the flight. Forgot to ask for Amanda until they started serving drinks. But, as it turned out, they had complimentary rum swizzles, so I was fine. Amanda, whoever she was, never showed herself. We finally set down at the airport in Kingston. Talk about hot. A thin, short-sleeved cotton shirt felt like it weighed a ton. I had no passport, only my driver's license. They made me wait. The immigration officer wanted to know why I was in Jamaica. I told him I'd come down to get away from my wife. "Why no baggage?" he asked. "I didn't want her to know I was leaving," I told him.

"Where are you staying?"

"The Pegasus."

"You have a resevation?"

"Sure." What the hell, I thought, I had nothing to lose. Besides, I had to tell him something.

The son of a bitch called the Pegasus. I mean this African with his British-style white shirt and epaulettes, khaki shorts, socks to his knees, and dark shoes was one cool customer, and he wasn't letting me off the hook by any means. Not easily, anyway. To my utter amazement I was confirmed at the Pegasus. Well, that gave me tremendous credibility in his eyes, as it turned out. But I wasn't out of the woods yet. He checked with his supervisor, who went looking through books. Then he came back. When last had I had shots for typhus, influenza, hoof and mouth disease and God knows what? That over with, how much money did I have. That worried me. "The money's coming down," I said.

He looked at me as if I were a fool. "You don't even have a round-trip ticket," he said.

"I know. That's coming down too."

"I'm afraid I won't be able to let you land," he said with finality. I thought about making a dash for it but, of course, I wouldn't even know in which direction to run.

"Look, if my round-trip ticket and my money show up on the American Airlines flight which gets here in an hour, how about that?"

"What American flight that gets in here in an hour?"

"Don't you have an American Airlines flight coming in from New York that'll land in an hour?"

He looked at his chart, made a call, and then said, "No."

Well, well, Regina had struck again. I had to think fast.

"Oh, isn't that silly of me. I forgot. My bag came down on the Air Jamaica flight that left New York at two-thirty." He looked at me unbelievingly. Then he called Air Jamaica. There was an unclaimed bag there. He got the baggage claim number, asked me for the stub. I had it—to my utter astonishment and amazement. I started to reconstruct what had happened before Regina and I had separated. She had paid the price of the air fare to get the bag on the plane, using a credit card. She used my name and gave me the claim check. At the time I hadn't thought anything of it. Now it was beginning to loom large.

We walked over to Air Jamaica. A young lady came up and hailed us just as we were getting there. She and the immigration officer knew each other. Then she turned to me and said, "Marlene said hello." At that point if Santa Claus had showed up and asked for a dance, I would have been ready to say yes.

My official British colonial gentleman didn't like that at all. He had me on a plane to New York and no question about it. I had news for him. I had me on the same plane.

The sweet young thing—God I hadn't seen an ugly woman yet—was, as it turned out, Amanda. What the hell was going on I didn't know. She followed us to the baggage check area. She, of course, knew everybody. What had started out as a sentence of death had suddenly turned into a red carpet, replete with smiles and politeness, almost to the point of being unctuous.

I got the bag, asked if I could take it to the men's room. Was told I could not. That's when I began to sweat. If Regina wanted me in irons, all she had to do was have something in that bag that I couldn't explain. She did.

We went into a small, bare room. He opened it and there was

a suitcase full of money. American. It looked like about a hundred thousand dollars. I couldn't be sure.

"Are you trying to buy up the island?" he asked.

"No, of course not."

"Well, I can't let you in with more than fifty thousand, unless you have a business visa and documents authorizing you to make commercial purchases. Even then it has to go through the Bank of Jamaica."

I suddenly had a bright idea. "What if I converted all of this to Jamaican dollars here and now?"

"Then you would be more than welcome."

"The government would get the dollars and I would have Jamaican currency to spread around and help the old economy."

"Something like that. But that too would have to be handled by the Bank of Jamaica in town."

"O.K. So let me get to my hotel and we can do it in the morning."

"What about the money?"

"You take me to the hotel and we lock it up there. Then you come for me in the morning."

He bought it and went to talk it over with his boss. Amanda slipped in with a rum while I waited, all smiles, and winked at me. She had dimples an inch deep. And she was more gorgeous and just as petite and leggy as the other one whose name I hadn't even gotten.

He came back and it had all been settled. The three of us got into an official car and drove off. I still didn't believe it was happening. I looked back instinctively and there was a police car behind us.

"Escort?" I asked.

"Of course," he said.

I sat back and relaxed and looked around. It was just turning dusk. From what I could see the land was lush, but the colors were not too brilliant. The airport was on a palisade with a large bay on one side and the sea on the other. There were sand dunes and scrub on the sea side. The road was a narrow, winding, single lane affair going in both directions. The night breeze hadn't started up yet. I was hot. Most of the cars were small British makes: Austins, Morrises, English Fords, Opels. Every now and then a big Buick or Mercedes would lumber around a corner and look completely out of place.

When we got to the hotel it was dark. The porter couldn't get his hands on the bag. Amanda got the key as soon as I checked in and said she'd go up and make the room "comfy," as she put it. I think my official friend was going to put me back on a plane at that point just to get rid of me, whether he had a good reason or not. Not that he had something going with Amanda. He just didn't seem to like foreigners poaching on local gaming preserves.

We found the manager, an Englishman, and gave him the suitcase. He didn't want to open it, but the immigration officer insisted. He did. Then he didn't want to take it. We all three counted the money together. It was exactly $119,000, U.S., as they say in the islands. The immigration officer gave him a letter of authorization from his superior. By now I was sure that the whole island was in on it. I was still in yesterday's clothes so I told the manager I wanted to open an account in the clothing shop. He handed me a card that he said gave me unlimited credit in all the stores in the hotel, whether they were run by the hotel or not. Then he locked the money away in a heavy safe while we watched, and he tucked the key in his pocket. That done, we all shook hands.

Back in the lobby, my epauletted friend gave me a temporary visa that was good for ten days. If I stayed longer, I had to report to Immigration. Then he smiled and said, "But of course, I'll see you in the morning."

"Of course you will," I said and went up to my room.

Amanda had opened the sliding glass door and had a bottle of rum, glasses, ice, and a tray of hors d'oeuvres on a table on the balcony ready and waiting. And there was music coming from a radio built into the headboard.

"Hi," she purred.

"Hi."

She fixed me a drink, then said, "I told room service to send you up pajamas and slippers and a robe. In the morning we'll get you some swim trunks and with the robe and slippers you'll be able to go shopping. What about dinner?"

"What about it?"

"Well, there's a buffet by the pool, but how could we get you in? I have an idea. Why don't you slip into a towel—there's a large bath size in the shower—and let me see if I can manage something."

Before I knew what was happening, she had taken off my jacket and tie and was unbuttoning my shirt.

"O.K., O.K., I'll do it," I protested. I left the jacket on the bed. There wasn't anything in it that she couldn't see. I took off my pants in the bathroom, kept my wallet, and gave her everything else, including my New York City tokens.

She actually went through the pockets, complaining as she did so that American coins weren't worth anything in Jamaica, only American paper. I suddenly got the feeling that she was looking for something.

"Do you actually think that you can get those cleaned tonight?" I asked.

"Maybe just the shirt and underpants. That should get you through. But I must admit, it's a gamy lot." And she held her nose and disappeared through the door with all of it.

I went out onto the terrace and poured another drink, had an hors d'oeuvre, and looked out. I was way up, about seventeen stories. It was an immense view of the town, stretching down to the sea and the palisade beyond. I could see the airport with the grounded planes in the distance. Endless lights were twinkling all over the lower plains. Below me, about eighty feet down, was the swimming pool. It seemed very large. There were some last-minute divers. Off to the side they were making ready for the poolside dinner. And at the far end the musicians were just setting up.

The phone rang. I went to it and the operator said, "One moment please, long distance calling." I waited. There was static and then Marlene's voice came on, but it was a bad connection. The last words of almost everything she said were lost.

"Can you hear . . . ?" she asked.

"I can hear you, but not too clearly. Can you hear me?"

"Yes."

"Thanks for making the trip so comfy."

"I don't understand . . ."

"Your friends. They saw to it that I didn't have a chance to feel neglected one step of the way."

"They did? What . . . ?"

Just then we were cut off. I waited, then called the operator, but she said the problem was in Miami or New York. I didn't believe her. She promised to try again and call me as soon as she got through.

I wandered back to the balcony, sipped some more rum. Then a knock came at the door. I turned and said, "Come in," assuming it was Amanda. The door opened and three men were standing there, then a fourth one appeared. One was in uniform, like the immigration officer's, but he was police. He had a cap, the short-sleeved shirt with epaulettes was light blue, and he sported a cane. He also had the long socks and the black shoes and black short pants. The fourth man was in long pants and shirt, open collar. Two were in suits. They stood there. The one to my right was a light-brown-skinned man in his forties, about six feet, reddish coloring, freckles. He was in a light tan tropical suit and a shirt and tie that didn't particularly match. He was casual.

"Mr. Cinquez."

"Yes."

"May we come in?"

"I don't know. What's it all about?"

"Allow me to introduce myself. I'm Charles A. H. Macfarlane, Bank of Jamaica. Here's my card."

He came in and gave me a card that read SPECIAL ASSISTANT TO THE GOVERNOR OF THE BANK OF JAMAICA. The card was very well done. And it was newly printed.

"Yes, of course, please come in, by all means."

"Allow me to introduce my colleagues. This is Mr. Percy, aide to the prime minister."

"Mr. Percy." We shook hands.

He was perfectly matched in grays. Everything expensive and tropical, light. He said nothing, but he took my hand and nodded. He had an Indian or a Portuguese look to him. I hadn't been down long enough to be sure which. His hair was very straight and slicked back.

"And this is Inspector Collins from the constabulary—CID division."

Inspector Collins was one hundred percent black, about five feet ten, fifties, piercing eyes, inquiring manner. Something about him was familiar.

"And Captain Brown from the Treasury Department." Brown came forward and shook hands energetically. He was wiry, about five feet eight, the oldest of the four from the look of him.

I sat in a chair and told them to make themselves comfortable. They, of course, could do anything but that. The room was not large. And there were only two other chairs in it. The prime minister's man stood. Macfarlane took one chair, Brown another, and Collins sat on the edge of the bed. Before he sat down, Brown closed the door.

"You came about the money, I suppose."

"Yes, we did." Macfarlane.

"Is it counterfeit?"

"Not that we know of. Are you telling us that it is?"

"No, not at all. Is it being examined now?"

"No, but it will be in the morning." And he turned to Brown, who nodded.

"Go on."

"We've had a currency problem for some time now, Mr. Cinquez. The prime minister is most insistent on solving the problem. He's a man who insists on solving problems. There are problems and there are problems. Once a problem gets to the top of his list it gets solved or heads roll rather quickly and inexorably."

"And the currency problem is now at the top of the list, and some of the heads that are in danger of rolling are in this room?"

"Quite right."

Just then Amanda came back in. She had taken the key. She was as unperturbed as ever. She did a broken field run through the various bodies and put the robe, slippers, and a pair of paper underpants on the bed, commenting on the last with, "Look what I found."

"They're a touch too big, I think."

"Just cover them up. Hello, Ralph," she smiled at the prime minister's man as she headed for the door. Ralph didn't respond. She turned and said, "I'm working on your costume for dinner," and left.

"Excuse me," I said, and put on the robe, slipped into the paper underpants, put on the slippers and threw the towel over a chair on the balcony. "Anyone for a drink?" Brown said yes. He took it straight, not too much ice. I was on my third. After I'd settled back into my chair, we were ready to resume the discussion.

"Where were we?"

"At the top of the prime minister's list of problems," Macfarlane said.

"Right."

"The parallel market is draining all the dollars that come into the country."

"I'm sorry, that's not a term with which I am familiar."

"You call it black market," Ralph said, "but we have to be more racially sensitive in Jamaica as we are a country that is over ninety-five percent black."

"I see. How much are they giving for a U.S. dollar?"

"It varies," Macfarlane said. "Anywhere from three to one to six to one."

"And you want the dollars in the banks and the shops, which means they end up back in the Bank of Jamaica, rather than on the street where the government never gets any of it."

"Roughly speaking, yes."

"So how can I help?"

"Your one hundred thousand U.S. in the bank is very tempting, but we'd rather you keep it and spend it."

"In any manner I choose?"

"Not quite. We don't expect to solve all of our problems with this ploy. Actually, we're going to let the banks go into parallel marketing."

He paused, and thank goodness. I found the term ludicrous —although I understood the reason for it—so it was all I could do not to laugh when he said it. Then he continued, "But we want to get some of the money off the street. A sort of clean-up operation."

"You actually hope to catch them at it?"

"We know who the main dealers are," and he looked at Collins, who nodded twice. "But they're much too smart to get caught."

"How much are you losing a day?"

"Roughly a million and a half."

"That is a lot."

"But most of it is in five-hundred-dollar amounts or less. Sometimes it's as much as a thousand, but not too often."

"So the big operators have networks?"

"Quite extensive and well organized."

"Then what good is my one hundred thousand?"

"Because it's in one person's possession, namely yours, and because you are not known to our friends on the street, we thought we'd ask you to cooperate with us. We're convinced that there's someone in the immigration department who's helping to identify some of the big spenders when they come in. They'll all be convinced that you aren't working for us. Which actually is the case at present."

"Your only problem is that my story was so inept that I still can't believe that I'm here."

"Yes, we know all about your story. And that has caused us some concern. But we decided it's our best bet. Our chief problem is that we don't know much about you."

"But you certainly learned about my arrival quickly enough."

"I told you, this is top priority right now. We're all of us on the line, and we're working round the clock to solve this thing. We have to have it under control before the P.M. announces the new regulations allowing the banks to set rates of exchange on their own."

"That could give you a bigger problem in the long run."

"If they abuse the privilege we simply withdraw it. It's only temporary."

"I see. What's your plan?"

"We thought," Ralph said, "that if you did a few five-thousand-dollar deals, say two, and indicated that there was more where that came from that you'd have to meet some of the big boys without even trying."

"How much do you want me to negotiate for at one time?"

"After the initial five thousands, do two or three tens and then jump to half of what's left. Do that twice."

"And?"

"By then," said Brown, "we'll have them."

"How?" I asked.

"We'll mark the money, and we'll wait until the men we want show up."

"You think it'll be that simple."

"It won't be simple at all," Brown continued. "And we have to worry about your safety as well."

"What about my money?"

"As we understand it," said Ralph, "you were willing to convert it all to Jamaican currency anyway."

"Okay, but do I get to keep whatever I negotiate?"

"Of course. After all, it is your money," said Macfarlane.

"My only problem, gentlemen, is that I came down here on another matter and I don't know if I'll have the time."

"Well, tell us what it is and we'll help you." Macfarlane.

"I'll have to think that one over."

"Client confidentiality." Ralph.

"Sort of." So they knew. They had to. They wouldn't have been so willing to use me otherwise. But when and how did they find out?

Collins finally spoke up. "Do you carry a gun?"

I hesitated, but decided it was silly to do so. "I'm licensed to carry a gun in New York. But I don't have one with me."

He said no more.

"Our problem," Macfarlane said, "is that we have to put our plan in motion tonight."

I was afraid of that and asked, "What specifically needs to be done tonight?"

"The money has to be marked, serial numbers taken down." Ralph.

"What else?"

"We'd like to do certain other things to ensure getting the men we want," Macfarlane said. "Setting the trap, as it were."

"How many are we talking about?"

"Only two or three." Macfarlane again.

"I still have to think it over. But you can go ahead with the marking of the money."

"I can get the men ready and tell them not to make a move until I give the signal." Collins.

"Well, that's about it," Macfarlane said as he got up. "Will you come down with us while we mark the money?"

"No, I trust you."

"Very well." He moved to the door.

"You'll let us know tomorrow?" Ralph.

"I'll try."

"What kind of gun do you carry, when you're carrying one?" Brown.

"Right now it's a .38 automatic, but I'm not partial."

No one else said anything. Brown closed the door as Macfarlane said, "Until the morning then."

"Until the morning then," I replied and they left.

I wandered back to the balcony. The night had completely fallen. It was as if a jet black curtain had descended from the sky. The lights of the city seemed like earthbound stars constantly twinkling. Cars moving about on the roadways and in the streets seemed to be moving at random, through gullies and streams and buildings. The band had started up. There were sounds that seemed to be everywhere, but I was too far up to really hear them. They were the sounds of the tropics, of birds, insects, the wind through the leaves of the trees, the water on the sand and gravel of the shore.

I threw out my drink and made a fresh one. I was standing there, feeling like an ugly version of James Bond when the phone rang again. I went to it. It was Amanda.

"Well, all through?"

"Yes."

"Good. I just talked to Marlene. She wants me to show you the sights."

"I'd just as soon pass on that. I'm a little bushed."

"Not allowed. You're in Jamaica now. We party in Jamaica every night. We work hard and we play hard."

"I'm exhausted already."

"That won't last long. Some good hot food, a shot of white rum, the music, and you'll be fit, man, fit."

"Oh, I work out in the gym on a regular basis."

"When we say *fit* in Jamaica, we mean *ready*, not in good shape."

"Oh."

"Anyway, the pants and the shirt are almost finished. It was the best I could do."

"I'm not complaining."

"They'll start serving in about half an hour. I'll send the clothes up. Meet me in the Jon Konnoo Lounge in forty-five minutes."

"What's the name of that lounge?"

She spelled it.

"Okay. In forty-five minutes."

Marlene never called back. Maybe they weren't letting her get through because they wanted to keep their stories straight. I couldn't finish my drink. I kept thinking about the dead bodies: Mrs. Hylton, Josephs, Kathleen, Reg O'Connor, and about the unanswered questions: Where was Mrs. Hylton's three million dollars? Who had the map and what was it a map of? Maybe I had it. Maybe I didn't. Was there a formula and was it worth anything? What exactly was Regina's game? Was I falling for Marlene? Would that turn out to be a big mistake, big enough to cost me my life even? Why *was* Reg killed? Who killed Mrs. Hylton? Where did Trevor and Snakey and Gretchen fit into all this? And why had Regina stuck me with a suitcase full of money and practically put me in the hands of the Jamaican police to boot?

I met Amanda in the Jon Konnoo lounge in forty-five minutes as agreed. I was dressed absurdly. My gabardine slacks and business shirt, open at the collar, and heavy leather brown shoes, just didn't read the tropics. At least the shirt was clean, the pants freshly pressed, and the underpants comfortable. The socks had gotten lost, so I had none on.

The maid who had brought everything up said her name was Esme. She was the most voluptuous woman I'd ever laid eyes on, black or white. How any man worked around her on a continuous basis without losing his dignity, I couldn't possibly imagine. She was all smiles and sweetnesses. She wore the same uniform that the rest of them wore, but on her it was a piece of couturier art. She couldn't have been more enticing if she had appeared in a negligee.

She said she wanted to go to America and she was looking for someone to "sponsor" her. My response was noncommittal. I simply told her that we could "discuss" it. She seemed eager. I told her I had to leave, however, as I had an appointment in the lobby. She said not to worry, she'd be in touch. I was sure she would.

The hotel lobby had more people in it than Madison Square Garden on a Saturday night in the middle of the basketball season. There was a round staircase going down from the center of the lobby to the pool and the shops. Off to the right were more shops, a pub room called Bull & Board, and a theater across from it with a live performance going on. The Jon Konnoo Lounge was also right and fronted the pool. There was a huge glass panel that looked down to the pool area. Straight ahead was the formal dining room. The Jaycees were having a dinner or something. There were a lot of people with ribbons in their lapels. Everyone was dressed as formally as one can be in the tropics. But you needed an invitation to get into that party. I stood there for a brief moment, taking it all in, when someone bumped me. I turned to see who it was and felt something sticking out of my waist. It was a small piece of paper. I looked at it and it said, "Best rates. Ask for Cool Boy at the Calabash Lounge, right across from the Hot Pot Restaurant." I stuck it in my pocket and crossed over to the lounge. Amanda was at the bar holding court. She ushered me into her little circle of friends—all airline types. A stewardess and steward and one co-pilot. The steward and stewardess were light-skinned Jamaicans with that same mixture of either Portuguese or Indian, I couldn't be sure which. The co-pilot was East Indian. I told her not to bother with names, I'd never remember them anyway. We had a round or two. I decided to try the local beer. It was called Red Stripe. It was quite good. It had body, but it wasn't heavy, and the aftertaste was excellent.

The music by the pool had started up with a vengeance. We could hear it all the way in the lounge, even though the whole area was closed off by solid glass windows. Every time the door to formal dining opened, the music from that room blared out too. Add to that the dozens of groups milling around and you had quite a cacophany. But there was more. Booths had been set up next to the bell captain's station to sell tickets for a jazz concert. The group was from New York and they would play in the hotel in two weeks. I felt as if I were in the middle of all the important activity on the island. No wonder everyone said, "I'll be at the Pegasus." Everyone was. I tried to pick out suspicious-looking characters, but couldn't. I never saw who gave me the note announcing Cool Boy's whereabouts.

"The social mix is very interesting," I offered to no one in particular.

"Oh, yes," replied the pilot. "There was a time when anyone very dark couldn't get in the front door, unless he was Indian."

"Oh, John is exaggerating," protested Amanda.

"But it's true," offered the steward. "You see that fellow over there?" And he pointed to a young man dressed in what seemed like cheap khaki, with sandals, his hair in cornrows.

"Yes," I said.

"Well, he would have been kept out on three grounds, five, six years back. One, he's black-black. Two, the way he wears his hair. And three, the way he's dressed."

"I see. And now that democracy has come to the republic?"

"People don't change that much," he said. "What do the French say? 'The more things change, the more they remain the same.' My grandfather was such a racist that he used to get girls from the country as servants and never allow them to wear shoes. He said black people weren't really comfortable in shoes. The servants in his house were always in slippers or bare feet and they couldn't leave the premises without his permission, not even to visit their family."

"What about their days off?" I asked.

"They never had days off," he said.

"But that's all in the past," Amanda insisted. The other woman didn't say anything. I don't think she particularly cared. The pilot spoke up again.

"Yes, things have changed, but it still takes a while for it all to disappear psychologically. I remember lower-caste Hindus being tied to a tree by my uncle and beaten."

"You're mad," Amanda protested.

"I certainly was after I saw it," he said, sipping his beer. The stewardess wanted to dance, so we all went down the circular staircase and came out on the ground floor right in front of the pool. The food was to our right. People were sitting on both sides of the pool.

The band was playing a calypso and a famous singer from Trinidad named Sparrow had just started his first show of the evening. He was quite good. The song was an infectious number about the West Indian man's predilection for salt fish: "Take my woman, take my money, but you can't take my salt fish," said he. People were milling around but no one was dancing. There weren't any good tables left and the waiter tried to put us in a corner, but Amanda would have none of it. She hailed what passed for a maître d' and he had a table set up at poolside right in front of Sparrow. The pool was lighted, which gave a nice romantic touch to everything, but of course no one was in the water. Sparrow was in high gear and he had the audience with him all the way, when shots rang out. People screamed and started scattering and ducking under tables. There had been two shots, then four more. They seemed to come from the other side of the pool. It was dark over there. After the first two shots, I saw a man standing who began to stagger backward. With each additional shot his body jerked as it continued to stumble backward. The last of the four knocked him into the pool. I finally picked up the guy who was doing the shooting. He was short, but muscular, and he had on shorts and sneakers and a T-shirt. He was in his twenties from what I could tell. He skipped over a wall and disappeared behind a garden and a gazebo. There were security guards at a gate back there. They fired at him, but he skipped away down a side street. They did not pursue.

The dead man was old, short and bald. He was in suit and tie. They fished him out of the pool and the ambulance and the police were there in a matter of minutes. After the body had been removed, the musicians and the singer packed up and left. The hotel put recorded music on. They kept the buffet open, but no one was interested in either.

We went back upstairs. People buzzed around, talked about it, then went back to what they'd been doing. It didn't seem to bother the Jaycees. They were going great guns. We went into the Bull & Board, sat in a corner booth, and had beer. They were all silent.

"Anyone know who he was?" I asked, finally.

John, the pilot, spoke. "The assistant commissioner of the CID."

"You're kidding," I said.

"No. This is a big one."

"They're declaring all-out war," said the steward.

"Who is?" I asked.

"The black market boys," said John.

"Parallel market, my dear," corrected Amanda.

"What had he done?" I asked.

"He was trying to stop the dollar drain. We had chaos here three years ago. There weren't enough dollars to pay for our minimal needs. The whole country was close to literally starving. No meat in the shops, no credit, no fuel coming in. We're a big, beautiful island, as islands of the Caribbean go, but we're energy poor."

"So the fight for who controls the U.S. dollars that come into the country is a fight for control of the country itself," I said.

"Right!" he replied.

Just then Inspector Collins came in and crossed over to our booth.

"Your boss got it, Inspector," I said.

"Were you there?"

"Yes."

"Did you see it?"

"Some of it. Want me to tell you about it?"

"Please."

"Okay. Here?"

"No, we'll go upstairs."

I excused myself and followed him. Amanda was about to say something, but changed her mind.

We went up to a room on the second floor. Everyone from the earlier interview was there and they were very solemn. There were two uniformed policemen standing guard in the hallway.

Macfarlane started in right away. "I'm afraid we have to have an answer tonight, Mr. Cinquez. As you can see, they don't intend to give up without a fight."

"Yes, it was pretty daring, I thought."

"The assailant has been described as very dark, about five feet nine, a hundred and forty pounds," Collins said.

"No, shorter. Five-six or seven, I'd say, and heavier, maybe twenty pounds heavier," I said.

"That much?" Collins asked.

"Definitely. He was well built."

"Anything else?"

"Yes. He wasn't that dark, I don't think, but I'm not really sure."

"What was he wearing?" Macfarlane.

I told him.

"Well, that much everyone agrees on anyway," he said. Then he turned to me. "Well, Mr. Cinquez, will you cooperate with us?"

"Under the circumstances it seems like the only decent thing to do. Although, as a rule, I'm not given to letting the decent thing dictate what I do."

"Good," Macfarlane said, rubbing his hands together. "Then we can go to work."

I remembered the slip of paper. I took it out and showed it to them. They passed it from one to the other.

"When did you get this?" Collins.

"Just as I came down, shortly after you gentlemen had left."

"Did you get a look at him?" Brown.

"Or her." Ralph.

"No, I didn't."

"That's good. Means they think you're ready to do business." Macfarlane.

"Maybe." Ralph.

"It also means that your idea about the immigration department leak is right," I said.

"You're supposed to meet with the officer who handled your disembarkation in the morning. Is that right?"

"Yes. Do you suspect him?"

"He's definitely a possibility." Macfarlane.

"Maybe yes, maybe no." Brown.

"So what happens?" I asked.

"We'll have everything checked and put back. All you have

to do is go through the formality with him. And then have dinner at the Hot Pot, go discoing at the Calabash Lounge, and let them show their face," Macfarlane said.

"All right."

"Let's go over the ground rules once more." Brown.

"Let's."

"And we have some equipment for you," he added and displayed an absurd array of espionage paraphernalia. "Here's a microphone built into a wristwatch."

I pushed a button on the wristwatch they gave to me, then I stopped it and played back what had been said. It was working perfectly. "What's the range?" I asked.

"It will pick up anything said in a room twelve by fourteen." Brown.

"Pretty good," I offered.

"Amanda will be your date," Macfarlane said.

"Oh, so that's how that is," I said.

"Yes." he said.

"And if you're in trouble, you can set off a signal in the car that will be following you by pressing this ring, which we hope will fit one of your fingers." Macfarlane.

"What kind of car?"

"A rented English Ford. It won't attract attention."

"I see. Well then, I guess I'm ready."

They were hesitating. I didn't know why. Brown spoke up. "We thought about giving you a gun, but decided it would be a mistake."

"No question about it," I agreed.

"Just the same," said Collins, "here's something that could help." He gave me a pair of sunglasses. "If you look at the right stem of the frame, you'll see a knife inside. It's barely visible from the inside of the stem but it's big enough to kill a grown man. You press that little button on the hinge and the knife is ejected. The folded glasses become your handle."

"That means I have to take the glasses off before I'm ready to strike?"

"Right."

I took them and pressed the button and a fairly good-sized knife shot out.

"What if it's nighttime?" I asked.

"The glasses look as if they are prescription lenses. You have photophobia." Collins.

"I do?"

"You do."

"Okay."

"Well, that wraps it up, good sir," said Macfarlane. "We'll be right behind you, day and night. Here are the pictures of the men we want most of all. Study them well, they're dangerous men."

"I will," I said, and we broke it up.

I went up to my room, relaxed, had a rum, turned on the music, and looked at the pictures. They were sinister-looking fellows all right. One light-skinned, one medium brown, and one jet black. They were dressed in open-collar shirts with hair cut to ordinary length. Their names were ordinary Anglo-Saxon ones.

But their sobriquets were another matter. The light one was Mas Busta, the brown one was Teeth Man, and the black guy was Rude Boy. I watched the night from the balcony. Most of the lights had gone off. But there were still enough to set the plains aglow. The occasional car that moved through the darkness seemed to have purpose now. The sounds of the island night were stronger and seemed all around, even eighteen stories high.

I turned off the light and went to bed. Before I could fall asleep, something soft and sensuous slipped in under the covers next to me. It was Amanda. She put her clothesless body next to mine and lulled me to sleep. And so ended my first night in the tropics.

7

When I awoke she was gone. I called room service and ordered a hearty breakfast of ham and eggs and coffee and the newspaper—the *Daily Gleaner*. The killing was all over the front page. The prime minister would lead the country in mourning the death of a hero of the nation. In a separate article he declared all-out war on the killers. Yet a third article talked about the issue of black market money and how it was keeping the country from making an economic recovery. But it was not linked as an issue to the death of the CID commissioner.

I flipped through some of the other pages, trying to get a feel for the place in general. The sports section was filled with articles about cricket matches in the country. The entertainment page listed at least five separate performances of live theater, all in the same week, in the capital. That seemed like a lot for an island of just over two million people with a land size no bigger than Connecticut. Then there were ads for dances and concerts in Montego Bay, which was on the other side of the island. The plane had landed there first and more than half the passengers had gotten off. They were strictly the tourist crowd, secretaries from New Jersey and the like.

In the obituary column I saw an In Memoriam notice and the picture of an Englishman. It read: "The late, lamented Dr. Eric Gillesslee, who died, a long way from England on this day Sept. 10th, three years ago. Bemoaned by his daughter, Prudence."

I tore that item out, headed for the shops on the ground-level arcade—they were just opening up—and got myself the most garish tropical shirt imaginable and the most absurd pair of Bermuda shorts and the newest-looking and klunkiest pair of sandals, replete with buckles. I mean I looked the ridiculous tourist if ever anyone did.

I went up to the front desk and left a message, for anyone who wanted to know, that I'd be at the poolside sunning myself. Before I got two steps, I was hailed by the bell captain. There was a call for me that I could take in the lobby. He pointed to the phones. I went over and picked up the one indicated. It was Marlene. She came in loud and clear.

"Hi. You sound as if you're next door," I said.

"I'll be down tomorrow," she said.

"Did you get the package?"

"Got it and did what you told me to."

"Good."

"You sure you don't want me to bring it?"

"No, just proceed as we arranged."

"Okay. What was all that talk about my friends? What friends?"

"You didn't tell friends of yours to take care of me on the flight coming down?"

"No, how could I? I didn't even know you were going until you were practically on the plane."

"Right. I just didn't think anyone else . . . Well, anyway, are you all right?"

"Yes."

"Do you know anyone named Amanda?"

"Amanda Nasrali."

"I don't know her last name. Describe her."

She did.

"Sounds like her."

"How'd you get hooked up with that tramp?"

So that's why she was so good last night, I thought. What I said was, "She knew when I was going to land. And she also knew that I knew you. She used your name. Or, at least, the one on the flight to Miami did and then she used Amanda's name."

"What are you ranting on about? Have you been out in the sun?"

"Not yet, it's too early. But there's a dollar war going on over who controls the millions that tourists bring in every day—the government or the guys on the street. They killed the assistant commissioner of the CID last night. I was there when it happened."

"Where, at the Pegasus?"

"Yes, right by the pool."

"And what did you and Amanda do after that?"

"Nothing."

"I'll bet. The bitch."

"Please, this is a long-distance call, remember."

"As if that mattered to you."

"Anything else you want to tell me?"

"Yes, your friends called."

"What did they say?"

"They said de Souza was sorry he followed them, and you'll be sorry too."

I wondered if that meant that something terrible had happened to de Souza. I'd find out eventually, of course. "I'll feel a lot safer when you're on that plane," I said.

"I'll be careful."

"Stay someplace else tonight."

"I will."

I wanted to say more, but never got it out. I finally managed "Bye."

"Bye." And she hung up.

I made it to the pool this time. I think some of the help were laughing at me because of the ridiculousness of my costume. But I didn't care. I sat in the sun, my shirt open, eyes closed. Someone came over and stood in front of me, blocking my tan in process. I looked up and it was Esme, lots of love, no squalor.

"Can I get you something?"

"Yes, a Bloody Mary."

She went for it while I watched the effects on her hips of her perambulating. It was quite delightful. When she came back and bent over to give me the drink, I smelled eucalyptus oil number 41. She couldn't have been in New York when Josephs was killed.

"Were you ever in the Brooklyn Union Gas Company building?" I asked her.

"Excuse please?"

"Forget it."

She smiled and gave me the check to sign. There was a note sticking out from under it. She looked at it, indicating that it was for me. I took it, smiled and she left. I sipped my drink and read the note after I'd covered it with the newspaper.

It said, "You can't beat my price. If the amount is big enough, I'll even go ten to one. Just ask for Count at any record store in the shopping plaza."

Just then my name was announced over the loudspeaker. I got up and went to the phone that the guy who handed out the towels for swimmers had. It was the immigration officer. He was on his way. Would I meet him in the lobby in ten minutes. I said I would and went back to my drink and the sun.

Esme came perambulating back. "You want a next one, please?"

I wasn't sure if that was a request or a demand, but I said I was fine.

"Can I get you some snacks?"

"No, no snacks, thank you."

"But you mus' want something?"

"Oh, I mus'."

"Yes, you mus'."

"Why I mus'?" I wanted to know.

" 'Cause I can't come out with the message if you don't order something."

"I see. Well, then bring me a lemonade."

"After the Bloody Mary is lemonade you want? That don't make no sense."

"Oh, now it has to make sense too."

"O.K., lemonade." And she perambulated back. I waited and she returned presently with the lemonade and another note stuck under the coaster. It read, *"If you get tied up, make Esme bring you to a jump up tonight."*

"What's a jump up?" I asked.

"A dance."

"Hm. Tell him I'll make it this afternoon. If I don't, come by the room around nine."

"I cahn't."

"Why cahn't you?"

" 'Cause I won't be here. But I can call you."

"That's even better. Between nine and nine-thirty. Keep calling till you get me."

"Aw right." And she perambulated back. Every man on that side of the pool ogled her, whether the woman with him dared him to or not. That's the kind of statement she made. I was convinced that the manager would either fire her or fornicate with her before the week was out—if he hadn't already done one or the other.

I sat there thinking about what I'd gotten myself into. I couldn't believe my stupidity. I had been trying to find out how Mrs. Hylton had been killed. In the process, someone or someones had killed a lot of other people, and what I was left with was a mess of a case that didn't make a damned bit of sense. I'd probably thrown away Regina's five hundred dollars for nothing. How was I to know I'd land in the damned island loaded, the whole place ready and willing to do business with me. Yet there it was. I'd probably never find out why Reg was killed or why the guardians of the peace had done such a flip flop on me in Manhattan. I wasn't too worried about helping out the authorities in Jamaica.

All I had to do was stand still and every guy hustling dollars within a radius of fifty miles would be all over me. Prudence, that was my first move. But Prudence who? Gillesslee? Or was she married?

I sat up, having had enough of the sun, took off the silly glasses—God, they weighed a ton—and took a last sip of the Bloody Mary, which was mostly water by now, got up and crossed over to the side of the pool where the CID commissioner had been shot. A foot path led up to the gazebo. There was a children's wading pool back there and the gate, guarded by a lone guard. It was the morning after, after all. The fence wasn't high, so leaping over it had been easy. The hotel wasn't really trying that hard to keep anybody out. Maybe now they'd have to rethink that. I looked on the ground around where I saw the guy take off. There was a jogging path that circled by the fence and the back entrance of the hotel—where the supplies came in. It went round to the other side of the pool and came full circle. I sort of ambled along it for a little, came back across the grass, when my eye caught something. I bent down and picked it up. It looked like a piece of costume jewelry. I wasn't sure, maybe a stud earring. It was about where the guy could have been hiding. I stuck it in my Bermudas and headed back down to the pool.

Amanda was crossing over in bikini and heels as I came past the gazebo. She had her suntan lotions and the rest of her equipment with her.

"You finally got up."

"Yes."

"We have a busy day. You'd better go meet immigration and get that over with. And put some of this on my back before you do." And she lay on her stomach, undid her top, kicked off her heels, and gave me the lotion. While I was giving her a salacious rub, I told her that Marlene was coming down.

"When?"

"Oh, Friday," I lied.

"By then we should have concluded our business."

"You expect results that quickly?"

"Macfarlane does."

"I see. I need a favor."

"Yes."

"An English doctor who taught at the university died here three years to the day. His daughter, Prudence, took out an In Memoriam notice. It appeared in the *Gleaner* this morning."

"And?"

"I want to talk to the daughter."

"If she's in Jamaica, that won't be hard."

"Why wouldn't she be?"

"A lot of people who leave the island send those notices in. It's kind of a custom."

"But that's only if they're Jamaican."

"I see what you mean. If she's English and she's gone back to England, what would be the point?" she said.

"Well, let's put it this way. If there is a point, I want to know what it is."

"What's the name?"

"Prudence Gillesslee."

"Today's paper, you say."

"Yes."

"Okay."

I looked up and saw my immigration friend in the hotel lounge at the window signaling me. I gave her a last pat and left.

Inside, he, the manager and I went through the formality of counting the money over again. After he was satisfied that it was all there, he seemed to hesitate. It was the first time that he had appeared unsure of himself.

"Now what?" I asked.

Something was on his mind. Whatever it was, he wasn't talking about it.

"We have to wait for a representative from the Bank of Jamaica," he said.

"I see. Will the conversion take place here or at the bank?"

"I don't know. I wasn't told."

"Well, are we just going to stand here or put it back or what?"

"I'd feel a lot better if we put it back," said the Englishman.

"So would I," I agreed.

"It just seems like a waste of time to keep opening and closing the safe," he said.

Then we heard someone at the door. A voice on the other side said, "Bank of Jamaica, here."

The Englishman went to the door and unlocked it. There were two men in uniform. One had a briefcase, the other had a rifle. The man with the briefcase was a captain or something. The man with the rifle was a sergeant. I was still a little confused by their uniforms. The shirts were short sleeved, pale gray-blue, with stripes and pockets. They were smartly starched. The guy with the briefcase had a lanyard around his left shoulder. They were both in pale blue shorts, dark shoes and dark knee socks. The officer held out a card. The Englishman looked at it and gave it to the immigration officer. He handed it back to the other officer. They exchanged documents, each signing on their respective documents. The briefcase was handed to the officer and he, his sergeant, the immigration officer and I left. I got in one car with the money and the two soldiers. The immigration officer followed in another car. He was alone.

We went left out of the driveway, then right, then left again and we were on a major roadway. There were a lot of cars about. It was suddenly very hot and the streets were noisy. There were many vendors on the road and lots of bicycles, a few donkey-drawn carts, but not too many. The street we were on was a large enough thoroughfare—two lanes in each direction. We passed many low, one-story residential homes with an occasional large official building—some older with a tropical pink stucco effect, some new with gleaming glass and large darkened windows. The immigration officer was right behind us.

"Let's bypass Crossroads," the officer told his sergeant.

"Yes, sir," the sergeant replied and made a sharp left onto another wide road. There were houses on one side and a large sports arena type soccer stadium on the other. Then we seemed to be passing a soldiers' camp of some sort. I thought we were going to turn in, but we kept going. That's when another car cut in front of the immigration officer's car. It began immediately to menace us. There were four men. Two in front, two in back. They weren't showing any guns, but they were bumping us. The sergeant tried to get away, but couldn't. All the side streets were to our right, and they cut him off every time he tried to turn right.

"Why doesn't one of us use the rifle, captain?" I asked.

"Not a good idea," the officer said."

"Why not?"

"They may start shooting back."

"Well, if we wait long enough, they may shoot anyway. But if we fire first, even one well-aimed shot could throw them off and give us a chance to get away."

But before he could answer, we neared a major intersection. The sergeant again tried to go right, but was stopped by a car that was actually blocking the street. And two guys were behind it and opened fire on us. It was a wild west show, for chrissakes. The sergeant had no choice but to turn left. The street in front had suddenly turned into a one-way street coming in our direction and there was a full line of cars waiting for the light. So we were back on the airport road. The first car stayed right behind us. The guys from the second car got in and joined the pursuit. By now we were going very fast, scattering donkey-drawn carts, bicycles, and pedestrians with an abandon that defied the odds against any of us ending up alive. We hit the open road with the sea to the right and rock quarries to the left.

"Stay on the St. Thomas Road," the officer said. He had to be kidding. Good old St. Thomas. I was going to get there a lot sooner than I had expected.

"When are we going to get rescued by the marines?" I asked.

"Word will get back to town soon enough," the officer said.

"Well, can't you call them?"

"No."

"No two-way radio in the car?"

"No."

"Can't you signal for a helicopter?"

"No."

I finally remembered my ring and started pressing it like hell, but we were probably out of range, or they hadn't even geared up yet. We'd all been caught by surprise and no doubt about it. I'd expected to at least sneak into one or two smelly booths in sleazy restaurants and pass notes or looks, or some such, until money began to change hands. It was high-speed roller coaster time again, and all I wanted to do was relax and enjoy the scenery.

We were heading out into open country now. The surf, when we were close to it, was strong. To the left the rock quarries gave way to coconut groves. Long rows of coconut trees with cows and pretty white birds lowing in them. The cows were lowing at any rate. I suddenly thought of the painting in the empty room beneath Kathleen Campbell's. That's when we saw a roadblock up ahead. So they'd finally sprung their trap. Well, it had certainly taken them long enough.

"What about the guy from immigration?" I asked. "You think he'll get help?"

"Let's hope so," the officer said. "Turn in where you can," he told the sergeant, and *he* immediately made a wicked left into the grove, dodging the coconut trees as he did so. I knew we were trapped. It was just a matter of time before we'd hit a ditch and lose a wheel. But the sergeant had a side to him that I hadn't seen before. I mean driving where there was no road was his thing. He was twisting and turning to beat the band. I looked back and they were having trouble keeping up; then I looked ahead and we came to a big ridge and I closed my eyes. We went over the top like a jeep getting off the beach at Iwo Jima and landed on two of the four wheels, but ole sarge kept us right side up, and down the little hill we went. But, alas, when we got to the bottom, we hit a ditch and the wheels began to spin. I looked back and the first car came over the top, but didn't land right. They ended up on their side, passenger side up, and skidded down to a tree and smashed into it. The officer and I jumped out of our car and pushed it out of the ditch. They got out of their car and scrambled to get out guns and started to open fire. We were just getting back into our car when the shooting started. We moved off, only to get stuck again. That's when I grabbed the sergeant's rifle, got out and got behind a tree stump and fired at them. They scrambled behind the car and fired back. Then the sergeant got out of the car and he and the officer pushed it out of the second ditch, and onto solid ground. I aimed for their gas tank and their car exploded just as the second one came over the hill and ran right into a tree, and then hit a huge rock, and it too exploded.

Well, if anyone was in the sky looking for us, we shouldn't be hard to find with all those fires blazing. The sergeant was yelling for me to hurry up and come on. I tried to run crouching down, but my back was too stiff, so I straightened up only to hit my head on the limb of a tree. I wobbled, fell, got up, when a bullet landed in the trunk of the tree and splattered wood splints on my face. That cleared my head and sent me flying into the car and we were off. We drove over gullies and around trees and past abandoned shacks, but no one was following so we slowed down. Then we found a dirt road that went left. We followed it. It wound around a few times and eventually brought us out onto the main road. We stopped and looked left and right. It was clear both ways. The sergeant and the officer talked it over. They decided to turn right and come in behind the blockade. I was about to open my mouth and make a slight suggestion, but a big Buick came charging around a corner and barrelled toward us. Sarge did a quick U turn and headed east on the St. Thomas Road again, away from town. The Buick was serious. They had one guy up front who had a machine gun, and he started firing at us like mad, but he was out of range. Even though the road was a smooth adequate one, there were many twists and turns and bevels and ditches, and if a truck came from the opposite direction there really wasn't room for both of us, unless the truck hugged his side of the road.

The machine gun didn't really have too many chances because of the twists and turns in the road. Just when he was getting a good aim, we'd turn a corner. The road suddenly went inland, away from the sea and climbed quickly. We were churning up a hill full throttle. I looked down and the drop to the sea was quite considerable at that point. The other side of the road was solid rock going up to higher ground. We were coming to a blind curve and just as we got close, a huge truck came chugging around the corner carrying twice the weight it was built to carry. There were bananas and workers hanging off the sides, and you expected to hear the axle go any minute. But he was right down the middle of the road, not taking any chances either way. And he wasn't about to make a quick move in either direction. He couldn't if he wanted to. I knew we'd bought it. There just wasn't enough room for us between the truck and the edge of the drop. And the road had no guard rail. So what did ole sarge do? He moved over and passed the truck on his right, using the embankment for two of his wheels. We were leaning way beyond forty-five degrees and I thought we would fall into the truck, but we defied gravity long enough to get past it, and sarge righted us immediately. I looked back and the Buick tried to slam on his brakes. He ended up skidding into the truck, bouncing off, and flying down to the sea in his ship. Wonder of wonders, he didn't explode, but there was a lot of smoke.

"That should do it," said the officer. "How's our gas?"

"Good," said sarge.

"Okay, head over the mountain. We'll go to St. Ann's Bay and call in from there."

St. Ann's Bay, I thought. That's where the Germans are. But I said nothing. We drove over mountain fastnesses in really beautiful, quiet terrain, green, dewy country roads. The mountain road kept turning and going up and up. We had to take curves at twenty-five miles an hour because of their treacherousness.

"The engineer who built this was drunk," I said.

"There are only two roads that link north and south other than going by the coast. This one is called Mount Diablo."

"I can see why," I said.

Presently we stopped at a small roadside stand. The vendors were selling fruit, roasted corn on the cob, roasted yams, sorrel. I remembered that from Mrs. Hylton. They got out and started buying refreshments.

"Hey, guys," I said, "with all this money sitting here, shouldn't we keep going? Maybe there're more of them."

"I've been thinking about that," said the officer. "Maybe you'd better give the money to me." He reached for it.

"Not so fast. Where I go, the money goes. Who's your superior at the bank?" I asked.

"Oh, there are many of them," he said with a clever gleam in his eye.

"I think we'd better keep going," I repeated.

"No, man. First you must have some dasheen and some sorrel and some roas' corn."

"This is hardly the time for a picnic," I protested. But the sergeant seemed to agree with him, so I sat there like a fool while they visited with the local entrepreneurs. They ate, drank, paid their bill, and then we were on our way. I suddenly felt hungry, but I didn't say anything.

We pulled into St. Ann's Bay two and a half hours later. It had been a dusty, dirty ride once we got off the mountain. They were grinning.

"You'd have had a much more pleasant time," the officer said, "if you'd joined us at the roadside stand. It's the only way to make the journey over Mount Diablo."

"Now you tell me," I said.

The St. Ann's Bay Police Station was a converted wood frame house. The phones were old handle receivers with a crank box and all kinds of wires for a switchboard, overhead fans and a lot of flies.

We were ushered into a rear room. A captain got on the phone to Kingston, and got his headquarters. They told him to call back. He hung up and we waited. I didn't know what the hell was going on.

Finally, my officer suggested some rum. The captain buzzed and a young man in disheveled khakis with a towel over his shoulder and a small tray in his hand came in, with a bottle of what I assumed was white rum; it had no label. He also had a bucket of ice, some small glasses and some cut limes in a small dish. He shuffled in, expressionless. He was definitely a member of the servant class. It was as if *he* wasn't there, in anything but body. I suppose he was an example of what the pilot had been talking about at the hotel the night before. In any event, this time I didn't pass, but I wished I had. That rum was pure alcohol. When I reached for my third drink, I knocked it over by mistake and the rum spilled out onto the table and took the varnish off it. I shuddered at the thought of what it was doing to the lining of my stomach. But I was stuck, so I had my third and my fourth.

I was about to reach for number five when I was mercifully rescued by the phone. The captain picked it up, then passed it to my officer, who then passed it to me. It was Macfarlane.

"How are you?" he asked.

"Still alive," I said.

"Well, that's some comfort, isn't it?"

"I suppose so."

"Our friend from immigration skipped."

"I see, so he was in on it."

"Apparently."

"Rather than waiting for five thousand here and ten thousand there, they decided to grab it all."

"Precisely."

"So what do we do now?"

"Sit tight. I've sent out reinforcements. We'll have you back in town by nightfall."

"I wonder if you could tell me something about the Germans who live near here?" I asked. Everyone in the room looked up when I said that.

"Why do you want to know about them?" Macfarlane asked.

"You will remember that I am here on other business."

"Yes, well, I'll tell the captain to give you every assistance possible. Perhaps you'd like to drive 'round there?"

"Very much so."

"Good."

"About the money . . ."

"Yes, I was coming to that. I think we should leave it in St. Ann's Bay. I'll see that it gets back to Kingston safely."

"Then you assume responsibility?"

"I do."

"But I have no proof."

"You have my word."

"I think I'd like to see the prime minister just to make sure I'm not dealing with a gang of imposters."

"There's no problem there, but it can't be arranged until day after tomorrow at the earliest."

"Okay, you keep the money."

"Right. Just put me onto the captain."

I handed the phone back to the captain. After he had finished, he handed it back to my officer. When he hung up, he turned to me and smiled. "Well," he said.

"Looks like you're always right," I said and gave him the money. He gave it to the captain. And they actually made up a receipt and signed for it. What good that was going to do anyone if it got lost I didn't know.

The four of us all got into a very small car, a Morris Minor, I think it was called. The captain drove. Why we changed cars, I didn't know. But we took a circuitous back road route. We were in different country now. Drab, dirty, dusty, even depressing. Suddenly we were near the sea. I saw a sign in front of a small dilapidated concrete building that read ALLIGATOR POND POST OFFICE. And everyone looked as mean as the reptile the place was named for. But they were all black. There was an other-worldly, lost in time sense about the place. And everyone seemed to belong to the same family, more by manner than by look. And outsiders seemed definitely not to be welcomed.

We stopped in the center of town. A man came over and talked to the captain. I couldn't understand a thing he was saying, the accent was so thick. "Is he speaking English?" I asked my officer.

"Yes."

"You're kidding."

When they finished the conversation, we did a U turn and went back into the interior. We rode over a little hill, then a bigger one, then we went around another, even higher one, and finally descended into a valley and there they were, a whole group of blue-eyed brown-skinned people, some dressed in rags, the children mostly, others in drab khaki and cotton. A lot of them were mixed. But you could only tell that by the hair. It was red and short and woolly in about half of them. The houses were like little shacks. Some of them were on the hillside, some down in the valley bottom itself. I didn't think they had either running water or electricity, but I couldn't be sure. We pulled up and stopped right at the edge of the houses in the center of the enclave. Nobody moved. The captain turned and looked at me and said, "Here we are."

"Can I get out?" I asked.

"Sure, but stay near the car. They don't like strangers."

I got out and stretched my legs. I didn't see any men, but I'm sure they weren't that far away. Finally, a woman in her early sixties came up to me. She was a little on the plump side, about five feet seven, leathery face, straight hair, brown eyes.

"Is wha you wahn't, sah?"

That I could handle. "You know Gretchen Schultz?"

"Gretchen. No. She not from around here."

"You sure?"

"Yes, I know everybody."

"Well, she went to America a long time ago."

"How long?"

"Maybe five, ten years."

"You have something fe the pickney?"

"Yes, of course." I reached into my pocket, but, of course, I didn't have a sou. I turned to my officer and he gave me a Jamaican dollar.

"Come on, you can do better than that," I protested. He came up with a five. I gave it to her. She put it into her apron pocket. The pocket started at her waist and went all the way down to her ankle. She kept a lot of things in that pocket.

"Gretchen, you say. Wha she look like?"

I described her.

"But that sound like Dorothy Pinto. She went America from she was small, but she come back all the time. She look fe her

| 238 |

mother, bring her plenty presents. But is not here she stay when she come back, is Kingston."

"Can I see her mother?"

"Her mother not here again. She remove."

"Where to?"

"St. Thomas. Yallas in St. Thomas."

"How would I find her?"

"Ask by Missa Mac."

"How will I find Missa Mac?"

"Him have the only shop in town, except fe the Chiny man."

"What kind of shop?"

"Shop, shop. Is what do this man, sah?" she asked my officer.

"Is an American, mistress. Him don't know what is a shop."

"Eh, eh. Then them don't have shop in America?"

"Them mus'," he assured her. And she shook her head, took two of the children by the hand and wandered off. The interview was at an end. I got back into the car and we headed up the hill and down the other side, and up and down again until we got back to Alligator Pond. We stopped and the captain talked to his friend again. Then we returned to the police station in St. Ann's Bay. When we got there, Macfarlane was waiting for us.

"That was quick," I said.

"Helicopter," he said. "I hate to be unceremonious, but we might as well catch the light."

I said my goodbyes to the captain, my officer, and especially sarge, he'd saved my life, and we left.

We were back at the Pegasus in an hour.

8

The lobby was as filled as it had been the night before. I was glad to see it again. I wanted to go right to my room and shower and shave, not that I had anything suitable to put on, but everyone was either elegantly dressed for the evening or at least adequately dressed for it. Not so me. I was still the absurd tourist in my boxer shorts and peuce shirt. One ludicrous, the other garish. Macfarlane suggested a conference as soon as I was able to find something suitable to put on. But I never made it to the room. I went to the front desk to get my key and there was a message in the box. "I'm in the Bull & Board. Prudence Gillesslee."

Macfarlane saw me as I did an aboutface and crossed the lobby and went into the pub. She was sitting in a corner alone. A mousy blond, glasses, tall, on the thin side, not unattractive, but pale and dressed quite unprovocatively.

"Ms. Gillesslee?"

"Yes."

"I'm Joe Cinquez. Good of you to come."

"I got a call from the ministry saying it was important, so I came."

"Yes, well, I'm grateful all the same. Does your drink need refreshing?"

"Yes."

A waitress came over. She was cute, but she wasn't in Esme's class.

"The lady's having another. I'll have a Red Stripe."

The waitress looked at her. "Scotch and water," she said.

"What kind of scotch?" the waitress asked testily.

"Johnnie Walker Black."

The waitress left and Prudence Gillesslee said, "So, you're drinking the local beer already. And I understood that you just got down yesterday."

"Well, a thing like that only takes one night."

"You like it then?"

"Yes."

"I can't say I agree with you. It just doesn't hold up to English beer."

"I'm sure it doesn't."

"So, what's this all about?"

"Does the name Iris Hylton mean anything to you?"

"It certainly does. She's the voodoo bitch who drove my father out of his mind and ran off with all his money."

"When was this?"

"It started about four years ago. It was quite a scandal. The papers ran front-page stories on it for weeks."

"Are those papers on file?"

"Yes, at the *Gleaner's* office on North Street."

"What happened exactly?"

"Oh, it's pretty much of a sordid affair. Father had come out from his post at London University five, six years ago, after mother died, just to get away. But he was lonely. There had never been anyone else in his life. He wasn't really used to being in the world. And he made the mistake of thinking of these people as harmless natives, if you know what I mean. They're anything but harmless, let me tell you."

The waitress came back with the drinks and Prudence Gillesslee eyed her suspiciously. They didn't like each other, that was obvious. When the waitress left, Ms. Gillesslee said, "Bitch," under her breath.

"You've been here since your father died?"

"Yes."

"When did you come out?"

"About a year after he did."

"And you've stayed down here all the while, feeling the way you do about the people?"

"I only get like this around the time of Father's death. Actually my first two years were wonderful. I fell in love. We were going to be married, then someone else came into the picture and he left me for her."

"I'm sorry."

"No need to be. I've gotten Charlie out of my system completely."

"Charlie."

"Yes, the prime minister's cousin. Do you know him?"

"Of him."

"Oh."

"Yes. Tell me, Ms. Gillesslee, exactly how did she come by the money?"

"She insinuated herself into his confidence, took control of his life, kept him isolated from family and friends. And just completely dominated him."

"Weren't you around?"

"Yes, but I was in love, and on the other side of the island. When I finally got wind of it and came down to town, she already had most of the money. We tried to get it back, but he died before we could manage it, and then she skipped."

"Can you give me more specific details on just what went on?"

She seemed annoyed at that, but went ahead anyway. "You've heard of their obeah rituals, I take it, and their pocomania?"

"Yes, I have."

"Well, that's how she managed it."

"Did you not like her at any point?"

"She was all right, I suppose, at the beginning. But she changed once she got him under her power."

"It's hard for me to believe we're talking about the same person. I lived in her house in Brooklyn for almost a year. She was kind, generous, well liked, with a giving nature. The only thing willful about her was her tendency to run your life for you."

"That's what I mean."

"Not in the sense in which you mean it. In little benign ways. Being a busybody, things like that."

"That's only because you didn't have a million dollars U.S. for her to get her hands on."

"A million?"

"A million."

"But I thought it was three million."

"No, only one million. We stopped it from going any further than that."

"Who did?"

"Charlie and I."

"Didn't someone from England have to come out to help?"

"No, not at all. I was already here. You must be mixing it up with that other case."

"What other case?"

"The Jamaican widow who owned half of Trelawney."

"What's Trelawney?"

"A parish."

"And one woman owned half of it?"

"Well, enough."

"That must have made her immensely rich."

"Immensely."

"What was her name?"

"Lady Musgrave."

"So where did Iris hold her rituals?"

"In the backyard."

"You're kidding."

"No. And it was very clever. For even though the neighborhood was exclusive and the neighbors complained, there was nothing they could do. And up there in Red Hills, with the mountains, the lovely trees, the rugged terrain, it all added to the power of the music and the drums and the chanting. It was the perfect backdrop for getting the optimum effect."

"But Iris didn't do much dancing herself, surely. She was so heavy, and she always had bad feet."

"You're not talking about Iris, you're talking about her sister, Enid."

"I am?"

"Yes. Iris was the small, thin one; Enid was the big, heavyset one."

So, I thought, Enid was the one who led the obeah rituals. "But I saw a picture in the newspapers that mentioned her as Iris and also mentioned the scandal."

"Well, if they said she was Iris, they made a mistake."

"I see. Did you ever go to any of the rituals?"

"Yes, it was the only way I could even communicate with Father toward the end."

"Tell me about them."

"The music was a steady, insinuating drum beat that seemed to capture the beat of the heart itself. And it kept thumping and thumping insistently, but with a hypnotic effect, not loud or vulgar. And you just gave yourself over to it, finally. It was a total release from all the tensions and frustrations of the real world. I even allowed myself to be drugged by it. But, of course, once you are, you can't communicate with anyone. You're aware of what's happening, but you can't control it. You go to sleep eventually, and when you wake up, you're at peace with yourself and the world."

"Sounds like a good thing."

"I suppose, in a way it is," she admitted grudgingly.

"If Enid became Iris and Iris became Enid, why did they assume each other's identity and continue the deception long after they had left Jamaica?"

"I don't know," she said. "But I can tell you one thing, that money never left the island."

"How do you know?"

"Because Charlie saw to it that Iris never got a visa to leave the island."

"Well, then, doesn't that answer the question?"

"How?"

"My Iris, who's your Enid, took the money out," I said.

"But as Enid or Iris?"

"That we have to find out."

"That shouldn't be too difficult since you're working with the top boys in the government on this black market thing."

"You're supposed to say 'parallel market.' "

"I'll be damned."

"Did Charlie hurt you that much?"

"Oh, Charlie isn't black, he's Lebanese."

"I see. What then?"

"I told you. I get this way around the time of Father's death."

"And that's all?"

"That's all."

"Why haven't you left, gone back to England or someplace else?"

"Why should I? This is a great place to live if you're white. You always get preferential treatment. You can always get work. Oh, they resent you from time to time. But for the most part the odds are in your favor."

"I would have thought that with the trend to socialism that all of that has changed."

"Yes, but it's back to normal now."

"By normal, you mean the way things were?"

"More or less."

I thought of the airline pilot's remark about *the more things change* and wondered if, indeed, things were back to the way they were or not. "You can't really turn back the clock," I said.

"And nobody wants to. But in a strange way, even if the changes in social progress remain and there's more equality, things still go back to what they were in the unspoken ways, in the attitudes in a sense. Do you know what I mean?"

"Yes, I do. It's what happens in America after an election, regardless of the laws of the land. If a conservative Republican is in the White House, Wall Street is bullish, psychologically confident. They feel that he's their man and he's not going to give the place away to the people on welfare and their ilk. If a liberal Democrat is in power, no matter how sound the economy and how high the Dow Jones average, Wall Street sulks all the way to the bank."

"Exactly. The culture doesn't really change, not in one generation. It may evolve over a period of a hundred years. But short of that, forget it."

"What do you do, Ms. Gillesslee?"

"I'm a social anthropologist by profession. But right now I run the art gallery at Devon House. You should come round some time. We have some very fine artists in Jamaica. Sculptors and painters."

"Anyone doing masks?" I asked eagerly.

"No, you have to go to Haiti for that."

"What about faces that would be masks if they weren't on canvas?"

"Some."

"Can you give me a name?"

"Well, it's not my speciality. We only handle the approved artists, so to speak. But there are some fine talents that work out of shacks, in the hills and that sort of thing. We're having a reception tomorrow night. If you come round about seven I should be able to put you in touch with someone who could help you."

"Till seven tomorrow then."

"Till seven." But she didn't seem to be ready to leave. When I hesitated, she said, "I'm going to just sit a while and finish my drink. It's been a long time since I've been in here, or in the hotel itself for that matter. This is the closest thing to an English pub that there is on the island. Think I'll just stay and enjoy it for a while."

"As you wish. I'll have the waitress send you another."

"Thanks," she said.

I thought her a curious blend of English hauteur and a woman alone in the world who seemed afraid to pack up and leave a place that had so many sad memories for her: a dead father, a lost lover.

"Are you staying at the hotel?" she asked suddenly, almost as an afterthought.

"Yes, I am." I caught the waitress's eye and she came over, taking her own sweet time about it. "Bring me the check, please, and put one more drink on the bill for the lady."

"So you don't want a next drink?"

"No, I don't."

She didn't seem to like that very much, but she was willing to accept it, for the moment anyway. She came back with the bill and another drink, which she sort of dropped on the table.

"Hey, I didn't say I wanted you to give her the drink now. She's still got half to go on the last one. It'll be water by the time she gets to it."

"Then why you nevah say that before I bring it?"

"I never asked you to bring it. I asked you to put it on the bill."

"Then if I put it on the bill and you pay for it, I no mus' bring it."

"You no mus' do nothing but satisfy the customer within reason."

"Ah not tekin' it back. My feet too tired fe go walk up and down fe foolishness." And she turned and stalked off.

"Well, if she thinks she's going to get a tip from me, she's crazy," I protested.

"Oh, she's got her tip."

"She has?"

"Look at the bill."

"Gratuities, fifteen percent," it read.

"Whether you like it or not," she added.

"A pox on socialism." I snorted.

"It's all right. I know the bartender. He'll fix me another." She called to him and he came over. "Trevor, we paid for this drink, but we didn't want it just yet. The waitress refused to take it back."

"Don't worry, I will fix it fe you. Jus' let me know when you want it. And make that one stay." And he went back behind the bar.

"See, it worked to your advantage. You got two for the price of one."

That made me feel a little better. I signed the check and left her to her scotch. Trevor, I thought, must be a popular name in Jamaica. When I went up to my room, the message light on the phone was blinking. I called down to the front desk. "You have a message for me?"

"Just one moment please."

I waited. She came back on. "A Mr. A-u-b-o-c-h- . . ." She hesitated. "O-n," I told her. "Aubuchon."

"Right. In room 1013. He asked you to return his call."

"What time was this?"

"About an hour ago."

"Thanks." And I hung up. I put my pants and shirt on, but kept to my klunky sandals. Washed my face and went to the tenth floor. I rang Aubuchon's bell, but no one answered. I went back to my room. Called the manager. They had to find him. "I'd like to get into room 1013."

"I'm afraid that's impossible," he said.

"Macfarlane's in the first floor conference room; ask him to okay it."

"Mr. Macfarlane has no authority in that regard."

"It happens to be of the utmost importance. Can't you do it as a favor to me or to him, whatever?"

He hesitated. "All right, I'll get him."

Macfarlane came on presently. "Mr. Cinquez, I thought we had an appointment."

"Yes, but something's come up. I need to get into room 1013 in a hurry and I have no tools of the trade with me."

"Which would be illegal."

"At least."

"It's important, you say?"

"Very."

"I think we can arrange it."

I met the two of them back at 1013. The manager opened the door and turned on the light. Braithwaite was lying on the bed, fully clothed, face up, dead. One bullet through the chest. He'd been dead for at least an hour. Macfarlane called down to Collins. The Englishman seemed shaken. I looked around feverishly. There was nothing in any of the obvious places: drawers, closets, under the bed. I sat frustrated. They removed the body, but I got permission from Collins to stay in the room as long as I didn't take anything. The door was left open and a uniformed officer placed outside. Collins, Macfarlane, and the manager went back down.

Finally, after the tenth time searching, I found it. His attaché case was taped under the bedsprings. I got it out and opened it in the bathroom. It was filled with Jamaican dollars. It looked like about two million. I told the officer to get Macfarlane back up to the room.

"Well, Mr. Macfarlane, it seems as if our paths have really crossed this time."

He studied the money carefully.

"They certainly have," he said.

"What do you make of it?" I asked.

"Someone had something pretty expensive to buy."

"What do you think it was?"

"Oh, it could be almost anything. Ganja, American dollars, land, art."

"If it were land or art, wouldn't the money most likely have been in the bank?"

"Yes, but not necessarily. It's the seventies all over again. Half the place selling out at ridiculous prices and the other half buying everything they can put their hands on."

"That bad, huh?"

"That bad. Tell me about him."

"His name is Smedley Braithwaite. He was an attorney. I was told that although he came from Jamaican stock he was probably raised somewhere else. He handled the financial affairs of a woman whose murder I am investigating."

"Here or in New York?"

"In New York. But I think there was more to it than that. I think there was money down here that someone was trying to get his or her hands on and that the two million was involved with it, somehow."

"Why exactly are you in Jamaica, Mr. Cinquez?"

"I wish I knew. All the trails seemed to lead here. There are a lot of Jamaicans in New York, in Brooklyn in particular. There's a club on Empire Boulevard."

"I've heard of it."

"Have you really? Well, some of their members own land in Jamaica. And we had a meeting just before I left, at which they expressed the fear that they might be killed by parties unknown in order that the land could be gotten hold of."

He suddenly seemed very interested. "Go on."

"Well, one of their group was killed that very night. And they told me of incidents of other Jamaicans they'd known of who were beaten up, threatened, or killed outright so that their land could be taken."

"Mr. Cinquez, our paths have indeed crossed. Are you finished here?"

There was nothing else in the attaché case but the money. I'd looked everywhere else. "I would like to see the contents of his pockets," I said.

"No problem. Shall we?"

Downstairs we went back into the Englishman's office. The room had been registered to Aubuchon, but no one knew where he was.

"We have to take a little ride," he said.

He and I got into a large limousine with a civilian driver. We drove to another side of town, farther up in the hills. It seemed like a residential area. We turned into a driveway and pulled up to a large, flat building that was newly built. There was a guard at the front. As we went in he saluted Macfarlane.

The air conditioning was on, even at that late hour. It was a building given over to a tremendous amount of records. And there was a skeleton staff still at work. No one stopped work or looked up as we came in. He turned to me and said, "This is the nerve center of our operation. We've coordinated all our efforts into this one spot. Every area in the island where ganja can be grown in a considerable quantity is on this map."

He showed me a huge map on a wall. "We have records of everyone who owns property on the island. The official deeds are somewhere else, of course. Every time there is a change of ownership, we have a record of it. We are constantly monitoring all real estate activity on the island."

Then he led me to another part of the building. "This is our laboratory. Here we are constantly testing soil conditions, effects of climate, rainfall, and sun on the growth of the weed. And we do our experimental work in here."

He led me into a smaller room where two women and a man were working feverishly.

"And here is where we experiment on new varieties of ganja."

"Tell me about the super sensy."

"It's a hoax."

"It is?"

"Yes. Something the ganja crowd thought up to fight the Colombia competition. They just packed it tighter, cut it finer, gave the customer more for his money, changed the color a little bit and then charged five times what it was selling for before. And that added a two hundred percent profit on an already successful enterprise."

"Very clever."

"Very."

"But I've heard of formulas and the like."

"Smokescreens."

"What about the land?"

"The gang that runs the black market in money is trying to move in on the ganja trade. They've decided that the best way to do it is to get their hands on land owned by Jamaicans not in Jamaica."

"So that would explain why the properties that people were being killed for were in such different and varied parts of the island."

"Exactly."

"I take it then that ganja is grown in almost every part of the island."

"Yes, it is."

"If I had a list of properties and names, could you identify them for certain as being possible ganja areas?"

"Within a matter of an hour."

"So we have the big picture. All we need to do now is fill in the gaps."

"That may be your problem," he said. "But mine is to break the back of the black market ring."

"What about the ganja boys?"

"They stay."

"What?"

"We have no choice. We need that money coming into our economy. After bauxite and tourism, it's the leading earner of foreign exchange."

I almost laughed. "Then why not legalize it?"

"Your country wouldn't like it if we did."

"I see. Would you also have a social problem with it if you did?"

"No, very little of our crime, teenage or otherwise, is caused by smoking ganja. Poverty, that's the biggest cause of crime. And tribalism. The warring factions who want to control the ghetto."

"So why are the black market boys more of a threat than the ganja boys?"

"For one, their siphoning off of the tourist dollars robs us of our second largest foreign exchange earner without benefit of any advantage. In addition to that, the amount of bloodshed that would follow that type of gang war would be very disruptive to our national security."

That seemed to make sense.

"And finally, the ganja trade, as it now exists, while it has built-in risks, and while there are occasional killings connected with it, that trade is on the whole quite stable. And the amount of dollars that come to us from the sale of ganja, even though those sales are illegal, is considerable."

"How so?"

"Well, much of the money is spent on better living. For example, if a man builds a hundred-thousand-dollar home out of savings and a loan from the bank, that's all right. But if he spends a million, that's even better. More people employed, the building industry benefits. Construction increases. The value of property goes up. All in all it's good for everyone."

"And having all that ganja money around makes such purchases possible?"

| 253 |

"Quite right."

"Aside from the disruptive factor and the large amounts of money that go into the economy, are there any other reasons for the 'favored-nation status' of the ganja crowd?"

"I would think that would be enough."

"Oh, it is. But is there more to it than that?"

"I don't think I follow you."

"Well, are the ganja boys better connected?"

"With whom?"

"Mr. Macfarlane, really. In a small country the government either sees all, knows all, and can control all, or it quickly loses power."

"We are one of the few remaining true democracies in the Third World. The vote has always counted in Jamaica. That's a legacy the Englishman left us, when he finally decided to let us vote in the first place."

"You mean you have a real two-party system?"

"Exactly."

"That still doesn't answer the question."

"I suppose it would not be incorrect to say that some of the most powerful men in the ganja trade have friends in high places."

I played a hunch. "Like the prime minister's cousin Charlie, for example?"

He quite suddenly became very quiet. Then he said, "I wasn't aware that there was any connection between the gentleman you just mentioned, who incidentally is the prime minister's favorite cousin, and the ganja traffic."

"Oh, I'm sure you're right," I hastened to reply. "So what's our next move?" I asked. But he was deep in thought. I had said something that disturbed him.

"I think we had better hold off on any further action until tomorrow."

"Of course. Do you want me to return the glasses?"

"No, not at all."

"What are you going to do about the money?"

"It will be impounded until a proper investigation is made of the matter."

"Look, I'm sorry if I said anything to upset you. I'd still like to know what was in Braithwaite's pockets."

"Please don't misunderstand me, Mr. Cinquez. Our arrangement hasn't changed. It's just that I have a thought that makes me want to check a few things before we proceed further."

"A thought that came to you as a consequence of my mentioning the prime minister's cousin Charlie?"

"Maybe."

"Well, is he involved in the ganja trade or isn't he?"

"He is. It's common knowledge."

"And?"

"And that's as far as I care to take it. Shall we go back to the hotel and see what's in your friend's pockets?"

We were back at the Pegasus in no time. The body had been kept in a giant freezer in the basement while they waited for an ambulance to show up. They wheeled it out for us. His wallet was still on him. Inside there was a slip of paper with the words "Aquinas first" scribbled on it. And tucked in one of the secret pockets was a mate to the earring I had found on the grass near the fence where the man who shot the assistant commissioner of the CID had been hiding. I asked Macfarlane to join me in the Bull & Board for a drink. He knew I had something on my mind.

"Look," I said. "Braithwaite and Aubuchon probably wanted to get their hands on Iris Hylton's money for something other than simple theft, which was why she was killed so crudely. They were in a hurry. Seeing that two million makes me realize that if the move in the black market sector was to ganja, then a lot more people wanted to play than the established boys. That two million represented a payoff of some kind. Either for services rendered or to buy into the action. My guess is that someone in the government is involved."

"That would eliminate the prime minister's cousin. He's already in," he said, sounding relieved.

"I found a stud earring—the kind some men are wearing these days—near the fence where the man who shot your assistant commissioner of the CID was hiding. Braithwaite had the mate in his wallet. And the feeling I had about him was verified, in effect, when I observed Aubuchon in close contact with him. Look for a homosexual connection in high places. That will probably answer a lot of questions for you."

He really got silent then.

"One more thing. What does the name Aquinas mean to you?"

"Nothing offhand. Why?"

"The name has come up twice during the course of this case. Once in New York and again here. Which means the reference is probably to Jamaica."

"Well, there's St. Thomas Aquinas, of course."

"Yes, I thought of that. The parish of St. Thomas."

"Quite right."

"That's where they're going to concentrate when they make their move. Get your staff to zero in on St. Thomas and make a list of all the vulnerable properties there on which ganja could be grown. The properties in other parts of the island could either be a smokescreen or a backup play."

"I see. Very good, Mr. Cinquez. We need you in Jamaica working for us."

"You could definitely afford me, but I'd probably get bored with the beauty. Nature's, of course."

"Of course."

He left and I strolled to the bar downstairs by the pool. I was still drinking local beer. It had been a long day, but I was just too wound up to go to sleep. I thought about Westchester. I suddenly found myself missing her for the first time. Then I thought about Marlene coming down in the morning, and I didn't feel as lonely.

Trevor was now working the outside bar. When he brought me my beer we started chatting.

"She leave a number fe you."

"Who did?"

"Miss Prudence."

"Oh. But I'm going to see her tomorrow."

"She leave it all the same."

He gave it to me. It was a seven-digit number. "Do I dial all seven numbers?"

"If you in Kingston, only the last five. If you not in Kingston, you need all seven."

"Is there an area code?"

"No. Only the first two numbers."

I put the number away while he went to take care of another customer.

Why had Regina let me land with all that money, a veritable fortune in U.S. currency for dollar-starved Jamaica? Since she didn't tell me about it, it stood to reason that I was supposed to get caught. The bag was on one plane and I was on another. But I had the claim check. Was there to have been a switch before I got to it? Was the immigration officer supposed to impound it and then it would disappear? What went wrong? Did Amanda get there too late? Or because she was there the immigration guy didn't dare make the switch? He had disappeared from sight from what Macfarlane had said. Well, I had her hundred thousand, so that meant she wasn't too far behind. If they lost it or tried some sort of ruse to separate me from it, that would be a bridge I'd have to cross when I came to it. I was beginning to have less and less conviction about the syndicate threat that Regina had tried so hard to sell me on. But if she had the money, then what was all the fancy footwork for? The goons who followed us to the airport seemed real enough. And the two at her apartment were certainly serious. I was getting closer, but it wasn't time to start celebrating just yet.

Trevor came back. "A next one?"

"No, the beer is boring me. Rum."

"What kind?"

"What about that white stuff? The overproof. I had some in the police station at St. Ann's Bay earlier today."

"But that's the real thing. We can't serve anything that strong in here. We'd kill the tourists." And he laughed.

"Well, give me the strongest you have."

When he came back, I brought up his odd first name. "Is Trevor a popular name in Jamaica?"

"Yes, and no. Some people favor it, but some think it's too English." He seemed to sneer when he said "English."

"Don't you like the English?"

"No, why should I? They've never given the black man a real break. Anything they do is for show. They don't really mean it."

"But you like Prudence Gillesslee?"

"Yes, I have nothing against a person as a human being."

"I see, just as a group."

"When they don't treat me right."

"I can't argue with that. Suppose I wanted to find out about a man named Trevor, how would I go about it?"

He laughed again. "That's all you know about him, his first name?"

"No, his last name is Hylton. He's late thirties, early forties. I can describe him."

"Well," he said, a twinkle in his eye, "actually you in luck."

"I am?"

"Yes, about five years ago the United Nations chose Jamaica as a test site for developing techniques on gathering data on everyone in a country."

"Everyone!"

"Yes, you see we were the right size, just over two million people, and they had a new computer that they wanted to test.

So not only do we have births and deaths recorded, but we have schools, professions, and information on all kinds of things: awards, honors, distinguished services to the community."

"Is it up-to-date?"

"They keep updating it as best they can."

"So all I have to do is plug into the computer and I can find out everything I want to know?"

"Well, you can't plug into it. You must fill out forms and get permission from the proper authorities."

"It's just an expression. When we say plug in, we don't always mean it literally."

"Is jus' a figure of speech?"

"Exactly. So what is this place called where I can get all of this great information?"

"The Bureau of Statistics and Naturalization—Special Section."

I thanked him, paid for the drinks, and wandered out by the pool. They'd emptied it so there was no sense of beauty that a large body of water sometimes creates. I was just meandering. The wind was up. It was dark at the far end where the killing had taken place. I wasn't really looking for anything in particular, but even if I had been, it was impossible to see back there. I turned to go back and looked up at the hotel. Two people were struggling on a balcony close to the top. I couldn't make them out. Both seemed to be men. One was much bigger than the other and wore a cap. The bigger man picked the smaller man up and threw him over the side. He landed just beyond the bar on solid concrete. I was fifty feet away. The killer looked down, then around, then out. He saw me, but I was just a body without a face from that distance. He tried to peer into the darkness, but I was moving toward the body. I saw two other men come into the room and argue with him. Then all three left just as I got midway between where I had been and the body. I was sure he was dead on impact. He never moved. As a good view of the

| 259 |

room passed out of my line of sight because I had gotten closer to the building, I suddenly realized that the room was in the very definite vicinity of mine.

The dead man was Aubuchon. He had landed on his back, but he fell in an upside-down position and broke his neck when he hit.

Someone screamed and several people from the bar rushed out. I kept them back and told someone to get the manager. A security guard showed up and shortly afterwards the Englishman.

"This is Aubuchon," I said.

"Well, the ambulance just arrived, so we can get rid of both of them at the same time. What a nightmare. I can't believe it. I've been in the business thirty years and nothing like this has ever happened to me."

"I'd like to look through his pockets before you take him away."

"If you can do it and get it over with, fine, but he's not staying in the hotel a minute longer than he has to."

While the guard kept the crowd at a distance and the Englishman went back to get the ambulance attendants, I quickly went through Aubuchon's pockets. Money and keys were in the pants pockets. I put the money back and kept the keys. He had a billfold wallet in his jacket pocket. It had credit cards and scraps of paper in it. The scraps of paper were memorandums to himself mostly. I kept them, got up and told the guard I would return them to Inspector Collins. That reassured him. He knew who Collins was and he saluted me. I was too embarrassed to return it. I slipped through the crowd. The Englishman was returning with the ambulance attendants and a stretcher. He was determined to get the corpse out of his hotel.

I went up to my floor only to find a mob scene in front of my room.

A smart young police officer in uniform accosted me. When I identified myself, he wanted to see my passport. When I told him I didn't have one, he was on the verge of arresting me.

Luckily Collins came to my rescue. They were a strange lot, these Jamaicans. On the one hand, I was given access to things it would have been almost impossible to get in New York. On the other hand, they could be as strict and as insistent on enforcing the law to the letter as any New York City desk sergeant.

When the dust had settled, Collins closed the door and he and I got down to cases.

"I was down by the pool, just taking a stroll before going to bed. I'd had a beer and a glass of rum at the pool bar and chatted with the bartender. Trevor is his name. Then when I finished my poolside stroll, I just happened to turn and look up. And that's when I saw them struggling on the balcony. But they were so far up that I couldn't tell what floor they were really on."

"Were there just the two of them?"

"At first, and when the other man threw Aubuchon over they were still alone."

"Once he threw him over, what did he do then?"

"He looked around and saw me. But we were just shadows to one another."

"How much of him did you actually see?"

"He was about six-three. He seemed well built, and he was wearing a cap."

"Could you tell anything else?"

"Not from that distance in the night. I had a feeling that I had seen him before, but it's probably just my imagination."

"Why do you say that?"

"Because I've never been to Jamaica before in my life. Anyway, the guy I'm thinking of is in New York."

"What's his name?"

"I don't know. But everybody calls him Snakey."

He wrote it down. Then the phone rang. It was Macfarlane. I filled him in. Told him Collins was here and had everything under control.

"So those two men were together in New York, you say?" he asked.

"Yes, they're both lawyers, and they shared an office in Manhattan. I think you should ask around in the legal community. I had the feeling that they were known here professionally."

"Very good. I talked to the P.M. and we are back on GO. You will make your first contact tomorrow. Who are the people who have approached you and where were you to meet them?"

"Well, there's the Calypso Lounge and the record store in the Plaza."

"Let's take the Calypso Lounge first. I'd say around noon."

"That would be Rude Boy. You know him, of course."

"Oh yes, quite well. He's medium height, brown skinned, with freckles and a big smile. He's chubby and dresses in a nondescript fashion."

"Okay. Anything else?" I asked.

"No. Put me on to Collins, please."

I gave Collins the phone and went to the balcony and looked at the railing and at the floor itself. When Collins got off the phone he joined me.

"There are fragments of clothing here that seem to come from Aubuchon's suit. But you can't tell without a microscope."

We both looked.

"I'll have someone come round in the morning and dust for prints and take samples."

"Good. I'll try not to muck it up by poking around too much."

"It's all right. We'll be able to separate them from yours."

"Yes, but the other two men were out here also."

"Well, we'll do the best we can. Did you get a good look at them?"

"No, I was on my way to the body by then. They argued with the killer and then all three left. But they were in business suits, shirt and tie. They could have been non-Jamaicans."

"Why do you say that?"

"Manner mostly. It seemed American. But again, that's just a guess."

"Okay, Mr. Cinquez, you've been very helpful. See you at noon."

He left and I closed the door behind him and put the lock on. I changed into my robe and fixed myself a rum. Sat and looked out on the cars and the sky and listened to the sounds, the ones that reached up to me at any rate.

Aubuchon and Braithwaite were both dead. What the hell did that mean? Well, Marlene would be down in the morning. Hopefully she'd have some answers in that map. Regina and Jay were alive. The P.M.'s cousin Charlie was alive. Enid, who it now turns out is Iris, was alive. Snakey, Trevor, Gretchen, and the members of the club, all except Josephs, were all alive. The police in Manhattan and Brooklyn were involved somehow. Reg O'Connor's wife was missing. De Souza might be missing too. Was there anyone else? I couldn't think offhand.

My mission was to find a murderer. It meant finding what had happened to a lot of money, and it probably also meant finding out who killed Kathleen Campbell. If I solved Braithwaite's death as well, Aubuchon's was hardly a mystery, all well and good. I didn't like to leave loose ends around. It usually meant that the job wasn't really finished. Reg's death and Josephs's should wrap it up. Six deaths. That was a lot. Were they all related? I was falling asleep thinking about it. I jumped up when I heard someone at the door. It was Amanda. She couldn't get the chain off. I let her in and we had another salacious night in the tropics.

9

Sitting at breakfast, after finally getting something presentable to appear in by way of attire, after all I didn't need to attract attention anymore, I tried to convince the waitress that all I wanted was coffee.

"But you mus' try the smorgasbord," she insisted.

"What have they got?" I asked.

"Plantain, ackee and saltfish, herring, h'eggs, 'ahm, assorted fruit, Johnny cake, steak, sausage, bacon, coffee, tea, ovaltine, paw paw, mango, ugly fruit and dessert."

I wasn't going to ask what was for dessert. "Okay, okay, I'll try it." So I wouldn't be able to wear a swim suit for a week. You only live once.

I was just finishing up when I saw Gretchen at the other end of the smorgasbord getting seconds on the steak and eggs and paw paw and Johnny cake. She seemed perfectly relaxed. I sat and played with my coffee. The waitress came back and refilled the cup.

"Look," I said, "I'm finished, but I'd like to sit a while. Is it all right if I move to another table. One that's smaller?"

"No, me love, you jus' res' youself. Stay as long as you like. Afta all, don't you going to pay fe you smorgasbord?"

"Yes," I admitted, "but . . ."

"No 'but' don't in it. You goin' pay so you can stay."

"You don't seem to understand. I want to move to a smaller table."

"Look, this is my station. Once you leave my station, I don't get nothin' outa it."

"Oh, don't worry, I'll pay the check before I move."

"Well, once you pay the check you gone clear."

"Well, bring it!"

She did. I signed and moved to a small table in a corner, where I could see Gretchen, but she couldn't see me. No sooner had I settled in than another waitress came over to take my order.

"You want the smorgasbord?" she asked.

"No, I've eaten already. All I want to do is finish my coffee."

"But you can't finish it here. You mus' finish it where you had your smorgasbord."

"The other waitress said it was all right if I moved."

"She can't tell you is all right if is my station. If it don't all right with me, then it don't all right. You unnastan'?"

"I understand, but . . ."

"No, 'but' don't in dey. You want the smorgasbord or you don't want it?"

"I don't want it."

"Then you having the continental breakfast?"

"How much?"

"Ten dollars U.S."

"But I just had the smorgasbord for twenty-five dollars U.S."

"Is not my problem that, you know, backrah."

"Can I see somebody in authority?"

"I am in authority. This is my station." And she began to raise her voice. "You either have the smorgasbord or the continental breakfast or you leave. It simple."

People looked up, then away. She finished off by shouting, "Well?"

When Gretchen finally got curious enough about the commotion to ignore her steak and eggs for a minute and look around to see what all the fuss was about, she quickly turned back again as soon as she saw me, got up and disappeared through the service entrance.

I got up, told the waitress that the table was now all hers and tried to catch up with Gretchen. But a waiter stopped me. And he was huge and smooth.

"You can't go in there," he said.

"But I just saw another guest of the hotel do it," I protested.

"I didn't see another guest of the hotel do it, but I did see you." He smiled back.

The Englishman was just coming in with a party of what seemed like dignitaries.

"Shall I get the manager in on this?" I asked testily. "He happens to be a friend." I thought that would surely move him. The big hulk.

"Maybe Englishman frighten you," he replied, imperiously, "but a rule is a rule. Him cahn break it anymore than I can break it. Otherwise is no point in having it. Y'annah stan'?"

"I unnastan'. I also unnastan' that she's probably gone by now. But I want to know who saw her. And either you let me in or he will. But I'm going in, backrah."

He laughed. He'd had his fun. "No, you is backrah." And he moved off.

Well, *backrah* wasn't universal, that much I'd found out. It was somewhere between *tourist* and *enemy*. Gretchen, of course, was long gone. No one knew anything. I followed the trail through a couple of swinging doors until it led to the first floor behind the front desk lobby where the administrative offices were. When I got to the front desk my old friend the bell captain was at his stand.

"She didn't come by here," he said.

"Are you sure?" I described her.

"Yes, I'm sure."

"Maybe you were reading the paper and didn't look up when she passed by."

"I always read the paper without looking up. But I don't have to look up to see what's going on, and I tell you that in the last ten minutes she didn't pass me."

"Then where could she have gone?"

"She couldn't get out through the rear, that door's still locked. And you have to have the key to open it."

"Then where?"

"Back upstairs."

"How?"

"Through the service elevator."

"Where is that?"

He showed me, leaving his station to do so.

"Won't you get into trouble if you're not at your post?" I asked.

"No, the backrah say is all right to help you."

"Who the hell is he?"

"The manager."

"Oh, the Englishman."

"Right."

"So Englishman is backrah?"

"Not exactly."

"It's a bit too complicated, this language of yours."

He pushed the button and sent me on my way. It stopped at every floor. And it wasn't set to do anything unusual. So that didn't help me. I got out on my floor and wandered through the hall, then went down the stairs, methodically, coming back out again on the first floor.

"Any luck?" he asked, not looking up.

"No."

"Jus' a minute." And he got on the phone. When he hung up, he said, "Just go round to the cashier window and ask for Mr. Francis." I did as I was told. Mr. Francis was an East Indian, very pleasant, very well dressed. Open faced.

"No one by that name at the hotel. But I'm just going off. The day manager will be on in half an hour. He can ask around if anyone remembers her," he said.

"You're the night manager?" I asked.

"Yes."

"Then what about the Englishman?"

"Oh, he's the general manager."

"And there's a working manager for each shift?"

"Yes."

"How many shifts are there?"

"Three."

"So there are two other managers besides you?"

"Right."

"Thanks, I'll be back in an hour." I went up to my room and made some calls. The second one paid off. She was going by the name the old woman had used in Alligator Pond, Dorothy Pinto. And she was registered under that name on the twenty-fifth floor. She tried to disguise her voice, but I recognized it. I hung up. So it *was* Snakey I saw. I tried to get in touch with Collins, but couldn't. I left messages for him everywhere I could think of. It was Brown who finally got back to me.

"Hello, Brown here."

"Yes, Inspector Brown—"

"We're not as formal in Treasury as the CID."

"What does CID stand for anyway?"

"Criminal Investigation Division."

"Right, the British system."

"Right."

"A man was killed last night. He was thrown from my balcony. I was downstairs by the pool at the time, but I saw it."

"Yes, I heard."

"I thought the killer looked familiar, but, of course, from that distance I couldn't be certain. Now I am. Well, more so at any rate."

"What's his name?"

"I don't know. But he's called Snakey. He had to have arrived in Jamaica sometime between Wednesday morning and the time the murder took place in order to have done it, because I saw him in New York Sunday night, or at least I heard him."

"What makes you now feel more certain that this Snakey is the same man you saw committing the murder?"

"Because his girlfriend has suddenly appeared."

"Where did you see her?"

"Here in the hotel. She's registered under the name of Dorothy Pinto. I knew her in New York as Gretchen Schultz. I think she was born in St. Ann's, one of the German Jamaicans who go back one hundred years to the time the British brought a group over as indentured servants to work the plantations."

"I see you know a lot about our history, sir."

"Only bits and pieces."

"What room is she in?"

"2521."

"Do you want me to pick her up for questioning?"

I was so startled by that question that I hardly knew what to answer.

"Well, I don't know. I'm sure that if you took her in, you could possibly get her to tell you where he is. But getting your hands on him might be another matter. On the other hand, if you just follow her, she should lead you right to him. They are very close to one another from what I can tell."

"Yes, but do you want her questioned for your own reasons?"

"Oh, I didn't understand. Yes, I do, but then again I don't. I won't get the answers I want from her under those circumstances."

"So you don't want her questioned?"

"Not officially. But you'd better get someone over here right away. She's a slippery one. She might not hang around."

"I'll get right on it."

"Let me know when your people are in place. I have an idea."

"Very well." And he hung up.

My idea was to get the woman from Alligator Pond to Kingston to identify ole Gretchen. But Gretchen had to be around for it to happen. I called back down to the front desk and asked for Francis. When he came on I asked him to let me know when

Dorothy Pinto checked out—room 2521. He told me to wait, then came back on and said, "She's got the room for a week. She's scheduled to check out next Wednesday."

"Yes, but she might check out before."

"Oh, of course. And if she does, I'll have you alerted."

"What's the name of the manager who takes over from you?"

"Espeut."

"I've never heard that name before."

"It's not that common, but there are several families on the island."

"Who's in the room besides her?"

"Oh, there's no way of telling that."

"No, I mean offically."

"She's registered as a party of one."

"I see. Who's in charge of hotel security?"

"A Mr. Richards."

"Would you have him call me or come up?"

"Yes." And he hung up.

There was a knock at the door presently. A very young man, mid-thirties tops, strongly built, but quite relaxed, with a calculating smile that somehow was appealing nevertheless, about five feet ten, very dark, handsome, introduced himself as Mr. Richards, in charge of hotel security. I asked to see a card, since everyone on the island seemed to have one, and he produced it with a smile. I asked him in, told him I was working with Macfarlane, Collins, and Brown. I left out Ralph Percy. He was impressed. I told him that it was important that the lady in 2521—I described her—not slip away without my knowing. He wanted to know what authority I had to interfere in the personal comings and goings of guests of the hotel.

"I thought I just explained it. Macfarlane and—"

"Yes, yes, I know all about that, but that don't concern the hotel."

"Look, while we're standing here arguing, she could be on her way out the door."

"Which would be her right."

"I don't want to interfere with her right, I just want to know where she goes."

Just then the phone rang. It was Francis. "She's checking out."

"Does she have a car or did she call for a taxi?"

"She didn't call for a taxi."

"Where is she now?"

"In her room."

"Come on," I said to Richards, "she's checking out." I grabbed my weapon posing as a pair of sunglasses, and pushed him out the door.

"Once she's checked out she's no longer my problem," he told me.

"The picture's a little bigger than that, my friend. The reputation of the hotel is at stake. Speak to the Englishman if you want."

"Can't, he's not around."

"Then figure it out for yourself. I have to know where she goes. And I need your help if Brown doesn't get here in time. Hell, I'd get lost on these roads trying to follow her. You guys drive on the wrong side of the street, for chrissakes, and I don't know how you tell a one-way street from one that isn't. I sure as hell can't."

"I can't leave the hotel because you want somebody followed."

"Good, then get me a driver and a car . . ." We were waiting for the elevator. I looked up and it was standing on the twenty-fifth floor. "Let's not go this way. I think that's her getting on." He had a key to the service elevator and we took that down and got to the lobby before she did.

I told Francis my problem and he persuaded Richards to co-operate.

"On your authority," Richards insisted.

"Yes, on my authority," Francis replied.

"Okay." And he was gone like a shot.

"Hey, wait for me," I yelled, but Francis reassured me, "He wants you to wait out front. He'll be across the street. When you see her get into the car, cross over."

"You know the routine?" I asked.

"Yes, I guess I do."

"Look, a Marlene Campbell will be joining me, I think, sometime today. Tell her where I've gone and that I'll call her as soon as I can."

"Yes, she's due in at one."

"Oh, and do you know Ms. Campbell?"

"Quite well. Quite well, indeed!"

I didn't like the way he said that, but there was no time to dally. The elevator had finally left the twenty-fifth floor and was on the way down. I went outside and stood off near some trees and waited. When she came out she headed for the car park, the porter trailing with the bags. She got into a small blue, beat-up Austin. Snakey was behind the wheel! I crossed over and got in with Richards. "I hope you have a radio hook-up of some kind because there's a man wanted for murder driving the car she just got in."

"No radio," he said.

"But you can send up a flare if you have to?"

"No flare."

"Smoke? Pigeons?"

"No. If I have to I'll push you out at thirty miles per hour and you can find the nearest phone."

"And what good would that do? The phones probably don't work either."

"Ever been to Philadelphia?" he asked.

"Occasionally."

"Well, the phones there don't work either."

They were out of the driveway by this and had turned right and headed north in the direction away from the airport, up toward the hills. If there were stop signs or red lights Snakey didn't see them. I mean from the time he made the right turn he was gone! He cut behind corners, through gas stations, down lanes that weren't big enough to hold a bicycle, and he had her full out to the floor. He was using a clutch, that was for sure, and as old and as absurd looking as the car was, that boy knew how to drive her. And they never looked back. We came to a big intersection and Snakey went right through it. That's when my friend Mr. Richards stopped.

"What's the matter?" I demanded.

"He's going up to Red Hills. If I follow him up there, he'll see me for sure."

"Maybe he's already seen you."

"But I'm not trying to overtake him. He's done nothing wrong."

"You're right. Find a phone for me." He did and I took out Prudence Gillesslee's number and called her. "What's the address of your father's house in Red Hills?"

She told me and reminded me to be at the gallery around seven. I promised her I would, gave Richards the address, and we slowly made our way into the hills. When we got to the shaded lane all was quiet, even in the middle of the morning. The Austin was parked in front. I made Richards stop.

"Okay, you go back and get help. I'm staying."

"But you can't do anything but watch. You have no authority."

"I know all about the authority I don't have. Now get out of here, will you?"

He reluctantly made a U-turn and headed back down. I went through some trees down to a little brook that flowed behind the house and came up on the rear. I heard sounds but didn't know where they were coming from just yet.

I went down to the creek and crossed over to the other side and came up behind trees and bush. I had a clear view of the house, but there was no one in it. Where were the noises that I heard coming from? I waited. Nothing. I went back across the creek. The back door was open; I went in. They were chanting and it was coming from beneath me. I saw the door that led down, but decided to have a look around upstairs first.

The living room was furnished simply and seemed hardly used. It hadn't been dusted in a long time. I went up the stairs to the second level. There was one room up there, a bedroom. It had a huge round bed in it without legs, that just sat on the floor. The room was a mess. There were discarded match sticks and cigarette butts and ashes everywhere. Very little in the way of furniture. There was nothing up there of any consequence. I went back down. Got to the door and it was all much louder now.

I went down to the basement and there was no one, just a tape recorder, an old reel to reel model. It was playing a voodoo ceremony of some sort. What Prudence called obeah, I guess. But that room had been used for some sort of ceremony. The lighting was purples and blues and greens. Some of the bulbs were painted, others covered with colored cellophane paper. In some cases the paper had come too close and burned through. It was a haphazard affair, all in all. There were benches and a round, benchlike table in the middle of the floor. The floor itself was a reddish clay dirt. The kind Prudence had said was used in the rituals. The tape came to a part where there was cackling laughter and screams and moans, then it ended suddenly. Standing there in the sudden quiet with the lurid lighting, I tried to understand what was going on. Then I heard sounds upstairs. I ran up just in time to see Snakey and Gretchen get into the car and speed off.

I went back inside. Now I was really confused. I looked in the refrigerator. There were molds, plain water in a bottle, bread that was crusted over and a hypodermic needle. Not a reusable one, the cheap plastic kind. But it had never been used. I took it out and it had the name of a local pharmacy on it. The date was a year old. But there was no prescription number or any other means of identifying it. I kept it.

Outside I was just about to send up a flare when Richards showed up.

"What brought you back?" I wanted to know.

"I called the hotel, and just as I was about to get back in the car I saw them."

"Which way did they go?"

"They headed towards Half Way Tree."

"Where's that?"

"Well, it's west of here. But it's a major intersection. From there they could go back north into the hills, they could go south into town, or they could continue west and go into the interior of the island."

"Had Brown gotten anyone to the hotel yet?"

"Oh yes. He was there himself. He's on his way."

I went back in. Richards followed me. I tried the phone. It was dead. We went back out and Brown pulled up in a matter of minutes. He was sitting in front. He had a driver and two men in the back.

"The man I told you about, he was here. The woman checked out and he was waiting for her. They gave me the slip."

"Which way did they go?" he asked. I turned to Richards.

"They went down Hope Road towards Half Way Tree," he said.

"What kind of car?" Brown asked.

"A beat-up Austin," I told him. I gave him the license plate number. "But the phone in the house isn't working."

"Don't need it," Brown said and went back to his car. He had a phone. Well, well, the guys in Treasury knew how to travel. He called it in, left one of his men there and we all started back to the hotel. Halfway there I had a brilliant idea. Well, maybe not brilliant, but at least it was better than the kind of hunch

Marlene would have laughed at, or that wouldn't even have crossed Agatha Christie's mind. At least I hoped it was.

"Pull up," I said. Brown gave the order. "Where does Prudence Gillesslee live?"

No one knew. But I had a phone number. Brown got on his phone, had them check it. We waited. It seemed like an eternity. Then they came back on with it.

"Is that in the direction the car went?" I asked.

"It certainly is," Brown said.

"Then let's go," I said. We told Richards to go back to base and headed for the house. At the corner of the street we slowed down and took a peek. It was parked there all right. I suggested we not show ourselves just yet. Brown had the driver continue down the cross street in the direction away from the house and pull up around a corner out of sight. He had the driver make a U-turn and stick his front end out, just enough so that he could see the traffic coming in his direction.

"Well," Brown said, "what do you think?" I just wasn't used to having policemen, of any stripe, ask me what I thought. I almost asked him to repeat himself. But I cleared my throat and tried to think for both of us.

"We need to know what's going on. Surveillance, that's our first move. And while we're waiting, let's get some help. And see if you can find out who bought this, and where and why." I gave him the hypodermic needle with the drug store label on it. He turned to one of his men and gave him instructions. The man got out and walked down the street in the direction of the house. Then Brown got on the phone again. He was waiting for someone to get back to him when the driver said, "A car coming. It look like Mr. Percy driving it. He turned into the street." We waited. Someone came on the phone. Brown tried to talk as quickly and as quietly as he could. Not that he could be heard.

"Yes, put him on," he said. Just then the driver spoke up again. "He's coming back." We leaned forward and Percy's car turned right furiously and came in our direction. As he drove past he looked right at us and then looked back, but he never stopped or slowed down.

"You want me to follow him?" the driver asked.

"No," Brown said. "Check Banjo." The driver got on his walkie talkie. "Authority one to Zed," he said.

"Zed in. Condition static. Am proceeding accordin' to plan. Zed out." And he clicked off. Aw right! Now these guys knew about the fourth quarter of the twentieth century.

Then we heard Macfarlane on the phone.

"Hello, hello."

"Yes," Brown said.

"What's up? Is Mr. Cinquez there?"

"Yes. Need your assistance immediately. One back-up car equipped. Murder suspect under surveillance, we think. Percy seen in the area. He drove off without acknowledging."

"You did say Percy?"

"Ralph Percy, yes."

"Anything else?"

I quickly pointed to the hypodermic needle.

"Yes, please check Nelson's Drug Store for nonreusable hypodermic needle purchased twenty-one/seven last year."

Twenty-one/seven, I thought, then I realized it was the British system again, the month after the day, not before.

"You want to know who purchased it?"

"Mr. Cinquez does."

"Okay. What did you do about Percy?"

"Nothing."

"I understand," and he hung up. We waited for about ten minutes, then Zed came on again.

"Zed in."

"Go ahead, Zed," the driver said.

"One Reggae, one Calypso getting into car. Have a bag. Driving off towards Constant Spring."

Brown grabbed the walkie talkie. "Take cover. You will remain at post." The driver had moved off without being told to, and we were around the corner as Brown started his next sentence. "Wait for back-up. Tell them to contact Red Gal Ring. Authority out." We passed him and he stood up and pointed left. We turned left, didn't see them. Brown decided to go north. We did. A lot of small turns on side streets. Then we stopped. They obviously could have been a lot of places, but Brown seemed certain that he hadn't lost them. He got onto Zed, who said they hadn't doubled back, so we waited. Presently we saw them two streets down, heading west. We moved off cautiously. They passed us while we were still a block away, going north.

"I was right," Brown said, almost to himself. "Red Gal Ring it is." We turned right and headed north behind them. Snakey was still driving aggressively, but he seemed less suicidal at that point.

"Reggae and Calypso?" I asked.

"Reggae is our code for a black male," he replied, "and Calypso is a white female."

"Suppose the male had been white and the female black?" I asked.

"That would have been Quadrille and Jump Up."

"Quadrille for the white male and Jump Up for the black female."

"That is correct."

Sounded racist and sexist, both, and at the same time, to me, but of course I said nothing.

They went straight past a shopping mall and a big open market, right through a red light, scattering pedestrians and dogs at will. We followed in similar fashion. People yelled at them and at us and then continued on about their business.

"When we get to Red Gal Ring we stop," Brown told the driver.

We began to ascend into the hills. Then we came right up to

the mountain, and the road took a tremendous turn of about 130 degrees left and then right again. All the while going up the mountain. We stopped at the first turn as they disappeared up the hill. The police station was right there facing the road. Brown jumped out and disappeared inside. The phone began to beep. The driver picked it up. It was Macfarlane. He was at Prudence Gillesslee's house. I asked to speak to him.

"If you're planning to join us, I'd like to know what's in that house before you do," I told him.

"Yes, quite right. Where are they now?"

"They've gone up past Red Gal Ring, I guess. Brown's inside the police station."

"Tell him I'm on my way."

"I will." And we both hung up.

Brown came to the steps and motioned me in. The driver stayed in the car by himself.

"We have a station just at the top of the climb before the road turns inland and goes into the country. They didn't pass it yet."

"Is there any other way over the mountain?"

"No, they either pass him or come back through here and pass us."

"Then we wait."

"Then we wait."

He got out some cold beers, gave me one, took one to his driver, and had him move off the road and came back up. He called his man on the other side just to make sure. No, they hadn't passed him.

"They've gone off somewhere," I said.

"That's possible. There are a lot of side roads and houses up there. But short of abandoning the car and going on foot there is no other way out."

We waited. Macfarlane was on the phone again. "There doesn't seem to be anything of particular interest in the house from what we can tell. But we just took a cursory look. However, your hypodermic needle turned up an interesting bit of information. It was purchased by Prudence Gillesslee along with some insulin."

"Over a year ago?" I asked.

"No, she gets it filled regularly. That must be an old needle that somebody forgot to use."

"I see. Well, we're still waiting for them to come out. It's Snakey all right. The one I saw throw the lawyer over the balcony."

"And you're certain?"

"I'm certain."

"We may have to go in and apprehend him."

"I understand."

"I'll be there in fifteen minutes."

"Can you find the doctor who wrote the prescription?"

"Of course I can," he said and he hung up.

"What's up there?" I asked Brown.

"It's a residential area mostly."

"What kind of residential area?"

"Substantial, very."

"What else?"

"There's a tourist spot at the top where our man is waiting. It's a quite lovely botanical garden called Castleton."

"And that's it?"

"That's it, except for Casa Monte."

"What's that?"

"It's where we train people to work in hotels."

"Is it a hotel?"

"Oh, yes. One of the best in the island. It's in a lovely spot, on a hill overlooking all of Kingston."

"Does anyone stay there?"

"No, not really. We have to have people there from time to time so the trainees can actually get first-hand experience."

"Who does?"

"Who does what?"

"Who does stay there when you have people staying there?"

"It's usually reserved for members of the family of government officials and their guests."

"Do a lot of them stay there at one time?"

"No, usually about ten or twenty tops."

"How big is the hotel?"

"Oh, I'd say it was built to hold about one hundred, but a lot of it is boarded up."

"Who's in charge of deciding who stays there?"

"Someone in the prime minister's office. I'm not sure who."

We finished our beer and had a few more. Marlene should be landing about now, I thought. I was getting restless. Nothing seemed to be going according to plan. As soon as I thought I was on a road that led somewhere, something would come along and sidetrack me. It was getting very discouraging. God, if I started thinking about all the loose ends in this case I'd head for an out island and dig a hole and crawl into it.

Somewhere along the way I started spreading myself too thin and just never recovered. It's as simple as that. I could think of no conceivable way in which an Irishman wanting to run for mayor of New York City, a prime minister of a small West Indian island arrested for narcotics trafficking, a dead Englishman who gave away a small fortune while he was dancing to an ancient African ritual, a crazy mixed-up kid who got me to take $100,000 in U.S. currency into a foreign country without my knowledge, a super strain of ganja, a pair of twin sisters, one dead, one alive, two homosexual lawyers, one black, one white, both dead, acquisition of land rights in a foreign country, and half a dozen other deaths had to do with each other. Maybe I ought to call Westchester and take that job with her father after all. But Macfarlane showed up and I was ready, once more, and again, for the chase.

Macfarlane, Brown, and I went into a back room and closed the door.

"Have you talked to Jamaica House about Ralph yet?" Brown asked.

"No," said Macfarlane. "I won't be able to do that until tonight. By the way, the prime minister is having a small dinner party tonight, Mr. Cinquez. You're invited."

"I'm supposed to be at the art gallery at Devon House at seven."

"You can make both."

"And I'd like to get a message to a Miss Marlene Campbell who came in on the noon flight from Kennedy. She should be checking in at the Pegasus about now."

Brown and Macfarlane exchanged a look when I mentioned her name, but I said nothing. "Well, can you see that she's told?"

"Of course. What's the message?" asked Macfarlane.

"Tell her I'll see her for dinner."

"But you'll be at the prime minister's."

"Well, can't I take her along?"

"You'd better talk to her about that first."

"You mean because of Cousin Charlie?"

They both looked surprised that I knew.

"Check Castleton again," Macfarlane told Brown. He went out to do it. "Well, Mr. Cinquez, here we are once more."

"Yes."

"How long have they been up there?"

"Not long. About forty-five minutes."

"Tell me about this Snakey character."

I did.

"Would you know the woman if you saw her?" he asked.

"Mrs. O'Gilvie?"

"Yes."

"Probably, unless the picture was taken so long ago that there's no longer any resemblance."

"What connection does it all have to the murder you're trying to solve?"

"Other than the fact that Gretchen is connected to Snakey and

Mrs. O'Gilvie is involved in something that seems to be some sort of inheritance scheme that I really know nothing about, I can't tell you."

"I think we have to find them, even if they do refuse to talk."

"I think you're right. Tell me about the hotel, the Casa Monte."

"It's not a good hideout, if that's what you mean."

"Why not?"

"Because there are too many people around."

"Unless Snakey or Gretchen have an inside contact."

"Yes, that would change things."

"Anybody else around that comes to mind?"

"Well, a lot of people live in the area."

"Reputable, noteworthy people who could possibly have a connection to a ganja war or a U.S. dollar war?"

"Yes."

"Then shouldn't we make a list and start checking?"

"That could get tricky."

"You don't want to embarrass someone of influence who might be involved?"

"Well, 'embarrass' isn't quite the right word. Let's say we wouldn't want to confront anyone unless we were absolutely sure of our ground."

"How much surer do you have to be than murder?"

"Well, if we find him, then we will certainly arrest him, no matter where he is. What we don't want to do is go charging in somewhere with very little to go on."

"Do either Ralph Percy, the P.M.'s adc, or Charlie, the P.M.'s cousin, live up there?"

"Yes."

"Which one?"

"Both."

That stopped me.

Brown came back in, shaking his head. "No one's been through, not even a tourist." That bothered Macfarlane. He didn't want to go into the residential area where so many important people had addresses. But he had to.

"What about a helicopter?" I asked.

"No, no, we couldn't chance having an aircraft buzzing overhead. That could set off a panic of major proportions. Someone might even think there was a coup of some sort in the making."

"As sensitive as that?"

"Yes."

"So what do we do?"

"We find the car. Get a map of the district," he told Brown. Brown went to the door and called to someone, who brought a map. He laid it out on the table and we looked at it.

"Where are their homes?" I asked.

Macfarlane paused. "We won't start there," he said.

"Why not? Ralph came charging up and when he saw Brown's man in the street he did an aboutface and flew right by us and kept going. And Cousin Charlie used to be Prudence Gillesslee's boyfriend."

There was a pause. Then Brown spoke up. "He's right."

"Damn it, suppose we get there and we find nothing?"

"Oh, come on. We could drive up and just simply ask him why he didn't stop. As for Cousin Charlie, I'd like to meet him anyway."

"Aw right." And he took a pencil and marked two X's. "Let's set up two roadblocks. One here in front of the police station and one at Castleton Gardens."

"Roadblocks. You want to go that far?" I asked.

"Yes, if we're going to do it, let's do it right."

Once he'd made up his mind, he suddenly became quite determined.

"Then what?" I asked.

"Then we go in and stay in until we find them. We'll only need one car. It shouldn't take us more than ten to fifteen minutes tops to cover the entire area."

"What do we do if we find the car and there's no one in it?"
Brown.

"Take it out of commission."

"Then what?" I asked.

"Go in, no matter whose house it is. Take two men fully
armed."

It wasn't going to be enough, but we didn't know it at the time.

When the car was ready we went out. The two officers were
in the back. One had an automatic weapon and one had a shotgun. Brown drove and Macfarlane and I got in beside him. I was
in the middle. Brown turned to the men and one of them handed
up three pistols. We each took one.

As we moved off they were setting up the roadblock. It wasn't
very substantial, but of course they were only trying to stop one
car. We took the hill slowly. It was some ring—the ole Red Gal.
In my constant thirst for knowledge of the Caribbean, I wanted
to ask where they ever got the name from, but I really had my
mind on other things. We drove right through, staying on the
main road, got to Castleton, and Brown, Macfarlane and I got
out. They conferred with their man up there. He was waiting
for the roadblock contingent to come from his police station.
They got walkie talkies going and we decided not to wait. Back
in the car we turned around and headed down the way we had
come. Halfway down we took a right up a winding road, past
houses until we came to a steep hill with a small entrance that
had two stone posts on either side that read CASA MONTE. We
drove in. The roadway was very narrow and steep. The hotel was
on the left, sitting on the very edge of a cliff. When we pulled
up in front I saw that the swimming pool and tennis courts were
across the road opposite the main building.

Macfarlane got out and went inside.

"What's the manager's name?" I asked Brown.

"It's never the same person for more than a month. I don't
know who's doing it this month."

"Well, where do they get them from?"

"Other hotels. It's an arrangement that's made with the government."

There was no one about. No one at the door, no one on the grounds.

"The place seems deserted," I suggested.

"Yes, it's like that often. They only keep a skeletal staff here most of the time."

From what I could see it was a showplace. The grass was cut to absolute neatness. Everything seemed freshly painted or scrubbed or polished. But still there was no one about. Then Macfarlane came back out.

"I spoke to the manager. He'll check the staff and find out if there's anything unusual going on."

"Is he good enough to find out if there is?"

"Oh, yes, he's a very reliable man."

"What's his name?"

"Whose, the manager's?"

"Yes."

He looked at Brown, hesitated, then back at me and said, "Espeut."

"Not the same Espeut who works at the Pegasus?"

"Yes."

"I see. Is he more than just a manager?"

"Well, let's just say that he's reliable in a situation of this sort."

"Very well, let's just say. So where to next?"

"Ralph Percy." And he took a deep breath when he said it.

It was back down to the gate and out. But this time Brown made a right turn and continued on the road we'd come in by. We got to the end and made a left and then another right. It was a quiet street with a dead end. The houses seemed quite substantial indeed. All set away from the road, with well-groomed trees and lawns. The beat-up Austin at the end of the cul de sac was definitely out of place.

"Is that Ralph Percy's house?" I asked.

"Yes."

We drove right up. Everybody got out. Macfarlane and Brown hesitated, then Macfarlane had the two officers follow him. Brown and I brought up the rear. He went to the front door and knocked. No one came to answer it. He sent the men around back, one on each side, and we waited. I looked through a front window, but I saw no one. The men came back. There was no one in the rear. Macfarlane was close to panicking.

"Well?" I asked.

"We can't just break in."

"That car says we can."

But Brown came to the rescue. "I think I have a key that fits." And he did.

Inside all was quiet.

We searched the entire house, but no one was home.

"What do you make of it?" I asked.

"I don't know what to make of it," Macfarlane said. He turned to Brown, but he just stared blankly back in return.

"Let's try Cousin Charlie's," I said.

"I suppose so," Macfarlane replied.

We got back in the car. Brown got onto Castleton, told them to get the car and take down both roadblocks, and we headed for Cousin Charlie's.

As we turned into the street, I thought I saw someone dart behind a tree to the left about four houses down.

"Which house is it?" I asked quickly.

"It's just here on the right," Macfarlane said.

"The second one or the third one?" Brown asked.

"The one with the St. Julian mango tree in front."

The house turned out to be directly opposite the one where I thought I saw someone lurking. "Keep an eye out across the street. I thought I saw someone over there when we turned into the road," I told the men in back.

We got out and used the same deployment—the men at the rear and the three of us in front. Macfarlane put his hand on the door and it swung open. It was a magnificent house with a winding staircase and a sunken living room, furnished with the very best that money could buy. The chandelier must have been worth a small fortune by itself.

"So this is how the other half lives," I found myself saying.

"Yes," said Macfarlane.

We went into the waiting room on the right. Snakey and Gretchen were lying on the floor in a huge pool of blood. That's when they opened fire.

Why they had waited until we got to the house, I didn't know. But we scooted in and closed the door behind us. Macfarlane, who was in the lead, got in first. I was in second and Brown last. He got nicked on the shoulder, but it was only a flesh wound and didn't seem to bother him much. It wasn't the shoulder he fired from. I looked out from a window and there was no one in sight. Then we heard what sounded like the Battle of the Bulge coming from the rear. I rushed back there and opened the kitchen door. I tried to look out but there was machine gun fire coming from the bushes in the rear. I could hear what sounded like our two policemen returning the fire, but I couldn't see them. In desperation I yelled, "The back door's open. Can either of you make a run for it?"

"No," one of them shouted. I moved to a window and saw him—the one with the shotgun—behind a tree. He was not in a good spot. His shotgun couldn't help him. He wasn't in range. And it was the kind of weapon that he couldn't fire from cover too effectively. But I could hear the machine gun firing away. He was to my left, but he was too near the house for me to see him. I moved to another window to get a better angle. He was almost below me. I opened the window.

"Throw me the gun. I'll cover you, then you jump in." He threw in the machine gun. I caught it and went down. I saw him ducking as they opened fire. It seemed like an army back there in the bushes, but I couldn't really tell. I came back up firing and he leaped through in one jump, as if he was diving into a clear pool of water. I gave him back the gun, told him to go to the door and cover his partner. I'd try to pick off anyone I could with the handgun. He opened the door and yelled to the other guy to run for it. One of them came up and I fired, but I didn't think I got him. The shotgun made his move, but he never got more than halfway. There were just too many of them. They came up shooting. He never really had a chance. His partner closed the door, cursing. I was trying to figure out a way to get my hands on that shotgun, but it didn't seem possible. Not with that many of them out there—all willing to show themselves, guns blazing away no matter what.

"Give me back the machine gun and check out the front," I told him. He did. I gave him the pistol. I waited, expecting to be rushed, but no one moved. He was gone a long time. It was suddenly very quiet. Then he came back.

"Well?" I asked.

"He's not there."

"Who's not there?"

"Macfarlane."

"What do you mean he's not?"

"I went upstairs and back down again. I tell you he's not there."

"What about Brown?"

"He's dead."

"You're mad!" And I ran into the front. Brown was lying face down. Not shot through the back, I didn't think. But the bullet had gone clean through. That meant it was fired from extremely close range or from an extremely powerful weapon.

"They're leaving," he yelled.

I opened the front door and they opened fire. I threw the door closed and hit the floor. As soon as the door closed they stopped firing.

| 289 |

"Stay back there," I yelled. I went over to Snakey and Gretchen. They were holding hands. Each had been shot once, through the head. Gretchen still had her purse with her. I went to the window and looked out. There was no one moving. I came back and searched Snakey. He had nothing on him but money and reefers. No wallet, no papers of any kind. Gretchen's handbag was another matter. Tucked under the bottom flap on the inside was a key. It looked like a key to a safety deposit box of some sort. Nothing else seemed to be of any consequence, but I had a feeling the bag had been rifled. But why search it and close it afterwards, and then put it back on her arm during that melee? Unless the search happened before we got there.

The policeman in the rear came forward. "All clear in the back." And he had the shotgun to prove it.

"Let's test the front."

We got to the door and I pushed it open with my foot. I stuck my head out and pulled it back as a bullet flew past. Then we heard firing again in the back. We closed the front door and both of us ran back there. Then we realized what had happened. There was a helicopter overhead firing in the area where our would-be assailants in the rear had been.

Brown had the keys to the car on him.

"Come on," I said.

"When we get to the door, I'll go first. If I make it to the car, I'll pull it up and you can jump in. If the car won't start, I'll have to come back. When I give them a shotgun blast, you cover me coming back. The shotgun probably won't hit anything, but it might make them duck."

He nodded. I threw open the door and ran for the car all at the same time. He was with me all the way. He stood full up in the doorway a good eight seconds, firing away, then he ducked back in and shut the door just as they riddled it. I got to the car, put the key in and it started up. I backed it up and he ducked into the rear. We drove off, but they didn't show themselves.

I headed straight for the Casa Monte. I drove right up and jumped out and ran inside. I was still holding the shotgun. I heard my newfound ally on the radio reporting Brown's death and Macfarlane's disappearance. He wanted instructions.

I ran up and down stairways, kicking in doors, but I found no one—absolutely no one! I came back out. I was breathing heavily.

"I called the station," he said. "Inspector Collins will be here shortly."

"We're not waiting. You drive."

"Where to?"

"The Pegasus Hotel."

"But shouldn't we—"

"No. Brown's dead and we don't know what the hell is going on."

He got us there so quickly that I wasn't able to solve any puzzles before I found myself at the hotel entrance. I left him and the guns in the car, found the Englishman, and showed him the key. It was one of theirs all right. We opened it and there were all of Iris Hylton's papers. Only they weren't Iris Hylton's, they were Enid Hylton's.

"The woman who left these with you, Dorothy Pinto, she's dead. Inspector Brown's dead. Macfarlane has disappeared and all hell is breaking loose. Will you trust me with these?"

He hesitated. "Well, it's usually not done. But you do have the key. Strictly speaking we could be sued by a next of kin or an heir."

"But she checked out before she died."

"Yes, well, we're still responsible." And he paused. And before I could do something foolish, he said, "Go ahead, but don't leave the hotel with them whatever you do."

I promised him I wouldn't. Told the officer to send Collins up as soon as he arrived. Then I went up to my room, checked the pistol. I had five shots left. I put it on the table. Poured myself a stiff drink of rum and began to carefully go through everything. It made fascinating reading. Better than any novel I had come across in the last ten years.

Two sisters had married two brothers, on the same day. One brother owned a fortune in land. The other brother had nothing. The brothers were twins. My Mrs. Hylton was in fact Enid. And her sister, who was still alive and in Brooklyn the last time I saw her, was in fact Iris. There were pictures, letters, marriage certificates, wills, everything. Enid and her husband divorced. But she stayed in Jamaica. When Gillesslee came to the island, he hired her as his housekeeper. His daughter, Prudence, wanted him to make her his heir in fact. She and Cousin Charlie had plans. But he said no. Only she wouldn't take no for an answer and the good doctor began to worry about not only his money, but his health. Enid tried to help, but when Prudence found out that she might, at the doctor's request, take a large chunk of his money out of the country, she had Cousin Charlie arrange to have Enid's passport revoked. So Enid became Iris and was able to get out using her sister's identity. She put the money in trust under her name. The doctor could claim the money with her consent or, if she died, by proving his identity. So Enid came to America as Iris and sat on the money, waiting for Dr. Gillesslee to show up. She used the interest, with his permission, to live on. She couldn't do anything to help him because, by rights, she shouldn't have even been in America.

Iris, who had helped her sister with the switch, found out why her sister needed to change her identity and tried to get her hands on some of what was left, but the cow was already out the barn door by then. And the doctor only got involved in the pocomania rituals as a way to make up for the loss of Enid.

My mind was racing ahead, but I stopped it to read some more. Many of the letters were written from a Mr. Williams in Yallas. And reference was constantly being made to an Aunt P. It was getting tricky and there were big jumps in time. Much of what was being made reference to I could only guess at the meaning of. But then I got lucky with one letter that had no last page with the signature on it. Apparently the reason for all the letters was the fact that Enid had to keep her identity secret, or her where-abouts. I wasn't sure which. But in that letter, written to her a year after she left Jamaica, there was a discussion of her husband's death, which was never reported. Then there was a mention of the land he had that Iris couldn't sell because there was so much in back taxes owed on it. So, the letter went, "they did it all for nothing, but everybody knew that it wasn't the brother who died, but her husband. But you know country people. They keep their mouth shut. They don't even tell police what they know 'cause they still have to live there after."

I thought about that for a long time.

If the brother who owned the land, Enid's husband, died and the death had never been reported, then how could the land have been sold anyway, taxes or no taxes, since the wife was in New York. If, as the letter seemed to indicate, the penniless one was alive, was he posing as the brother who owned all the land? Since they were twins, it obviously was feasible. And in the village where they both lived it was common knowledge who was alive and who wasn't. What village was it, though? Yallas? Or some-place else. That I had to find out. Then I remembered what the bartender at the pool bar, the one named Trevor, had told me. Everyone was listed somewhere, their births, deaths and a lot of other data. All I needed was a name. Hylton? What was the first name?

How had Dr. Gilesslee died? Where was he buried? How much money did Enid actually take out and how much had been left? What was Gretchen's connection with it all? Why were she and Snakey killed? And finally, what had happened to Macfarlane, and how was Brown killed? Was there anyone left to trust? How could I tell? And what was I being used as a pawn for and why? And by whom?

I called the front desk and asked if Marlene Campbell had checked in yet. She hadn't. Then I asked about the morning flight that was to have arrived at noon. I was told it was late leaving New York. And they had no further information on its arrival. I could call the airport if I wished. I didn't wish. Not yet anyway.

I was going to have some graves dug up. I was going to have to get tax records, marriage and death certificates, visa information, a list of passports issued and when, and God only knew what else. And I was going to need a lot of help. But who to ask for it, that became the burning question.

The phone rang. It was Collins.

"Where have you been? I've been trying to catch up with you all day," he said agitatedly.

"Are you friend or foe?" I asked.

"What sort of question is that?"

"Just answer it."

"Where's Macfarlane?"

"You mean you don't know?"

"Know what?"

"About Brown."

"What about him?"

"He's dead."

"Dead!"

"Dead. And Macfarlane was the last person to see him alive. And Macfarlane has suddenly disappeared. If he hasn't, wherever he is, he hasn't gotten in touch with me."

"Where did you see him last?"

"Where Brown was killed."

"Where was that?"

"In Cousin Charlie's house."

"The prime minister's Cousin Charlie?"

"The prime minister's Cousin Charlie."

"How do I know what you're telling me is true?"

"Check it with one of your men from the Red Gal Ring Police Station."

"What's his name?"

"You know, we probably saved each other's lives and I don't even know his name. But he should be parked outside. Have the front desk send someone out and get him to come to the phone."

He was quiet. I could hear him thinking. While he was still at it I had another question for him. "When did you last see Ralph Percy?"

"He's right here beside me."

"Can I talk to him?"

"Of course."

"Yes, Percy here."

"Tell me, Percy there, why did you run away when you saw Brown's man in the street in front of Prudence Gillesslee's house?"

"I'm afraid I'm not at liberty to discuss that."

"Brown's dead."

"So you've just been telling us. But how is it we know nothing about it? Surely—"

"I knelt down over the corpse. He was shot once through the chest, somewhere near his heart. The bullet came out the other side. And unless someone moved him, he should still be lying there face down. And Snakey and Gretchen should be right beside him."

"Who're they?"

"I haven't got time to go into that now, but if you're a good guy, then I think you should worry about Macfarlane. He disappeared under what can only be described as peculiar circumstances. If you're a bad guy, then you're somebody else's problem. But I need someone to open some graves and look into some tax records and get me information on a passport that was issued three years ago."

"Macfarlane would be the man to do all that."

"And now that he's disappeared?"

"Now that he's disappeared it's going to take a lot longer, I'm afraid."

"You know I think you guys have let Macfarlane do too much. And since he was willing and able the rest of you got lazy, and before anyone looked up he'd become the indispensable man. Somebody should tell the prime minister what's going on. I think he might be interested." And I hung up.

Whether Percy and Collins were helping their country or not, I didn't know. And hoped I wouldn't have to care.

I took the papers back downstairs. Told the Englishman that he had better not surrender them to anyone. "And I mean even a lawyer, an heir presumptive or Macfarlane." That shocked him. He wanted to ask why, but didn't. But I didn't think that any of those reasons would have made a difference, so I added, "I'll make you a deal. You promise me you won't let anyone near that box and I'll solve the murders for you, all three of them."

"All three of them?"

"Well, at least two. Everyone has a general idea of why the CID commissioner was killed, although no one's actually sure. But the two lawyers, one thrown from my balcony and one killed in his room, are a different matter."

"I would like that very much. You have my word on it."

"Good," I said and we shook hands.

I went looking for the bell captain. He was just sitting there reading the paper the way he always was. I didn't think he ever had a day off.

"I need a car and a driver," I told him.

"For when and where?"

"For now. I want to go to Yallas."

"That's a long way. It'll take you at least two hours."

"I still want to go."

"Okay." He sent one of his men out to get someone. We waited. Then an old man came in who could hardly walk. He was bent over with arthritis and he couldn't move his neck in either direction sideways. I turned to the bell captain, but he stopped me. "You want to go to Yallas, he's your man. Whatever you need to know when you get there, he's the man who can see that you find it."

There wasn't very much I could say to that, so I went with him. When we got outside, I looked around for the policeman, but he wasn't there.

The old man had a Packard. A Packard! I had never even seen one before except in magazines. It actually had a running board, was open at the sides and with a canvas top! Where the hell he got that relic from was beyond understanding. As old as he was, even he wasn't that old.

We got in and I waited while he tried to start it up. It took him a long, long time. He pumped and kicked and coughed, and the old buggy shook and sputtered, but between the two of them she made it.

"She starts funny, but once she hits the road, she's as smooth as a peach."

I decided I would let him show me.

We got out of the city without too much difficulty, but it wasn't until we were on the open road that the damned thing seemed like it was going backwards. Maybe it did 30 m.p.h., maybe, but cars were passing us so fast that I was getting wind burns. I decided to sit back and close my eyes so that I could keep my courage up. When I finally looked up we were on the same road where I almost got run over by the overloaded bus.

The traffic had thinned out and it was actually becoming a pleasant ride. The car was made for the tropics. You were covered from the sun, but you got the breeze and you didn't travel much faster than a donkey.

I decided to lean forward and talk to my pilot.

"When we get to Yallas, I have to find a man."

But he couldn't turn around and I wasn't sure if he understood me. I know I didn't understand him. He mumbled something and I repeated the question. He stopped the car, turned all the way around and looked directly at me.

"We'll take care of it when we get there." And he turned back around and continued driving.

We finally arrived in the center of the town and parked. He got out, I followed. We went into the local rum shop, had a couple of rums, and then left. The next stop was the post office. Well, that was a good idea, I thought. He moved quickly, even with his impediments. Over a short distance he might even beat the car.

When we got inside, he took me through a side door and into a back office, where a man in his sixties, suspenders and belt, bald, glasses, was sitting on a stool sorting letters.

"Andrew, this gentleman needs to find somebody. I'll be at Maud's," and he disappeared!

Andrew turned and looked at me skeptically. Then his manner changed.

"Yes, sir, can I help you?"

"I'm looking for a man who uses your post office as his mailing address."

"Everyone in the village does that."

"Everyone?"

"Everyone."

"You mean there are no street names or house numbers?"

"There are, but you don't need them if you're from Yallas. It's only useful to outsiders. What's your man's name?"

"Williams, A. Williams. He wrote several letters from Yallas to a woman in Brooklyn, New York. The last one was about three months ago."

"He died last week."

"Did he?"

"Yes."

"Any relations?"

"A sister."

"Had she been living with him?"

"No, she was in Brooklyn herself."

"What's her name?"

"O'Gilvie."

Well, well, I thought. At least that trail had come full circle. "Where is she now?"

"At the house."

"Is she planning on going back to New York?"

"You'd have to ask her that."

"Can you have someone tell me how to get there?"

"I'll tell you how to get there." He got down from the stool and went through the front door and out into the street. I followed.

"You go down past the square. The church is on your right, and the first road on your left you take. You go up five, six houses, then turn right and the third house on the left is it. The street is called Anthurium Street, but there's no sign."

"Is there a number on the gate?"

"Number six."

"Thanks."

I found the house without any difficulty. I went in and stood on the small front porch and knocked on the door. Eventually a young girl, dressed like a maid, came to the door and unlocked it.

"Is Mrs. O'Gilvie in?"

"Yes, jus' a minute, please," she said and disapeared.

Then an older version of the woman I had seen in the picture came to the door and asked me in.

It was a very small living room with thin chairs and end tables and a couch. We sat across from each other.

"Gretchen's dead," I said.

She said, "Oh, dear," and then she began to cry softly.

I gave her a chance to regain her composure.

"I'm sorry," she said, drying her eyes.

"I don't really want to upset you, but I felt it was easier to just say it and get it over with."

"Yes, you're right. It is easier in the long run." Then she paused and said, "I can't say I'm really surprised."

"You suspected that something illegal was going on."

"Yes, I did."

"How are you and Gretchen related, Mrs. O'Gilvie?"

"We're not."

"Then how did she come to live in your apartment in New York?"

"Oh, she's lived with me on and off ever since I took her out of Alligator Pond."

"You come from Alligator Pond?"

"Well, not exactly. I come from near there. From a place called Marchfield. Gretchen was the daughter of my best friend, Dorothy Pinto. Dorothy was a very pretty woman. She was very light skinned, like you, almost white. Her husband was one of the Germans from Alligator Pond whose ancestors were brought here one hundred years ago by the British as indentured servants. She was educated, ambitious. Schultz was just a country boy who happened to be white. He sat around and drank rum with the fellas and that was about all. Dorothy got tired of that life and went to Kingston and became involved with the prime minister's cousin. She left her daughter in the village with the father. I took the girl in and raised her. From time to time her mother would send for her, but after a week, a month, six months, she'd send her back. Dorothy eventually married the prime minister's cousin but something happened that no one really knows about. It was something illegal. Anyway, the prime minister cleared it up and Dorothy was sent away. Don't ask me why she had to leave the country and not Charlie, but after she left the incident was forgotten. Everyone agreed that she was made the scapegoat. After that Gretchen lived with me until I took her to New York.

But she was never happy. When your own mother doesn't really care for you, that hurts more than anything else. I tried to make it up to her, but it was never enough. Maybe if she hadn't known her mother, she might have just accepted me as the real thing and that would have been that. But she knew her mother, had lived through the rejections. I think that's what made it so hard for her."

"Tell me about your brother."

"Albert. I know what you're thinking, that Gretchen was involved in a scheme with that no-good tramp she was running with to get Albert's land so they could grow ganja on it. Everyone around here has been trying to get that land to grow ganja on it. They have been for years. There's nothing new in that story."

"Where is the land?"

"Just a few miles from here."

"How much land is it?"

"Quite a lot, about two thousand acres."

"And what had he done with it?"

"Nothing. That was Albert's way. He was a relatively wealthy man. But he was very casual about his wealth. He worked hard, was a lifelong bachelor, but wasn't overly ambitious. The fact that he had the land and wouldn't do anything with it bothered everyone but him. He had a construction business and a fishing business and he was content to just let the land sit there."

"What was his relationship with Enid Hylton?"

"Enid or Iris?"

She obviously knew about the switch. "The sister who was killed in her brownstone in New York a week ago."

"He loved her all his life. When she married Hylton it broke his heart. He . . . he committed suicide when he found out she was dead."

"You mean he spent his whole life alone because she married another man and then when he found out she was dead, he killed himself?"

"Yes. He got up the morning after I called him with the news and put a bullet through his head, as the poem says." And she started crying again. I waited.

"Who's his heir?"

"I am."

"Had you promised Gretchen that you would give her anything after you came into possession of the property?"

"No."

"Had she asked you for anything?"

"No."

"I think she had her eye on those two thousand acres."

"But I had no intention of allowing the land to be used for anything illegal, certainly not anything that would have gone against what my brother would have wanted. Some of the community leaders in the area were talking about a camp for poor children. A work camp. The plan was to sell off a lot of the land to pay for it."

"Who was helping you with this project?"

"A gentleman in the government."

"Does he have a name?"

"Yes, Charles Macfarlane, he's—"

"I know who he is. Do you know him . . . well?"

"Yes, quite well. We've been friends for years."

"What kind of friends?"

"People come and go in and out of each other's lives in Jamaica, almost for as long as they're alive. The island itself isn't that small, but if you're part of a certain circle, a certain class, then it is definitely quite small."

"And you and Macfarlane were from the same circle."

"Yes, we were."

"So you trusted him."

"I did and I still do."

"I believe that if you allow him to handle the selling of the land for you, all will go well, but if you don't, your life could be in danger. Have you made a will?"

"Yes."

"Who is your heir?"

"Gretchen was."

"Does the will include your brother's property?"

"No, it was made before he died."

"So unless you changed the will to specify what you wanted done with what you inherited from him, that would automatically go to her also?"

"Yes, I suppose so. That's the way wills work. But Albert's death was so sudden that I hardly had time to think about anything like that. So you think Gretchen was killed because of Albert's land?"

"Yes. Gretchen's boyfriend, Snakey, might have had plans to get the land for Gretchen by getting rid of you. But if Macfarlane is involved, removing Snakey and Gretchen would obviously give him a clear field to pretend to buy the land for a good cause and still use it for ganja growing."

"Gretchen would never have done anything to harm me."

"Snakey might not have told her about his plans."

"And Charles has always been a reputable, upstanding man."

"Maybe, but the amount of money to be made growing ganja is almost beyond comprehension. It makes for an irresistible temptation to some men. Especially if they live in a world where everyone around them is getting rich from it."

"Well, there certainly is a lot of it growing, and it doesn't seem as if the government is that particular about stopping it, either."

"Who was your brother's lawyer?"

"A man from Kingston, Audley Johnson."

Well, that was the wrong name. But I wasn't going to let that stop me. "Where will I be able to find him?"

"I have his card right here." And she went to a small table, opened a drawer, took out a card and handed it to me. I copied down the information.

"Does he have anyone working with him, a partner or someone like that?"

"Only his nephew."

"Nephew?"

"Yes, but he's not much help to him because he's an American lawyer. He was born here but he grew up in America, as I understand it."

That rang a bell. "Do you know his name?"

"I can't remember it."

"Smedley Braithwaite?"

"That's him."

I didn't bother to tell her that he was dead too.

"When did you last speak to Macfarlane, personally?"

"He called only yesterday. He said that they had gotten a group together to make the purchase. They were going to work out the details with Audley Johnson soon. This week, in fact, and that either he or Johnson would get back to me."

"Whatever you do, Mrs. O'Gilvie, don't cause trouble."

"What do you mean?"

"You intend going back to America, I take it."

"Well, eventually, yes."

"I suggest that if you trust Macfarlane that you sell him the land and take him at his word. If it turns out that he is not honorable, I would wash my hands of the whole thing and get on with my life."

"But that's . . . wrong! If I thought for one minute that Charles or anyone else was actually going to use that land to grow ganja, I'd hold onto it if my life depended on it."

"It may very well."

"What may very well?"

"Your life. It may very well depend on it."

She looked at me still not appreciating the severity of the situation.

"Look, Mrs. O'Gilvie, Gretchen is dead, her boyfriend is dead, the assistant commissioner of the CID is dead. The whole island is on the edge of an allout drug war that's going to determine who's going to control all the tourist dollars that pour into the country every day by the millions. The country's very stability is at stake. The government is at stake. I don't know all the answers, I may never know them. Half of them don't even concern me. But I'm in it, much more deeply than I want to be, and I tell you nothing or no one is sacred. The old Jamaica, the one you grew up in, is no more, not from what I can see. The ladies and the gentlemen of the inner circles and the right class get killed today along with everyone else. I saw the CID commissioner killed. I was there. It happened beside the swimming pool at dinnertime. The place was crowded and there were at least twenty eyewitnesses. But that didn't stop them. It was daring, bold, and they pulled it off. One man alone who came and went like the night. You're alone here in the country. Please don't be foolish. There's nothing you can do to stop them, nothing. Don't sacrifice yourself for your dead brother's wishes. He spent his entire life waiting for a love that never returned, and when it could no longer be he ended it all. But it was his choice. There's some satisfaction at least in that. My advice, ignoble as it may sound, is to pack up your tent, like the Arabs, and as silently steal away, as the poem says."

She was quiet, then she began to shake her head. "No, no, absolutely no. I won't do it."

At that point I was sorry I had opened my mouth. Macfarlane could probably have gotten the land without her ever suspecting that he was doing it. Now it was too late. She was going to ask questions.

"Aw right, but do me a favor. Call me at the Pegasus if anything happens to make you suspicious, and don't discuss what I've told you with anyone, including Macfarlane. I may be able to solve your problem for you."

She was so glad to hear me say that that she smiled and cried at the same time, and she took my hand and squeezed it.

"Oh, thank you, thank you. Let's have some tea."

"I can't. I have to get back to town and . . ."

But she waved me off and disappeared into the back. Either it was waiting on a tray or the maid had anticipated her because she was back in a flash, with brown sugar, milk, cookies, and tea.

I sat reluctantly and agreed to one cup.

"Why did Gretchen use her mother's name to register at the Pegasus?"

"I don't know."

"Is Pinto her mother's second husband's name, the prime minister's cousin?"

"Yes."

"When did she divorce Schultz?"

"She never did, I don't think. That's why they could get her to do what they wanted."

"There was a woman I spoke to at Alligator Pond who seemed to confuse Gretchen with her mother."

"They looked very much alike."

"And Gretchen's mother used to come back and visit her mother?"

"Yes, the mother's still alive."

"Really!"

"She must be ninety now."

"Who's Missa Mac?"

"He owns the general store in town."

"The woman in Alligator Pond told me that I would be able to find Dorothy Pinto here by asking him where she was."

"They have a house near here, or at least they used to."

"Who does?"

"Charlie and Dorothy."

"When they were married?"

"Yes, it's down near the sea. If you ask in town anyone will show it to you. Just ask for Charlie Pinto's place."

"What's your first name?"

"Evadne."

"I never would have guessed it."

"Oh, why should you have had to?"

"It's not important. What do you do now?"

"You mean once things here are settled?"

"Yes."

"I don't know. I'm a widow. We never had children. And now, with Gretchen gone and Albert, I'm all alone. Maybe I'll go back to New York, Maybe I'll . . . stay here."

"Isn't there anyone, anywhere?"

"There's a cousin in Canada. We write but I haven't seen her in ten years."

"Then maybe it's time you took a trip."

"Not if they're going to grow ganja on my brother's property!"

"No, I mean after you've straightened that out."

"Oh, after. Maybe."

I took a last sip, got up and said my goodbye. I made her repeat her promise not to let anyone think that she knew what was going on, if anything happens to be going on, and to let me know as soon as anything did go on that shouldn't be going on. She said she would, kissed me on the cheek and I left and went to meet my pilot face to face at Maud's.

10

So Cousin Charlie, also Charlie Pinto, not only had a house near Red Gal Ring, but he also had one in Yallas. I hoped someone was home. As we drove down there, my arthritic friend and I, I decided I had better tell him what kind of league we were playing cricket in. I made him pull over to the side of the road and turn around so there'd be no chance of his not understanding me.

"I said we may run into trouble down there, so I don't want you to drive all the way in."

"What kind of trouble?"

"I'm not sure, but I think you should park nearby and wait."

"Wait for what?"

"Wait to see what happens. If you hear shooting, or anything that sounds like violence, screams for instance, then get the police and tell them to contact Chief Inspector Collins"—I hoped he was a Chief Inspector—"at headquarters in Kingston. Collins. Remember that."

And he nodded and then said, "Yes" he understood.

We drove a little farther and then he pulled up on the side of a dirt road and told me to get out. We walked about ten yards and stood at the edge of a clump of trees. He pointed to a low beach house tucked behind a sand hill just below it and to the left of us.

"How long should I wait?"

"For as long as it takes. But don't wait here, go back to the main road and park by the bus stop we just passed. If anyone sees you, they'll think you're waiting for someone to come in on the bus."

"Pretty smart, pretty smart." And he trundled off, mumbling to himself, "I hope I'll be able to hear the shots that far away."

I went down to the edge of the sand hill. The roof of the house was just a little higher than where I was standing. But it was too far away for me to jump without making a noise. There was a tree, but I decided against cat and mouse. Besides, the house didn't seem to be that big. I checked the revolver, stuck it in my waist, pulled my shirt out and over it, and went around to the side. I couldn't see up over the window once I got down on the level with the house. The house itself was very wide. The front porch went all the way across, from end to end. It seemed an expensive affair from the outside. Charlie believed in going first class all the way, I guess, all the time.

But there were two levels. A flight of stairs led from the beach right up to the porch. Beneath it was a second level where the showers were and the equipment. And the biggest piece of equipment was a bruiser posing as a lifeguard. He was sitting in a beach chair under the porch, with only a pair of swim trunks to cover his muscles. And were they ever bulging. I waited. He moved to his right to get some lotion to make the muscles gleam even more, and that's when I got in behind him. He turned while sitting, the lotion in his right hand, he in the act of coming back to an upright position. I had the gun out and I was just standing there waiting for his first move. He was about to make it. I was all for letting him—at least he would no longer be at my back —but something made me stop him.

"Don't. Charlie doesn't pay you that much money. And besides, you'll never live to find out how much fun your grandchildren are gonna be."

He dropped the lotion. I motioned him up. He stood. I looked in his eyes all the time. It takes a hell of a lot of practice to disguise the eyes. I've looked at a man's hands and he's still been fast enough to beat me, even though I saw it coming. But not the eyes. It's not only that they tell you when the other guy's going to make his move, but they tell your eyes. And your eyes move a lot faster when they get the signal from other eyes. I guess eyes believe eyes more than they believe anything else.

Anyway, his eyes said he had ideas. And he thought he was good enough to take me, gun or no gun. And he probably was, if he got lucky. I was going to take away his luck and fast. I motioned him to put his hands behind his neck. He did it. Just then a man came onto the porch and called down, "Donald, Donald." I motioned "no" with my head.

"Donald! Where the rass that bway gahn?" And he started down the stairs.

Donald's eyes got excited, but I smiled, cocked the gun, and pointed at his head. He froze. The man came halfway down, I motioned Donald back inside the door, crossed in front of him and stood with my back against the window, the gun pointing at his head as I held it in my right hand across my chest. The man looked between the stairs, but didn't seem to see us. He called again, then stalked back up. I motioned Donald inside. It was gleaming with tile and marble. There were bicycles, charcoal broilers, beach chairs, umbrellas, mopeds, showers, a sauna, everything.

"Is that Charlie Pinto, Donald?"

He said nothing. It wasn't going to work. This son of a bitch was just too hard a case. I picked up a beach mat, doubled it and put it over the gun, and fired straight at him. But I held the gun just far enough back so that the bullet lodged in the mat. That was his last chance. The fool jumped me with his hands! He couldn't get to the gun because I had the mat in front of it, so he tried to choke me to death. I dropped half the mat and fired again. This time I dug the gun into it. The bullet blew out his chest. He fell against a moped and made a hell of a racket. The second shot had been muffled enough so that it sounded like it could have been a limb snapping from a tree.

The man came back and yelled through the stairs, "Donald, if you got some gal in there, get rid of her and bring your ahse up here, fas'!" And he stalked back upstairs.

I looked down at Donald. He was menacing, even in death. Then a door at the rear caught my eye. I went to it and opened it slowly. I smelled food. I looked up and there was a small staircase just wide enough for one adult to use. I heard the man again. "Gwendolyn!" He was in the back now. "She put on the pot, but she gone. Suppose it catch fire and burn down my house. Bway, you can't get good help these days. Everybody, rass, independent. Is equality them want. Them betta learn fe work fe it first."

"You sent her to town, remember." It was a woman's voice, and while I couldn't be certain whose it was, I really was. But I had to see for myself. He went back to the front and I came up the stairs. I put the gun away, opened the narrow door and looked in on the kitchen. He had turned off the fire, but the room was filled with an aroma that almost took my mind off business. I looked right and there was one big room with a sliding glass door separating it from the room I was in. The glass door was open. He had his back to me, and I saw her legs, the right one over the left and swinging back and forth. They were the right legs all right, but I still wanted to see the face to be sure. I moved forward, staying to my right, and saw the thighs, waist and breasts, arm holding a drink. Then she leaned forward and it was none other than good ole Regina!

She turned and saw me and dropped the glass and said, "Oh, my God."

Charlie, for that's who it had to be, turned, saw me, and ran to a desk drawer. I pulled out my gun and fired once, hitting the front of the drawer. He stopped, not knowing what to do, but he didn't turn around.

"Relax, Charlie, play the host, offer me a drink, and you won't get hurt."

He looked at Regina, over his left shoulder, and she nodded. He immediately assumed a calm manner and went to the other side of the room where the bar was. I came in, crossed the room, opened the drawer and took out the gun—an automatic, very expensive, very light, very compact. I put it in my side pocket and put the pistol back in my waist. I felt like a ten-ton truck, but I was out there in no-man's land, with nobody to call on for help, so far as I really knew. I was feeling insecure and unsure of myself in no small measure. That's when you really get mean. As I looked back on it, Donald didn't really have to die, but my margin of error was too thin, so he was dead.

Charlie fixed me a drink. He didn't even ask what I wanted. I watched him. It smelled all right, good old scotch. I took a sip, decided not to finish it, even though I didn't think it was drugged. Put it down and leaned against the top of the desk that the gun had come from.

"I'm afraid, Charlie, that that shot is going to bring the police."

Charlie all but laughed in my face when I said it, although he tried to hide it. He probably owned every cop on the island.

"And I know what you're thinking, but Macfarlane can't help you. Collins just went to your uncle with the evidence. He's going to ask for Macfarlane's resignation before he puts him under house arrest. What he's going to do with you, well, that's between the two of you. Comes under the heading of a family affair. But you tried it once before, didn't you? And he forgave you. He won't do it twice. Setting yourself up as a feudal lord with an independent empire in ganja, and this time adding a fortune in tourist dollars—doesn't it undermine the system, throw off the balance of power? After all, he's got enough problems, does the ole P.M. With all of his other enemies, he really can't afford an enemy within, can he? Certainly not one who's been punished, once, but just won't behave himself. I think your number's up, Charlie boy. But calling it in is not my job."

Then I turned to Regina. "So I got your hundred thousand

dollars in for you. The mob boys in New York City gave it to you to give old Charlie. It was the final payment on the deal. And Charlie was to deliver the ganja, all of it, and the black market action, all of it, in one fell swoop. Only you had to play it close, both of you, because a lot of strange faces suddenly popping up would have ruined it.

"I wonder what happened to the immigration officer who found it in the suitcase you gave me? I bet the poor boy's dead, even though he was plan B. But there's a leak in Charlie's operation somewhere. There has to be, otherwise once the money got here, he would have gotten it and I would have disappeared without a trace, or else the money would have and I wouldn't have been able to prove that I even had it in the first place. Who's giving you trouble, Charlie, huh? Let me think. Not Macfarlane. No, the two of you have to be working together. Who's causing the trouble, Charlie, huh, who?"

"Look behind you, and you'll find out."

I had moved away from the desk in my overzealousness, my back to the front porch. I turned and there was Marlene, holding a gun on me.

"Now careful, Joe, I know how tricky you are, so don't force me to ruin that beautiful body."

"He has two guns," Charlie said quickly. He was about to move toward me.

"No," Marlene shouted. "Don't do that! You get between us and anything can happen. Where's the first one, Joe?"

I carefully raised my shirt and pointed to it.

"Take it out slowly, and watch how you hold the handle. Throw it on the floor at my feet. Careful now."

I did as I was told.

"Good, now where's number two?"

"In my pocket."

"Okay, take it out, just like the first one, steady!"

I put my hand in my pocket, drew the gun halfway out, slowly, looking her right in the eyes as I did so. When I got it halfway, I fired through my pants pocket and got her in the chest. Her gun went off, but the shot was wild. She fell against the door, raised her arm and aimed at me again, but the pain was too great and she couldn't steady her hand. The second shot went by me and hit Regina, who was trying to get out of the line of fire. That's when Marlene gave it up. She dropped the gun to her side and sank to the floor. She was bleeding badly. I looked over at Regina. She was dead.

"You'd better call for an ambulance, Charlie."

He was horrified by what he'd just seen and it paralyzed him.

"Charlie!" He roused himself and got on the phone. But he wasn't calling an ambulance. Then I heard sirens screaming and we were suddenly drowning in policemen of every stripe and variety. Weapons everywhere. I was handcuffed and put in a corner. Charlie had disappeared. And no one knew what to do. But they did take Marlene away to get her medical attention. My arthritic friend finally appeared and managed to get over to me and whisper in my ear, "Collins is coming."

Collins and Percy finally showed up. I was uncuffed and made to feel at my ease.

"So you were a good guy after all," I finally said. "Both of you."

They said nothing.

"Where's Charlie?" I asked.

"We don't know. The fool of a lieutenant let him get away," said Collins.

"Well, you didn't expect him to actually arrest the prime minister's cousin, did you?"

"No, but he could have detained him."

"How many women was Charlie, uh, shall we say *associating* with?"

"Who knows?" Collins again.

"How many stars are there in the sky?" Percy.

"What are we hanging around here for?" I wanted to know.

"We're waiting for a report on what, if anything, is in the house."

"You won't find anything here. You'd better round up all those black market boys and tell them Charlie's no longer a threat, so they can relax. That was the real problem, wasn't it? Everyone was gearing up for war because they thought big boys from across the pond were moving in?"

"Half of them wanted to fight and half wanted to sell out."

"Why did you go through the charade of giving me eyeglasses with a knife and the rest of it, and pretending that you wanted me to help you catch them at it?"

"That was Macfarlane, trying to eliminate some of the competition." Collins.

"So he was in it with Charlie?"

"It was a decision he made at the last minute, which is why we were fooled." Percy.

"Brown and Percy both got suspicious at about the same time," Collins said. I looked over at Percy and he nodded agreement.

"Somebody had been tipping off the key guys, the ones who were going to sell out to Charlie," Collins continued. "So we were doing their work for them, knocking off the ones they wanted knocked off and leaving their group intact so that they had an in-place operator with which to do business with the boys from New York."

"Yeah, the New York boys don't like to come into anything that's too clean. They want someone left over to do the go-fer work."

"What's that?" Collins.

"Fetching and carrying."

"Exactly." Percy.

"Where's Macfarlane now?"

"Disappeared." Collins.

"So why did you drive off like that this morning?" I asked Percy.

"Because I thought Brown was protecting Prudence Gillesslee. Collins had a tap on Charlie's phone and he heard Charlie tell Prudence she had to come up with the money tomorrow."

"That would be the money that Snakey killed Braithwaite for, but couldn't find. How and why Snakey, Gretchen and Prudence were working together is your little puzzle. But I think Braithwaite and his partner, Aubuchon, were going to use the money, which they separated from Enid Hylton before she died, somehow, to buy the two thousand acres that are sitting just a few miles from here, left by one Albert Williams, who killed himself last week."

"How did you know about that?" Collins.

"That's why I'm down here, remember." Then I paused. "So you and Collins were sure of each other," I said to Percy, "but neither of you knew whether or not to trust Brown or Macfarlane."

"Macfarlane used Brown two ways. First, he led Brown to suspect us, then he pointed a finger, very discreetly, you understand, at Brown for us to see. So that we ended up suspecting Brown and Brown ended up suspecting us."

"And I guess he killed Brown when it was time to make an exit."

"Exactly!" Percy.

The lieutenant reported that there was nothing in the way of money or ganja to be found on the premises, so we left. Back at the Pegasus I changed, ordered up dinner, and tried to eat some, but had no taste for it. I wandered out onto the balcony. Night was coming down again: the twinkling lights, the moving cars, the sound of the tropics, the sense of sand and sea and shore in the distance.

I had a cognac, but there was no taste to it. I changed and went to bed. The phone rang about an hour later and woke me up. It was the overseas operator. Westchester had called several times. She couldn't get me, but she had found a way to leave a message with an operator in Miami who, for a fee, would see that I was contacted within twenty-four hours and given the message. The message was: "When do you return to New York? Please contact me as soon as possible."

Well, I was awake, but I was wiped out inside. The Marlene thing had been a real shock. I still hadn't put all of that together yet. Then I heard a key in the door. My guns were somewhere in Yallas, and I had forgotten to put the chain on. I stood there in the dark and waited. The door opened. She came in, closed it behind her, and put the chain on. Crossed the room, undressing as she did so, got to the bed, realized I wasn't there. Stopped, looked around. Saw me. Came over. Took me back to it, and, emotionally wrought as I was, when she was through with me, I slept like a baby.

The next morning, after Amanda had left, Collins called. The prime minister sent his personal thanks. Both Charlie and Mac-farlane had fled the country. The threat of a New York mob takeover of the ganja trade in Jamaica was over, and so was the threat of a dollar war, I supposed. They had the situation under control and most of the money spent by tourists would now go into the economy instead of into the pockets of the local hoods.

"What can I do for you? Ask for anything you want. You've got it," he declared.

"What's going to happen to Marlene Campbell?"

"I don't really know. No charges have been filed yet. Unless you want to file some."

I assured him I didn't.

"Where is she?" I asked.

"In the main hospital in town. Sedated and under guard."

"May I see her?"

"Of course." And he gave me the information. "What else?"

"I still need to know who's buried in Dr. Gillesslee's grave and who is buried in Enid Hylton's husband's grave. I don't know where he's buried and I don't know his first name. But a Mrs. O'Gilvie, Albert Williams's sister, should know."

"Check. If she doesn't, we'll find it for you."

"That's it. And thanks for Amanda."

"She was actually Macfarlane's idea initially, but she apparently enjoyed her work so much that she went beyond the call of duty. But then you would know about that better than I."

"Well, thanks anyway."

Marlene was bandaged up and not very talkative.

"I'm leaving for New York today, Marlene. Is there anything you want to tell me?"

"Anything about what?"

"Well, your sister, for one."

"She knew what she was doing."

"Did she?"

"Yes."

"Why was she killed?"

"Because she had control of the money."

"And?"

"And they wanted it."

"But no one actually made her an offer. At least when I talked to her they hadn't."

"Maybe, but the Hylton woman told her the risks and she foolishly went ahead anyway."

"And you?"

"I wasn't an heir."

"No, but someone thought that Mrs. Hylton had given me some of the money to keep for her. That's how you got into the act, isn't it? You were supposed to find out what I had and separate me from it. Isn't that how it was supposed to have happened?"

"Leave me alone. I'm in pain."

"I'm sorry. I think I could have liked your sister if I'd gotten to know her." And I left.

| 318 |

Back at the hotel, Collins was waiting for me. We went into the pub and sat in front of a couple of beers.

"I have the court orders. We can go out and dig up the graves this afternoon. When had you planned on leaving?"

"I thought of leaving today, but there's no rush. Look, I don't want to be crass about this, but I haven't any money. Not with me at any rate."

"Come, come. It's true we've confiscated the hundred thousand, although Macfarlane almost got his hands on it."

"It was mob money intended for Charlie."

"Yes, we know that. Which is why we're going to be so generous with it and give you ten percent."

"Well, that's certainly a good day's pay."

"If it were up to me, you'd get it all."

"No, ten percent is more than generous."

"And while you stay on the island everything is on the house."

"That's tempting, but I have to get back to New York."

"What's the hurry?"

"Believe it or not, I still have a murder to solve."

"I would have thought you'd solved enough murders to last you a year."

"Oh, I have. But this one comes under the heading of a debt unpaid. Have you talked to Prudence Gillesslee?"

"No. Can't find her."

"I still don't know why she put that In Memoriam notice in the paper after her father had been dead for three years."

"Sentiment."

"No, she didn't love him. She just wanted his money so she could buy back Charlie boy."

"I'm a policeman. I have a policeman's mind. That means I like things to be orderly. And I like all the pieces to fit into place when it's all over."

"That's asking a lot."

"It must be because this one is a bit too complicated for me."

"Maybe, but . . . but let's go back a bit. An English doctor dies and leaves a lot of money. His housekeeper was in America with some of it before he died, waiting for him to show up and claim it. But he can't because he's dead. Yet she continues to wait. She doesn't spend it or give it away. Why?"

"Because the doctor isn't dead," he offered.

"Right. That's why she's waiting. She knows he's alive but she can't do anything to help because she's using her sister's name."

"Right."

"Well, we'll certainly find out when we open the grave."

"Right again."

"If he's not in it, we have to find him."

"It's a big island. He could be dead and buried someplace else."

"And Hylton?"

"His grave is in another parish."

"Well, let's get going."

All the time that we were driving to the cemetery to find out if Dr. Gillesslee was actually in his grave, I kept thinking that if he were alive, three years was a long time to keep someone under wraps, especially against his will. What had happened to what was left of his property? Did it go to Prudence? If he was legally dead, then it didn't matter whether they kept him alive or not. The heir could collect everything there was to collect in three years. And where was the other Hylton brother, Iris's husband, the one with no money of his own? According to his wife he was in Jamaica somewhere. She didn't know where.

The two men were tied together somehow. I was sure of it. By the time we got to the cemetery, I was getting closer to it. But I still needed help.

We waited while they dug it up. The grave was empty. Collins found a rum shop and we sat in front of a couple of them this time.

"Well, orderly mind, what have you got?" I asked.

"I told you, this one's too complicated for me. Besides, I only know half of it."

"A lot of Jamaicans, little people, working people, were beaten up, threatened, in some cases killed, for Jamaican property. Who was it all going to?"

"Charlie."

"All of it?"

"Most of it."

"And the rest?"

"Who knows?"

"Macfarlane would know."

"But he's skipped, I told you."

"Has he?"

"If he's still here, the only future he has is a long stay in the penitentiary. And remember we have no parole system in Jamaica. What you get, you serve."

"I bet you he's going to call your prime minister to make a deal."

"My prime minister doesn't make deals."

"Not even a deal to get Cousin Charlie? You see, somebody's got to show up to explain the loss of the hundred thousand to the boys in New York. They don't believe in keeping sloppy books. It would have been Regina's tab to make good, but Regina's dead. So TAG, Charlie's it. That's why Macfarlane can deal for him. He's got no place to run to. They don't want Macfarlane, they want Charlie. Charlie's got no future, either in New York or Kingston. Macfarlane might be able to land on his feet in either town."

I was underestimating Charlie, but I didn't know it at the time.

"Let me see if I can guess what you're getting at. If Gillesslee is alive, his daughter would know it."

"Right."

"And since she was trying to deal herself in with Charlie, and since she's also disappeared, maybe she knows where he is too."

"Right."

"That's as far as my orderly mind goes."

"Where would a Charlie, or even a Macfarlane, go to hide?"

"Oh, there are too many places. I wouldn't know where to begin."

"What about the hotel, the Casa Monte?"

"No, it's used too often for official functions."

"Tell me about Espeut."

"Espeut?"

"Yes. Isn't he managing the hotel now?"

"I wouldn't know. Why?"

"Macfarlane talked to him yesterday, when we were supposedly looking for Charlie."

"Espeut. You mean the Espeut who works at the Pegasus?"

"That's the one."

"He's been Charlie's shadow for years."

"Well, well. So Macfarlane was telling Espeut to tip off Charlie to get out."

"And since we were closing in, he had to get rid of Snakey and Gretchen or take them along."

"Right. They hadn't come up with the money, but Snakey had Gretchen, who had the two thousand acres to deal with."

"So then why kill them?"

"Because Macfarlane had another way to get to it, by buying it from the dead man's sister, Mrs. O'Gilvie, or pretending to, at any rate."

"Right."

"And even if he did have to buy it, it probably was the easier way out at that point."

"So what do you want to do now?"

"Have somebody you trust check the Hylton grave. If there's a body I need a medical identification to the degree that it's possible. But you and I have to tail Espeut."

"Now you're playing my game. Let's go."

And he meant it.

After he'd set the wheels in motion on the Hylton grave exhumation, we drove to the Casa Monte. This time there was a man out front in khaki. Collins talked to him, then we parked and went in.

Espeut was sitting at a desk in a room that was marked Manager's Office. He was a little man with glasses and a moustache. Collins introduced me. "This gentleman is a detective from New York. We're trying to find Prudence Gillesslee. Didn't she used to work for you at one time?"

Espeut seemed nervous and removed. He wiped his glasses. He didn't get up. "No," he said. "She did public relations for the hotel."

"Right," Collins came back. "She's not at her home and she's not at her father's house. And no one's seen her. Does she have any friends or the like that she might go to that you know of?"

"Is this official?"

"Yes, it is, I'm afraid. And we'd appreciate any help we can get."

Espeut looked at me, sweated some more, then coughed. "Well, if I hear anything, I will certainly pass it along."

"Thanks. And if you know of anyone who might be trying to help her stay out of sight, please tell them for me that we will not be understanding about it. Not at all. I know that you don't come under that category, but if you know of anyone who does, pass that word along for me, that we will not deal lightly with that sort of disruption."

Espeut looked very solemn as he nodded.

Then we left.

"What about the phone?" I asked him.

"I doubt it. Besides that phone only goes to an office in Government House. It was a measure instituted to cut down expenses."

"So what's the plan?"

"The man out front is mine."

We drove to the Castleton Gardens Police Station and waited. Half an hour later we got the call. He was coming our way. Would pass us in about five minutes. We had to scramble to get the car out of sight. He passed right in front, driving a small Austin, relatively new, dark blue. When about two minutes had elapsed, one of Collins's motorcycle boys took up the trail. We followed behind a few minutes later. We drove at a leisurely thirty, thirty-five miles per hour. We never saw either the motorcycle or Espeut's blue Austin. After fifteen minutes, I got worried. "Suppose we've lost them?"

"There are several side roads that go into small, interior districts. But there's nothing in there except farms and little villages and some large plantations here and there. If he'd turned off into any of those I would have been contacted."

"Suppose your man lost him?"

"I would have been contacted."

"So no contact means he's got him in his sights."

"That's what it means."

"Where does this road lead?"

"It leads to the north coast. It's called the Junction Road. It's a bit tricky, but it's not as bad as Mount Diablo."

"Yes, I went over that one. Talk about hills going straight up. How long before we get to the north coast?"

"Two hours."

"You're kidding?"

"No, we're crossing the entire island from south to north."

"Are we prepared for a trip like that?"

"We will be. Settle back. Unless you hear him beeping in, there's nothing to do but enjoy the scenery."

Just when I was about to relax and put my head back, I saw a flashing yellow light. "What's that?"

"That means we stop."

"Oh."

| 324 |

"He's probably getting gas."

"Suppose he spots your man?"

"There's always a chance of that."

We waited for a good twenty minutes, then the yellow began to blink again.

"They're off."

We pulled into the gas station and Collins put his watch on —a timer—had the guy put in gas, got beers and beef patties, and we were back on the road in less than six minutes. We sped until we saw the motorcycle in the distance, then we slowed down again and it stayed that way for the next two hours.

When we descended from the mountain down to the north shore it was getting on early evening. A breeze had whipped up. As we came off the mountain, we descended into a large seaport town. The motorcycle policeman was at the interchange sitting and waiting for us. We pulled up beside him.

"He's on his way to Montego Bay."

"Call it in to St. Ann's Bay. Use the same code."

"Right." And he saluted Collins as we drove off.

"We're heading due west as you can see. The sea to our right and more small districts of the interior to our left. Of course he could go inland and double back to Kingston. He'd have to drive all night to do it though. There are no direct roads."

Night was falling fast.

"How well are the roads lighted in the interior at night?"

"Not well at all. A thousand to one he's going to Montego Bay."

It was a good, flat road. And with the breeze behind us, we were really moving. Every so often the road would veer inland, only to return to the sea. There were times when it spread out to a four-lane highway, two in each direction. But he was no-where in sight.

Collins called St. Ann's Bay. They hadn't seen him.

"We've lost him," Collins said.

"But how?"

"He went inland somewhere between here and St. Ann's Bay."

"St. Ann's Bay. Could he have gone to Alligator Pond?"

"Yes."

"Then that's probably where he's headed."

"It'll be tricky. You can see a light moving for miles up in there at night. Once he gets into the hills, he can look down and there we'll be."

"But if he can see us, we can see him."

"True, but the object is not to let him see us."

"But he won't know for sure."

"I suppose you're right. It's the chance we'll have to take anyway, isn't it?"

He told St. Ann's Bay what he was doing in code. "Just in case he's on to us and tries to double back." And we took the road to Alligator Pond. Fifteen minutes after we were on it, we saw him. He was going at a steady pace. He was above us. Of course we only saw the lights, but it was a good bet, as Collins pointed out.

"You can tell by the way the lights are set that it's not a truck or a van or a bus. It's about the right size. We'll soon know." Then his yellow light flashed. They were warning him that he was getting out of range.

"We can go on and risk losing contact. Which means that if he has given us the slip and they spot him, they won't be able to tell us. Or we can sit here and wait, and hope he comes back, if he's up there."

"I say we go on."

He told them to pursue if they couldn't contact us, and Espeut reappeared, and we went on.

The car kept disappearing and then reappearing around curves. Then it left the main road, Collins said. He could tell by the herky jerk motion. Then it stopped and the lights went out.

"Now what do we do?" I asked.

We were at least three minutes away.

"Hope that another light comes on."

It did and none too soon. We were about to take the wrong road when we saw it, it was a house light. Collins pulled over and stopped and turned out his lights. "We can't go in there," he explained. "If they see us coming we've gone through all this for nothing."

We waited, then we saw them, a man and a woman, get into the car, followed by another man who seemed like Espeut. Then the car started up. It was startling when they did it, the night had been so deadly quiet with no one or nothing moving for miles around. No lights anywhere, not even a house light, just empty darkness.

They came back toward us, high beams on. But we were well hidden. They turned left and went back the way Espeut had come. It was the same Austin, license plates and all. We waited for a long time, then Collins started up. And we slowly went down the mountain behind them. As soon as we got within range of the radio contact he called ahead and told them to be at the main road ready to go in either direction, but still tailing, then we took it easy. We lost them down near the end, other cars coming and going, and we didn't get close enough to tell the Austin from the rest.

When we got to the main road we were told that they had continued on toward Montego Bay. We had no way of telling who had gotten into the car at the house or even if Espeut was still driving. St. Ann's Bay had used an unmarked car to trail them. Their man, who met us, gave Collins the license plate number of the unmarked car.

"Good, now we're set all the way into Mo Bay," Collins said, smiling.

Two hours later we pulled into Montego Bay and stopped at the first gas station when the phone buzzed. It was the Montego Bay police. They hadn't stopped, they were going right through.

The unmarked car was still behind them. They were picking up speed. He didn't know if he'd been spotted or not. Collins looked at the gas gauge and said, "We'll just have to chance it," and we sped off.

We were moving again, passing the well-lit, thickly populated tourist area and heading due west. As fast as we were going, we never saw the unmarked car. Somebody else must have been driving the Austin, that was for sure. An hour later we were heading into a town called Negril, when we passed the unmarked car. I don't know how Collins spotted him on the side of the road, but he did. He slowed down gradually, pulled to a stop, waited, then carefully did a U-turn, came back up and pulled across from him. They talked to each other by radio.

The Austin had stopped at a beach house down the dirt road that he was parked in front of. There had been two people in the back of the car, he said, but he couldn't really tell much more about them than that. There was a big hotel to the left. The field separating the road from the water was flat grass with a few trees. The house sat near the water. There was a smaller house to the right and a boat on blocks up from the beach. Water seemed to be all around us.

"Are we close to the western tip of the island?" I asked.

"Very close," he said. "Another ten miles and you've got nothing but water."

"Well, the orderly mind has done its job. What's our next move?"

"A closer look."

He told his man we were going in. He was to stay put. We got out and crossed the road. Collins asked him, "Any dogs?"

"Didn't see any."

"O.K. You know what to do."

"Yes, sir."

There was no gate as such, just the dirt road for cars. The fencing, what little there was, was just one or two pieces of barbed wire with simple posts holding it up. You could pick your spot to enter; it was all open.

"Is that private property or what?"

"Out here things are pretty informal. They own the land the house is on. How much of anything else they own is anyone's guess. Even that hundred-million-dollar hotel next door doesn't have a fence around it. And there are no fences on the beach anywhere on this part of the island."

"So coming and going by land or sea is pretty simple."

"Even simpler by sea. As you see, we can block a land route at several points along the road in this area, as it gets quite narrow."

Well, if they were leaving by sea they'd picked a good spot for it. And no question.

"Have you seen the car?" I asked him.

"No."

We took the road and went right to the smaller house first. It was a boathouse. The equipment seemed new. But the boat that was on blocks hadn't been in the water for quite some time. We were standing there, making sure we hadn't missed anything, when a huge dog suddenly appeared from nowhere. He was quiet and staring. But he didn't seem to be about to do much of anything else other than sniff us out for good or bad intentions. We pretended our hearts weren't beating a mile a minute and he went away.

"We were lucky," Collins said. "In Kingston or even Montego Bay he would have been all over us. But out here, it's very casual. They even train the dogs differently."

"Of course, he could always change his mind and come back," I offered.

"True, but I doubt it."

We moved to the larger house, one eye on the dog and one on the house. But the mutt disappeared as he had come, silently and effortlessly.

The car was nowhere in sight. There were tire tracks on the hard sand, in front of the house, that led to the hotel.

"Espeut must have driven over to the hotel. I guess he decided to spend the night. It would certainly be a long drive back to Kingston."

"And maybe his job isn't over," I suggested.

"Maybe."

We looked in through the side window. There was an older white man, who could have been Gillesslee. Collins didn't know him and the newspaper photos I'd seen were no help. This man had a stub of beard and he was dressed shabbily. Then Prudence came into the room. She seemed solicitous of him. But he was distant. He acted like a man who hadn't seen the sun in years.

Then I felt something at my leg.

"Don't jump, whatever you do," Collins said.

The dog had returned. When he finished sniffing me, he sniffed Collins. We waited. He waited. Finally, we sauntered off. He did too, in a different direction.

"Let's see what our friend is up to," Collins said.

When we got to the line that separated the hotel from the part of the beach we were on, a guard suddenly appeared and stopped us. Collins identified himself and asked the man about Espeut.

Espeut was well known at the hotel and had been let through. He drove his car around to the parking lot. He's spending the night, the guard thought, but he wasn't sure.

We went round to the front desk and asked for the manager. When the three of us were behind closed doors, Collins told him, in no uncertain terms, that he did not want Espeut to know we were there. Collins then told him that he wanted to know what phone calls Espeut made, as soon as he made them, and where he made them and to whom. And if he left the hotel, he wanted to know that too, and right away. The manager didn't seem to want any trouble. He was more than willing to cooperate, but he told Collins that when Espeut drove down like that and spent the night, it was usually for only one reason.

"What reason is that?"

"To meet Charlie Pinto," he said.

"Where do they meet?"

"Charlie brings his boat in from a small island off the north coast and docks it at the marina just up the beach."

"Which island?"

"Cayman Brac."

Bingo, I thought. Another trail come full circle. The same island whose prime minister had been caught in Florida smuggling dope. But I said nothing.

"How does Espeut know that he's coming?" Collins asked.

"It's usually prearranged, I guess. Sometimes Charlie calls him and he leaves soon after."

"But does he ever call Charlie first?"

"Sometimes."

"We'll be at the pool bar. Call me there when something happens."

"Will do."

We went to the pool bar and some of the young people were swimming nude. They'd get close to the pool, take off their suits, and quickly jump in the water and then swim to the bar and sit under the the water up to their waist and order a drink. The women showed breasts in most cases. But everyone pretended that they'd been used to seeing such pulchritude in public all their lives. Collins was enjoying it immensely when the phone rang. It was for us. He took it and talked briefly, keeping his eye on the main attraction as he did so. Then he came back.

"Espeut called Cayman Brac. The operator said she thinks he's coming over tonight."

"How long does it take?"

"About forty-five minutes. Charlie has a cruiser launch that makes very good time."

We had to tear ourselves away from the breasts at the bar, but there was no help for it. We went back to the car and Collins called Montego Bay. We needed a launch, but we couldn't wait for them to send one. They called back. There was one at the lighthouse at Negril that wasn't being used. It was kept as a spare in case the regular launch that patrolled the western tip of the island broke down.

Collins checked with his man in the unmarked car, then we drove to the lighthouse and got the launch and a pilot to go with it. We left the car there and came back by sea to the marina and docked just north of it, behind a jetty. Close to forty minutes had gone by. As soon as we docked we saw a boat come out of the distance. It was about five minutes away. Immediately Prudence and the older man appeared on the dock and Espeut came across from the hotel. The man piloting Charlie's boat was young and muscular. We didn't see Charlie anywhere. Espeut handed the man an envelope and Prudence and the older man got into the boat. Espeut stood there watching as they turned around and were off.

Espeut stood for a while, then he went back across to the hotel. We waited another few minutes, then we followed the other boat. Our pilot told us that there were a lot of boats out doing moonlight cruises with young tourists, so we wouldn't arouse suspicion once we got to sea. We stayed at a distance. It was a clear night in the tropics. They put into Cayman Brac and we stayed out to sea and waited, pretending that we were giving some young couples a Caribbean night under the stars. Our boat had binoculars, but we weren't near enough to see anything. We moved closer, gradually, then we focused in. Collins took a look first, then handed the glasses to me. The pilot was closing up shop for the night. I gave the glasses back to Collins.

"Well, I think it's time we went ashore," I said.

"That could be tricky."

"True. Of course, I could go alone and you could sit it out and wait for me to make it back, one way or another."

"Not practical. We have the entire resources of the island of Jamaica at our disposal if we can get them here in time. I say we go together and send the boat back for help."

"All right. What kind of weapons do you have on board?"

Collins turned to the pilot, who produced an array of handguns, rifles, and plenty of ammunition. We each took a handgun. Collins also took a rifle.

"Now how do we get ashore?" he asked.

"There's an abandoned wharf about a mile down on the leeward side. I can let you off there," said the pilot.

Collins looked at me and I nodded.

"Where's Pinto's house?" Collins asked.

"About half a mile directly inland from where the boat is docked."

We got to the abandoned wharf and jumped out. It was mostly dry rot and we had to be careful where we stepped. The launch turned around and headed back to Jamaica. We were in a different country. Collins had no authority on the island. But we weren't going to let that stop us.

"What's the story over here since the prime minister was arrested for drug running by U.S. narcotics agents?"

"Pretty chaotic."

"Did you know that Charlie had a house here?"

"Yes, but I never gave it much thought. It wasn't connected to a case that I was working on in any way."

"How does it tie into the Jamaica situation?"

"Charlie could run everything from here without any difficulty. His money, his men, his drugs, it's all here. The gossip says he got the prime minister arrested because he wouldn't cooperate with him and they needed a free hand on the island."

Now that made a lot of sense. Regina would certainly want to shield Charlie's name from me while at the same time telling me about the prime minister's problems. I was getting excited. Now I felt close, closer than I'd felt since this whole thing started.

We treaded our way back, following the coastline.

"The damned island seems abandoned," I said.

"This part is fairly well deserted. The population is mostly on the east end and around the other side."

"So Charlie's got a perfect spot in which to do as he pleases."

"Pretty much."

We got up to the house and stopped about twenty yards away.

"I've broken every rule in the book tonight. And now I'm about to break the one rule that should never be broken."

"I know, and for what it's worth you've got my respect for doing it. Most chief inspectors wouldn't cross a road even with an army protecting them."

"Actually, it's been a long time since I've been in the saddle, so to speak. It feels great."

"True, but you're really just helping me. You have no stake in what's going on. If you want, I can go in alone."

"You saved us. By exposing Charlie the way you did, you probably made it possible for us to beat this thing. It's the least I can do. Besides, if we get rid of his operation once and for all, then my job will certainly be a lot easier."

We looked around for dogs or wire fences or some sort of security, but could find none. We were in close now, so close that we could see silhouettes through the curtains.

"Where are the bodyguards?" I asked.

"He probably thinks he's safe. Charlie was always a gambler who believed that no matter what happened, he would never get hurt."

"I see. But if he got the prime minister arrested, how come he's still here?" I asked.

"Good question. Maybe the prime minister doesn't know that Charlie was responsible."

"Maybe. But if he's being protected, he probably bought it. That would account for the lack of concern over security."

"Yes, it would."

We heard shouting and moved closer. There was certainly no one protecting the grounds that we could see. I guess Charlie assumed that once out of Jamaica, he had nothing to fear from Jamaica. Maybe he was right. The house was a simple one-room affair. Really just a bungalow. The curtains on our side were drawn halfway. We went right up. I found a building block made out of brick and stood to get a good look. Collins watched my back.

There was a very heated argument going on. Charlie was pacing, but he wasn't doing the screaming. The old man was sitting in the center of the room looking blankly ahead. Prudence was on her feet and banging on the table with her hands. Who she was yelling at I didn't know. It was someone to my right. I could hear her calling Prudence a bitch. And calling Charlie a bitch. I knew the voice, and then again I wasn't sure. I tried to lean to my left to get a better angle. That's when she charged Prudence and the two of them started pulling each other's hair and scratching and clawing. Before long they were rolling on the ground. The old man never moved. Charlie finally broke it up and seemed to give all of his energy to the other woman. Pushing her back and threatening to give her a good sock in the jaw if he had to. She was none other than Caitlin O'Connor. My old friend Reg's wife, who had disappeared from their New York apartment after her husband was killed. But the lady's Irish temper was up and there was no stopping her. She got a huge knife from the table the old man was sitting at, but Charlie managed to get that away from her. He forced her into a chair. She suddenly got quiet. Charlie relaxed. As soon as he turned his back, she ran to a bag on a bed and took out a gun. Charlie just stood there while she pumped three bullets into Prudence's body.

Collins and I rushed in, but she didn't raise the gun again, once she'd killed Prudence.

"I'm taking you back to Jamaica," Collins told Charlie.

"You don't have the authority," Charlie said.

I looked at the man sitting there. "Dr. Gillesslee?"

"Yes."

"Your daughter's dead."

"She's been dead to me for years."

"Enid Hylton's dead too."

"Oh, no!" Then he started to cry.

What a mess!

I turned to Caitlin O'Connor. "Is that the gun that killed your husband?" She thought about using it on me, but Collins was too quick for her. She let him take it when he pointed the rifle at her.

We left Prudence's bullet-ridden body there and the five of us made a strange sight as we headed for Charlie's boat. His man came charging up, but once he saw Collins he lost his nerve. That's when Charlie began to panic.

"If you bolt, Charlie, I'll shoot, so help me," Collins warned.

Charlie decided to go quietly.

We landed at the marina just as a flotilla from the Jamaican navy was about to invade its smaller neighbor.

Charlie was put under house arrest while his uncle decided what he was going to do with him. It certainly left Macfarlane in the lurch. The game was up and all he could do now was make a run for it.

Collins allowed me to have some time alone with Dr. Gillesslee before the reporters got to him. Caitlin O'Connor was held incommunicado. She had killed an English citizen in another country. And she would probably be extradited to New York for murder there too, once the bullets that killed Prudence were matched with the one that killed her husband.

But Caitlin and Prudence and Reg and Regina and even Marlene were no longer my problem, although I counted on Collins to get all the details for his orderly mind and pass them along to me once it had all been solved and worked out.

Gillesslee was shaking visibly, shaking and sobbing intermittently.

"My God, my God. All these years. I let them keep me a prisoner in Schultz's house because of Enid. What a fool I was. What a fool!"

"But why did you pretend you were dead?"

"So Prudence could get the rest of the estate."

"Why not just give it to her?"

"We were in a court battle that would have lasted for years. Then they just kidnapped me and said, sit still or they'd kill Enid. They promised me that if I cooperated they'd let her live. She sent me letters every month, sometimes every week, for three whole years. It's the only thing that kept me alive."

"How much money did Prudence get?"

"Half a million pounds."

"And Iris?"

"Almost a million."

"Pounds?"

"Pounds sterling."

"What is that in dollars?"

"At the time about two and a half million."

"What happened to Enid's husband?"

"They killed him, poor man. Enid never loved him. She loved me. But they wouldn't let us live in peace. That's why she left. And I was too weak to go with her. But I wanted her to have the money. It was a gift outright. A gift of love. If I never saw her again, it didn't matter. Her happiness was all that mattered."

"She kept your money, doctor. And now that you're alive, you can go to New York and claim it."

"If I could bring her back by giving it all away, I'd gladly do it."

"You loved her that much?"

"More."

11

I caught the first plane to New York that I could get. When I got back to my "rooms," I called de Souza. He was still alive, thank goodness.

"When did you get back?"

"Just this minute. I think I know who killed Mrs. Hylton and Kathleen Campbell and even Josephs."

"You're kidding?"

"Nope."

"Well, Black and the boys will be glad to hear it. Although there hasn't been any pressure lately on anyone."

"That's because the danger no longer exists. The prime minister's cousin was behind it all."

"You're kidding?"

"No. What's Quinn been up to?"

"Quiet. The commissioner hasn't been running so hard lately. He hasn't withdrawn from the race outright, but there're rumors."

"Really? I wonder why?"

"Don't know."

"So who and what was the FBI after?"

"The FBI had a major crime boss that they had wire taps on. And an informant and a witness both ready to testify. They were going to indict him. His money came from the Florida action. He had a big piece of it."

"He was ambitious."

"Very."

"And now?"

"Now he's in retrenchment."

"Is there a tie-in?"

"With what?"

"With him and the police commissioner."

"Not that I know of."

"What's Iris Hylton been doing?" I asked.

"You mean Enid. Iris is dead, remember."

"No, Enid's dead, but we can talk about that later."

"Well, if you mean the sister who's alive, she's been shut up in her house, not answering the phone or even going out. She's got two chains on her door and a dog."

"When did all this happen?"

"Just since you disappeared."

"I'll call you later at the club."

"Okay." And he hung up.

I took my gun out of the cookie jar and rushed over to Iris Hylton's apartment. I banged on the door and leaned on the bell until she answered.

"Go away. Go away," she screamed. "Go away or I'll call the police."

I had to wait until she stopped screaming and then talk fast. "It's me, Joe. I just got back from Jamaica."

"Talk again, mek a hear you."

I repeated it. There was quiet, then she unlocked the door. The dog was straining at the leash, but she held him. She took a good look at me. "You alone?" she asked.

"Yes, I'm alone."

She seemed to want to look around corners, but finally relented and let me in. The dog was very aggressive. She stood all the while, holding the dog by the collar.

She moved to a couch and sat on the edge of it, leaning forward, holding the dog's collar. I sat.

"So how long you was in Jamaica?"

"Only four days."

"So what you do and who you see?"

"I saw Dr. Gillesslee and his daughter, Prudence."

"You got around."

"The daughter's dead. Albert Williams is dead too."

She was immobile.

"The man who lived in Yallas, and who loved your sister all his life, he committed suicide when he heard that she had died. And your name is Iris. Your sister's name was Enid. That's how she got out of the country. She used a forged passport with your birth certificate, your identity. Now that she's dead, you're going to try to get the money that she was keeping for Gillesslee by just being yourself—Iris Hylton. If the bank never finds out she's dead, it should be easy."

"Not true. I was never going to do that."

"Then who, who was going to do it?"

She didn't answer.

I got up, paced. Then I turned to her. "Where's your husband?"

"Didn't you find out when you were there? He's dead. Dead and buried in the country."

"I know somebody's dead and buried in the country. They're digging up the grave today. Since they were twins, your husband and your sister's husband, it might be tricky telling who's in the grave. Unless the birth records are really accurate. Or someone shows up who can tell the difference. Even if the man who's dead is your husband or isn't, where's the other brother? Whichever one he is. Nobody seems to know. When I find him the puzzle should be complete. All of it.

"Your sister was killed for the money. That's why Kathleen was killed too. If you get it all, then you know who was doing the killing, whether it was you or someone else. But now you've got another problem. Gillesslee. He's alive. So the money reverts to him. That's how Enid set it up. You went to all that trouble for nothing."

"I didn't. I never. It wasn't me."

"Then who?"

"It was Trevor."

"Trevor. O.K., Trevor. How do we prove it?"

"I don't know. You're the detective."

"Then let me ask you, how do you know it's Trevor?"

"The cutlass."

"That's how Kathleen died, not your sister."

"I don't know. I don't know."

"Why all the security? Who're you afraid of?"

She said nothing.

"Well, I'm waiting."

She began to tremble. The dog got restless, but she held him.

"I'm going to ask you for the last time. Do you need or want my help in any way?"

She shook her head no.

"Are you in any danger? Do you fear for your life?"

"No."

"Of course not. Why should you? You're in no danger, not now. Now that Gillesslee's alive. You wouldn't have been killed in any event, just threatened maybe, beaten up. But not killed. What happened to the partnership? What broke it up?"

She looked at me as if she were about to let the dog loose.

"I have a gun. I'd shoot before he made the leap, so hold onto him if you still think you need him."

And I left.

I went back to the house, searched it from top to bottom. Locked all the doors as best I could, went up to Enid's bedroom, and waited. Night was beginning to fall. Snakey had gotten into the house through a means that I never figured out. But I didn't think he was the only one who knew about it.

Well, the word should be out. De Souza and his crowd knew I was back. Iris and whoever she was or wasn't working with knew. All I had to do was wait. One by one I'd reduced the suspects or they'd been reduced. My friend would either run, hide, or get rid of me. He or she couldn't afford to have me hanging around anymore asking questions, digging up skeletons long dead. If the killer didn't feel me breathing down his or her neck now, he never would. I heard the phone ringing downstairs. And that's all I heard. Something flat and cold hit me on the head and stunned me, then I saw his shoes again as I fell into that deep pool that kept spinning around and around and around.

When I awoke, I was tied and gagged.

Well, at least I was alive. I was downstairs in the back room, the one they had laid Enid in. The double mahogany doors were closed, but not completely. There were two people in the front room arguing. I recognized Trevor's voice. The other voice was a man's also. But I'd never heard it before.

"Killing. All this killing has got to stop. You say Snakey killed my mother, well, I don't believe it. I believe . . . I don't want to say what I believe."

"Your mother worked for that man for three years. He gave her that money. That money belongs to us, to you and me."

"How're you going to get it, by killing her sister?"

"I'm not going to kill anybody."

"Oh, no?"

"I love you. Believe me. Help me with this and we can get it, all of it. There's almost three million dollars sitting in a bank here in New York." And he got intense when he said it.

"But where are the papers?"

"I told you, Snakey stole them from me."

"Why would you have anything to do with that slimy bastard in the first place?"

"I thought I needed him. There were too many people to take care of. The lawyers . . . Josephs, Marlene Campbell, but he double-crossed me."

"So who took care of the lawyers? Who took care of Snakey? Who took care of Josephs?"

"Marlene killed Josephs. That was her down payment for getting in. And she's sitting in a hospital in Kingston now with a bullet in her that they can't get out because that bastard in there put it in her."

"Yeah and what was she holding on him when he did it?"

"Never mind about that. We've got to get the papers. Then we can deal with Iris."

"And how are you going to get them, you don't even know where they are? And how are you going to get Iris to help you when you do, kill her too?"

"Will you stop saying that? I told you I didn't kill anybody. Is he dead?" I guess that meant me.

"Of course not. You need him. He's going to tell you where the papers are."

"I know where the papers are."

"Where?"

"In Kingston. I think a man named Macfarlane's got them."

"Who's he?"

"Never mind. But I've got to make sure before I make a move. And that bastard in there is going to help me make sure."

"How's he going to do that?"

"There's a white cop in Brooklyn who hates him. I'm going to convince the cop that he killed Snakey."

"What good would that do? Snakey died in Jamaica. A white cop in Brooklyn couldn't give a damn about that."

"Well, there's more to it than that. There're the answers to some questions about ganja that the cop's interested in. If he can hold our friend for extradition it could prove hot for him."

"I've seen that guy. You're not going to bluff him with any crap like that. Besides, he's probably got half the policemen in Jamaica on his side."

"Look, I'm not saying that we'd have to go through with it. But if you talk to him maybe he'll tell you. But one way or the other I'm going to get it out of him. I'll cut that red nigger ten ways from Sunday if I have to."

"O.K., O.K., I'll talk to him. Why don't you go get something to eat, like you said you were going to do?"

"I knew I could count on you."

He left and Trevor opened the mahogany doors, turned on the light and came over to me and sat on a table. He saw that I was awake and cut the gag. He couldn't think of anything to say so I started the conversation.

"Who is he?"

"My uncle."

"Really, not your father?"

"No, my father's dead."

"Well, well. Imagine that. Who's buried in the grave?"

"My father, of course."

"Under what name?"

"Under my uncle's name, Walter Hylton."

"And what's your father's name?"

"Robert Hylton."

"You mean your uncle killed your father, buried him under his name, so he could assume his identity, take over his land, and you have just sat by and let it happen, and now you're even going to help him? Didn't you ever read *Hamlet*?"

"You don't understand."

"I guess not, but cut me loose and I'll tell you where the papers are."

"Promise?"

"Promise."

He did. As I was getting the blood back in my arms and legs, the uncle walked in with his cutlass. Trevor froze. The uncle raised the cutlass and came at Trevor.

"You promised!" he yelled.

I wasn't sure if he was going to scare Trevor, stun him, or just give him a flesh wound, but I wasn't taking any chances. Trevor tried to get away, but he didn't quite make it. The uncle chopped him in the arm as I hit him with a vase that was made of solid milk glass that was on a table next to where I was standing. I caught him on the side of his skull. His feet buckled and he tried to bring his arm up again, but couldn't.

I called an ambulance and got Trevor to a hospital in spite of his protests. He was in danger of losing the whole arm, as it turned out. That's how deep the cut went.

I got de Souza to arrest the uncle, Walter Hylton. I was the complainant and the eyewitness. Late that night Collins called.

"The man in the grave is probably Walter, not Enid's husband, but her sister's husband."

"Well, I've got a man in custody in Brooklyn who should be Robert, not the brother but Enid's husband, only Enid's son says he is the brother, Walter, and that it's his father, Robert, who's dead."

"Well, he's probably right. Walter killed Robert to get his property and assumed his identity. Sounds reasonable."

"Maybe, but there's one way of telling."

"How's that?"

"When did he die?"

"Two years ago."

"O.K. Now this part's tricky. Prudence was an authority on Jamaican art. She said there were very few artists doing landscapes. There's a landscape here in New York by R. H. dated a year ago. Find out from someone in the artistic community which brother was the painter and you'll know who's buried in that grave."

"You say the picture was dated a year ago?"

"Right."

"And you've seen it?"

"I have."

"Describe it."

I did.

"O.K. Call you tomorrow."

There was an article in the morning paper. The FBI had gotten

a confession from the prime minister of the small island impli-
cating an attorney at the law firm that the police commissioner
used to be a senior partner of in the trafficking of drugs. The
commissioner denied all knowledge and refused to withdraw from
the race. But no one was taking his candidacy seriously anymore.
Someone even suggested they were thinking of replacing him
with a black man as police commissioner. That'd be the day, I
thought. Turns out I was wrong about that one too.

Poor Quinn and his captain in Manhattan. They had been
working on a case, the solution of which almost destroyed their
boss.

I found Jay at his mother's house in Queens. I traced him
from the hospital records.

"Regina's dead."

"So I heard. You did it."

"No, Jay, but I was there when it happened. You want to hear
about it?"

"No."

"Why were you beaten up?"

"I don't know. Regina kept saying we were setting a trap for
you and I kept getting beat up. It never made any sense to me."

"She was probably trying to use us as a way out with the mob,
if she needed it. She really loved Charlie."

"The guy in Jamaica?"

"Right."

"I figured."

"I guess she told you one thing and told those hoods something
else. This way she always had two exits. Who knows. But whatever it was that she did, she did it for Charlie boy."

"They tell me he was quite a ladies' man."

"That he was. The count at present is five."

"Five women!"

"Five. And of the two who're alive in Jamaica, one's in the
hospital and one's in jail."

"And where's he?"

"Oh, he's alive. But he's in jail too or close to it. Although I wouldn't count on that lasting too long."

I left Jay and haunted a few new bars in Manhattan, trying to change my luck. It was either that or join a monastery.

So Marlene was one of them. Nobody knew where the papers were because Snakey had taken them. Did Aubuchon and Braithwaite think that Marlene had the papers or that she knew where they were? She couldn't tell me that or I'd realize that she was in on it, if not with them with someone else. Well, some of it I'd never know for sure. But I still had a murder to solve.

Collins called a day later. It took him a while. The man we had in jail was Trevor's father! Collins had confirmed it not only by Robert Hylton's reputation as a painter, but by the types of landscapes he painted. Strange. When it came to his art he was an honest man. He couldn't lie about the date he painted a picture!

"What about Macfarlane?"

"Disappeared. But you remember you said he might try to bargain for his freedom by ratting on Charlie."

"Yes."

"Looks like it might be the other way around."

"No kidding."

"Yes, we'll need you to come down and testify, of course, but with any luck we should be able to prove Macfarlane killed Brown."

"Especially since he actually did."

"Right."

"Thanks, I'll be in touch."

"Oh, by the way, Marlene Campbell left the hospital this morning. She sent me a note addressed to you. Shall I read it?"

"Please do."

"It says . . ." and he hesitated while he opened it, "you want to know who killed Mrs. Hylton, ask her sister."

| 347 |

"That's all?"

"That's all."

"Thanks again, Inspector."

But I didn't ask the sister. I asked the son, after I'd talked to Quinn.

"Well, well, Lieutenant, how are the Irish running this week?"

"Whadda ya want?"

"Those fingerprints you found on the doorknobs. Check Robert Hylton's and the sister's, see what you get. The cutlass that killed Kathleen made a wound that's probably a match for the one that slashed Trevor Hylton. Not that that would prove anything. Kathleen's dead and her wound is just a statistic now. But there are his shoes. Unusual, like orthodics. That print should tell you something. If you've found them in both rooms, now you're close. Let me know and I can probably nail it in for you."

He got back to me in minutes. Yes, Hylton's fingerprints and shoes matched in both accounts.

I went to see Trevor, who was ready to get out of the hospital. They'd saved his arm.

"Why were you shielding your father?"

"Because I loved him, why else?"

"But he's a butcher!"

"You don't want to believe things like that about your own father."

"I guess not. Only you know who killed your mother. It's up to you to see that justice is done. Simply go to the police and tell them."

"But I don't know."

"Think. She was hit over the head with a blunt instrument. One swing. She grabbed the inside of the bed with her left hand. What was used only the killer knows. Whatever it was, it's probably been destroyed by now. The blow could have been made by a short or tall person. The angle, according to the lab report, would indicate a short person. But all the prints were wiped clean after. Who was afraid of leaving prints in that room?"

"My aunt."

"How do you know?"

"My father always wore gloves when he wasn't painting, to keep his hands soft, he said, so they wouldn't hurt when he painted."

"He didn't have them on when he hacked you."

"They were in his pocket, he'd just taken them off. If he'd wanted to kill my mother by hitting her over the head from behind, he'd have put them on first. Even if he didn't, he wasn't the one to go around leaving his prints all over the place. He was very fastidious about things like that. Besides, he hadn't been in that room in years."

"You knew it was your aunt all along."

"No, I just hoped it wasn't my father."

"But he killed Kathleen."

"I guess so."

"What happened between his brother and him?"

"His brother posed as my father so my father could do his Pocomania rituals incognito. It would have been bad for business if he was associated with that sort of thing. But one night one of the women went into a trance that turned into a coma and she never came out of it. There was an investigation and my father, posing as my uncle, was held responsible. So my father killed his brother, took back his own identity, and was free and clear."

"I see. If your aunt did kill your mother, the question now is how do we prove it."

"I don't know."

"She's sitting there with that dog. She's no longer in any danger. She knows we know, but she knows we can't prove it. She was in the room. They probably argued. Your aunt struck her, but she didn't take the papers because she wasn't supposed to know her sister was dead. They would be found in due course, given to the proper authorities, and she would inherit the money. But by leaving them there she allowed your father to get them. No one knew where the papers were. Snakey searched and he didn't find them. I came along, found them, and your father knocked me out and took them from me, and Snakey got them from him. They ended up in Jamaica with Gretchen. Macfarlane killed Gretchen for them. Why? He had to be working with your aunt."

I called Collins back. "I think we both need to find Macfarlane and I don't think Charlie's going to help."

"Oh."

"No. Someone put a notice In Memoriam in the newspaper for Dr. Gillesslee the day after I got there. Find out who did it and if one had been placed the year before. I'll wait for your call."

An hour later he was on the phone.

"It wasn't his daughter, but there doesn't seem to be a record of who it was, and no, there had been none the year before."

"When did Walter Hylton die, even though he was supposed to be Robert?"

"I'll check it." He did and called back. "Six months from now would be the right month."

"Put an In Memoriam notice in his name anyway, tomorrow if you can. Make sure it's in Friday's New York edition."

We had to wait a day for it to come out in New York. But the notice was there.

With the help of the Jamaican government and the FBI we put a tap on Iris's phone. Then we waited. Two days after the notice came out she called a number in Brooklyn and asked if there were any messages for her. She gave her name. A woman answered, asked her to wait a minute, and then Macfarlane came on. He knew nothing about the notice. He knew where the papers were, but they wouldn't do anyone any good now. He told her to forget it and be thankful she was alive, and hung up.

I had to work fast. I called de Souza. We got a woman to approximate Iris's voice and a man to approximate Macfarlane's. We called them both and told them to meet each other at the house on Hancock Street. Our story was that all the papers weren't in Jamaica and they could still probably salvage some of the money if they acted quickly.

Then I enlisted Trevor to put the icing on the cake. He showed me how his father and Snakey got in through an old iron trapdoor that used to be used for coal deliveries before the house was converted to oil.

Iris and Macfarlane showed up around the same time. She got there first and was waiting when he arrived. They were in the front room.

"Is our friend downstairs?" he asked.

"Not that I can tell. Why did you want to meet here?"

"I didn't want to. . . . You called me, didn't you?"

"No, I thought you called me."

Then they were quiet.

Trevor opened the mahogany door and came out of the back room.

"I called both of you."

"How did you know my number?" Macfarlane asked.

"My aunt gave it to me."

"He's lying," she said.

"Why did you have to kill her? Why?" he pleaded.

"Say nothing," Macfarlane said. "Nothing. I assume that Mr. Cinquez is somewhere on the premises. Is there a recording device of some sort in the room? Well, he needn't have bothered. There are no charges against me in Jamaica. There will be no extradition attempt. None whatsoever. The prime minister doesn't want me to return ever. You see, I know where too many skeletons are buried. So if you have nothing further to say, I think we should leave."

I was downstairs with de Souza. We had opened the area

around the hot water pipe leading from the basement all the way up to the top floor and had a crude tape recorder and microphone hooked up so that we could hear everything. But Trevor was hanging in there.

"You went to all that trouble for nothing. But I am going to dog you, Auntie. One dark night—"

"Trevor, don't be stupid. The afternoon that your mother died, I was at the beauty parlor. If anybody had asked me, I could have told them."

That stopped old Trevor. I had news for him. It stopped me too. An alibi. Come on. At this late stage in the game. She had to be kidding. But if it was true then I'd really been fooled. But Macfarlane saved me. He sounded nervous when he said, "Uh, I don't think we should say anymore." And they left.

Why, I kept asking myself, would he be nervous because Iris had an alibi? When I shared my thoughts with de Souza and Trevor, they had no answers either. Then I got a serious hunch.

"Let's go back to the precinct and look through the personal effects."

"At this time of night?" de Souza said.

"Sure. You solve the murder case and you can get a promotion, and Quinn won't be able to tell you what to do anymore."

We went to the precinct, all three of us, and de Souza managed to cajole the key from a sergeant and get into the safe that had Enid's personal effects. There was nothing there but clothes and a bracelet.

"No, this isn't what I want. I want the stuff the lab boys picked up."

"But they're just samples."

"O.K., so let's see them."

It took him twice as long, but he got it. There were a lot of dust particles. Samples from the window, the rug. I was sifting through it all with a pencil when I saw something. "Well, well. Lookee here at what we've got." De Souza got me a tweezer and

I picked it up and put it on a clean sheet of white paper. Then I opened my wallet and took out one just like it.

"This stud ear piece, gentlemen, as you can see, is the match to this one. And where did this one come from, you ask? Why, from the grass near where the commissioner of the CID was killed in Kingston. There was a third one in a dead man's wallet. But we don't need to bother about that."

"I don't get it," Trevor said.

"Hank?"

"The stud you found near the dead commissioner was left by the killer."

"I've always thought so."

"And now that you've found the mate, you're saying it's the same person who killed Mrs. Hylton."

"That's what I'm saying."

"But how? Who? Why?" asked Trevor.

"It's Macfarlane obviously."

"You mean Macfarlane killed the commissioner and my mother?"

"No, Macfarlane had them killed. The killer is light brown skinned, about five feet nine inches, almost two hundred pounds. I saw him as he was escaping. He's got to be Macfarlane's hit man. Why did Macfarlane want the CID commissioner killed? Because he stood in the way of Macfarlane's empire in ganja and tourist dollars. Maybe the commissioner knew about Macfarlane. Collins can probably tie up that loose end. But he was Iris Hylton's accomplice, and he had your mother killed so Iris could get the money."

"So how do we prove it?" asked de Souza.

"We obviously have to find the young man."

"How?" de Souza insisted. Macfarlane won't fall for any more traps. And the killer could be anywhere.

We left the precinct and went to the club. The group was there. While we were on the third round of white rum and everyone was feeling relieved because no one's land was going to be taken away, not this year anyway, I brought up my problem.

"Describe him," Chin said.

I did.

He thought about it, then he shook his head.

I looked at Black, who said, "No, I don't know him. But I do know Macfarlane. We went to school together."

"Who's he living with here in Brooklyn?"

"A brother."

"You know the address?"

"No, but I can get it."

"Please do. I'll be at home all morning." And I left.

I got back to my place and called Jamaica. I was only able to get the Pegasus at that time of night. Mr. Ellis, the bell captain, was on duty! I didn't believe it.

"Don't you ever sleep?" I asked.

"Yes, sitting up. What can I do for you?"

"I need to talk to Collins right away. Can you get him at home?"

"No, but I can get him first thing tomorrow."

"That's good enough."

"When you coming down again?"

"As soon as this is over. You need anything?"

"Yes, a hair dryer for my wife."

"That's easy."

Collins called before nine.

"Macfarlane has immunity from the prime minister," I told him.

"I was afraid of that," he said.

"I think the CID commissioner was on to him."

"If anyone would have been he was the man."

"Well, his killer's my man too."

"Then we do indeed want the same man."

"Especially since it gives us Macfarlane also."

| 354 |

"Especially."

"Can you come to New York?"

"Yes."

"Catch the first flight. I'll meet you."

We drove in on the expressway while I told him what I had in mind.

"I'm double-checking his address against the one that he answered the phone from. I should have it by the time we get back. We've got to tease him out again. He's a shrewd customer, it won't be easy."

"True, he is shrewd, but he's also rash."

Black called as soon as we got to my place. The address he gave me was the same as the one that went with the telephone number. He wished me happy hunting. We got there and waited outside for a while. But no one came or went. Collins then went to a phone and called. He asked for Macfarlane. He came on. He was surprised to hear Collins's voice.

"Mr. Cinquez must be giving out my number on street corners. How he got it, I'm still not sure."

Collins held the phone so that I could listen. "Trevor's convinced that you killed his mother. He's going to kill you. I just thought I'd warn you."

"Does the P.M. know you're in New York talking to me?"

"Yes."

"Did he give you a message for me?"

"Yes."

"What is it?"

"He'll keep the bargain. You have nothing to worry about."

"That's not good enough. I thought I was going to come into some money. But those plans didn't quite materialize."

"He's not going to give you any money."

"I think he will."

"Well, I'm not taking back any messages. Whatever you want to tell him, you'll have to tell him on your own."

"Why are you here?"

"I'm here with Gillesslee. He's trying to get back the money that Enid Hylton kept for him."

"Oh. How long will you be in town?"

"A week."

"Well, let's get together for a drink."

"Sure, Mac."

"I'll meet you at your hotel. Where're you staying?"

"The Parker Meridien in midtown."

"Right." And he hung up.

I smiled. "It might work," I told him.

Quinn gave me an elderly English-type operative. "But you guys pay for the hotel," he demanded.

Collins assured him his government would pick up the tab.

Poor Quinn, class was not a strong point of his, never was and never would be. He needed a transfer from Brooklyn and fast.

We waited two days. Macfarlane finally called and he and Collins had their drink. Then Collins got a message from the front desk. Dr. Gillesslee needed him. Collins excused himself and left. Macfarlane stayed at the bar. De Souza and I were in the security booth overlooking the lobby. I think he knew he was being watched. But he was cool. Collins called down. He went to a house phone. Gillesslee wasn't well. The house doctor had been sent for. He was sorry. Macfarlane said he understood and left.

The next night our friend struck. He got in posing as a delivery boy. He had flowers for the man in room 702 who wasn't feeling well. The clerk at the front desk checked. "Dr. Gillesslee?" He said yes. She sent him up. He opened the door. Saw the operative under the covers and started shooting as we came out of a closet down the hall. The operative tried to get his gun out but our friend was too fast. We ran after him. He crossed the room, crashed through the window and landed on a small roof three stories down. We were at the window as he disappeared over the side.

"We went through all that trouble for nothing," de Souza said.

"I almost got killed for nothing," the operative said, crawling out from under his bulletproof blanket.

We went back down.

Collins had stayed in the lobby in case the killer came back that way.

"It was him," I said, "but he got away."

"Tough luck."

"I don't believe in luck. Let's go," I said.

We got in a car, the three of us, and drove to Iris Hylton's apartment. She wouldn't open the door. I broke it in. She let the dog go and I killed it with one shot. She panicked and ran for the phone. De Souza took it away from her. She said she was going to get the police and have us all arrested. He told her he was the police. That's when she sat down.

"We don't have much time," I told her. "Macfarlane just tried to have Dr. Gillesslee killed."

"That's crazy. He said nothing to me."

"Tells you something, doesn't it?"

"Did he get him?"

"No, Gillesslee never left Jamaica. The man was a policeman. But Macfarlane's young killer made the attempt."

"And he got away."

"He got away."

"And you want me to tell you where he is?"

"That's what I want."

She was tired. She was weak. She'd had enough. She gave us the guy's name and where we could find him.

Collins and I waited while de Souza called Quinn and went to meet him. They caught the guy later that night. He confessed to the one murder and to the other attempt. We weren't interested in Jamaica. Besides, I'd seen that one with my own eyes.

Macfarlane was extradited. Discredited as he was, since the killer was doing his dirty work, the prime minister was able to withstand the attempted revelations of the secrets on him that Macfarlane had.

Collins and I said goodbye at the airport.

"Well, we got our man."

"Yes," I said. "I feel good about it. Even though I called her by the wrong first name for the short time that I knew her, she was a wonderful woman. I'll think of her fondly for the rest of my life."

He got on the plane with Macfarlane. Trevor called when I got back to my "rooms."

"I want to sell the house, but I won't if you don't want me to."

"Sell it, I'm leaving Brooklyn."

"You sure?"

"I'm positive."

The boys made me show up for the Saturday night dance. De Souza was up for a promotion. Everyone was in high spirits. Then Trevor walked in with my East Indian beauty. I left, even though they all tried to get me to stay.

Well, Iris Hylton would have a long winter and summer to contemplate her loneliness. Gillesslee wanted to give the money that Enid had kept for him to the New York Rastafarians, but Trevor felt that that might be overdoing it.

It was a quiet day. The summer had finally ended and the autumn leaves were covering the sidewalks of Brooklyn. When I woke up the next morning, there were two funerals at the same time. A Jamaican one on my side of the street and a Jewish one on the other side. They were both going to mourn the dead similarly, I thought. The Jews by sitting shiva. The Jamaicans by sitting nine night.

I went to Manhattan and sat in every bar on the Upper West Side, one by one. When it was all over, I was cold sober and miserable.

I went home. As soon as I walked through the door, the phone started ringing. I didn't answer it. I didn't have to.

It wasn't that I didn't like her father. It was just that the guy didn't drink. How could you work for a man who didn't drink?

When she called again, the next afternoon, I finally answered.

She had a lot of plans. All of which had a million options. All of which could be discussed from every and any angle imaginable. About the only thing that wasn't negotiable was whether or not we should try again. We had to, she insisted, and that was that.

I said yes, God help me. But I knew that there was only one reason why I was doing it.

I was still in love.